London Borough of Tower Hamlets

91000008169544

KU-534-372

WITHDRAWN

BLACK
THORN

By Sarah Hilary

BLACK THORN

SARAH HILARY

MACMILLAN

First published 2023 by Macmillan
an imprint of Pan Macmillan
The Smithson, 6 Briset Street, London EC1M 5NR
EU representative: Macmillan Publishers Ireland Ltd, 1st Floor,
The Liffey Trust Centre, 117–126 Sheriff Street Upper,
Dublin 1, D01 YC43
Associated companies throughout the world
www.panmacmillan.com

ISBN 978-1-0350-0388-4 HB
ISBN 978-1-0350-0430-0 TPB

Copyright © Sarah Hilary 2023

The right of Sarah Hilary to be identified as the
author of this work has been asserted by her in accordance
with the Copyright, Designs and Patents Act 1988.

All rights reserved. No part of this publication may be reproduced,
stored in a retrieval system, or transmitted, in any form, or by any means
(electronic, mechanical, photocopying, recording or otherwise)
without the prior written permission of the publisher.

Pan Macmillan does not have any control over, or any responsibility for,
any author or third-party websites referred to in or on this book.

1 3 5 7 9 8 6 4 2

A CIP catalogue record for this book is available from the British Library.

Typeset in Arno by Jouve (UK), Milton Keynes
Printed and bound by CPI Group (UK) Ltd, Croydon, CR0 4YY

This book is sold subject to the condition that it shall not, by way of
trade or otherwise, be lent, hired out, or otherwise circulated without
the publisher's prior consent in any form of binding or cover other than
that in which it is published and without a similar condition including
this condition being imposed on the subsequent purchaser.

Visit **www.panmacmillan.com** to read more about all our books
and to buy them. You will also find features, author interviews and
news of any author events, and you can sign up for e-newsletters
so that you're always first to hear about our new releases.

To Erin Kelly

abandonment, n.

1. the act of leaving a person, thing or place
with no intention of returning

2. the state or condition of being abandoned
by a person or people

3. the surrender or devotion of oneself to
an influence, passion, emotion

20 AUGUST

Five days before abandonment

1

From a distance, the screaming could've been seagulls, a familiar enough soundtrack on this coastal road with its shaggy moorland to the right, the sea's long horizon on the left. Rory was running late, the satnav sending him up a lane barely big enough for a car, let alone a van, hairpin bends bringing him close enough to the water to wish he'd worn a wetsuit. Choppy out there, waves like white horses; if he went over, it was a sheer drop to rocks as big as boulders.

Brambles screeched against the van's side, thorns scoring the paintwork. He slowed to a crawl but it made no difference to the damage, other than putting him further behind schedule. At this rate, he'd be home after dark. Again. The satnav's route had plenty of potholes and mud too, a slippery juddering under his tyres. He kept picturing the van seesawing at the cliff's edge, back wheels churning empty air, *The Italian Job* transposed to the Tin Coast.

No gold in the van, just a couple of hundred cardboard packages sorted into a dozen plastic sacks. Back at the beginning of this job, he'd tried to guess at some of the packages, a game to keep him company on the long drives. He'd soon given it up; the punishing schedule didn't allow for games, or even comfort breaks. Four plastic drinks bottles rolled around the passenger footwell, one already filled. Most drivers chucked the full bottles out into the road – a charming new feature of Cornwall's highways and byways – but Rory always emptied his down a gutter. It felt like a tiny triumph when he did that, though there wasn't much to be triumphant about, he supposed, standing in the dark emptying a bottle of pee down the drain outside his own back door.

'I'm a responsible driver,' he'd said at the interview. 'A safe driver.'

'A fast driver?' they'd quizzed.

Not asking, as he'd thought, about penalty points or convictions. Just keen to know if he'd make it through their schedules, which seemed angled more towards time travel than traffic conditions.

Two months ago the job had been a godsend, coming as funds were drying up. No one needed more travel agents but home deliveries were booming, everyone signing up for stuff to take the edge off isolation, conjure the illusion of luxury. He'd been glad of the work, still was, but it was knackering, far tougher than selling package holidays. His last drop-off had been a tower block, rare in this part of the world, sea views but you had to climb seven flights to get them. Lift out of order and a grumpy git at the end of it, asking what took him so long.

'Christ!' An oncoming car, blaring its horn, backed him into the hedge before weaving past and away. 'Bastard!'

He stopped the van to catch his breath, heart hammering in his chest. Light-headedness, like altitude sickness, had him gripping the wheel even with the engine off. He was high on the cliffs above the sea at what felt like the edge of the world but was only West Cornwall.

Gulls screamed somewhere inland. An eerie sound, he'd always thought. He peered through the windscreen, expecting to see the birds wheeling off the water but the sky was empty. A big sky, the kind he used to rave about: *Blue skies and endless sunshine . . .* The summer was endless all right, hadn't rained in weeks. The air had a pizza-oven hotness which said a storm was coming and his van had no air-con in front, only in the back; the driver could fry as long as no one one-star-reviewed a melted box of Black Magic or whatever passed for posh chocolates these days.

Rory rested his chin on the backs of his hands, taking a moment. Dead ahead, the cliff edge crooked its finger, beckoning that *Italian Job* image back into his head, of the van's rear end swung out over the sea, box after box emptying out: foot spas, novelty LED lamps and crystal chandeliers all fleetingly airborne before taking a fatal nosedive to the rocks, washing up next morning on a tide of sodden cardboard.

'Good riddance to expensive rubbish . . .'

From inland, that sound again, sending a shudder up his spine.

Not gulls. Kids. Screaming.

He gripped the wheel, waiting for the noise to make sense. Just the happy sound of summer spent in the garden, dodging water from a hose or a Super Soaker. He bet there was at least one Super Soaker in the back of his van. He fired the engine into life. Home after dark? He'd be lucky if he didn't sleep in the cab. It wouldn't be the first time, forget the so-called Break Policy. The bottle he'd filled thudded in the footwell, reminding him how badly he needed to pee again. A pothole did its (un)level best to make matters more urgent. The satnav's route was taking him towards the screaming, which had to be coming from the new-build estate, Blackthorn

Ashes. It was his first time on this route and he was curious, having heard fellow drivers discussing the families living there. 'Money to burn,' that's what he'd heard, buying up everything from matching towel sets and hot chocolate machines to paddling pools and sun loungers. He squinted through the windscreen as the road twisted and turned, snaking between sea and scrubland. Wondering who in their right mind wanted to live all the long way up here, never mind building houses at what felt like the edge of the world. But as the van crested a curve and the ocean rose into view – miles and miles of sculpted silver – he began to see how special it might be to live with that view or just the prospect of it waiting behind your bedroom curtains. Just as suddenly, the road narrowed to a shriek of thorns and he reverted to his original judgement: 'You don't have to be mad to live here but it helps.'

Blackthorn Ashes was exclusive, that's what he'd heard. Being built in stages to spread the expense, and to talk up that exclusivity. By the end of the year, eighteen houses would be perched on the cliff, the sea's salt eating away at fancy floor-to-ceiling windows and white stone walls.

A straight stretch of road allowed him to call up the delivery rota, discovering just a handful of families were living in Blackthorn Ashes; a first phased occupation? Judging by the back of his van, those half dozen were spending a small fortune on the kind of miscellanea meant to make a British summer more endurable. His advice? Go to Portugal, or even Croatia. No matter how exclusive, Blackthorn Ashes was still stuck out on a cliff above the Atlantic. On a sunny day – he was certain the sales brochure said this – Cornwall took some beating. But the first snap of winter could close this road, cutting them off completely. Unless drones were delivering by then, there'd be no more yoga mats or ceramic diffusers finding their way into the hands of the lucky few living here.

Something thudded over his head.

'Shit!' He ducked, rolling his eyes as the sound sorted itself out into the padding of webbed feet. A seagull, leaving a one-star review of its own on the roof of his van.

'Turn right,' the satnav instructed, as if turning left was an option involving anything other than a short swim and a long afterlife.

Rory steered the van onto Ashes Road which deserved a special award for somehow managing to be more blighted by potholes than the road he'd just turned off. It forked this way and that, giving tantalizing glimpses of the destination ahead. There was a word Rory missed: *destination*. In his old job, it'd meant exotic, worthy of the notion of 'destiny'. Now it was just a word the satnav snapped at him: 'You have arrived at your destination,' a tower block with a broken lift; 'Your destination is on the right,' a clapped-out trailer in a caravan park.

'Arrived,' the satnav said now.

Two seconds later, it repeated the word more firmly: 'Arrived.'

Dead ahead, two recently planted blackthorn bushes were staked either side of a wide gateway where a granite boulder had been tortured into a signpost: *Blackthorn Ashes*, the 'o' a stylized wreath of thorns. He bet the sales brochure rhapsodized about the architect's soaring vision, the strength of nature encircling the houses, protecting all those who dwelled here from invasion. For 'invasion' read 'reality'. It was a promise Rory had made to countless holiday-seekers over the years. The thorns were carved deep into the boulder, striking a seam of pink in the granite, making him wonder if the sales brochure referenced *Sleeping Beauty*, always assuming they could wrest the appropriate copyright from Walt Disney. He was being cynical but as soon as he was through the gates, he could see what the fuss was about. The hedges hiding the view ended abruptly and there it was: sloping red roofs under a spotlessly blue sky, a green forest of ash trees crowding behind. The homes were spaced apart, each elevated from its neighbour. The first impression was of an alpine village, that irresistible combination of Scandinavian warmth and coolness. The houses themselves were a blaze of sunshine, every window gleaming, every lawn an emerald. Big, bold houses lush with glass and timber but charming, not aggressively modern, and packed with light. The perfect houses for the location, soaking up the sea views, snug to the cliffside. You couldn't see the sea but you could hear it and you could smell it. SOLD signs outside a couple of the houses were fading in the salt air. More signs asked visitors to please park here, 'Children Playing', and go on foot. Brick dust was specking his windscreen but the building site for the second and third phases was well hidden to anyone driving through the gates. And since there wasn't any other way in or out of Blackthorn Ashes, that's what mattered. Rory was impressed, in spite of himself. It had nothing on the real Scandes, of course. But for West Cornwall, it was really something. It'd taken a dreamer to make this, a dreamer and a doer. He wondered about them as he parked up – the architect and the engineer – wondered if they were part of the noise he could hear up ahead where a wide ribbon of tarmac turned west towards the sea. His bladder reminded him of more pressing matters.

He released his seat belt, climbing from the van.

An arch of blue and white balloons joggled in the near distance, voices carrying on the breeze. He stood for a second, giving his spine time to readjust before swinging open the van's rear end in search of the afternoon's deliveries. It was approaching three o'clock. He was almost two hours behind schedule but reluctant to rush, wanting to soak up some sun, maybe a little of Blackthorn Ashes' gloss and glamour. The tower block from this morning felt miles away, as if he'd entered another country or another continent. There were actual goosebumps on his forearms as he loaded the cardboard boxes into a sack, setting off in the direction of the nearest house.

A short walk down the sloping tarmac brought him to the front door of Hawthorn, the first address on his app. Seaside-blue door, brass letter box not quite big enough to take the book they'd ordered. Rory guessed it was a book, too heavy for a DVD. The address label said V. Prentiss.

He rapped on the door, watching the breeze bounce the balloon arch. Someone's birthday, he guessed, or a street party. The smoky smell of a barbecue blew across the communal garden: a circle of pampas grass and palm trees that hid the lower half of the houses from his view. Living here, you probably found excuses for parties every other weekend. The weather was especially good right now but he could picture wood-burners in sitting rooms (the houses had the right chimneys), fat sofas, slouchy beanbags for the kids. He had an urge to press his nose to Hawthorn's windows, see if the houses were just as special inside.

And yet there was something . . .

A strange sort of silence, stifling, punctuated by the semi-hysterical sound of the party.

Red dust freckled the windows. The same dust had gathered in high triangles at either side of the door. A shiver travelled up his spine – someone walking on his grave. The isolation up here was too much. Oppressive, claustrophobic.

No one was answering his knock, no footsteps coming down the stairs or from the garden at the rear of the house. He rapped again because that was the drill but he already knew he was going to have to leave this particular package with a neighbour.

He dropped the book back into the sack, bringing out the next delivery, this one small enough to slot through a letter box. Weighing it in his hand, he took a punt at . . . iPhone charger.

Addressed to Trevor Kyte, care of Redthorn.

Redthorn was sporting even more dust, plus dirty windows. Rory posted the package through the letter box, knocking in the hope of leaving the first delivery with Mr Kyte. No answer here either. This time he put his nose to the window, squinting inside. What he could see of the sitting room looked like a squat: boxes, sleeping bag, piles of clothes. Paradise was a work in progress.

The next package was bulkier than the first but weighed less. A plastic kid's toy, he reckoned, or a cheap toaster. For J. Mason at Maythorn.

He followed the curve in the road, looking at each house's name as he went past – Quickthorn, Silverthorn – finding Maythorn nearly at the end, where he also found the street party, on a long island of communal lawn that ran in front of the houses.

He saw the kids first. A boy of about ten and a younger girl staggering about between trestle tables where plates and cups were stacked. Two steel planters stood in as ice buckets, beer and fizzy drink cans floating on a sea of melting ice cubes. The two kids were chucking ice at one another half-heartedly, as if the game had been going on a long time. They looked like brother and sister, the girl maybe six or seven. Both kids wore one-piece swimsuits, the kind with built-in sun protection. The boy's was blue camouflage, his sister's pink pineapples. A couple stood to one side, holding tall glasses with paper umbrellas perking the rims. A youngish woman in a red vest and yellow sarong balanced a baby on one hip. The youngish man next to her had half an eye on the battle with the ice cubes. He called a warning to the boy as Rory approached.

'Felix, calm down . . .'

From the sound of it, it wasn't the first warning he'd issued.

Behind the trestle tables, a dark-haired woman in a green dress was slicing buns with a bread knife while a man in a navy apron over chinos and a T-shirt worked the barbecue with gusto, his hair curling in the heat.

'This's almost hot! When's the meat coming?'

This provoked a snigger from a blonde in a hot pink bikini and cut-off jeans, lounging in the lap of a third man who sat in a deck-chair with a bottle of beer glued to his lips. Baked-in tan, faded jeans and cowboy boots – like the Marlboro Man took a wrong turn and ended up in Cornwall.

'No clue, mate,' he said in answer to the question about the meat. 'You're in charge of the menu, like you said. I'm just here for the beer.'

'Oi!' The blonde in the bikini cuffed his shoulder, wriggling deeper into his lap.

He ignored her, necking a long mouthful of beer. 'Organic burgers, wasn't it? Local venison . . .'

'Coming up!' The man at the barbecue spun his utensils like a pair of pistols, a big grin fixed on his face. 'Soon's the delivery gets here.'

No one had noticed Rory standing with his sack of deliveries like an out-of-season Santa whose need to relieve himself was now desperate.

'Felix, Chloe . . . Calm down.'

The baby began to cry weakly, its mother lifting it to her shoulder, cradling its head. The woman in the green dress finished with the buns and started on a bowl of sweetcorn.

'S'cuse me.' Rory stepped closer, hefting the sack. 'I'm looking for V. Prentiss?'

Their faces turned his way, more or less at the same time, giving him the feeling he'd intruded on something so private it should never be spoken of, almost as if he might be asked to sign a non-disclosure agreement to that effect.

The blonde in the bikini wet her lips, Marlboro Man narrowing his eyes until his face became lupine. The young couple shielded their eyes with their hands, moving closer to their kids who'd stopped racing and were standing open-mouthed, staring at Rory. The woman in the green dress was the first to recover, wiping her hands on a tea towel as she appraised him.

'You'll find Val Prentiss at Hawthorn, the first house as you came in.'

'No one's in, I don't think. Could someone take their package?'

The sun drew a shadow from the timber lintel of the nearest house so that for a second the house was frowning at him, all the houses were, wanting him to leave and let them get on with whatever secret business he'd disturbed.

'I can pop a note through the door?'

'Of course!' The curly-haired man came out from behind the

barbecue. 'Welcome to Blackthorn Ashes. I'm Adrian Gale, this's my wife Ruth. Our kids're round here somewhere . . .'

Rory shook the man's hand even though it was odd being greeted like a guest.

'Thanks, I'm Rory. If someone could take . . .' He fumbled in the sack for the package he'd failed to fit through Hawthorn's letter box. 'Looks like a book. Sorry . . . This.' He held it out.

'Have you tried knocking?' Adrian's wife Ruth added a brisk smile like an afterthought. 'They should be home.'

'They're not . . . At least, I don't think—'

'Gale!'

The shout cut him short.

'I want a word with you!'

Rory turned to see a stocky man on crutches swinging his way towards them. When he reached the barbecue, he waved one crutch at Adrian Gale.

'This's your answer to my question, is it? A bloody street party?'

He wore a short-sleeved shirt and beige shorts like a scoutmaster. And one slip-on leather shoe, on his left foot. His right foot was strapped inside a black plastic walker boot. They sold the boots on the website Rory worked for. He'd often wondered how many of those who ordered them actually had broken feet.

'What about that bloody death trap in my garden? No explanation there!' The man snarled in Ruth's direction. 'Perhaps I should fill it with baps, since that's what you're all so busy doing.'

'Luke, let's talk about this.' Adrian started to untie the apron from his waist. 'I've been wanting to talk about it, as you know . . .'

He glanced at Rory, a hint of apology in his expression. Luke swung to fix Rory with a stare. Every inch of his face was red and, since he was bald, every inch of his head too. His eyes and nose formed a furious triangle in the dead centre of his face; he looked like an angry bowling ball.

'Who the hell're you?'

'Delivery guy.' Rory held up his sack. 'Just looking to drop off a few packages.'

It distracted Luke, momentarily. 'Anything for Dearman?'

'Um . . .' Rory checked his app. 'Which house?'

'Silverthorn. The one with the deathtrap garden.' He jiggled his crutch in Adrian's direction. 'Right, Gale? Bloody deathtrap!'

'Something for Mason but not Dearman.' Rory pocketed the app. 'Sorry.'

Luke snorted, turning his attention back to the barbecue. 'This's your idea of dealing with the problem, I suppose, fiddling about with sausages while the rest of us burn . . .'

'Let's talk,' Adrian said again. 'C'mon, Luke. Have a lager.' He reached for the nearest bucket, scooping up a can. 'It's cold!'

'You're a bloody disgrace.' Dearman leant on the crutches, stretching his neck in the other man's direction. 'I wouldn't treat an animal this way—'

'That's enough.'

Ruth Gale put the tea towel down, speaking quietly but with enough steel in her voice to make everyone pay attention. 'There are children here.'

'Your husband needs to face up to his responsibilities!' Luke's face turned a deeper shade of red. 'I've informed Health and Safety, so you know. I expect they'll be round soon enough. Then we'll see what's what. *Children!*' But he swung to one side, away from Ruth's husband.

'Meat's here.'

Marlboro Man pointed his beer bottle back the way Rory had come, to where a white van was parking up. Adrian hung his apron over a deckchair.

'Stay and have a burger with us,' he told Rory. 'You can freshen up at our place.' He wiped his hands on his jeans, smiling. 'Come on, you're probably running late as it is. And don't you guys have to take regulation breaks?' He was an irresistible force. 'Leave the packages at ours, use the bathroom, grab a bite to eat. How's that sound?'

Rory's bladder settled it. 'Thanks, that's very kind.'

He fell into step at Gale's side, anticipating a sales pitch since this was clearly the man whose vision had made Blackthorn Ashes a reality. Not the architect, he guessed, but a head honcho in sales maybe. They walked under the arch of blue and white balloons.

'You're still building here?'

'Twelve more houses to come.' Adrian rubbed a hand through his hair, looking tired all of a sudden. 'But then that's it. We're keeping it small. Friendlier that way, you know?'

Neither of them mentioned the angry man on crutches.

Adrian took him to a big house on a corner plot where the floor-to-ceiling windows were splashed with sunshine.

'This's us.' He opened the front door with one hand. 'We don't bother locking our doors here, everyone's a friend.'

'Can't remember the last time I saw that,' Rory said.

He bet Luke Dearman locked his door, though.

'We've got biomass boilers, sheep's wool insulation . . . I won't bore you with the details. Ruth says I'm like Alexa . . . Come on in.'

Adrian was toeing off his deck shoes on the doorstep.

Something flashed at the periphery of Rory's vision. Coming

up the side of the house across the street – Silverthorn? – was a boy in a faded blue T-shirt and jogging bottoms. Older than Felix but not much. Thirteen, fourteen at a pinch. Seeing them outside Blackthorn, he dodged back up the path.

Adrian's kid, Rory guessed, looking to get out of whatever chore he'd been given at the party. Adrian hadn't noticed and Rory didn't enlighten him, following the man into the house which was exactly what he'd expected. Three walls of the sitting room were windows, bringing in the bright blue of the sky. A right-angle of sofas jumbled with cushions, low tables holding lamps. Just that glimpse was enough to have Rory imagining his family here, soaking up the last of a spectacular sunset, stomachs stuffed with a home-cooked meal. Easiest sales pitch in the world. Forever homes.

Except Luke Dearman didn't think so.

Rory wondered what'd gone wrong in Luke's garden. He considered asking Adrian but couldn't afford the time it would take to listen to the answer; something told him it wasn't a short story.

'Loo's through there.' Adrian pointed. 'Let me fix you a cold drink. Coke okay?'

'Just water, thanks.'

The downstairs cloakroom was small but Rory knew there'd be a family bathroom upstairs, probably with sea views. He emptied his bladder, washing his hands thoroughly at the basin before drying them on a pebble-coloured towel.

'Through here,' Adrian called.

The kitchen had been polished to within an inch of its life, winking with quartz. Shuttle-sized fridge, central island sporting a tombstone-sized slab of marble, instant hot water tap, the works.

Rory gulped down iced water in a long glass.

'Thanks for this. I shouldn't, really. Against the rules.'

It'd occurred to him that Luke Dearman might file a complaint, complaints being his thing.

'I'd better get going. You said I could leave the packages with you?'

Adrian reached into the fridge, taking out a bottle of water which he pressed into Rory's hand. 'For later. And let me fix you a burger to take away, won't be two minutes now the meat's here.'

Back outside the house, Rory saw a group of young people gathered around the white van that'd parked alongside his. Two young white women and a black man, all in their twenties by the look of them. The sun had gone behind a cloud, blotting the shadows and making everything easier to see. Luke Dearman was limping away from the barbecue. The hot pink bikini was still wedged in Marlboro Man's lap.

'That's my daughter, Agnes, helping down at the van.' He heard the pride in Adrian's voice. 'My son's round here somewhere . . .'

Hiding, Rory thought, *and good at it.* Maybe the smell of the burgers would lure him out.

'Thanks for the comfort break but I really ought to get going.' He paused, to take the obligatory photos of the parcels inside Blackthorn's open front door.

Adrian held out his hand again. 'Good to meet you, Rory. Thanks for driving all the way out here, I know it's not the easiest of routes.' His smile was strained, as if he was dreading getting back to the street party and would've liked to hitch a ride in Rory's van.

When Rory reached the van, the three young people were laughing together. One of the women was skinny, her hair in a buzz cut that showcased high cheekbones, wide dark eyes. Dressed in black jeans and a grey hoodie whose cowled neck gave her the appearance of a novice monk. Adrian's daughter, Agnes, he guessed. She had her dad's eyes.

The other woman was in cycling gear, built like an athlete. The man was the one you looked at, though, even if, like Rory, you weren't attracted to men. Over fraying jeans he wore a silk robe madly patterned with peacock feathers. His hair was dark-blond dreadlocks cut short, his skin shockingly smooth, his bare feet as beautiful as the rest of him.

'You'll have to excuse her,' he was saying, 'she's a vegan.'

He said *vegan* in the hushed voice of someone saying *virgin* at an orgy. It brought a bubble of laughter from Agnes who swiped at the man's arm.

'Not all of us love meat as much as you!'

The athletic woman joined in the laughter after a tiny pause that told Rory she was a stranger, although possibly not for long.

'I'll let you in on a secret,' she said. 'I'm vegan too. This,' nodding at the meat van, 'is just a favour for a friend. I promise it's not my real job!'

Rory felt the way he had inside Blackthorn, drawn to the promise of this place where beautiful people greeted strangers like old friends. But it was Luke Dearman who was on his mind as he climbed back into his van, the furious way the man turned the party into an interrogation. Most people had a neighbour they'd prefer not to spend time with. But all the way out here, in a place like this, how did you avoid a man like Luke? And what happened when you couldn't?

Rory checked his schedule, finding ten minutes left of his mandatory break. He could've had that burger after all. He wasn't vegan like Adrian's daughter, and he was hungry enough to eat two burgers. What was in a vegan burger? he wondered. Mushroom, probably. He watched the young people, finding it hard to believe the athletic-looking woman was vegan. Whether she was or not, her hands were a mess from handling the meat Adrian was waiting to grill. In the bright sunshine, the blood looked almost indelible.

Agnes studied the rusty stains on the other woman's hands, thinking, *Where did you come from?*

Iris (she hadn't given her surname) was a couple of years younger than her, and a couple of inches taller. Chestnut hair in a ponytail, sunglasses pushed up into an Alice band, almond eyes, a pink-tinted mouth. Snakeskin leggings to just below her knees, neon vest stopping short of her slim brown waist. Bare shins, tan leather ankle boots. She glowed with good health. It hurt Agnes to look at her; she felt old and pale, her skin papery under her clothes, her bones like glass.

'Seriously,' Iris was saying. 'Sorry about this, hazard of the job . . .' She held up her hands, their palms wet from the meat she was unpacking. 'I couldn't use your bathroom, could I?'

She smelt of rust, and underneath of spices. The scent came in colours: burnt amber with a hot red thread of chilli or paprika. Errol was telling another joke, making Iris laugh. Her whole face lit up when she laughed. Agnes could see flecks of gold in her green eyes.

Errol turned neatly to raise his eyebrows at Agnes, his peacock robe swinging. 'Yours, I think,' that's what his eyebrows were saying. Iris was like the drinks Dad was serving at the barbecue:

long and cool and refreshing. Agnes hadn't seen anyone like her. Nor had she felt like laughing in a long time, although Errol invariably helped with that.

The other delivery van remained parked in place. She'd seen the driver chatting with her father, the two men coming out of their house together. Dad, she knew, couldn't resist inviting every visitor into Blackthorn. The van driver lay back in his seat now, dozing. On a break. Agnes wondered whether Iris was due a break.

Errol, as if reading her mind, said, 'You can freshen up at Agnes's place before you join us for the party. You are joining us for the party?'

'I'd love to but I'd better get this to the barbecue before it makes any more mess . . .' Iris scooped a shallow crate from the van.

Errol made a shield of his hands. 'Look away, little vegan.'

The three of them set off for the street party which'd been Dad's idea, a way of bolstering morale after all the small disasters of the past five weeks. Agnes bit her lip. Could disasters be called small when so many of them kept happening?

'Wow. It's amazing here,' Iris said. 'These houses! Which one's yours?'

Errol waved in the direction of Quickthorn. 'Not really, though. Bette and I live up the road.' He waved again, this time in the direction of the coastal path.

'Who's Bette?'

'My grandmother, their housekeeper.' He sent a serene smile across his shoulder to Agnes. 'Everyone's housekeeper. She's staying on site, some of the time anyway.'

'Really?' Iris carried the crate of meat as if it weighed nothing at all. Agnes could see the smooth shape of the muscles in her shoulders. 'You have a housekeeper, living on site?'

'It's temporary.' Agnes felt embarrassed. 'Bette gets the new houses ready before they go up for sale.'

'She's Cornwall's leading cushion-plumper.' Errol was swinging a plastic bag filled with sachets of sauce for the meat. 'My lovely grandmother.'

'And you stay here too?' Iris asked him.

'Sometimes,' Errol said. 'For my sins.'

A slap of wind brought dust from the bottom of the estate. Iris dipped her sunglasses into place, squinting in that direction. 'You're still building?'

Agnes saw her staring at the blind spots and no-go zones, fences warning you to Keep Out. Floodlights too, mounted on scaffolding that looked like watchtowers.

'It's a bit of a war zone, isn't it?' Iris said. 'A gorgeous war zone but still . . .'

Agnes liked her even more for seeing through the surface gloss to the dark heart of Blackthorn Ashes. She waited as Iris handed the crate of meat to Dad who was keeping the barbecue hot. Her mother, Ruth, was preparing mushrooms. Trevor and his girlfriend were kissing in a deckchair. Barry and Janis Mason stood together, talking about the baby, Sasha, who was sleeping against Janis's shoulder. Tim and Val Prentiss had been here at the start of the party, helping to set up tables, but there was no sign of them now. No sign of Luke Dearman either, which was a good thing. Agnes crouched to put her hands in a bucket of ice, fishing out cans of Sprite. She handed one to Errol, the other to Iris who was explaining to Dad about the meat. He was quizzing her on its provenance even though he'd done this already by phone. 'And how're animal welfare standards being met exactly?'

When Iris finished explaining, Agnes said, 'You wanted to use the bathroom?'

Errol came with them to the house, sitting on Blackthorn's kitchen island while Agnes showed Iris to the bathroom upstairs. When Agnes came back down, he said, 'Ask her.'

'Ask her what?'

'How animal welfare standards are being met . . .' He rolled his eyes. '*On a date*. Ask her on a date.'

'I don't have the energy.' Just walking upstairs had exhausted her. 'She's nice, though.'

'Sprite is *nice*. She's gorgeous. Like this war zone we all live in.' Reminding Agnes that Iris was on her side instinctively, despite the bloody hands. 'Plus, she's vegan . . .'

'I still don't have the energy. For the explaining, apart from anything else.' If she'd explained herself to Laura in London, she might still be there, rather than trapped in Blackthorn Ashes.

'You're autistic,' Errol said. 'You're not contagious.'

He said it simply but with fierce affection, defending her, the way he always did. Whatever else she might regret about moving back home, she'd never regret finding Errol. They'd only known each other five weeks but he felt like a best friend, the kind you kept for life.

'Where'd I take her? I wouldn't want her here with everything that's happening. It's unsafe.'

She could say this to Errol, knowing he'd understand. She couldn't have said it to her parents, or to anyone else in Blackthorn Ashes.

'Take her to the pub. Go in her meat wagon. You can light a candle to Linda McCartney as penance when you get back.'

'Linda McCartney was vegetarian, not vegan.'

Errol rolled his eyes. 'So you can light a candle to . . . Woody Harrelson.'

'A soya candle.'

'Of course *soya*. I'm not a monster.'

'Thanks for that . . .' Iris came into the kitchen, scrubbed and clean and, yes, lovely.

Agnes was about to ask how long she could stay when Christie burst through the back door, kicking it shut behind him. He ignored them, going to the fridge to get one of his Monster cans and a six-pack of Dad's Brew Dog which he hung from his fingers as if it was an afterthought.

He left the way he'd come, Brew Dog bumping through the door after him.

Errol murmured, 'Exit, pursued by beer . . .'

'Who was *that*?' Iris laughed.

'My brother,' Agnes said. 'Christie.'

'Your brother? But isn't he, like, twelve?'

'Thirteen,' Errol corrected. 'Going on thirty.'

'My mum had trouble getting pregnant the second time.'

Too much information, Agnes. She bent to scratch her ankle, and to hide her embarrassment.

'Doesn't he get lonely out here?' Iris asked. 'There aren't a lot of teenagers around. And doesn't anyone have a pet? I thought you'd all have dogs. My boss warned me to watch out because they smell the van coming for miles.'

'We had a rabbit,' Agnes said. 'But she died.'

'We have a dog.' Errol slid off the island. 'He isn't allowed in the houses here, you'd understand if you saw him . . . I'm starving, shall we go?'

He held the door for the pair of them so Agnes and Iris could leave together.

Back at the barbecue, her parents were plating up chargrilled sweetcorn and baked potatoes. Trevor had moved Sandra off his lap onto the grass at his feet. He was rolling a cigarette.

'Where's Christie?' her mother asked.

'He's around. We saw him at the house just now . . . Dad, can Iris have a vegan burger?'

When they had food in their hands, Errol offered Iris a guided tour. He was trying to get Agnes away from Ruth, and Trevor. He knew she was on edge around them, even if he didn't know why. He did his best to steer her clear of the stress that was everywhere in Blackthorn Ashes, no matter how hard Dad tried to plug the gaps or seal the leaks with his smile and his generosity, his unsinkable optimism.

A door slammed in the street.

Silverthorn. Agnes felt her shoulders stiffen.

Errol took a bite of his burger. 'Don't Luke Now . . .'

Iris turned to Agnes for an explanation but she shook her head. 'One of the neighbours . . .'

Luke Dearman was fighting with his crutches, gearing up for another round with Dad. He couldn't leave it alone, as if he drew strength from constantly confronting people. Agnes was aware of her father turning sausages on the grill, one eye on the commotion. She'd lost count of how often he'd let Luke shout at him, flinging insults for everyone to hear. Even at a distance, the man's fury managed to transmit itself, making everyone except Trevor tense up. Janis cupped baby Sasha's head, turning away. Only Iris watched, curious to see what Luke was doing. He planted the crutches in the tarmac one after the other, as if he were planting flagpoles on the moon. Before he'd even reached them, he was shouting.

'Right, I've been on to Health and Safety! They've asked me to file a full report, so I'll be taking photos of what's gone wrong in my garden and I'll be asking you lot for witness statements!'

'Come on.' Errol ducked out, Agnes at his heels.

Iris lingered but in the end she followed too. When they were out of sight of the party, she said, 'Okay, so I have to know, what exactly's gone wrong in his garden?' She was laughing but her eyes were serious. Luke did that, sucked the joy out of everything and everyone.

'Holes,' Errol said. 'In the lawn. He blames Agnes's dad but it's just as likely he dug them himself in a frenzied search for his sense of humour . . .'

'Holes in the lawn,' Iris echoed. 'Is that how he broke his foot?'

'Allegedly,' Errol said.

'And he blames your dad?' Iris looked at Agnes, puzzled.

'Because Dad sold the houses. That makes everything his fault, according to Luke.'

'He sounds bonkers.'

'Putting it mildly . . .' Errol's mouth was full of burger.

'Is he living alone here—?'

A scream interrupted Iris, the pitch of it high enough to make Agnes cringe. A child's scream, full of terror, coming from the back garden at Maythorn.

'Chloe.' Agnes put her food down and started running.

Errol was on her heels, up the side of the house and into May-thorn's garden where the paddling pool was full and the sandpit had spilt pale sand onto wet grass.

Six-year-old Chloe Mason was squatting in the sandpit, both arms raised in the air. Her hands were a bright shiny red, her mouth wide with screaming.

'Shit.' Errol skidded to a halt on the lawn.

Agnes crouched at the side of the sandpit. 'Chloe, it's okay.' But it wasn't. Her little hands were covered in blood and it was too bright – Agnes had to blink as she reached to help. Then Janis and Barry were in the garden, Chloe being scooped up into her dad's arms, Janis searching through the sand for whatever it was that had cut her little girl and it was a can, a torn tin can, deckled with sand and cherry-red blood. Errol and Agnes moved back, making room for the Masons to comfort Chloe.

Iris had stayed on the side path, out of the way. Her face was frowning, shocked. She wouldn't want to come back here, not after this. It wasn't the end of it, either.

As Chloe began to calm down, someone on the street gave a long bellow of pain.

Investigating, they found Luke sitting by the barbecue with his right arm buried in an ice bucket. Smoke rose from the grill, along with the horrible sweet smell of meat cooking.

Luke had lunged for Dad and missed, Mum told them, his fore-arm hitting the grill.

'I've only just ordered a first aid kit. I'm surprised it wasn't in one of the packages that man brought . . .'

'Rory,' Adrian said automatically. He was phoning for an ambu-lance. 'His name was Rory.'

*

Rory had missed the excitement, after backing his van onto Ashes Road. Dodging potholes, he found himself swerving when a white face pressed up against his windscreen.

'Christ!'

But it was just a balloon escaping from the arch at the street party, drifting aimlessly away.

The acoustics were weird on the road, the drag of the sea fogging the sounds of the party back in Blackthorn Ashes. What he took to be their chatter trailed after him like the balloon. He drove until the sea was back at his side, half dreaming of what it must be like to live in one of the houses with the wide windows, woodburners, ice makers in the fridges . . .

A few miles further on, a gunfire burst of sirens split the road in two. He had the van wedged in the hedge before he knew what was happening.

An ambulance swept up the coast road at speed, lit all over by flashing lights.

The van's passenger side was blacked out by the thorny hedge he'd dodged into, dust rising from his tyres. The ambulance pushed past and away. Headed for Blackthorn Ashes and at speed.

Something had gone very wrong at the street party.

So much for paradise.

Rory waited until the dust settled before he eased the van from the hedge, thorns protesting against the paintwork. Just up ahead, a little way along the coast road, the white balloon was waiting, hanging like a child's sock from the branches of the blackthorn.

1 SEPTEMBER

Seven days after abandonment

———

2

A thick pelt of condensation had grown on the inside of the caravan's windows overnight. Agnes drew a face in it, watching the mouth and eyes run wetly. Rain oozed from the roof, drilling holes in the mud outside. Everything in Indigo Park was grey. Even the hedges, after rain brought the fields down in a river, were skeleton-stiff with drying mud. Ghost hedges.

'What're you doing?'

Christie was in his pyjamas, rubbing sleep from his eyes.

'Spying . . .' Agnes trained the binoculars on the caravan across from theirs. 'Last time it rained this hard, someone stole our duckboards.'

Christie came close, peering out through the face she'd drawn in the condensation. 'It'll dry up.'

The mud wouldn't dry, not for weeks. Better to be surrounded by water; you could swim in water. In mud, you could only drown. Agnes swept the binoculars to the west, watching.

'You're doing it again.' Her brother wiped her face from the window, drying his hand on his pyjamas. 'Being a bit mental.'

'Well, you know me . . .' Agnes narrowed her field of vision to Bette's caravan. 'Always suspected of being paranoid.'

She intended it as a joke: *Just because I'm paranoid doesn't mean . . .* But Christie didn't laugh. She couldn't remember the last time he did.

Bette was waiting for her dog to finish peeing up against her decking. It peed in the same place every morning and again in the evening. You could set your watch to it.

'Seriously, though.' Christie ran his finger down the window, leaving a white streak. 'Who'd want to steal any of our shit?'

'People will steal anything' – Agnes waggled the binoculars – 'that's not nailed down.'

'That'll do.' Their mother was listening from the caravan's kitchen. She didn't like Christie swearing. He was thirteen, still young in her mind. Not like Agnes who'd left home swearing eleven years ago and come back no better. 'Sit and have your breakfast.'

'He's right, though,' Agnes said to herself as her brother loped to the kitchen. 'There's nothing here worth stealing.'

For that, you had to walk twenty minutes in the direction of the sea. She set her teeth around the name, gritting it out: 'Black-thorn Ashes.' She couldn't bring herself to use the word *home*. In the big houses with the pretty names – Maythorn, Silverthorn – treasure was stashed in every room. Like these binoculars left out on Hawthorn's kitchen island with the reed tumblers and glazed olive dishes, the last new things Tim and Val Prentiss ever bought. Professional binoculars with excellent optics and rubber armoury, a wide field of view. Ideal for spying on your neighbours.

Bette's dog splashed through puddles, nosing in the mud. A flash of colour said Errol was up. Happiness leapt in her chest, swiftly dampened by guilt: she'd no business being happy, none of them did. Dad expressed it best, sitting with his shoulders slumped, misery in his eyes.

Bette was hanging out her washing – a crimson skirt – and suddenly Agnes saw the ghost of a red gingham dress, ruched at the waist, her mother's favourite sundress from years ago. She could smell Mum's suncream, feel the smooth roll of pebbles under her feet.

'Breakfast.' Her mother didn't need to raise her voice, the caravan wasn't more than eight metres from the galley to the front door, but she raised it anyway. 'Agnes.'

She joined her mother and brother at the table where the binoculars looked much bigger than they had on Hawthorn's marble island. Everything was bigger in the caravan. Her mother's moods, Christie's snoring and his farts, Dad's silence. Breakfast was beans on toast cooked on the gas ring, tasting of the gas ring. In Blackthorn Ashes, they'd breakfasted on fresh fruit and French toast, American pancakes. She wondered what Val and Tim's favourite breakfast had been, what they'd cooked on the ceramic hob or in their built-in double oven. She'd never know, now.

'I'd better be off . . .' Mum poured coffee into a Thermos, screwing the lid flush. 'Remember to dry the plates after you've washed them. We can't afford to get ill, there's too much to do.'

Droplets of undried water could grow mould, become a breeding ground for germs and bacteria. E. coli. S. aureus. There was a whole alphabet of illnesses and they'd seen enough sickness to last a lifetime. In Blackthorn Ashes, they'd been the lucky ones. But luck never lasts.

'What about Dad?' Agnes chased a baked bean around her plate. 'Is he going to want breakfast?'

'He can sort himself out,' Mum said shortly. 'There's plenty of bread for toast.'

Agnes couldn't tell if she was exasperated with Dad or simply preoccupied. She knew her parents had been arguing, even before the street party that ended with Chloe screaming in the sandpit, Luke's barbecued arm.

Her mother pulled on a jacket, resting her eyes on Christie. Her face softened and there she was: Agnes's mum from long ago, a red gingham dress and the orange smell of suncream.

'Look after your brother.'

'Of course.'

'You might see if Bette needs anything.'

Mum wanted to make certain Agnes would stay in the caravan park, that she wouldn't wander off with Errol, or with Christie, getting into God knows what trouble. Like sickness, they'd seen enough trouble to last a lifetime.

'What about the police?' Agnes asked.

'What about them?' Her mother held the flask in both hands, not a flicker anywhere in her face. Her self-control made Agnes ashamed of the sweat in her own armpits.

'What if this's the day they come?' Panic shivered in her throat. 'Or the investigators?'

At the table, Christie had his head down, scrolling through his phone. He was tense, listening for Mum's answer. Her eyes rested on him before returning to Agnes.

'We have been through this.' She spoke slowly, her voice rinsed of emotion. 'They are not just going to turn up at the caravan. There is a process to be followed. We answered all their initial questions to the best of our ability—'

'Six people died.' The panic tasted metallic, shiny in her mouth. 'Children died.'

'It was horrible.' Her mother's expression didn't change. 'A horrible accident.' She spaced the three words apart from one another, sounding out each syllable. 'It was one night, a week ago. We're here now and we need to make the best of it.'

'The papers called it a tragedy. An atrocity.'

'They use words like that as clickbait. We know better.'

'Do we?' She pushed, wanting her mother to react. Not wanting Ruth to leave her alone with Dad and Christie and everything that'd happened. She didn't understand how Ruth wasn't panicking, why her mother's mouth wasn't full of metal and fear like her own.

'We were there. So yes, we know better.'

'Tell me.'

Anything to keep her here, stop her from leaving. Even if it meant a lecture. Her mother was holding in a sigh; Agnes saw its shape in her throat, knew what she'd say next.

'Have you taken your meds?'

Always the same question, since she was sixteen and newly diagnosed. She was trying to be helpful, because sometimes Agnes did forget and then the inside of her head was like the windows in the caravan, fogged up. Fuzzy thinking.

'I took them, yes.'

'And you know what happened. Carbon monoxide leaked into the houses through faults in the flues.' Ruth tamped each word down as if Agnes's panic were a flapping sheet of nylon. 'Bad ventilation exacerbated the effect but it was most likely caused by land contamination. Subsidence put cracks in the flue pipes, that's how the carbon monoxide was able to build up. The reports failed to show the true levels of land contamination. If they had, the developers would never have built there. Your father would never have sold there.' She paused. 'He sold those houses in good faith.'

'Six people died.'

Agnes didn't understand how Ruth could keep the ghosts out of her head, how she was able to stop seeing Tim and Val and Emma. Felix and Chloe and baby Sasha.

'The police won't come here. It is in the hands of the investigators now. But it was an accident.' No margin in her mother's voice for doubt to wriggle through, every crack covered, sealed tight. 'Blackthorn Ashes was not what we thought it was.'

Paradise, a forever home. Bad enough when the money dried up and the work ground to a halt, Trevor doing what he could to keep it going, Ruth seeking new sources of funding when they should have been looking closer to home, at the danger lurking in the houses already built.

'I'm worried about Dad. He hasn't got up from the sofa in three days. I don't think he's—'

'Your father's fine.' Ruth rubbed the back of her hand across her forehead. 'He's exhausted, as anyone would be after everything. Look, love, I have to go.' She forced a smile. 'Bette says the supermarket might need someone but the good shifts go fast. Just as well we've still got the car.'

Christie kicked a foot at the table leg, turning up the volume on his phone: a sudden blast of sea shanty. The caravan was full of the static crackle of fear.

'I'm sorry.' Agnes forced her hands to her sides. 'I'll take care of things here. We'll ask Bette if we can walk her dog.'

'Yeah!' Her brother looked up, his phone forgotten. 'We can totally walk Odie.'

'Good.' Ruth bent to plant a kiss on his head.

Then she was gone, taking the flask of coffee with her.

Christie waited for the sound of her car pulling away before he said, 'Come on, then.'

He dumped his empty plate in the sink, standing five feet tall in his socks. 'Bet I'm dressed before you're done.' He raced the short distance to the room they shared, banging shut the door.

Agnes washed and dried the dishes, not hurrying. She took two slices from the loaf in the bread bin, spreading peanut butter into a sandwich which she cut into triangles and put on a plate, covering it with cling film. She put a teabag into a mug and filled the kettle, bringing it to the boil.

Mum thought Dad could sort himself out but it wasn't that simple. He was sunk in depression, under the surface of their lives. At least this way he'd see a meal waiting when he got up.

'You lose.'

Christie was in hoodie and jeans, empty backpack between his shoulder blades.

Agnes rolled down the sleeves of her T-shirt. 'Is Dad awake?'

'No.'

He was pleased because it meant they could sneak out without being asked awkward questions. Dad hadn't asked any questions in days, or answered any either.

'Okay,' she said. 'You go ahead. Let me get my boots.'

Her father was curled on his side on the sofa bed, one shoulder hunched against the day. He'd made an attempt to shave at some point: a rusty scab under his left ear. Agnes shut her eyes, seeing the bright blood on Chloe's little hands, hearing her wail echo up and down the houses like the noise Janis made, much worse, on the last night they ever spent in Blackthorn Ashes.

Outside, the day was warmer than it'd looked from the window.

Bette was wrapped for winter but that was her style, lots of layers in different shades of the same colour. Red, today. Orange boots, crimson trousers, pink fleece. She waved to Agnes and Christie while Odie sniffed around the Calor bottles, his arse in the air.

Errol moved inside the caravan like an exotic fish in a murky tank (Agnes made a note to tell him that later). Left to her own devices, she'd have spent the day with him, but there was Christie to think about. She'd see Errol when they got back, her reward for being a good sister.

'Sun's putting in an appearance,' Bette said. 'About time.'

She was in her late seventies, her skin soft and powdery but her eyes blue steel. The first time she'd seen them sneaking off, Agnes had been certain she'd tell Ruth. But Bette hadn't told, then or any time since. It was possible Errol had asked her to keep their secret. He didn't understand what Agnes and Christie were up to but he was on her side. Bette was, too. When they'd lost their home in Blackthorn Ashes, Bette was the one who'd found them the caravan here in Indigo Park.

Odie glanced up from the gas bottles before sprinting towards Christie.

'Hello, boy!'

Agnes waited while her brother petted the dog's ears. She was in no hurry to get going. This was Christie's idea, his compulsion.

She stayed with him, keeping him safe or trying to, with no real idea of what would happen if – *when* – they were caught. How they'd explain themselves, what they'd do. Flight, fight or freeze. When she tried to imagine it, her mind went blank.

'Yeah, Odie.' Christie fussed at the dog. 'You're all right, aren't you? You're okay.'

A little of the tension had left him but his jaw was bunched, the way it had been since the start of the trouble at Blackthorn Ashes. That was Agnes's fault: no one noticed anything wrong in any of the houses until she began pointing it out. Mum said no one was to blame but she had to blame Agnes for that – not letting them have even a few days of happiness before she started asking about the things only she could hear and smell and taste – before it all went to hell.

'Come on.'

Christie straightened from petting Odie. Then he stiffened, going still. He'd heard someone stumbling inside their caravan, knees knocking into stuff. Dad was up.

They stood and listened, not looking at one another.

Agnes told herself Dad didn't care what they did. He never noticed, would never tell. He spent all day with his shoulders caved in, wishing he'd been smarter or quicker or braver when it counted. Some days, she caught a look in his eyes like a plea. For understanding or forgiveness, or simply for peace. She couldn't help him but she wanted to, desperately.

'Odie!' Bette tucked the dog under one arm, going inside to Errol, leaving them alone.

'Come on,' Christie said.

They turned away from Indigo Park, shaking off Dad's silence as they walked. The only sounds were the keys in Christie's pocket and the hiss of the nylon backpack against his hoodie.

By the time they reached the coastal path, six minutes later, they were breathing normally. Up here, the air was washed by rain, hedges purple with sloes, smelling sharp and wet. Ahead, just out of sight, the sea rolled against the rocks. As the path climbed, they caught a flash of it, white-tipped.

Gulls barked overhead. They plagued the caravan park, scavenging for scraps and fried chicken bones. They'd have to wait for the half-term holidaymakers; Agnes's family couldn't afford fried chicken. A week ago, on the night they moved to Indigo Park, Mum bought fish and chips to cheer them up but the next morning she wrote menus based on a weekly budget that wouldn't have kept Christie in Monster Energy and Flamin' Hot Doritos back in Blackthorn Ashes.

Agnes walked as slowly as she could without losing sight of her brother who ploughed ahead, swiping a broken branch at the hedges, sending up a riot of raindrops. He couldn't wait to get back to Blackthorn Ashes. For her, this was the best part of their day, walking the coastal path in the fresh air. Rain didn't bother her, nor the wind thumping off the sea, inflating Christie's backpack until it looked like he might take flight. The dark hedges were pricked with colour, late-flowering sea campion in white knots, rusty-red stonecrop.

'There!' Christie pointed, his voice climbing. 'Come on!' He broke into a run.

Agnes called after him, 'Quietly! They might've put up cameras, brought in a guard . . .'

'What, since yesterday?' he scoffed, cocking his head at her, red fringe falling like a question mark. But he slowed to a crouch, hidden by the hedge.

Six more steps and they were at the back of Blackthorn Ashes, where there were only gardens. No fences or cameras or guards. Just houses separated by lawns, each with its roof shaped like a ski slope, the whole lot bracketed by ancient ash trees.

In Scandinavian mythology, the sales brochure said, ash is the tree of life. Over centuries, it colonized this part of the cliffs, springing up where other trees had fallen and died. Now, as autumn crept in, its branches were hung with bunches of ash keys: winged seeds waiting to spill and spread. In Celtic mythology, blackthorn is symbolic of protection and the overcoming of obstacles for a better future. Here the sales brochure became fanciful, suggesting Sleeping Beauty encircled in thorns, waiting to be woken by a prince's kiss. The houses were dead white, bone white. *Akiya.* That was closer to the truth. Ghost houses.

Christie crouched, using his branch to prod at the hole he'd made in the hedge before pushing his way inside and disappearing, branches closing tight behind him.

Agnes stood a moment longer on the safe side of what they were doing. Alone on the path, no Christie, no Ruth, just salt wind and a big sprawl of sky. Then she crouched to squeeze her way through the thin scratch of sharp branches, joining her brother on the other side.

Blackthorn Ashes: a time for new beginnings.

The whole place was shining, the way it did whenever the sun was out. House after house glittering, breathing, waiting. Shadows snagged here and there as clouds creased the sky. Where the shadows touched the houses, they shivered, windows like thin white skin.

'It's what we deserve,' Dad had said. 'What we've earnt.'

Not Indigo Park with its caravans sinking into mud. Agnes heard the mud when she was in her bunk at night, sucking at the underside of the caravan. Blackthorn Ashes, as it turned out, was built on slurry, soil rotted through with toxins and riddled with blight. She wanted to sink the whole place into a huge hole but first the site had to be declared safe enough to go in with specialist equipment, digging in the slurry for the secrets buried there.

The earth tells stories . . . Agnes was unsure where she'd heard that phrase but it was true. The earth had been the first to speak here. Before the worst of the cracks began creeping up the walls, tiles coming loose on the floors, pockets of dead air popping underfoot. It was the earth opening up, laying a long trench in Silverthorn's lawn, that broke Luke Dearman's foot.

A breeze slid through the young trees planted beside the houses, playing against her face for a second before it moved towards the sea. Above her, a gull cried, lonely as a lost child. They were in the back garden of Maythorn, where Felix had kicked a ball about the lawn; Agnes knew her brother missed his friend. Christie toed at the lawn now, his eyes off in the past, seeing this place as it was eight weeks ago when the billboards were up and the show house newly opened. 'Luxury living, between coast and country.' He'd memorized the sales brochure Dad brought home. 'Fall asleep to the sound of the sea.' *And never wake up.*

This time, the breeze brought a fistful of dust to their feet. Agnes pinched the skin at her wrist to quell a stab of panic.

Christie was poking in Chloe's sandpit with his branch.

Blackthorn Ashes didn't haunt him the way it haunted her. He'd invested so much in the idea of their new home, months of antici- pation, excitedly scoring down the days. Perhaps you had to accept a place was dead before its ghosts could haunt you. The sandpit was poked full of holes, not just from Christie's branch but the beaks and feet of birds. Crows and gulls, swifts and swallows and house martins. The smaller birds had left when the people moved in but the gardens were theirs again now, if they could survive the sparrowhawks. All the people were gone. Twelve half-built houses at the bottom of the estate were shrouded in tattered plastic. Each of the finished houses was a museum. The families left fast on the day of evacuation, no time for removal vans or bubble wrap and boxes. They left clothes and toys, books and toasters in the empty rooms. A pair of reading glasses propped on the open spine of a paperback book left by Tim Prentiss. A pot of face cream with the lid set aside, Val's fingerprints in the cream. A stuffed toy ele- phant at the foot of an empty cot. Some of it had been stripped by gangs from the local town but most stayed away, sensing some- thing wasn't right. Even if you hadn't heard the news, you sensed it. Something went very wrong here. Safer to rob the houses down the hill. Nearly everyone stayed away from Blackthorn Ashes. It was only Christie who kept coming, drawn by a need she almost understood, the way you almost catch sight of a thing from the edge of your eye. A need to snatch back the happiness he'd known here, was that it? Afraid to let it go. As a family, they'd been so glad to be back together after the eleven years Agnes was in London but it was over so quickly. Finished.

'Come on.'

Her brother led the way up the side of Maythorn, past the wheelie bins, out into the street.

Agnes looked towards Hawthorn, the show house, then turned in the direction of Quickthorn where Errol and Bette had stayed while Bette was working here as housekeeper. A flash of the street party – Iris and Errol laughing – came and went in the same breath, the tail end of their happiness. She understood why her brother wanted it back.

'We're going to get some cool stuff today.' He went ahead of her. 'Let's do Whitethorn.' He shaded his eyes. 'Shall we do Whitethorn?'

Whitethorn was one of the unsold houses made ready by Bette, a second show home, furnished and polished. Smaller than Black-thorn, the house where Agnes and Christie had lived. They'd been lucky, Dad said, getting one of the bigger houses on the plot, 'As if we knew you'd be living back home with us, love,' but it wasn't luck that had brought Agnes home after eleven years away. Unless it was bad luck, the worst of her life. Losing her job in London, losing Laura.

Christie broke into a run, looking like a thirteen-year-old again, her baby brother. Being back here made him jump and run, wrig-gling through hedges, under sofas, into wardrobes. Perhaps the ghosts found him after all, haunting him into a dervish, unstop-pable, fearless.

By the time she caught up, he was at Whitethorn's back door, Dad's keys in his hand. He separated out a key, fitting it into Whitethorn's lock.

Agnes suffered the usual clench of terror, acid flooding her throat, expecting the wail of an alarm. But there was just the *shush* of the door folding on its hinges to let her brother into the house, its kitchen dim and hushed.

'Wait,' she warned Christie.

If they could get inside so easily, why not someone else? Her skin twitched with warning. They shouldn't be here. This place was a death trap.

Christie jogged his leg impatiently. The key was in his pocket, ticking against the others on the ring. Dad should've handed the keys to the police. Instead, he'd put them into a toolbox for Christie to find. Dad and Trevor had been the developers' trusted duo, their golden boys, Dad promising paradise to friends and to strangers in the pub, reeling everyone in with talk of bi-fold doors that let light flood seamlessly from room to room, a special quality of darkness, wide skies, crisp sea air . . .

'Agnes, come on.'

Christie wanted her inside the house with him so he could shut the door. Six days ago, the first time they'd come back, he dug ice cream from the freezers, sitting on the marble islands to eat it, feet swinging. But then he'd wanted to go deeper into the houses, to the backs of cupboards and the bottoms of drawers, searching for whatever was small enough to slip into his backpack. CDs and books, paperweights, aftershave, ashtrays. His first treasure was a bottle opener shaped like a sea lion. His first *theft*. As the days went by, with no one to stop them and Mum in the dark, his courage grew. Last week in Maythorn, he'd emptied all the fridge magnets into his backpack with a single sweep of his elbow.

How was it possible for nearly new houses to feel so eerie?

Agnes shivered as her brother prowled the kitchen, his red hair reflecting in the pendant lamp, trainers squealing on the tiled floor. He picked up a sponge shaped like a lemon, dropped it back down. His fingers fidgeted at his sides, adrenaline making him electric. She wished he'd take a spoon or saucer, put it in his backpack. Once he had something – anything – as ballast, he'd calm down and grow tired, be ready to trail back to the caravan. Agnes hated the stealing but more than that she couldn't picture the look on Ruth's face if she could see them here. She didn't want to picture it. She tried seeing the red sundress instead but it hurt to remember. Not just Mum as she used to be. Binka, too. Agnes felt the warm weight of the rabbit in her arms, the wriggle of Binka's body as she escaped to nibble at the lawn. She'd put her ear to the ground, heard the shredding of Binka's teeth in the grass. And something underneath, a sound like cloth splitting apart. The memory pricked her skin with dread. It was mostly memories she was scared of now. Even happy ones, especially happy ones. Her family seven weeks ago. Christie when he was two years old, putting stuff in his mouth. Pebbles and grass and the red straps of Ruth's dress. Now he carried keys to half a dozen houses. The keys were always with him, tucked into a pocket or hidden in a console case, never out of reach. He'd known the back door to every house could be opened with the same key; Trevor taught him that. Front doors were different, secure, but every back door could be opened with the same identical key. It was crazy, but no crazier than anything else that'd happened here.

Christie had closed the back door behind them. Agnes opened it a crack, needing to know they could leave in a hurry if they had to.

In Whitethorn's sitting room, her brother was flat on his stomach, stretching a hand under the sofa for whatever was hidden there. Today's treasure. His feet kicked, putting pleats in the pale rug.

Agnes stopped at the threshold, not seeing an unsold house or not only that. Seeing the other houses – Hawthorn where Tim and Val Prentiss died, Silverthorn where Emma Dearman died – cringing at the thought of Luke sitting on the sofa, working himself into a rage over whatever was on the TV. Bette had put a tea tray on the low table in the centre of the room, made ready with cups and saucers, a white teapot with a square spout. Dust sat in the cups and saucers.

In Maythorn, Janis's yellow cardigan was still on the back of the sofa, its pockets patched with gingham. Left behind, like everything else, in the rush to leave.

Whitethorn's sitting room stank of stale air and dead flies. And the other smell, the one all the houses had. Disturbingly earthy like a badger's sett, a place of blood and bones. She heard the echo of Errol's voice in her head: *You're autistic, not contagious.*

The windows were bleary, a long streak of gull's shit against the glass.

'What is it?' she asked.

Christie wriggled free, holding out his hand. A diamond filled his fist, spilling a weak pink rainbow over his fingers. An acrylic diamond, designed to make you believe in the dream of luxury living. The scatter diamonds were part of the lies Dad and Trevor had told about Blackthorn Ashes, how life would be here. She watched her brother close his fist around it. When she came home from London, he told her about the bricks he'd signed.

'Dad let me lay the first one. I wrote my name on, like, a ton of bricks. Dad uses one in each of the houses. The first brick they lay – with my name written on it!'

Her heart hurt for him, remembering that. Every house with

a signed brick in its walls bearing his name. No wonder he felt
so tied to this place. She wanted to help him get better but what
if she was making it worse by letting him come here? She should
tell Ruth what they were doing but she didn't know how to talk
to her mother. Eleven years had passed since they'd stopped yelling at one another, fighting over everything and nothing at all. At
eighteen, she'd packed a bag and left for London, making sure to
let her mother know of her successes, the interviews she smashed,
the promotions. Never telling of the moments (so many) when she
hadn't coped, having no idea how to fix the things (so many) that
went wrong. Then there was Laura, and everything came upright.
She wrote home about the flat she and Laura were renting together,
the first flush of wedding plans. Nine weeks ago, when she turned
up on their doorstep without warning, Ruth hadn't recognized
her, Agnes was so unlike the picture she'd painted of herself. She
pinched the skin at her wrist, watching Christie zip the scatter diamond into his backpack.

He shrugged the backpack into place. 'Let's go upstairs.'

'You go. I'll keep watch.'

'For what? No one's here. There's never anyone.'

'You go, if you have to.'

The last thing she wanted to see was a bed like the one where
Val and Tim were found dead. Or where Luke and Emma had slept,
his pain medication on a bedside table, her nightie on the pillow.
She wanted to be in the fresh air, on her way back to Indigo Park
and Errol. This place was deadly at a level no boreholes or blood
tests could detect. Her family's fresh start had lasted less than a
week before Blackthorn Ashes began to show its true face. No
shadows spoilt the carpets, no crude handprints on the walls.

No one broke in after dark, swinging a hammer or wielding a knife. In Maythorn, the children died in their sleep. In Hawthorn, Tim and Val went to bed and never woke. Their deaths had been quiet, too quiet to account for the shouting in her head. She turned from the window, listening. Christie was light on his feet but the floorboards gave him away. All the wood in Blackthorn Ashes was noisy, as if it had absorbed the soundtrack of the horror that unfolded here. Her brother made the floor groan and shriek as he prowled from room to room.

Agnes breathed on Whitethorn's window, wanting to write, 'I warned you,' but it wasn't true. She'd tried to warn them but not about this. Not about what actually happened.

A sudden sound outside froze her, blood buzzing in her fingers.

'Christie,' she hissed his name up the stairs, 'We have to go!'

No answer. He was deep inside a cupboard or lying on a bed with his trainers on, playing on his phone because that was the other reason he kept coming back here – to feel normal again.

'*Christie!*'

The back door was open. She'd left it like that for a quick getaway. It was hard to breathe.

The house – huge compared to the caravan – felt small and getting smaller, walls and ceilings crowding in. They should've stayed away. Ruth had warned them to stay away.

A shadow was outside the back door. A man, broad-shouldered, his face in darkness. The sun turned him into an iron silhouette.

Agnes stayed at the far end of the marble island, gripping its chilly lip. Eighteen feet separated her from the man. Cold stone floor then bi-fold door. Butcher's block to her right: eight steel handles, eight sharp blades; she could taste their white metal on her tongue.

The man wasn't moving, his hands loose at his sides, head cocked as if he were listening rather than watching. Was it possible he couldn't see her?

A fly droned by the fridge. Anything inside would be rancid but the fly didn't know that. She slid her hand to her pocket, finding the hard shape of her phone. There was no one she could call, no one who'd get here fast enough to help them. And what would she say? She hadn't the words to describe her fear of being found, trapped here. Her fear of the ghosts inside, and of the man out there. He put up a hand, spreading his palm on the glass of the door.

Thick, blurred fingers. *Gloves.*

Fear shook her blackly from head to foot, a foul taste flooding her mouth.

Feet thumped above her, nylon hissing. Christie was coming down the stairs. She should stop him. Turn and run, push him ahead of her to find a room with a lock. The bathroom, they could hide in the bath, his body under hers, until it was over . . .

Her panic made no sense. If they were trespassing, then so was the man outside the door. But her fear was older than that, far older than the houses. It was made of tears and touching and the crisp chill of beer on her tongue. Her fear wore cowboy boots and was called Trevor Kyte.

The man's shadow shrank as he moved closer to the door, his breath on the glass.

The bathroom door wasn't strong enough to hold him, none of the doors here was. The wood unseasoned and tacky with sap, one of many corners cut to make Blackthorn Ashes profitable. Why was she thinking of that now? Why was she standing as if her feet had been hammered into place? She should be running, shouting at Christie to run too.

'Shit.' Her brother came to a halt behind her, breath hiccupping in his chest. 'Who is it?'

She shook her head, pushing her hands at him warningly.

'What're they doing?' His whisper was thin with terror. 'Shit, is the door *open*?'

The man wasn't moving but he was tenser than before, his body cocked in their direction. Could he hear them? See them? What was he waiting for?

'Agnes, we've got to go.' Christie plucked at her sleeve. 'Let's go.'

'You go. I'll stay.' Her brother was fast, he could get away. 'You go.'

'What? No.' He tried to pull her in the direction of the front door. 'Come on!'

'Christie.' She put her hands on his shoulders, making him still. 'He can't chase both of us, not if we split up. You need to run. Get back to the caravan park.'

He shook his head fiercely.

'*Yes*. Look, he's not coming in. That means he's not meant to be here any more than we are. He's trespassing too. Maybe he'll go away. If he doesn't, I'll make up a story. I'm good with stories. You go. Out through the front then back through the gardens. Stay out of sight.'

'I'll wait for you.' He bunched his jaw, reaching for her hand.

'All right,' she agreed. 'Wait by the lane. But if I don't join you in ten minutes, keep going until you get back to the caravan.'

'Mum'll—'

'I'll make up a story for her, too. *Go.*'

She watched him race to the front door.

When he was safely outside, she turned to face the man whose gloved hand was on the glass of the kitchen door.

She'd told Christie she didn't know who he was but she'd lied. She'd known as soon as she'd seen his silhouette, as soon as she heard the sound of someone creeping up on them.

She'd known, and she'd stayed.

3

It was the smell of his own body that drove Adrian from the sofa. He hadn't the energy to wash in the caravan's narrow shower cubicle, gripping the side of the sink as he swilled water around his teeth, spat it out. Four cheap toothbrushes hung from a rack bought at the supermarket. The electric toothbrushes had been left behind in the family bathroom in Blackthorn, where tiles started falling from the walls the week he moved his family in. He gagged at the chemical stink of the caravan's toilet but it was no worse than the stink of his own skin; he hadn't washed in days. He rubbed a water stain from the mirror, avoiding his reflection. Shame was a bad taste in his mouth, gritty like the sand from the site where they'd left a dozen houses half-built.

Blackthorn Ashes would always be half-built now, until they tore it all down. Their house would be gone, the bedroom with the sea view reduced to rubble. Christie's room with the cupboards and cabinets Adrian built – rubble. His daughter's room, earmarked as an office until Agnes came home, the kitchen he'd been so proud of – rubble.

'No choice,' that's what he'd kept repeating to himself, what he

muttered now as he dodged his reflection in the caravan's bathroom. He'd had no choice, none of them had. In the end, it was the
police who ordered them to leave everything and go, abandoning
Blackthorn Ashes to the gulls and crows, and the investigators who
would pick around in search of answers.

'Could've been worse,' Trevor kept saying. 'Could've been
Christie in a body bag like those other kids, like Dearman's wife
could've been Ruth.'

Trevor never mentioned Agnes when he was roll-calling their
good fortune but he kept roll-calling, wanting Adrian to see the
silver lining in six deaths over a single summer.

The sun was out, making the caravan's walls pop as they shook
off last night's rain. Adrian had listened to the rain all night, its percussion a special sort of torture.

The caravan was temporary, Ruth insisted, they wouldn't be here
for ever. She left each morning in search of work in the scrubby
little town they'd intended to avoid when they moved out here.
The kids left too (not that Agnes was a kid), leaving him alone,
a rat in a trap. He rubbed his thumb at the stubborn water stain,
making the mirror squeak. Outside, he could smell the sun heating
mud under the duckboards. Indigo Park was built on fudge, as far
as he could tell, but not one of the caravans was sliding towards
the sea. Between bouts of rain, when the mud dried, it didn't crack
into trenches deep enough to break your feet in. Somewhere, Luke
Dearman was shaking his crutches at Adrian, telling him he'd told
him so, hoping they hung him out to dry for what he'd done.

All summer, the sun had kept shining, leeching every last useful
drop of moisture from the lawns. That's what Adrian saw when he
shut his eyes: sun baking the roofs and roasting gardens, softening

tarmac in driveways. Plenty of rain fell during the building of Black-thorn Ashes but by the time the first families moved in, summer was in full force, blazing through every window, setting light to the chrome finishes; better even than the promises or posters, proper paradise sunshine. But then it didn't stop, didn't even slack off. Week after week of heat scorching frail new flower beds, paint flak-ing from everything in scabs. Ruth had closed all the curtains to keep the heat out. If they'd kept the curtains open, they might've seen what was happening before it was too late. Barry Mason's house was next door to Blackthorn. His kids were taken away in body bags. Even the baby, in a body bag. From Maythorn, where Adrian had planted the first brick for luck, the one with Christie's name on it. Trevor had warned him, 'Mate, you can't afford to be sentimental in this game,' but Adrian had touched the walls for luck and polished the fake diamonds with a sick sort of pride, going from room to room grinning like an idiot.

Rain shook from the caravan's roof.

He dropped his hand to his side, riding a fresh wave of shame that left him shivering as if from shock. He made himself think of the other families, the lives he might have lived or lost.

If he'd bought Hawthorn, the show house, where the problems didn't end with falling tiles and ruined lawns, where those were just the beginning of the nightmare.

If Agnes hadn't come home, with her acute hearing, her hyper-vigilance.

It didn't bear thinking about. But he forced himself to think, hammering the pictures into his head, the way they'd be in Barry Mason's head, for ever.

The caravan's plastic sink pressed into the bony part of his pelvis.

He could've lost them, Ruth and the kids. The thought reached into his chest to twist his heart. Agnes had only just come home to them, and he couldn't look at Christie without thinking of Trevor – 'Could've been Christie in a body bag.' But his hands shook like his legs because he could have lost them. Still could. They were lucky to have the caravan, he knew. Thanks to Bette Argall's quick thinking. And it *was* only temporary, for him anyway, until the police worked their way around to arresting him. That's what Ruth didn't understand. She kept saying, 'When this is over,' but it had ended back in Blackthorn Ashes, the day they took Barry's kids away.

Those little body bags. The sound of Janis screaming.

He left the bathroom, walking to the kitchen on legs that buckled as if he were on a boat. Wind rattled the front door. Then the sound changed, coming inside, snaking through the sitting room and kitchen to sit at his feet. He gripped the counter, blinking at the jug where knives were kept, redness pricking his vision.

'Adrian?' Ruth. It was Ruth.

He pulled his fingers free of the counter, wiping them on the leg of his trousers. 'In here.' It came out as a squawk, the words trapped in his throat, his heart beating everywhere in his chest.

His wife came into the caravan's kitchen, squall jacket zipped to her chin, car keys in her hand. Her face was small inside the purple hood of the jacket but her eyes were huge as headlights. He swerved his stare from her path, turning to busy himself at the sink.

'Did you forget something?'

'Charger. My phone won't last the morning without it.'

He nodded, running the hot tap into one of the cups Agnes had already cleaned.

'What's happened?' Ruth asked in the carefully neutral voice she used now, the voice you might use if you were carrying a very full basin of water across a carpeted room. Because Adrian was unpredictable, brim-full of emotions which might spill without warning, drown the pair of them.

'Nothing's happened.' He rinsed the cup, stood it to drain. 'Just slow getting started today.'

'Didn't Agnes do the washing-up? I asked her to.'

'Yes. I'm just clearing up my own mess.'

He winced as he said it, hoping she wouldn't notice. His weakness made her furious. He didn't even know why. It was such a small thing, after all the rest. She was quiet now, watching him with her eyes heavy on the back of his neck.

'Adrian,' she said finally. 'Where is Christie, do you know?'

She waited.

'Do you know where Agnes is, or our son?'

Each word was loaded with accusation. He knew nothing. He was their father and he knew nothing.

'Because they're not here. Your children. Do you even know where they are?'

4

In Whitethorn's kitchen, Agnes stood frozen, the man's shadow staining the glass of the door.

The door was unlocked but he didn't trust this or he knew he only had to wait, for whoever went in to come back out. Was he afraid the alarm might sound if he stepped inside? No, he knew the alarms were disabled. He knew all about Blackthorn Ashes, from its first brick to its last bloodstain.

His head turned in the direction of the path behind the gardens, where Christie was waiting for Agnes. Had he heard her brother running to the path? She pictured a heavy hand on Christie's shoulder. Her mouth was dry, evil-tasting. She stepped into the light.

'Hello?' She said it loudly, as Emma or Val might have done, seeing a stranger outside their window one morning before it went bad, before they all began jumping at shadows. 'Hello?'

He took his hand off the glass and stepped back, body language bristling. He hadn't seen her until now, she was certain. Just for a second, he was the one on high alert, caught off balance. She reached for the door and hauled it open, looking into his face.

'Oh, it's you.' Her voice was a shrug, dismissing him. 'I thought it was a trespasser.'

Trevor Kyte made an incredulous sound, not quite a laugh. 'Like you, you mean?'

He was Dad's oldest friend. She'd known him her whole life, felt him in the bones of her, the way she felt Ruth as dusty knees and nettle stings, pink cream on her scratches, a cool hand on her head, even though it was years since her mother had touched her like that.

'I'm not trespassing.' She framed a smile. 'I'm just checking on stuff for Dad.'

Trevor started to speak but stopped himself, sucking at the inside of his cheek, trying to be the same man he was a week ago. Everyone who'd lived through what happened here was the same – trying to get back to the person they were before. Trevor hadn't lived here, not properly. He hadn't owned Redthorn, just used it as a deluxe squat while he was working on-site. All the same, he'd changed, like the rest of them. His eyes were wary, pale as pencil beams in the dark of his face. His tan was fading, skin greyed by the beginning of a beard. Not shaving enough, like Dad. It took a steady hand to shave. Trevor still dressed like a cowboy but he no longer looked at home in his own skin. There was a new tension to him, a watchfulness. Agnes preferred him like this; he'd been too smooth before, like trying to scale an ice sculpture. Now she could see a dozen places to put her fingers and her feet. She held on to her smile. 'What're you doing here?'

'Same as you, checking on stuff.'

His shoulders blocked the sunshine, chilling her. 'You have keys?'

She shook her head. 'You have the only set, don't you?'

'But you're inside the house . . .'

He reached into his pocket and drew out a metal tin, battered blue and gold. Tobacco and cigarette papers. 'How'd you get in?'

'The door was open.'

Christie was waiting in the lane, wondering what'd happened to her. 'I came inside to check.'

Trevor opened the tin with his thumbnail. He began pinching shredded tobacco into a paper, not taking his eyes off her. The tobacco smelt sweet and leafy.

'You weren't afraid?' He ran his tongue along the paper. 'You're trespassing, you know.'

'Makes two of us. But no, I wasn't afraid. It's always just kids, isn't it?'

'Not always.' He rolled the cigarette with two fingers. 'Not today.'

She could taste the cigarette, a scorch of paper against her lips.

'We must be mad,' she said. 'To come back here.' She waited a beat. 'To keep coming back.'

'You've been back before?'

Every inch of him was steady now, no trace of the earlier scare in his face or fingers. He put the cigarette between his lips. His hand went to his pocket, came out with the lighter she remembered. Heavy scratched silver, worn at the sides by his thumb.

'A few times.' She glanced across his shoulder, squinting at the overgrown lawn. 'Not here. Our house.' She nodded in that direction.

He flinted the lighter, its yellow flame leaping. He was made of dry sparks, dangerous. Other people saw a solid man, capable, always happy to help. But she knew how near the surface his temper lay, coiled like an adder. He held the flame to the cigarette. The air was staticky, lifting the hairs at the back of her neck.

'You want it?' He took the cigarette from his tongue, holding it out.

She shook her head.

'Christie with you? He loves it here. No way he stays home and lets you come digging around for whatever you can find.'

'I'm not digging, I'm checking.'

'Yeah, that's what you said. But it was a lie, same as mine.'

He sucked at the cigarette, its paper sizzling red. He was still afraid, she realized with a jolt. He was smoking because he was scared and it made him feel a bit better, less sick.

'Christie loves it here,' he said again.

'He did.' She bent to scratch at her ankle, keeping her arms loose, letting him see she wasn't the one who needed nicotine to stay steady. 'Before everything that happened.'

'You should ask him' – hardness in his voice; he resented her show of calm – 'just how much he loved it.' The sly lick of a pause. 'Ask him how much he got out of it.'

Agnes moved from his shadow, letting the sun onto her face. 'You're not making much sense.'

He smoked until the cigarette was ash, flicking the final shred towards the decking.

'Ask your mum what I'm on about. Or your brother. He won't be too happy to find out you were round here without him. This's his private kingdom, comes and goes as he wants. I told him, "That's going to get you in trouble, mate," but he wouldn't listen.' Trevor wiped his hand on the thigh of his jeans. 'I tried to be a dad to him when Ade stopped stepping up.'

He was talking about his best friend, her father. The fear was hers, now. He'd sneaked it back into her somehow, as if he'd slipped his hands into her pockets and filled them with scribbled scraps of paper and pebbles, gritty against her skin.

'Heading home?' he said. 'I'll give you a lift.'

'Thanks, but I like to walk.' She started to move past him.

He shifted to stop her, until a noise from the end of the garden made him glance that way. She could've dodged in that second and run. But if it was Christie at the end of the garden and if Trevor chased her and found her brother with his rucksack filled with whatever he'd stolen upstairs . . . She didn't want to give him that hold over them, not over Christie. She stayed still, facing him.

'Remember.' He was angry now, for whatever reason, perhaps because the past had him in its clutches and he hated to be held. 'What I know about your dad and your brother. About you.'

'And you.' She brushed past him, whispering the next words: 'What I know about you.'

Christie was sitting picking stones from the path to fling at the blackthorn hedge. The sloes were bruised, their blackened taste hanging in the air. The backpack was squashed into his lap. He looked up when Agnes approached, scowling with every inch of his face. The legs of his jeans were dusty, a dark patch on the right knee.

'Are you hurt?' She crouched at his side. 'What happened?'

'I tripped.' He hunched away from her. 'What happened to you? I thought you were never fucking coming.' Anger helping him to hide the pain.

'It was Trevor.' Agnes sat at his side. 'The man outside Whitethorn.'

'Trevor? What's he doing there?'

57

'Same as us.' She put her palm to the path, rolling it over the sharp pebbles to placate the itching in her skin. 'He can't stay away.'

'I can stay away.' Christie threw another stone into the hedge. 'I'm just bored because there's fuck all to do in the caravan.'

Agnes waited a moment before saying, 'We need to stop coming back.'

He snorted but he'd fight, she knew. Her and anyone else who tried to stop him. One day it wouldn't be Trevor who found them. It'd be someone who wanted to teach Christie a lesson, as if he hadn't learnt enough in the last six weeks.

'We need to stop,' she said again.

'Why?'

'Because you're hurt.' She watched the sloes shaking and shivering as she tried to find the right words to make him listen. 'And I'm scared.'

'Of Trevor?' He moved his head, looking at her.

'He knows what we've been up to. He says he knows.'

Christie drew a quick breath. A taut second passed before he scoffed his tongue at his teeth. 'He's screwing with you.'

'Yes. Maybe.'

'So tell him to piss off.'

'You said you don't need to come here. If you're bored, we can go into town or to the beach.'

'You *never* wanted to come here.' Another stone launched at the hedge. 'To Blackthorn Ashes. It freaked you out, before anything even happened.' He dragged himself upright, dusting his hands on his jeans. 'From that first day at the show house, you hated it.' His anger was like Trevor's, full of smoke and sparks. 'You said you'd never come back but you did and you *ruined* it.'

She stayed down, letting him be the bigger one, towering over her. 'I didn't mean to.'

'Yes you did! You always do.' He bunched his fingers into fists. 'You only came back because you'd nowhere else to go. You said you'd *never* come back, that you'd rather be *dead*. You think I don't remember because I was only a baby but I do and I wish you were, I wish you *were* dead!'

'Okay.'

'You'd nothing else, that's why you came back. You'd *nothing*. But we had this' – pointing over her shoulder to the abandoned houses – 'we had *everything*. Until you ruined it.'

Let him burn through it. Better he was angry at her, better than being scared.

'Mum's right about you! She said you're *sick*. You ruin everything.'

'I'm not sick.' She didn't want him thinking that, it wasn't fair. 'I'm autistic. My brain works differently to yours but it's not broken.'

His face creased in confusion. He looked ten, not thirteen. 'It was *you*.'

'People died.' Agnes climbed to her feet. She felt battered like the sloes. 'How was that my fault?' She turned in the direction of the sea, away from the caravan park. 'Come on.'

She didn't stop to see if he was following but after a bit she heard his trainers grinding behind her. He knew where she was headed. It was what they both needed.

It took four minutes to reach the bend where the path sheared away to scrubland at the cliff's edge. Here there was no shelter from the wind that beat in from the sea, cold and solid, making rough crops of gorse creak under its pressure. Buried in the thickest part of the hedge, in a thorny tangle of branches, was a big trampoline.

Blown from a garden at Blackthorn Ashes on the night of the storm. The night before the police came, evacuating everyone left alive.

Seven days ago, only seven. She couldn't believe it.

The storm took out the power and ripped tiles from the roofs of the houses, upturning garden furniture, tearing down fences. It set off car alarms and burglar alarms, and it lifted this trampoline from Maythorn's garden, carrying it over the trees to bury it in this hedge.

Wind tugged at Agnes's T-shirt, like hands.

Below them, the sea ran into the rocks, its salt stinging her scalp. The trampoline looked as if it'd been in the hedge for years rather than days, its frame the same colour as the branches that held it, with its black rubber mat facing out towards the path. She walked up to it and drew back her fist, punched as hard as she could into the heart of the rubber. The impact rippled up her arm, jarring her elbow. She did it again, harder. Then switched to her left hand, tucking her thumb inside her fingers. Punched. Her feet skidded on the grit of the path, wind whipping at her clothes.

Trevor's stupid cigarette. *Punch*. His smile. *Punch*.

'Hey.'

His *threats*.

'Agnes!' Christie was yelling, the wind taking his words away from her. 'My turn!'

She fell back to let him take her place, watching as he thrashed his fists into the rubber mat over and over again, a tortured squealing coming from the hedge as it held on to the trampoline's metal frame. He didn't stop for a long time.

Agnes walked away, looking out to the horizon, sucking in the scent of gorse and water. As long as she could remember, the sea's scent had brought her back. Its wildness stirred a stick inside her head that somehow helped when everything was muddled and murky with distress.

In London, she'd missed the sea so much she'd wept. Laura took her to the coast one weekend, to a seafront hotel, pebble-dashed, net-curtained. Their room had a sea view but it wasn't the sea as Agnes knew it, barely moving, a limp dishcloth shoving at dirty shingle. They shared a white bed in a blue room. As Laura slept, Agnes stood at the window, watching the sea. She hadn't known it could be so flat, so . . . *nothing*. A child's first drawing of the sea, pale as a plate. It hurt her head, having no stick to stir there. Her thoughts fused, nothing breaking free. She leant her head on glass the same temperature as her skin. Another non-thing. She began pinching at her wrist just to feel something, to try and sort out the *blah-blah-blah* in her brain. Bring herself back.

Behind her, Christie panted, bouncing his shoulder into the trampoline, muttering under his breath. He was calm at last. They were done. They could go back to the caravan, to Dad.

Christie was limping by the time they reached the duckboards at Indigo Park. Agnes checked her watch, needing to know how much time she had to wash the blood from his jeans before Mum saw it. Hiding his limp would be harder. The wind tracked them, the tug of it agitated and remote.

'Shithole,' Christie said under his breath.

He swerved when he saw their caravan, heading out past the trailers to the edge of the park where plastic awning sat around the roof of the biggest trailer like icing on a collapsing cake. To the left of its steps, a curling rectangle of AstroTurf was implausibly green against the boiled brown of the field. At night, a blood-red neon pistol flashed above the trailer door, its muzzle firing the word

'Bang!' A banner with the legend *Graceland 2* showed Elvis with a half-eaten burger in his fists.

At the south-west edge of the field, sun glittered on the felted roof of an old groundsman's shed. Christie's hiding place.

The shed had been treated for age and rot, would be standing long after the decking in the gardens at Blackthorn Ashes had turned to mush. A group was seated outside the Elvis trailer: two men in football shirts and jogging bottoms, a woman in a white bandage skirt and a red halter-neck. None of them looked at Agnes or Christie as they passed.

'Come on.' Her brother was nearly at the shed, keys rattling in his fist.

Someone was hefting chain behind the big trailer – a heavy, slinking sound.

Agnes shivered, the sun damp on the back of her neck, like breath. She slipped into the shadows where her brother was waiting. Christie pulled the padlock from the shed's door, pocketing the keys as he went inside. Agnes followed, leaving the door open a crack, to let the light in.

Inside, the shed was dusty but dry, no tang of mould or damp despite broken garden furniture stacked under windows blacked out by dirt. A dented filing cabinet stood under the nearest window. Padlocked, like the door. Christie had found the padlocks with the keys in Dad's toolbox.

The sun stirred at the windows as Agnes moved deeper into the shed's shadows, her wrists clammy and stinging. Delayed shock, she knew, from what had happened at Whitethorn. She watched as Christie squatted in the dust to open the bottom drawer of the cabinet, letting out the smell of Blackthorn Ashes: unripe wood and rot. All its soft-closing drawers were crooked open now, nothing flush or fitted, the houses slowly slumping to one side like bodies after a shooting.

Her brother shrugged off his backpack and unzipped it, hunching his shoulder to hide whatever he'd taken from Whitethorn. Something more than the scatter diamond, since he'd let her see that. Agnes left him to it, looking through the window to the open sky. Their caravan was out of sight at the other end of the park. *Temporary*, but Agnes had seen it in Ruth's face: the full stop of their lives. They'd no money, no means to recover the losses at Blackthorn Ashes. Dad faced the threat of prosecution. *Corporate manslaughter* fizzed in her skull like language from another place, words whispered in the sand dunes whole summers ago as she smoked her first, stolen cigarette. She rubbed her thumb at the dirt on the shed's window, inspecting the tan stain on her skin.

Behind her, Christie straightened, locking the cabinet. 'Done,' he said.

Agnes wiped her thumb on her jeans. 'What about your leg?'

'What about it?' He was always at his cockiest in here, with his stolen treasure close at hand. Thirteen going on thirty. He fixed her with a glare through his fringe. 'What?'

'What'll we tell Mum?' She nodded at the stain on his knee.

He shrugged. 'I tripped.'

She followed him from the shed, waiting while he padlocked the door. Indigo Park was a sea of squat roofs, choppy and rain-ruined. They picked their way along its margins, staying wide of the family in the big trailer. Agnes kept her eyes on the ground where the strange shapes of the mobile homes were replicated in shadows, the stain of each one a grey bar on her skin as she walked and Christie limped back to their caravan.

They'd nearly made it when Odie tore across the duckboards, barrelling into Christie's shins. Her brother yelped and would've lost his balance but for her hand on his elbow. He shook her away. The dog kept jumping, snapping at the straps of his empty backpack.

'Odie!' Bette came down the steps of her caravan, wiping her hands on a blue cloth. 'Back up!'

Christie hopped away from Agnes then reached a hand to rub Odie's head. 'He's okay, aren't you, boy?' He was catching his breath, hurt.

'He's pleased to see you.' Bette's eyes narrowed at the stain on his jeans. 'Casualties?' She glanced at Agnes, her sharp stare like a tack.

'I tripped,' Christie said. 'It's nothing.'

'It's your good jeans,' Agnes said. 'Your best ones.' Her palms were sweaty. She wiped them at her sleeves then kept wiping because the friction helped to ground her.

Bette took it all in, their stiffness and the silence between them that grew and grew in spite of the words they spoke. 'Come along.' She looped her hand through Odie's collar and scooped him into her arms, nodding towards her caravan. 'Let's get you cleaned up.'

Christie went ahead of Agnes up the short flight of steps to the door that matched theirs. It made the same sound when it shut behind them, a muffled *thunk* of plastic on plastic. Bette's caravan smelt of fried bread, washing detergent and tortilla chips. Agnes hated their caravan but she loved Bette's. In the kitchen, the floor was yellow lino. Apple-green cupboards with black handles, a white stove under a triangle of shelving where brightly painted pots and pans were wedged. Bette had lived all her life in Cornwall, taking odd jobs over the years to pay the bills without tying herself down. She'd worked as a hairdresser and in an antiques shop, been a secretary and a teaching assistant. At Blackthorn Ashes, she'd dressed the unsold houses according to instructions left by the interior designer, polishing windows, picking stray leaves from the floors between viewings. She set Odie down on the yellow lino. He settled with his chin between his front paws.

The sitting room had corner sofas covered in orange and brown zigzags, and flowered curtains in different shades of the same colours. There was a low round table with books, and an ashtray filled with a litter of sweet wrappers. A high shelf running above the sofa held mugs with carved faces, woven dolls, straw donkeys, seaside souvenirs. The carpet was thin and hairy and dark brown. A picture hung on one wall, of a leopard prowling in a velvet jungle.

'Sit yourself there.' Bette nodded at the sofa. Christie sat. 'I'll get my first aid kit.'

'I can do this,' Agnes said. 'We have a kit.'

'I know. But now you can go and see himself.'

Errol, she meant.

Christie was poking at the bloodstain on his jeans, his bottom lip turning out the way it did when he was about to cry. He wouldn't cry, not in here. Maybe later with Mum, or maybe not at all. He'd changed so much in the years since Agnes went away. The backs of his hands were filthy from punching the trampoline. They'd missed lunch. Christie could have Dad's sandwich, if Dad hadn't eaten it. The thought of making another sandwich was suddenly overwhelming. Agnes could picture the slices of bread and ham, butter in a plastic box, cheese in a hard block. She could see the plate, and the knife she'd use to spread the butter. But she couldn't fit the pictures together, not in the right order. It was a warning sign, she knew. Her brain was telling her it'd had enough, needing a dark room somewhere quiet and safe; it was done for the day. She left Christie and went to the kitchen, where she found Errol in his paisley bathrobe, smelling of peppermint tea.

'You look thirsty.' He reached for a cupboard, silk sleeve slipping to show a forearm sleek with muscle. 'Tea? Or coffee?'

'I can't stay. I'm only here while—'

'Bette fixes up Christie. I heard. Plastic walls.' He brushed his knuckles at the nearest wall to demonstrate. He had the hands of a supermodel, long-fingered with perfect, polished nails.

'Tell you what.' He put his hand into the cupboard, brought out a pair of shot glasses. 'It's late enough for cocktails and I'm running low on gin so . . .' The hand that wasn't holding the glasses swooped for the freezer box, bringing out an electric blue and pink bottle. Absolut vodka.

'We'll manage with this.' He turned, holding the bottle and glasses over his head, as neat as a dancer in the narrow space. 'Keep me company?'

In the sitting room, Agnes could hear Bette fixing Christie's knee: a murmur of voices, her brother sounding less tired, happier now. She followed Errol into his bedroom, the beaded curtain chiming as she moved through it, metal beads tapping at her cheek.

Being in Errol's bedroom was like standing inside a jewellery box: watery blue silk on the walls, pink velvet cushions on the bed, animal print rug on the floor. A battered film star's dressing table stood against one wall, its mirror studded by silvery lightbulbs. Errol patted the bed next to him and she sat, taking the shot glass she was handed. He chinked his glass against hers. The vodka filled her whole mouth with vanilla and dried apricots. She drank it off in a single swallow.

'So . . . Agnes.' He pronounced it the French way: *An-Yes.*

'Errol?'

'Didn't I tell you my friends call me Jackie?' He refilled their glasses.

'Yes, but you've yet to tell me why.'

He arranged the shoulders of his robe, sending her a look through his lashes. 'Jackie O?'

'Oh . . . Of course.'

'Errol was for Errol Flynn, so it could be worse. But I'm more of a Jackie, don't you think?'

'Maybe . . . I like Errol.'

'I might start calling you *Sinead.* Strictly eighties, of course. Your cheekbones give me the envy.'

Agnes ran a hand over her head, where the pelt of hair was growing back. Its electric feel shocked her. She'd half forgotten the buzz cut, expecting to feel the curls she'd had when she was sixteen. 'It was a mistake.'

'A beautiful mistake.'

Errol lay back on his elbows. His gaze brightened but not like Trevor's, not like anyone's. He wasn't like anyone else. She should have hated that, the lack of cues and clues, but she didn't.

'What happened to Christie? I suppose you were back there.' He balanced the shot glass flat to his chest. 'Blackthorn Ashes.'

'Can't keep away.'

She used a light voice, trying to pass it off as a joke. But Errol had been at the street party, even if he wasn't in Quickthorn on the night of the storm. He knew how far from funny it was. She gazed at the poster above his head, of a black man in a green shirt. She recognized him vaguely, a movie star or a singer. She concentrated on his easy smile, pushing the words *Blackthorn Ashes* away.

'I keep thinking,' she said. 'That afternoon with Iris, the street party. When the ambulance came for Luke after he burnt himself on the barbecue . . . If we'd asked them to look at Chloe, check she was okay after cutting herself in the sandpit, they'd have known from her blood, how bright it was. That's what carbon monoxide poisoning looks like. Or if we'd told them Val and Tim were ill . . . They'd have known the danger we were all in. No one need've died. We could've saved everyone.'

Errol sat up, reaching for the vodka bottle. The bottle was cloudy with coldness. His fingers left marks on it. 'Maybe.' He sucked the frost from his fingers, frowning. 'But it still isn't your fault. Or anyone's, really. No one set out to kill anyone, did they?'

The beaded curtain made a sort of music before settling into silence.

'Trevor knew. About the corners they'd been cutting, to save money and time. He knew but he didn't tell Dad.' She tested the shape of the words in her mouth, like probing for the cause of a toothache, needing to know she wasn't telling a lie, fooling herself. 'Maybe Dad knew. Trevor definitely did.'

'From what you've told me about Trevor, that fits.'

'I haven't told you anything. Have I?'

'From what you've *not* told me about Trevor,' Errol corrected, 'that fits.'

She couldn't hold his gaze, looking instead at the fake tiger skin on the floor. 'I saw him today.'

'Trevor? At Blackthorn Ashes? What's he doing there?'

'Same as us. Same as Christie.'

Errol didn't ask what that meant. He knew, or he'd guessed.

'Is that how he hurt himself?'

She shook her head then nodded; Christie wouldn't have run if Trevor hadn't turned up.

'Is it safe?' Errol asked. 'To keep going back?'

'It's never been safe. But it's what he needs to do, and I need to go with him because it'd be worse if he was alone.'

'I could go with him,' Errol offered. 'If it would give you a break. I'm not being rude but you're starting to look a bit . . . see-through.'

'They call it autistic fatigue. It's all the rage in certain circles.' Her attempt at humour fell flat, like an arrow fired from a faulty bow. She massaged her temples. 'Ignore me. I'll be fine tomorrow.'

Well enough to lie to Mum about staying home and then to walk the cliff path with her brother, standing aside as he raided houses where people died.

'Have it your way. But I'm right here when you need me . . .' Errol rolled sideways to refill their glasses. 'Not just for Christmas.'

'I know.' She did.

He was the only person she'd been able to talk to about her autism. Even with Laura it'd been hard. Plenty of people thought they understood but very few did. Too often she was met with vigorous nods and sage advice about essential oils and going non-dairy and had she tried noise-cancelling headphones? Hardly anyone sat as Errol sat, and simply listened.

'Christie thinks I'm crazy, by the way. In case he mentions it . . . He's found my meds, now we're sharing a room.' She smoothed her fingers over Errol's duvet cover. 'I take anti-psychotics to manage my mood and because sometimes I see or hear stuff that's not there. It happens quite often with autism but it's not really understood.'

Ruth hadn't understood it when Agnes was sixteen. Christie didn't understand it now. What was it doing to him being made to share a bunk with someone he believed to be crazy, even dangerous? A lot of his anger was fear but how much was fear of her? Her skin crawled with self-reproach.

'What I'm doing right now, explaining all this to you, being factual and personal and oversharing . . . that's my autism, too.'

She took the refilled shot glass from Errol's hand. 'Of course, sometimes I clam up. I'm going to try that now, let you get a word in edgeways.'

'I like listening to you,' Errol said. 'And getting a word in edgeways is my superpower. Nice to have a day off, frankly.'

That made her laugh. 'I shouldn't drink this.'

She drank it. 'Okay, I'm ready to go back. I love you, so you know.'

'I know,' Errol said. 'And same.'

Back in their caravan, Dad was on the sofa, a ball of cling film at his feet. He'd eaten her sandwich. He looked like she felt – far away from everything but somehow still too close. Everything was touching her, all the smells and sounds, the stretchy fabric of the sofa, the plasticky ball of cling film. She pushed through it to her bunk, dragging the duvet over her head. Blacking out, or trying to, needing to black it all out, wishing she was in London with Laura, that she hadn't ruined everything there and here, that she could go back and fix it. Back to before she came home, when Christie and Mum and Dad were happy and excited and Blackthorn Ashes was just a brochure and a first brick with her brother's name written on it.

4 AUGUST

Twenty-one days before abandonment

———

5

Christie was organizing his Ultramarines when Mum knocked on his bedroom door. She did that now, knocked before coming in. He had proper privacy, at last. It was just one of the ways Blackthorn Ashes was better than their old house.

'Have you seen your sister? She's not eaten her breakfast.'

'I haven't seen her. Mum, look at this!' He'd stood the marines in battle lines.

She came across the room. 'They look brilliant!'

'Wait till I put the spots on . . .'

Dad'd fixed lights to the shelves, perfect for picking out the detail in the marines' uniforms, metallic paint flashing under the spots.

'Okay, that's even cooler.' Mum leant in to look. 'Seriously impressive.'

Christie nudged one of the marines closer to the others. He wanted her to stay, see all the work he'd done, the shades of blue in their shoulder pads, gold laurel on the sergeant's head. If she'd just focus on the details, she'd forget about Agnes. His sister was the bigger picture but they didn't need to think about that right now, should be enjoying being here in Blackthorn Ashes where every-thing was new like these spotlights, and the shower head with a hundred individual water nozzles. The bigger picture was boring, mortgages and how many miles to the nearest supermarket and what if he didn't make any friends at his new school? No one got excited about that stuff, let alone right after they'd moved. When you went on holiday and the hotel was further from the beach than they'd said or the buffet had blue prawns that gave you the shits – none of that mattered in the first day or two because you were on holiday. Soon's you start picking at stuff, you'll find things that're wrong. It'd been great having his sister home, until she'd started picking.

Mum was at the window, looking down into the garden. Agnes wasn't out there. She never went into the garden, not to sit or sun-bathe anyway. Only to poke about, finding holes. She was obsessed with finding holes. Like, the rest of the buffet was brilliant but she had to eat the shitty prawns. Forget the chocolate fountain and the ten different toppings for ice cream. She'd gone on holiday to get food poisoning, the way other people went to get a suntan. Christie'd seen her picking at the edges of the bathroom door, 'Here,' wanting him to touch the same spot.

When he put his finger there, it was sticky. 'So?'

'It's sap. They didn't season the wood properly.' Agnes ran her thumb along the strip of yellow oozing from the door. 'They should've treated it. It wasn't ready.'

'It doesn't matter, though, does it?' He pulled the door shut then pushed it open. 'It works, so what's the difference?' He pulled and pushed again to make his point.

'It wasn't ready. They should've waited.'

'They did.' He had to yank the door this time because it stuck. 'We waited months to move.'

He was on the house's side, not hers. She was the one who wasn't ready. She was the *sap* and he was sick of her going round looking like a ghost, haunting the house and Mum, making Mum frown and worry when she should be happy. He'd seen her eyes at breakfast, red, like she'd been crying.

'Christie. Doesn't it feel tight to you?'

'The door? So what? You're mental.'

'Not just the door, the whole house.' Agnes put her hands in her hair. 'The house is too tight.'

In his bedroom now, facing his Ultramarines, the memory made him hot. His mad sister with her scribbly hair and crazy theories. She embarrassed him but it was more than that. She made him ashamed to be happy here, to be *trying* to be happy.

'She'll have gone for a walk,' he told Mum. 'Down to the sea.'

'She always loved the sea.' Mum's voice was strange, like she was talking from another room. She turned from the window with a big phony smile. 'The models are great!'

As if he were a little kid who needed a pat on the head for some stupid Lego when he'd made a Legion Tactical Squad and painted every detail, even the safety pins on the grenades.

'She thinks the house is haunted.' He rolled his eyes. 'Like new-builds can be haunted.'

'Is that what she told you? Haunted?'

'Yeah, or something.' He shut the cabinet door. 'She wasn't making much sense.'

Mum hugged herself. It was the only time she looked like Agnes, when she did that. He didn't want her to look like Agnes. He wanted her to look like his mum.

'I don't get why she's here when she hates it so much. Why's she here?'

'She hasn't anywhere else to go. She lost her job in London.'

He pulled his cuff over his hand to polish his fingerprints from the cabinet. 'Can't she get another job?'

'It's not that easy.' Mum reached to stroke her hand up his arm, the way she did when he was upset. 'It'll be okay.' She waited a bit then put her arms round him in a hug. 'It will.'

He was too old for hugs; they made him want to cry. He was thirteen, for fuck's sake. But he let Mum hug him because she never got to hug Agnes. Except when she was a tiny baby but even then she hadn't liked it. As soon as she was big enough, she'd run from hugs and kisses. So Christie let Mum hug him even though it was weird with the Ultramarines watching.

'Are you going to look for her?'

'No.' Mum kissed the top of his head and let him go. 'She'll be okay, like you said. She loves the sea. The walk'll do her good.'

It didn't. A bit later, he found his sister in the garage, messing with boxes from the old house, in a black top and jeans with dusty scratches all over them. When she bent over the boxes, he saw the ridges of her spine through her top. 'What're you looking for?'

'Can't you hear it?' She pulled at the boxes.

It was like watching a movie about someone who hears noises and goes to investigate and ends up dead. A jump scare was coming, that's how it felt. It was how it always felt with Agnes. You wanted to laugh at her but she scared you.

'Hear what?'

'Like . . . fizzing.' She moved her hands, making shapes with her fingers. He saw a swarm of bees in the shapes she made. 'Like fire.'

'You think the garage's on fire?' He looked around exaggeratedly. 'I don't think so.'

'Not actual fire, just the noise of it.' She threw him a glance, her eyes big and black like a cat's right before it scratches you. 'Help me look?'

He was angry suddenly. Angrier than he'd been about the sappy door or Mum's red eyes. 'Just stop it. Fuck's sake! Stop pretending there's something wrong so you can make this our fault – our problem – when it's yours!'

She started shaking her fingers like she was trying to get rid of the dust from the boxes. 'Sorry,' she said. 'I'm sorry.'

Christie felt bad then but he couldn't just stop being angry, couldn't flick a switch the way she did. *Flick and I'm normal. Flick and I'm a freak.* Everything was meant to be better, brand new, in Blackthorn Ashes. *He* felt new. Why'd she have to be his old sister? He wanted a new one. Not someone who wasn't Agnes, just a different version. She had been normal when she was living in London. He wished she was there now, being happy. Why'd they only get to see her when she was freaking out, upset about everything? He watched her shaking her hands and he tried to stay angry but he couldn't. It was like her sadness was a germ and she'd given it to everyone in the house.

'What're you looking for? Have you lost something?'

'Like my marbles?' She gave a weak smile. 'I'm okay. Really. I mean, I will be. Sorry.' She cocked her head at the garage. 'You can't hear it?'

'There's nothing. Unless it's the freezer. They make weird noises sometimes. And Dad says the house's settling.' He knew about this. 'It can take up to three years, that's why they build expansion joints to control where the cracks form in the concrete. You've seen the cracks in my room?' She'd pointed them out, in fact. 'They're settlement cracks. Dad says the structural engineer puts expansion joints on the building designs. It's *meant* to happen. The cracks, and the weird noises. It's just the house settling in.'

'Like us.' She wiped her hands on her jeans. She'd stopped shaking. Her smile looked better, less like it might tear her face. 'Thanks.'

'What for?'

'Talking like that. It helped.'

Her head was angled like she was listening to whatever it was only she could hear but she wanted him to think she was okay.

He didn't mind her faking, he wished she'd do it all the time. He didn't understand why she didn't.

'Do you want to play basketball? Or go for a walk?' She was trying to make it up to him. 'Dad said you've been modelling. Can I see?'

Christie didn't want her in his room. She saw things. Things that weren't there, yes. But things which *were* there, too. Things you thought you'd hidden really, really well. He didn't want her in his room.

'We could watch something. There's Cartoon Network on the new TV.'

'Great.' Her smile was going to crack any second now.

He turned away so she could let the smile go. It felt odd, like when you're walking downstairs and your feet forget how to do it and you nearly fall. He still knew how to manage her moods, after all this time. Memory made knots in his stomach, taking him back to when he was little and she'd start winding herself up. Mum getting tense, Dad looking for an excuse to leave the house; like Agnes was a storm brewing and they each had to find their own way to a safe place until it'd passed. Only Christie didn't go. He climbed into her lap and put his hands in her hair so she had to look at him, and he talked and talked. About nothing, stuff he made up, just talking and talking until her eyes stopped doing that black cat thing and turned blue again. Until his sister came back.

She was watching the road now, the new road that snaked round Blackthorn Ashes, in and out of all the driveways. Her hands were twitchy, and her eyes. She was seeing things, he knew. Strangers or smoke from a fire miles away, maybe Dad and Trevor coming back from the building site. She could never just look at things. She always had to *see stuff*. It scared him, the things she said she could see. It scared him, and he hated her for that.

1 SEPTEMBER

Seven days after abandonment

———

6

'I asked you to do one thing, look after your brother. Was that so much? After everything that's happened, everything we're going through *right now*, you couldn't do one simple job?'

'I'm sorry,' Agnes said. 'I tried.'

'Did you?' her mother demanded. 'Because I need to know I can count on you. It's just the two of us, in case you hadn't noticed. You and me against all . . . *this*.' She thrust her hands at the caravan. 'We're all we have.'

There was a small, familiar pause like the pothole in a much-travelled road. You steered around it if you were quick. If you weren't, what came next rattled your teeth.

'You've not forgotten?' Ruth dropped her voice. 'What I told you the night we came here?'

Agnes hadn't forgotten. Just shoved it to the back of her mind, as if that were a safe hiding place for her mother's secrets, like the shed for Christie's loot. She felt with her tongue for an old pain in one of her back teeth. A sound came from her mother like the hiss of a zip, sealing Ruth tight. She'd seen Christie's limp, how pale he

79

was, on guard against her questions, siding with Agnes. That's how it looked, how it felt, to Ruth.

'Nothing happened,' Agnes said.

Her mother laughed, incredulous. '*Nothing?*'

'Today, I mean. Nothing happened today. We went for a walk. Christie slipped on the path.'

She knew her brother had told the same lie. They'd practised it together.

Ruth knew it was a lie. She rubbed the skin between her eyebrows as if this were the source of her pain. 'Why did you come back to us?'

Agnes probed her bad tooth with the tip of her tongue. 'I don't know.'

'You don't *know*? You came back because you needed us. Needed *me*. And we loved having you home with us, of course we did, but you had to start pushing at every little thing that looked wrong, making it bigger and bigger until none of us could ignore it—' She broke off, biting shut her lips as if she'd shocked herself.

The caravan was too small for this fight, Dad and Christie just a few feet away. Agnes wanted to be outside. She wanted to go with her mother to the trampoline trapped in the hedge, take turns punching it until the pair of them were limp and empty from exhaustion.

'It *was* wrong. The houses, all the things I was saying . . . Those houses *were* wrong.'

'If it'd just been the *houses*, we could've—' Ruth stopped, swerved. 'I know you can't help it. I know you try. We're both trying. It's just too much sometimes. For me, it's too much for me.'

'I'm sorry.' Her heart hurt. 'I thought a walk would do us good. It was just a walk.'

Her mother knew how hard it was for her to lie. Sometimes that meant she believed the lies, imagining Agnes incapable of telling them. But sometimes it made her angrier. She let out a sigh, moving her hands towards Agnes before stopping short. How many times had she told the story of how her daughter couldn't bear to be hugged? But that wasn't Ruth's fault. Everything couldn't be Ruth's fault. Laura had tried to make Agnes see that during their many talks in London: 'Your dad was there too, when he wasn't away working. Your teachers should've spotted something was wrong. It wasn't all on your mum.' She and Laura had fought over it, in the end.

'Agnes, please. I need you to help with this. I can't do it on my own,' her mother was saying. 'Your dad's no use right now, you can see that. I *need* you to watch out for Christie, there isn't anyone else. But if it's too much, you have to tell me. I'll understand but I have to *know.*'

Another mother would've demanded Agnes go out to work while she stayed home. But Agnes wasn't like other twenty-nine-year-olds. Mum had to worry about her as well as Christie and Dad.

'It's not too much to ask. Christie gets bored in the caravan, though. It makes him miserable. It's hard keeping him inside. I am trying, honestly, but it's hard.'

'Maybe if I take the two of you into town with me every so often? You could look around the shops, go to the harbour, see the fishing boats.'

Boats, people, cars. Colour, noise, crowds.

Her armpits were wet. 'That sounds good.'

'The shops aren't much but there's a Smith's. He can get a comic.'

There wasn't any money for comics. They were surviving on tinned food. 'He has comics and books back at the house.'

'We don't have access to the house.' Mum pushed her hair behind her ears, her face snapping shut again. 'You know that. The whole place is sealed off.'

It's not, Agnes wanted to tell her, *it's wide open.*

'Maybe once the investigators get to work . . .' Ruth stared out of the window, across the caravan park. 'I should chase them again, find out what's happening.'

Nothing's happening. This is it. The mud and duckboards. Dad sitting on the sofa. Christie getting angrier and angrier. You, worrying yourself to death. And me fighting you, making it worse.

'I could go, if it'd help. Back to London. Laura will let me sleep on the floor.'

The idea made her tremble, a high-pitched ringing in her head. She'd thought all the phantoms were at Blackthorn Ashes but there were ghosts right here, between her and Ruth. There'd always been ghosts between them.

'She messaged me after the evacuation. She'd seen it on the news, wanted to know how she could help.'

Agnes had messaged back, saying she was fine, afraid Laura would come out here and get sick like the others.

'She'd understand if I needed to go back.'

'You can't go. You have to be here, we all do.'

'For the investigation?'

Ruth turned away, her cheek rigid. 'For everything.'

*

They made supper together, sitting with Dad and Christie at the kitchen table to share the meal. Mum talked about the jobs she'd seen advertised in town: till assistants, warehouse staff. She'd been a marketing executive, running multiple client accounts. When Blackthorn Ashes began to struggle, she took on the task of raising finance so the building could continue; confidence in the project was collapsing, slowly at first then faster, like coastal erosion when storms keep hitting.

Dad and Christie ate in silence. The caravan's windows were grey, steamed up from the stove. It was like sitting in a cellar.

After supper, she washed up while Ruth sat at the table going through job ads on her phone. Christie disappeared to the bedroom, Dad to the sofa, an open book slack in his lap. When the work was done, Agnes took her jacket from the door. She liked to go out at this time. During the day, everything was glaring, all the edges hard, but the dark was so soft you could lean into it.

In Bette's caravan, the TV was on.

Agnes pictured Errol and Bette sharing a bowl of popcorn, his hip tucked neatly into Bette's side. She turned away, shining her phone's torch to the duckboards and then to the hedges.

Everything was different in the dark, all the thorns blunted and branches smoothed to soothing patterns along the cliff path. She could smell the sea rolling out there, volatile and electric. Distant lights winked on tankers sailing so slowly they looked anchored to the horizon. Her skin stopped itching, at last. During the day it was maddening – the sensation of being in the crosshairs of a stranger's attention. Or someone who wasn't a stranger, someone she'd known when she was sixteen, holidaying with her parents, Mum about to give birth to Christie. If she squinted, Agnes could see her sixteen-year-old self walking barefoot on the sand.

The moon was up, licking the path white under her feet.

Up ahead, the trampoline creaked in the hedge.

The barefoot girl was gone but on nights like this Agnes felt her moving under her skin, hot behind her eyes. She'd never gone away, not even in London. The tiny flat she'd shared with Laura was the first place she'd felt truly safe. Except *safe* had been so strange. Alien. She kept searching for its edges, where it ended and she began. *Safe* was too much and she ruined it. Not deliberately – as if it were a favourite jumper she'd worn to death because she loved it, worn through its elbows and unravelled its cuffs until one day it fell to shreds.

She crouched to pick a pebble from the path, rolling it across her palm until the panic receded. The darkness soaked up her strangeness, washing it away. When her pulse was steady, she faced the sea and spoke their names, the way she had every night since leaving Blackthorn Ashes.

'Tim Prentiss. Valerie Prentiss.'

Pausing between each name to picture the face that went with it.

'Emma Dearman. Felix Mason.'

Drawing the details out of the darkness.

'Chloe Mason. Sasha Mason.'

Until the path was peopled with the ghosts of those who'd died in the homes her father sold. Ruth wouldn't allow him his guilt. It was nobody's fault, she kept saying. So Agnes brought his pain here each evening: the six ghosts whose names he was afraid to speak. His silence took up all the space in the caravan, every surface and cupboard that wasn't already filled with the things her mother had salvaged from their home in Blackthorn Ashes. It was too much for him to carry alone.

Tim and Val, Emma and the three children, Chloe's hand in her brother's, sticky fingers squeezing tight. Agnes stood with them until she couldn't stand it any longer, until she wanted to scream and shove and fight her way free.

The wind found her, standing at the end of the path where gorse grew out of the stone, the sea seething softly in the darkness.

She'd loved the sea from the second she first saw it.

'You walked right out to meet it,' Ruth had told her. Agnes saw them hand in hand, making their slow way towards the sea, her baby self stopping to watch wet sand sucking at their footprints.

'That was you,' Ruth told her. 'Scared of nothing, meeting it head on.' Then she said something Agnes never forgot: 'They say there's no unmoving point in the universe, nowhere we can fix our focus. But I fixed mine on you and sometimes, just sometimes, you fixed yours on me.'

Everything was different now.

Agnes wasn't a fixed point, for Ruth or anyone else. She was like the rest of the universe, spinning to infinity.

Gorse creaked at the cliff's edge, growing from a crop of stone that bit like teeth if you pushed your hand against it. Bracken can grow through stone. Like acid grassland, it has to be beaten back to preserve historic sites. She could feel it pushing – the living land-scape beneath the rock, centuries old and savage.

She turned to look back at Indigo Park where light from the trailers lay like dust on the hedges. Her mother was there, alone with Dad and Christie until Agnes returned. A memory came to her: a tender, living thing with teeth and claws. Her mother standing by an upstairs window in the house where Agnes was born, staring out at nothing. Agnes was five, maybe six. She watched through the gap in the door, afraid to break her mother's silence. Ruth looked like stone, like a statue. Any second, Agnes was certain, she'd see a crack running down her mother's face, splitting her in two.

It's up to us, Ruth had told her on the night they were evacuated from Blackthorn Ashes. *The two of us. We're all we've got.*

On the cliff path, her lips were tacky, tasting of salt and iron.

The sea beat against the rocks, her mind feeling the same. Black and treacherous, stewing with an oily mix of past and present, gritty as if old sand had found its way inside her clothes from that summer long ago. She unzipped her coat to pull her T-shirt from her neck, shaking it to get rid of the sensation. The itch was back, that sense of being watched. She turned a slow circle on the path, searching, but the ghosts were gone. No one living was in sight. Only blackness and the warring, warning sound of the sea.

7

Adrian couldn't sleep. It was the heat or the cold or the hardness of the sofa. It was the weight of the blankets, of himself. Ruth had taken her anger out on Agnes, blaming her for whatever had happened to Christie. She had to put her anger somewhere, he supposed. Easier to blame Agnes than admit she had a gutless husband who couldn't keep his own kids safe. He pushed his fingers at his eyes, driving out the pictures before they could turn into Barry's family. Felix and Chloe in the pool shrieking until Ruth said, 'You're going to have to say something,' and Adrian taking round a six-pack of beer as an apology, explaining to Barry about her work, conference calls to London, 'You know how it is, mate,' and Barry shrugging back at him, 'I'll ask Janis to take them out for a bit,' and always this shame like a rash hot up his neck, pulling his scalp tighter and tighter until he thought it would tear. The caravan brought it all closer, the pictures splitting into pixels; he could no longer see Barry's kids, just the pink of their sunburnt faces, yellow heads of hair. Ruth wanted him to stop seeing, stop thinking, stop hearing – voices and whispers and the distant drone of police sirens. Adrian knew they were coming, no matter what she said.

Any day now a knock on the door would deliver him from this waiting, this pretence of life going on when six people were dead, three of them little, little kids. He *wanted* it to come, needed it. He'd never get better like this, waiting.

He stood, fumbling his way along the tops of chairs to the kitchen where he filled a glass from the tap and drank without tasting. He was thirsty all the time. The night they'd arrived here, he gulped down three glasses of water before realizing how bad it tasted. Ruth took charge of everything that night, making up beds, filling cupboards, fetching fish and chips to convince Christie it was an adventure and not a nightmare made by his own father. In one sense, Barry had it easy. You couldn't lose your family twice. But you could fear losing them for ever. That kind of fear never went away. His hand shook as he upturned the glass on the draining rack.

He should get out of here, walk across the fields to where Trevor was camped with cold beers in the fridge, a fire pit to keep them warm. Trevor would have a version of this horror story that was bearable, spinning it until Adrian could see a silver lining. That might be better than cringing in here pretending he'd nothing to feel guilty about, nothing to fear from a visit from the police. Trevor wouldn't let him feel guilty, not for long.

'I don't do guilt.' He could hear Trevor saying it. 'Too many ways it can come back to bite you.'

Adrian missed Trevor like he'd miss his own arm if he woke to find it gone. They'd worked on Blackthorn Ashes together, from the first brick up. The thought lit a fuse in his head, the heat of his shame building into rage. He wanted to smash something, to shout and smash his way out of the silence that'd been strangling him since the evacuation.

Trevor was wrong. 'I don't do guilt,' but he should. They all should. Even Agnes, who should've stayed in London. Then at least one of his kids would be safe.

His hands shook. He stared at their empty palms in the dim light of the caravan's kitchen, thinking of everything they'd held. Agnes and Christie as babies. The urn of his father's ashes. His mother's hand when he was a child. Ruth's shoulders when they slow-danced, leaving Trevor alone at the bar. His hands had held the first brick laid at Blackthorn Ashes, and the last.

A siren sounded from the main road, or out at sea, trailing off before he could process the prick of panic beneath his ribs. His whole life was like that now, poised on the brink of panic. Afraid to tip too far in either direction, towards or away.

As long as they stayed away, Ruth said, as long as none of them ever went back, it would be okay. As if Blackthorn Ashes had a perimeter, a way of containing its poison and its death. As if *they* weren't Blackthorn Ashes.

The siren had died now, gone in the night.

Adrian stood for a long time, listening for the sounds of his family sleeping, hearing water refilling the tank, a gulping sound like a drowning man.

26 JULY

Thirty days before abandonment

———

8

Christie emptied a can of Sprite into a glass, loading it with cubes from the ice maker. Everything in their new kitchen was brilliant but the ice maker was best. He sucked fizz from the drink, bubbles going up his nose. He could hear Felix kicking a football in Maythorn's garden. Part of him wanted to join in but it was babyish, playing with a ten-year-old. He hung out with Trevor when he got the chance, which evened things up. He finished the Sprite in six big gulps, set the empty glass under the boiling water tap, letting it run until the last of the ice cubes exploded.

Agnes came into the kitchen while he was doing this. She went to the other sink to fill a glass from the cold water tap.

He knew what she was going to say before she said it, cutting her off with, 'No, the water doesn't *taste funny*. Anyway, there's bottled stuff in the fridge.'

She watched him poke ice down the plughole. 'The water in the ice maker, is it filtered?'

'*Yes*. Dad said, remember?' He swivelled on the stool to face her.

She was paler than usual. Her hair wet from a shower, like a load of black knots all over her head. Her T-shirt had a wide neck that turned her collarbones into a kind of coat hanger and she was wearing shorts that showed off how skinny she was, and how white. It was like she wanted them to stare at her, like she was flipping off the sun and the garden with the new loungers.

'Can we go for a walk together?' she said.

'Where?'

'Down to the sea. I could show you the route I've found.'

'Why?'

'Why?' She looked confused.

'Why'd I go for a walk when I could be here watching TV or playing basketball?'

Mum'd told her to make an effort, that was obvious. Christie felt a pang of guilt; he should make an effort too. He just wanted everyone to be happy. Mum and Dad had started arguing. He'd heard them whispering in the bedroom. They hadn't done that in ages, not since Dad asked what'd happened at Christie's old school and Mum refused to snitch on him.

'We could play basketball,' he said.

'Okay.'

'Really?' He hadn't expected her to say yes. 'I'll get dressed.'

He ran up the stairs to his room, banging each banister rail as he went. For luck and to prove to her the house was solid, there was nothing wrong with it, they were here to stay.

Agnes stood still after Christie left the kitchen, needing to separate out the sounds – his feet on the stairs then in his room, wardrobe door sliding open, clothes dragged from hangers, empty hangers knocking on the rail – from the other sounds of the house settling, shifting. Ice cracking in the fridge, that was nothing. Plastic window frames popping as they expanded, the hum of hot water reheating, the kettle clicking as it cooled – all normal. It was the noise underneath that disturbed her. Stealthy, like blood beating in a place she couldn't see. It switched off when she went outside. The sound was in here. Living in the house with them. She moved around the kitchen, touching counters, cupboards, walls; it was easier to hear a sound if she touched it. She crouched to put her palm to the floor. The tiles were spongy, lifting when she took her hand away. Yesterday, she'd set a marble down, seen it roll from one end of the kitchen to the other. The house was settling but that didn't explain the sound. She wished her head was clearer, that she didn't feel nauseous all the time.

'What're you doing?' Christie was in the doorway.

'I dropped something.' She made a fist and stood, pocketing the imaginary object.

They played basketball until he won, victory-dancing across the tarmac.

The sun shone on him, turning his red hair gold, freckles crowding his nose. His happiness filled her throat. She could've watched him dance all day. When they went back inside, he took two cans from the fridge, forgetting she couldn't drink anything fizzy. She took the can and chinked it with his to keep the victory going. They sat together on the sofa while he flicked through the many channels on the giant TV, settling on a programme about the paranormal. She quickly learnt not to laugh at the stories of snow circles and strange lights in the sky. Christie was engrossed, his glass dripping down the front of his T-shirt. It was a good hour, an orange hour.

When he went up to his room, Agnes stayed on the sofa. It was rare to have the sitting room to herself. Dad was with Trevor, Ruth in Exeter for a meeting. Agnes was in charge, nominally at least. Christie didn't need a babysitter and wouldn't have accepted her in that role if he did. Basketball had been a good idea, she wished she'd thought of it sooner. It was exhausting, being hated. It had to be exhausting for him, too. The TV ticked and clicked, together with the set-top box and home hub, a symphony of tiny sounds like insects stirring. She could hear Christie sitting at his desk, the wheels of his chair pressing at the floor. She curled her legs onto the sofa, shutting her eyes. Easier to listen with her eyes shut. The blood sound originated in the garage, she was certain, behind the stack of boxes from their old house. Christie thought she was mad, scrabbling around in there. Her brain wasn't wired the way his was but that didn't mean it was faulty. In London, Laura had spent hours explaining why her brain was beautiful, 'Like the rest of you,' kissing the nape of her neck and her wrists, all the places she hurt when her difference became too much and her brain was on fire, burning all her bridges and her best intentions.

She sat upright, rigid on the sofa.

There – in the corner of the sitting room where the wall met the ceiling.

A thick, black throbbing.

She squinted upwards, half expecting to see a stain spreading. There was nothing to see but she could hear it, inside the ceiling or in the floor of the room above. A living, secret sound.

Very slowly, she uncurled on the sofa, putting her feet to the floor. No change in tempo or disturbance in the air, nothing to say for certain this wasn't in her head. It's what Ruth said, the first time Agnes told her about the noises she was hearing. 'Your meds help with this sort of thing, love. Is the prescription up to date?' She stepped off the rug to stand under the source of the sound.

Something was here in the house with them. It was here the night they moved in, stirring in the walls, shifting from place to place. Mice or a squirrel, she'd thought. They were surrounded by open fields, the building work disturbing wildlife. In the unfinished houses, there were gaps everywhere for things to get in. Christie wanted to take her inside the half-built houses, 'It's cool, you'll see,' but Agnes was sure she'd hear feet scurrying behind the sheeting, shadows running up and down the walls. She wasn't saying the houses were haunted, just that mice or rats or squirrels had crept inside during construction. She couldn't understand why that was so contentious.

'Shut up,' Christie had told her, 'stop looking for ways to spoil it.'

'I just want us to be safe.'

'No you don't. You want us to be like you, always looking for a reason to run away.'

She'd backed down, trying not to hear the noises or to feel the tightness in the house, a scratchiness in her throat, constant pressure under her fingernails. Blackthorn was too new, built while the bricks were drying. She'd tried asking Dad how many weeks it'd been from the first brick to the carpets going down but he sidestepped her questions, looking wary. His tan was yellow, his eyes red-rimmed. Some days, she saw bruises on his forearms. He said it was normal, he enjoyed being a physical part of the development, had put his sweat and tears and blood into Blackthorn Ashes. It scared her, when he said that.

She climbed the stairs, keeping pace with the sound in the ceiling. Each stair creaked under her, new wood protesting. In their old house, the windows rattled when traffic went past but the stairs never creaked. All the noises in the old house had made sense.

Upstairs, the sound was different. Less like throbbing, more like scratching. It was the sound of something getting settled, burrowing in. If they didn't find it, there'd be a nest with babies and if those babies died, there'd be maggots and bluebottles. She shut her eyes, pinching the back of her neck to ground herself. It was too much, all this hunting, fearing.

In her bedroom, the curtains were closed against the day's heat. She put her head on the pillow, cool cotton under her cheek. She should run a bath. Not a shower, where the water felt like needles. A bath, nearly cold, where she could lie and listen.

In a minute, she thought, *in a minute I'll get up and run a bath.*

From Christie's room, the churn of music drowned out the other sound. She followed the music's thumping down into sleep.

Christie spent the afternoon in the garden. Next door, Felix and Chloe were in the paddling pool playing with foam shooters. Darts kept coming over the fence. Christie picked up the first two and chucked them back but it got boring. Felix asked if he wanted to play football and Christie called back, 'Too knackered, mate,' which was what Trevor would've said. The kids went inside when their mum called from the kitchen. Water slopped in the pool for ages after they'd jumped out.

Agnes came to join him after it got quiet. She'd been sleeping but now she had a tray with cold drinks and chocolate chip cookies. He helped himself, watching as she lugged a lounger into the shade. When she picked up one of the foam darts he said, 'It's from a shooter gun. Next door.'

She leant back, turning the dart between her fingers like a

pencil. Christie ate a couple of cookies before lying down with an arm across his eyes to block out the sun. He could hear bees buzzing in the flowers Mum'd planted. He didn't want to move. Everything he needed was here. Magnums in the freezer, crisps in the cupboards. He was getting lazy but it was the summer holidays. Basketball had been an effort. He felt wiped out.

'Did you hear that?' Agnes said.

He knew from her voice she was sitting upright. He ignored her but she said it again, 'Christie. Did you hear that? In the house.'

'So?'

'No one's home except us.'

'Probably Dad come back early.'

'We'd have heard him.'

'Then it's next door.' He reached for his glass. He was too tired for this.

Agnes was sitting with her bare feet on the grass, the red dart clenched in her fist. 'It's not next door. It's in there.' She stared at the house.

'Shut up.' He was sick of her drama. 'You didn't hear anything.'

A flushing sound from inside the house made her stand, the lounger rocking on the grass.

'You must've heard that.' Her face was so pale it made her eyes black. 'Stay here.'

Like she was protecting him from some monster lurking in there. His big, brave sister.

'It's Dad, stop being stupid . . .' He followed her into the house, wanting to see her proved wrong. It was cold inside after the garden. He shivered then caught her looking at him. 'Shut up.'

The downstairs toilet was next to the kitchen, its door propped open. From the other end of the hall, Christie could hear the cistern refilling. He'd heard it flush too. They went towards it, Agnes first, one hand out behind her to try and keep him back. Goosebumps on her shoulders, matching the ones on his neck. She pushed the bathroom door open with an outstretched hand.

The loo was empty. Lid up, water gurgling in the bowl. It'd just flushed, you could tell from the smell of the lemon tablets Mum put in the cisterns.

'Dad?' Christie headed to the kitchen. 'You home?'

Dad wasn't in the kitchen, or the sitting room. He ran upstairs to check the bedrooms but Dad wasn't anywhere in the house. By the time he got back down, Agnes was washing her hands in the bathroom sink. She'd put the toilet lid down.

'It'll be the water pressure.' She dried her hands on one of Mum's towels. 'Dad'll be able to explain it.'

Christie stared at her with his stomach churning. His ears were popping from running up and down the stairs. He kept telling *her* to stop imagining things. Now she was trying to calm him down like *he* was freaking out over nothing? When she'd *made* him freak out? He'd been happy in the garden, hadn't even heard the stupid toilet until she'd made a big deal out of it, the way she did out of everything.

'Christie?' She frowned at him. 'It's okay.'

'It's not. It's not fucking okay. You're ruining everything.'

Her face fell into the slack shape he hated, her eyes blanking. 'Okay.'

'It's not fucking okay!' he shouted.

He felt himself getting bigger and hotter, his ribcage filling with fury. It seemed to come up from the tiles under his bare feet, fizzing in his shins and thighs, all the way to his face.

His sister backed away from him, out of the bathroom. She looked wild for a second, like she wanted to run. Good. She *should* run. Run and never come back. He should *make* her run.

'What do I do with this?' She opened her fist on the foam dart.

'Throw it over the fucking fence!' He hit the thing from her hand. 'I don't care!'

The dart bounced, smacking against the wall before it fell to the floor.

Agnes took a step back from him, before stooping to pick it up. 'Okay, I'll put it over the fence.'

He hated her even more when she was being calm, making *him* look like the unreasonable one. He hated her so much he couldn't see straight, just the skinny white blur of her. His hands made fists, knuckles burning with the need to punch. He'd punch her so hard she'd land on the floor, so hard she wouldn't get up again. Ever.

'Why don't you *fuck off*? No one wants you here. *You* don't even want to be here.'

'That's not true. I'm trying . . .'

'Yeah?' He pushed past, slamming her into the wall. 'Try harder.'

Agnes dropped the foam dart over the fence into Maythorn's garden. She needed to get out of the house. Christie would be fine as long as she wasn't here, enraging him. His anger was new but it felt old, like the granite boulder they'd carved into an entrance stone for Blackthorn Ashes. She'd been gone for eleven years. Of course he'd changed in that time; they all had. But it had scared her, the fury in his face as he'd knocked her out of his way. As if he was a stranger, someone she'd cross the street to avoid. She pushed her feet into trainers, pulling on an oversized shirt.

Outside Blackthorn, the sun was glaring. Dust spun in a shallow circle at her feet. She started in the direction of the woods, wanting shade. She'd only gone a few yards before she heard yelping and saw a dog limping towards her from the direction of Silverthorn. A scruffy little dog, stopping at her feet with one paw raised.

'What happened?' She crouched, feeling faintly ridiculous, as if she'd wandered into a movie where a lonely young woman is befriended by a biscuit-coloured terrier.

'Odie!'

The shout came from the direction of Quickthorn, one of the unsold houses. She turned to see a tall black man with short blond dreadlocks, dressed in an orange kimono printed with white birds. When he came closer, she saw that he was her age and the birds were cranes, and he wasn't wearing anything under the kimono.

'Is he all right?' He sank to his heels beside her, reaching one hand for the dog's head. Between two fingers of his other hand, a cigarette was burning. No, a joint.

Agnes shut her eyes for a second, breathing deeply.

'What'd you do, you little shithead?' He rubbed the dog's ears. 'What is it?'

The dog whined, holding up its injured paw. He examined it, making soothing sounds, stopping when the dog began to bark, turning its head in the direction of Silverthorn.

'All right, Lassie . . .' He sat back on his heels, taking a drag on the joint. 'Thanks for the heart attack.' He let the dog curl next to his leg, petting its flank. 'Sorry, he's such a drama queen, runs in the family . . . Here,' he offered Agnes the joint, 'you look like you need this more than me.'

She nearly took it, shaking her head at the last second. 'I shouldn't.' She was already hearing things, and her meds didn't mix with marijuana.

He took another drag, blowing smoke softly in her direction. 'How about that?'

'Actually, that's perfect.' She drew a deep breath, feeling steady for the first time in days, her heart no longer labouring in her chest. 'Thanks.'

'I'm Errol.'

'Agnes.'

'From Blackthorn.' He nodded in the direction of their house. 'Your dad's nice, Bette says he's the best employer she's had in years. Plus, he did all this,' waving his hand at the houses, 'which makes him a kind of genius.'

Odie stood, ears pricking at some sound Agnes couldn't hear. She wondered how he'd hurt his paw. The houses all had the same blank face, shadows criss-crossing hot tarmac.

Errol took a last drag, sending her a smoke ring.

'No offence to your dad,' he climbed to his feet, brushing dust from the kimono, 'but shall we get out of here before the Stepford Wives set the Midwich Cuckoos on us?'

It took her a second to realize the new sound was her own laughter, surprised and delighted.

'I thought no one would ever ask.'

2 SEPTEMBER

Eight days after abandonment

———

9

'Come on.' Christie was in his jeans and hoodie, empty backpack hanging from his hand. 'Agnes.'

'After yesterday? You know Mum said we shouldn't.'

'She says a lot of things.' He'd eaten his breakfast in record time after Ruth left. 'School starts in like a *week*. I'm not spending the last of the holidays in this shithole.'

School meant reality, an end to the game they'd been playing, and to the pretence that he was okay. His fear was like smoke shifting under the surface of his anger, filling the caravan with its flintiness. At night, Agnes couldn't breathe because of it.

'I could try and fix your Game Boy,' she said. He'd been fidgeting with the old console all morning. 'I used to be good at fixing things, remember?'

Christie pushed his arms through the backpack's straps. He was going, with or without her.

'We could go for a walk?' she tried. 'Down to the trampoline?'

He shrugged. 'Okay.'

Agnes put Dad's sandwich on the counter. She hadn't talked Christie out of anything, she knew. As soon as they were on the cliff path, he'd insist on taking their usual route to Blackthorn Ashes. She couldn't stop him, and Ruth wouldn't want him there alone. They would have to tell her they'd gone to the beach for the day. Another secret but what was one more?

'Go ahead,' she told Christie. 'Wait for me outside.'

She pulled on walking boots and a long-sleeved T-shirt. Trevor might be waiting at the houses, a prospect that made her fingers shake as she laced the boots. Her brain had caught up with what'd happened yesterday. At the time, she'd blanked out his threats but her brain served them back up, the way it always did. The experts called it 'a delayed response to sensory stimuli'. It had been getting her into trouble for as long as she could remember.

Outside the caravan, Christie was petting Odie. Bette stood in the doorway to her caravan, cradling a mug. 'You two off? Only could you take him? I'm starting a cold. Errol, too.'

Christie twisted sideways to look at Agnes, mouthing, '*No.*' He loved the dog but they couldn't take Odie into the houses. They'd have to stick to the path, go to the beach after all. Agnes pictured them falling in the sand, getting back up. A normal, happy picture, nothing scary in it.

'We can take him.' She ignored the pulse of rage from her brother.

'I'll get his lead.' Bette disappeared into the caravan.

Odie put his front paws on Christie's leg, tail whipping.

'Why'd you do that?' he demanded. 'You know we can't take him in the houses.'

'It'll be fine. You'll see.'

Bette brought a plaited lead and snapped it to the dog's collar, offering the looped end to Christie. 'You'll be doing me a favour.'

The curtains were closed at Errol's window. Agnes had a thirsty feeling in her throat. Since Blackthorn Ashes, she'd been afraid of people falling ill. Afraid of fevers and coughs, and air that carried invisible particles. 'Is he okay?'

'He's fine,' Bette said. 'Just doing his dying swan routine. He'll be up and about by the time you get back, I expect.'

Christie didn't speak until they were on the cliff path. The lead was the retractable kind, reeling out to let Odie run ahead at his own pace. 'We'll tie him up in the garden when we go inside. He doesn't bark much or we'd have heard him. It'll be okay, won't it?'

'I don't know. He might hurt himself.'

'He won't.' Christie turned his head away from her.

The sun was strong behind the clouds, summer dragging on, making her want the woods. Like the beach, the woods were full of memories from her childhood, standing with the honey scent of fungus, bank after bank of bracken droning with bees. She'd been in the woods on the morning of the evacuation, returning to find her family packing bags in a panic, police cars parked everywhere. She'd heard one of the police officers saying, 'It's a blood bath . . .'

On the cliff path, Christie pulled on the lead to stop Odie running too far ahead. The backpack hung limp between his shoulder blades. What treasure would he find to fill it today, what pieces of another person's life? He took things no thirteen-year-old boy would want – a faux diamond, a foam dart. Little pieces of that other life they'd lived in Blackthorn Ashes. Was he searching for something to explain the horror of what happened? As if there might be a single answer, a thing he could hold in his hand and say, 'It was this.'

Agnes shivered as she followed him along the path. Odie ran

on, nosing at everything, his tail in the air. Excited by all the scents, snuffling and scampering. She thought of the bones they'd find in Blackthorn Ashes, centuries from now. Binka's bones. And bodies, buried in the rotting plot of earth in a corner of the garden. Thousands of bodies. Dead wasps. She hadn't watched while it was done, hiding in her bed, stroking the pads of her fingers at her new buzz cut, her scalp hot against the cool of the cotton. Ruth had tried to make her watch (some idea of closure) but Agnes couldn't. She'd told them it wasn't safe, she'd tried to tell them. Christie had screamed at her, slapping the foam dart from her hand. His rage was a wall, unscalable. She'd dropped the dart over the fence as he'd instructed. Two days ago, he'd found it in the paddling pool in Maythorn's garden. The pool, filled with dead leaves, was trodden down on one side as if Felix had put his foot on the rim to watch a rush of water flood the grass. Or Chloe, whose red hands reached into Agnes's nightmares.

'Come on.' Christie was at the gap in the hedge.

On the other side, Blackthorn Ashes was silent, its windows blanked by sunshine, red roofs sloping over white walls where streaks of rust had wept. Stiff leaves moved in the breeze, tapping against one another. No birdsong, no bees.

Her throat clenched with premonition. Something worse than Trevor was waiting for them today. 'Wait . . .'

'You can stay here if you like.' Christie held out the lead. 'With Odie.'

Bette's dog was straining to go through the hedge, smelling the gardens and houses. On a hot day, the estate stank of plastic and bins, abandoned barbecues, garden furniture. When the shadows shrank, you could make-believe people were inside the houses going from room to room, living their lives. Odie dragged at her arm, whining. Christie was gone, out of sight. She ducked to follow him through the hedge.

Something had been digging in Redthorn's lawn. A squirrel perhaps, burying nuts for the winter. It was strange to think of Blackthorn Ashes in winter, snow lying over everything. Perhaps by then it would have been pulled down. All this would be gone, bulldozed back to earth. Wildlife would creep in, or it would stay away. Nature was smarter than people. This place might become scorched earth, blighted for a generation.

At the back of the house, Christie was fitting the key into the lock. His fingerprints were all over the door frames here, and inside the homes he'd ransacked. A foam dart, a faux diamond – what would the police call that? Petty larceny? If they were lucky.

Odie was scrabbling at the flower beds, soil pattering behind him.

Agnes looped the lead more firmly about her hand. 'Come on, boy.' She followed Christie into Redthorn's kitchen.

This had been Trevor's place while he was working on-site. Mostly he slept in his campervan, a few miles away. He hated to be tied down, that's what he said when Dad was selling the houses, 'Lucky for you, I'm in a minority.' He'd left empty beer bottles in Redthorn's sink, a big bag of salted peanuts on the counter. Christie stole a handful of the nuts, tossing them into his mouth.

A single trip, she'd thought eight days ago, to satisfy his curiosity. A salve for his sadness. He was grieving, for those who'd died but also for his home and family. She didn't know what it would do to Ruth to lose him too. She only knew that in some strange way, Blackthorn Ashes was keeping her brother alive. She followed him through the house, sidestepping the toolkit in the hallway, next to steel-capped work boots. Odie stayed at her heels, tail down, flank pressed against her calf. A shiver passed through him into her. He felt the same way she did, being here. An empty house has echoes. Sometimes it vibrates, as if the family has stepped out for a while and will be back soon. Redthorn had no echoes, nothing to hint at life going on elsewhere.

Christie had left via the front door. She led Odie out the same way, searching for the red of her brother's backpack against the white of the houses. *There.* To the south, where Blackthorn stood. He was going home? He never did that. All the other houses were fair game, he said, but not theirs.

'Come on, boy.' She let the lead go long but Odie stayed at her side.

Blackthorn Ashes bristled in the sunshine, its windows pale, its roofs dark. She could smell bitumen and rubber but all the cars were gone. Outside Silverthorn, a trailer sat uncoupled, nose bar resting on the tarmac, tarpaulin roped around the husk of an abandoned dinghy. Perhaps Luke couldn't imagine sailing it again without Emma. Agnes tried not to see the other pictures. Felix on tiptoe, sneaking a peek under the tarpaulin, risking Luke's wrath until Janis, carrying baby Sasha in her arms, warned him to get back inside the house. Emma standing on Silverthorn's doorstep in her dressing gown, eyes narrowed against the sun. Tim and Val grey-faced with exhaustion, excusing themselves from the street party. 'We're a bit under the weather right now.'

Odie had spied Christie going into Blackthorn. He pulled at the lead, looking up at her. 'Okay,' she said. 'Come on.'

She didn't want to be in their old house, had no idea what

Christie's mood would be. In the other houses, he was flushed with the hunt, rummaging for his treasure. Could Agnes make her mother understand that somewhere in the half-emptied sock drawers and on the doors of fridges was what he needed to survive this catastrophe? They all needed something. For Ruth it was work, to pay the bills and keep them fed, but also for herself. So she could leave some of the shame behind and move forward. For Dad it was silence, a place to lie and lick his wounds. For Agnes it was Errol, waiting at the end of each day to make her smile.

Christie had disappeared up the side of the house into the garden. From there he'd open the back door with the key from Dad's keyring. Ruth had the keys to the front door.

Agnes picked up the pace, letting Odie run ahead of her. By the time they reached Blackthorn's front door, Christie was inside, holding the door open.

'He can come in.' He nodded at Odie. 'Our house, our rules.'

He was master of the house now. Master of all the houses, their keys jangling in his pocket. He didn't have to follow Ruth's rules or anyone else's. He reached for the lead, crouching to unclip it from Odie's collar. 'There you go, boy. All yours.'

Odie stood for a second on the threshold. Then he did an abrupt U-turn, diving between Agnes's feet and dashing up the curve of road in the direction they'd just come.

'Shit . . . Odie!' Her brother slapped the door frame. 'Come here!'

The dog barked once before disappearing from sight.

'We'll have to go and get him. He might go into a field. If a farmer sees him—'

'Leave him.' Christie tossed her the lead. 'He'll come when he gets hungry.' It was a phrase he'd heard Barry Mason use about Felix.

'Bette trusts us to keep him safe!'

'It's your fault.' He threw the accusation over his shoulder. 'You were supposed to stay with him. Why'd you follow me, anyway?'

'Mum trusts me to keep *you* safe.'

'Sure.' He laughed. 'Whatever.'

Then he was gone, too deep inside the house for her to hear whatever else he was saying, perhaps that Mum might as well have put the dog in charge.

Agnes stayed outside, scanning the estate for Odie. The lead was heavy, hanging from her wrist. She'd walk in the direction Odie ran, keeping the house in her sightline in case Christie got into trouble. Odie was scared. Christie's fear was different; being here made it better, not worse. She crossed to where Luke's dinghy sat, its tarpaulin puddled with leaves like the pool in Maythorn's garden. A breeze lifted one edge of the tarpaulin, showing a flash of pink underneath. She'd forgotten the dinghy was pink. Shielding her eyes, she scanned the street. The back of her neck chilled and she turned, seeing her brother's silhouette at the window of the front bedroom. Their parents' room. What was he doing in there? Dad didn't keep much in the bedroom, only clothes. Mum worked there, though, it was her room. Agnes watched Christie's shadow, telling herself Ruth would have taken anything private and shredded it, she was too smart to leave her secrets lying around. Christie could look all he wanted, there would be nothing to find.

She tapped the lead against her leg, looking for Odie. Afraid to call him, not wanting the sound of her voice thrown back at her. Christie felt powerful here but she felt the opposite, exposed and ineffectual. Every window was an eye, watching. She squeezed her fingers into fists, focusing on breathing until her pulse slowed. Then she shook her fingers loose, relaxing her shoulders. There was nothing and no one here. Not even Trevor today.

Soon it would be time to go back. Her brother would be calm and happy. He'd walk ahead of her while she tried to guess what was inside his backpack. He might talk to her, more than just, 'Come on.' The only time he ever talked to her properly was after a visit to Blackthorn Ashes.

She moved away from the house, tapping the lead against her leg again. 'Odie?'

She passed Maythorn and Hawthorn, thinking of breakfasts and bedtimes, children lolling on beanbags. Dad grilling sausages for the street party, Mum unloading shopping into the fridge. An arch of blue and white balloons. All gone, wiped out by police tape and foil shock blankets, sirens and clouded oxygen masks. No one had happy memories of Blackthorn Ashes. Perhaps that's what Christie was doing here, paying homage to the happy memories, trying to retrieve something of those lazy summer afternoons when barbecues sizzled and kids splashed in pools while their parents stood in open doorways stunned by sunshine and their own good fortune.

'I thought you didn't have a dog?'

A woman stood outside Quickthorn, the sun hiding her face. Odie lay in her arms, unmoving. For one horrible second, Agnes thought he was dead; his fur looked dull and his eye was a flat black disc, unblinking. Then the woman tickled him under his chin and he stirred, lifting his head to lick at her arm. Not dead or hurt, just content in her arms.

'I found him down by the building site.' Her voice was familiar.

'He's yours, right?' She came closer, laughing when Odie licked her chin. 'He's too cute.'

When she stepped out of the sun, Agnes recognized her. Iris with the bloodstained hands, from the street party.

'He's not mine . . .' She took Odie, setting him down, clipping the lead to his collar. She straightened to see Iris watching her.

'You don't remember me.' She held out a hand. Her fingernails were painted dark blue, no blood on her hands today. 'I'm Iris. We met at the barbecue.'

'Of course I remember you.' She didn't shake the hand, keeping herself busy with Odie so she wouldn't look rude. 'Thanks for finding him. We were walking the cliff path and he ran off through one of the hedges.' She crouched to pet Odie's ears.

'It's kind of spooky, right? So different to the last time we were here . . .'

Agnes kept her head down, aware of a sharpness in Iris's voice, curiosity or superstition. At the street party, she'd felt attraction but this was like a cliff edge. She thought: *If Christie comes out of the house, if he uses the front door to come out of the house* . . . When she straightened, Iris slid her eyes away as if she'd been staring but didn't want to be caught. What was she doing here? Dust dulled her ankle boots. She wore the snakeskin leggings, a close-fitting vest showing off her strong brown shoulders. The same sunglasses pushed up in an Alice band. A child-sized quilted backpack, neon green, sat snug between her shoulder blades.

'Don't you think?' She tipped the sunglasses into place, their bottle-brown lenses hiding her eyes. 'Spooky.'

'I hadn't thought about it . . .' Agnes looked about her vaguely as if seeing Blackthorn Ashes for the first time. As if she'd never lived here, or left, or come back.

'It must've been awful for you.' Iris came closer, putting out a hand for Odie to lick. 'Terrible.'

Was she a ghoul? Ruth said lots of people were ghoulish. After the story broke and the estate was evacuated, some of those people came to see for themselves, in groups or alone. But even ghouls got bored; she and Christie hadn't seen anyone here in a long time. Only Trevor. She didn't want to think Iris might be a ghoul. Whatever she was, Agnes should get her away before Christie came out of the house. 'I'd better take him home.'

'He's Errol's dog, right? He said he had a dog. Oh, you're a good boy!' Odie had his front paws on her shins, fretting up at her. She laughed, reaching to rub behind his ears.

Dogs had good instincts. Odie had been afraid to go into their old house, his tail down as soon as he saw Blackthorn Ashes. But he'd found a friend in Iris.

'He's Bette's dog, really . . .'

The crunch of gravel made them turn. Christie, coming up the path at the side of Blackthorn, stopped short when he saw Iris.

Agnes said loudly, 'We found him!' as if Christie had been searching for Odie. She was close enough to feel Iris tense, her interest piqued. 'My brother. You nearly met him, at the barbecue.'

Christie, acting on her cue, jogged towards them. 'Odie, you bugger, where were you?'

'I'm Iris.' She wiped her hand on her leggings before holding it out. 'Edison.' When Christie looked blank, she added, 'Lightbulb moment?' Turning the bid at a handshake into jazz hands.

Agnes thought of the street party, the ease with which Iris made herself part of that gathering. Joking with Errol. Flirting with her? She was deploying the same skill now, navigating Christie and Odie, and the whole of this deserted place where disaster struck. Something wasn't right, something didn't click. Agnes told herself to be very, very careful around Iris Edison.

'Hi.' Christie dropped to his knees to fuss at Odie, and to avoid Iris's scrutiny, his instincts matching Agnes's for once.

'How's your dad?' Iris asked. 'And your mum? Are they okay?'

Agnes's heart rate slowed to a crawl.

Christie was frozen at her feet, his hands buried in Odie's fur, his head tucked into his chest.

'It must be weird being back.' Iris fine-tuned her smile to suit the stress in the air. 'But I get why you'd want to. I mean, look at it. It looks so . . . *normal*.'

Agnes was able to meet her gaze because her brain hadn't processed the threat, not fully, not yet. This moment would catch up with her tomorrow or the next day. The danger she and Christie had been in as they stood here with Iris, seeing the sky reflected in her sunglasses.

'We need to get back.' Christie took Odie's lead from her slack hand. 'This isn't our dog.'

'He's Bette's, I know.' Iris pushed the sunglasses back up into her hair. 'How's Errol?'

Everything she said was a question, Agnes realized, of one kind or another. She'd asked a lot of questions at the street party too. About pets and people and could she use their bathroom and didn't they get lonely and how did Luke break his foot? She had more questions now. Agnes could guess at some of them. What does your dad think about what happened here? Who's to blame?

How well did you know the people who died, the children and the others?

Christie didn't like it any more than she did. 'We're allowed to come here.' He squared his jaw at Iris. 'What's your excuse?'

'I don't think you are,' she said smoothly. 'Allowed to come. No one is. I'm trespassing but I do that a lot. For a living, in fact. You two on the other hand . . .' She shrugged, smiling.

For a living. She wasn't a delivery driver, or not only that. What was she?

'We've special permission to get essential items from our home.' Christie was sweating, Agnes could smell it. The back of his neck was spotted with damp. 'Actually.'

'So you have a key?' Her face lit as if he'd shone a torch under her chin. 'To your house?'

'It's none of your business.' He looped the lead around his wrist. 'Come on, Odie.'

'You're very quiet.' Iris looked at Agnes. 'Are you okay?'

'I'm fine. But he's right. We need to get back. It was nice to meet you again.'

Or for the first time, because you were lying before. Hiding in plain sight like these houses that killed six people.

'I'm a reporter.'

'We guessed.'

A flicker of surprise, the first Iris had betrayed. 'Clever you.'

Agnes kept the smile in place until their backs were turned. She and Christie walked away side by side, Odie going ahead, his lead unreeling with a *shush.*

'I'd like to talk to you!' Iris called after them. 'I can pay cash!'

'Bitch,' Christie said under his breath.

'It's okay.' The tarmac was rubbery, a shock absorber under her feet. 'Let's get back, like you said.'

To Indigo Park, to Bette and Errol, and their parents.

'Did she see me in the house?' Christie demanded.

'She didn't see anything.'

'If Mum finds out we talked to a reporter . . .' He was thrumming with stress.

'We didn't. We talked to a stranger. As soon as she told us she was a reporter, we shut up.'

He squinted at her. 'How're you not freaking out?'

'You know me. I'll be a mess tomorrow . . . Odie liked her.'

'He's a little shitbag.' But Christie sounded less panicked.

It was better now they were walking away, leaving Iris behind. They couldn't cut through the hedge, in case she was watching. She wasn't following which seemed odd, unless she was trained not to pursue. Or unless she knew they'd be back. Had she guessed they couldn't stay away? Seen them here before? It would explain the skin-pricking sensation Agnes so often had, that sense of being watched. She could picture Iris staying out of sight, spying on them as they went from house to house. What did she want, really? Any reporter would be interested in the nightmare story of Blackthorn Ashes. But Iris was here *before* the real nightmare began. At the barbecue, asking about pets and housekeepers and Luke . . .

Agnes felt a tick of true panic in her chest.

Behind her, the houses bristled like a forest, a place of thorns and danger. Iris was alone there, standing with her sharp eyes, waiting for their return.

A solitary car was parked in the space outside the main entrance. Nondescript silver, new enough to be a hire car. Empty coffee cup on the dashboard, satnav suctioned to the windscreen, yellow rain jacket on the backseat next to an overnight bag; Iris wasn't going away. A mountain bike was strapped to the rear bumper. Agnes could picture her cycling, ponytail horizontal, ankle boots on the pedals; she had that outdoor colour, the strength which'd first attracted her at the street party. How long had she been watching them? When Trevor stopped her outside Whitethorn, was Iris watching then? Agnes hadn't seen a phone but of course Iris had one, tucked into her quilted backpack. A phone with pictures of Agnes on it, Agnes and Trevor. A recording – had she got close enough for that? Laura's voice told her to keep it together, 'Stay in the moment. Don't spiral.' Agnes had spiralled in London. If she spiralled here, her family would pay for it.

'D'you think she knows?' Christie was staring at the hire car.

Agnes was thirsty suddenly. So thirsty she couldn't answer, tasting dust and smoke, ashes.

'Do you?' Christie tugged on the lead, pulling Odie away from the tyres. 'Think she knows we keep coming here?'

'I'm not sure.' *She knows.* 'But she was trespassing too, remember?'

'She's a ghoul.' Using Ruth's word.

'It's her job . . . Forget her. Come on. I'll manage Odie, you go ahead.'

She wanted him to run off steam. The backpack was slack against his spine but there was something new inside. Thin and square. A book, or papers of some kind.

'You were weird with her.' He gave her a sideways look through his fringe. 'Like you knew her or something. You're not like that with strangers usually.'

Tim and Val, he meant. Luke and Emma. Often Agnes would

blank strangers, even people she'd met, struggling to place them out of context. Perhaps she'd blank Iris the next time they saw one another. No, Iris was too vivid. Not someone you could forget.

'I met her before, remember? She was at the barbecue that day.'

'D'you fancy her?' Christie kicked a stone down the road, not looking at her.

'She scares me.' Not the whole truth but the newest part of it, the part that mattered.

Her brother half turned to squint at her, the sun in his eyes. He looked relieved. He'd assumed she was saying no, she didn't fancy Iris with her all-over tan that said she spent the summer out here by the coast where houses should never have been built, on land that belonged to the sea.

A gull lurched overhead, its shadow making Odie jump and bark as it wheeled away, over the roofs of the houses behind them. Rank after rank of houses, each emptier than the last. *Akiya*. And Iris, standing among the ghosts, waiting.

'I got this for you.' Christie took something shiny from his pocket: a steel padlock painted with a red spot. 'From Binka's hutch.'

Agnes had painted the red spot herself before fastening the lock through the wire on the rabbit's hutch, the way she and Laura had fastened padlocks to bridges in London. Binka's padlock was cool and heavy in her hand, weighted with memories. 'Thank you.'

Christie said, 'I thought you'd like it.' He walked ahead, following Odie's route to the cliff path.

She slipped the padlock into the pocket of her jeans. 'What other treasure did you find?'

'Nothing.' He shrugged. 'That's not why I came today.'

The backpack told another story, stiff with whatever he'd taken from Ruth's room.

'Why did you come?' Against their mother's wishes, at the risk of incurring her wrath.

'I just wanted to go home.' He kicked a pebble from his path. 'I'm sick of waiting.'

Shock travelled up her spine. He thought they were coming back here, to live. No matter what he had witnessed or what they were told, he thought there was a way back. And he *wanted* it. He wanted to live in that deathtrap. His *home*.

'We can still see Odie at the caravan park.' He twitched at the lead. 'We'll still see you, shitbag. But we're going to get a proper dog once the rest of the houses're finished.'

Agnes walked in his shadow. She should have said something, regurgitated the instructions given by the police, parroted the rules laid down for the families evacuated from the estate, 'You need to leave. Now.'

They weren't told the whole truth that day, just that it wasn't safe to stay. For Agnes, it was easy. She'd wanted to go, almost from the start. It was different for Christie but she had thought he understood there wasn't any way they could ever return. No one would ever live in those houses again. Blackthorn Ashes was over, finished.

Six dead bodies had put paid to any hope of ever returning.

How had her brother not realized that?

Twenty-five days before abandonment

———

10

Dad came home with the rabbit at the end of their first week in Blackthorn Ashes. They were celebrating, he said. He'd got a hutch and water bottles, bowls and straw and food – everything the rabbit needed. He brought other stuff too, wine and flowers and ice cream, but the rabbit was the main attraction. Mum watched him set up the hutch in a corner of the garden. She'd put a smile on but Christie heard her whispering, 'What were you thinking? You don't ask me first, just waltz in with a new pet?' Dad looked surprised, and a bit hurt. He said a house wasn't a home without a pet.

'Christie'll enjoy her. Agnes too. Come on, love.'

Dad'd been wired since before they moved in. He was busy on-site most days, checking progress on the unfinished houses, pep-talking the sales team. Christie had heard him and Trevor talking about how nothing was happening as fast as they needed it to. Dad was serious but it never lasted. You couldn't stay serious for long round Trevor. When he came home, Dad'd grab the basketball, shouting for Christie to come and shoot hoops with him.

'C'mon! *Move!* Nope, too slow!'

Sometimes, it was like he was mad at Christie. But mostly he was just buzzed, touching stuff in the house, grinning so hard you could see the teeth at the back of his mouth. Because he loved it here and because Agnes was back, making them a proper family again.

Christie was glad too, to begin with. Everyone went a bit batshit around his sister, turning down the noise, only using air freshener in an emergency because it brought her out in a rash – but it was cool having her home. He'd forgotten how much he'd missed her.

They named the rabbit Binka. She was pretty cute. Brown fur, long ears. Everyone fell in love with her, even Mum. Agnes was bonkers about her. Christie wanted a dog but Dad said not while the building was going on. 'When it's finished, mate. Then we'll get you a puppy.'

Christie didn't want a puppy. He wanted a proper dog, a big one he could take on walks, who'd growl at strangers and bark in the middle of the night. He'd never be allowed a dog like that, he knew. It'd freak his sister out. He could hear the arguments, 'We're trying to be a family,' when they'd been one for years, all the time she was in London and, yeah, it was cool having her home but other people's grown-up kids didn't come back. She spent more time with Binka than she did with them, sitting for hours in the garden with the rabbit curled in her lap.

'You used to do that,' Mum said. 'When you were tiny, you'd sit in her lap like that when you were upset or sad.'

'Why didn't I sit in your lap?'

'You did.' She smoothed his hair, stopping when he jerked his head away. 'But it was Agnes you went to, when you could.'

So that was batshit too, Mum treating him like a baby again when they'd agreed on a new bedtime, more freedoms. He had to listen to shit about his sister all day, which meant listening to shit about when he was a baby. It started getting old, really quickly.

They'd only had Binka a few days before it happened. Christie had stopped cleaning the hutch and changing the water bottles because the rabbit was hers, not his. It was *her* job to keep it safe. Her fault, what happened.

He was getting a Magnum from the freezer when he saw her in the garden with her head bent over her lap. Her hair was hanging, touching the grass. Mum was working upstairs, Dad with Trevor down the end of the estate. Agnes was rocking but she did that a lot. He'd learnt to ignore it.

The Magnum was getting sweaty in his hand. She was making this noise like scratching but coming from her mouth. He stared past her to the hutch. Its door was open. She was probably rocking the rabbit, singing to it. He wasn't going to freak out. He'd seen the way Mum and Dad got when she went into one of her states. At first they'd be extra smiley, making jokes to try and jolly her out of it. Then they'd go quiet, spying on her out of the corners of their eyes like they didn't want her knowing they were worried in case it made her worse. Mum would go stiff, her neck and fingers then her face. She'd get on with whatever she was doing – cooking or reading or looking at work emails – but she'd be getting stiffer and stiffer until Christie started to feel it too like cramp in his neck. All because Agnes was rocking or pacing or pinching her wrists. He bit the chocolate from the top of the Magnum but he didn't want to eat it now. He couldn't swallow without pushing past the lump in his throat. She sat there making that sound, bent double like some-one in a Japanese horror movie, as if she'd suddenly come upright by cracking her spine and turning inside out, bones snapping, head hanging between her legs as she staggered towards the house howling.

He dropped the Magnum into the bin and raced upstairs.

'Mum!'

She was sitting at her laptop with her earbuds in. She frowned and shook her head, mouthing she was on a call. He flapped his hand at the garden, mouthing back, '*Agnes!*' and she ended the call, dragging out the earbuds, dropping them on the desk. She did it so quickly he knew he'd been right to run up here. Panic was the only response that made sense where his sister was concerned.

He followed Mum down into the garden, staying back as she went to where Agnes was bent. Mum knelt three feet away, careful not to crowd her. She said his sister's name really softly and other stuff he couldn't hear from where he was standing, using the special voice she only ever used to Agnes, the one that made him think of someone lowering a dinghy into the sea really carefully so it didn't topple and fill with water.

Agnes kept rocking, her arms out of sight in her lap. Then she started to say, 'I told you,' over and over. Louder and louder until she was shouting, 'I told you!'

Mum put out her hands, not touching Agnes, just trying to calm her down. It was like a police standoff: 'Put the gun down and we'll talk.'

'I told you!'

Agnes rocked back, unbending and opening her arms at the same time so they could see what she'd been hiding in her lap. Binka. Brown fur and long ears, not twitching.

'Oh no. Oh, sweetheart.' Mum touched the fur with the tip of her finger. 'What happened?'

The rabbit was dead. Christie felt a rush of horror, hot and cold. He came closer, wanting to see what it looked like. He'd thought it'd look the same but it didn't. It looked bad, like it was already stiff. Agnes pushed her hands at it suddenly, as if she wanted Binka off her lap. She wasn't shouting any more but her face was making the shape of a shout, her eyes big and black.

Mum leant in and scooped the rabbit from her lap, holding it between her hands. She laid it on the grass very gently, stroking it like it was still alive. Agnes watched and after a bit, her shoulders went down and the shout slipped off her face.

Christie's heart was slamming. He thought he might be sick. He sat on the grass because it was odd to be the only one standing and because he was afraid Mum would notice and tell him to go inside the house. She didn't. She glanced his way and gave a tiny nod, telling him he'd done the right thing in running upstairs to fetch her.

'It's this place,' Agnes said. 'I told you.'

'Sweetheart.' Mum used the lowering-boat voice. 'It's horrible but these things happen—'

'It's here.' Agnes put the heel of her hand to the lawn, pushing until it left a dent in the grass. 'She died because of this place. It's not right. It's *sick*. It's going to make us all sick.'

'No, it's not.' Mum held out a hand to Christie but he shook his head. She'd touched the dead rabbit with that hand. 'These things happen. Agnes? It's very sad. I'm sorry.'

'You don't get it. None of you do. But I told you this would happen . . .'

Christie turned to look at the house. It looked the same as ever but he shivered.

They'd bury Binka in the flower bed in a shoebox; he'd seen it in movies. Agnes would paint a pebble from the beach and make a grave, a place she could point at next time she was freaking out about Blackthorn Ashes. There was poison here, that's what she kept saying. Coming up through the ground, seeping through the walls while they slept, rotting everything. She said it over and over, in a hundred different ways. It never seemed to occur to her *she* might be the poison. The cause of Mum's sore eyes and Dad's headaches. The reason the rabbit died. It'd start to smell soon. It would swell. Flies would come, then maggots.

Christie shivered. It was on her. *Agnes*. It was all on her.

2 SEPTEMBER

Eight days after abandonment

———

11

An ambulance was parked at the entrance to Indigo Park, its back wheels off the duckboards, sun splashed like paint across its doors. Odie barked at the sight of it, dashing forward until Christie dragged on the lead to bring him to heel.

Agnes was slow to react, the bark confusing her, throwing the picture out of focus. The last time she saw an ambulance it was in the aftermath of the storm when the only light came from next door, from Maythorn.

'Wait here,' she told Christie as Odie fretted at the lead.

'No way.' He walked with her, deeper into the caravan park.

Bette stood a short distance away, pink fleece zipped to her chin, red wellies on her feet. She raised a hand in greeting, smiling when she saw Odie. 'Come here, you bugger.'

Christie unclipped the lead and Odie ran to be scooped up, licking at Bette's face.

'You silly bugger,' she said. 'Did you have a nice walk, then? Did you?'

Agnes needed to turn and look at their caravan but she couldn't do it. What if paramedics were in there with Dad, trying to revive him? What if they were too late? Her head was thick with fear. Iris would get her story: Adrian Gale haunted to death. Agnes couldn't separate out what she had been afraid of at Blackthorn Ashes and what she was afraid of here and now.

'It's her from the flashy trailer. Jonelle.' Bette clicked her tongue. 'Her son's in a right state.'

Not their caravan. Not Dad. Her heart unclenched a little.

'What happened?' Christie asked.

'Not clear.' Bette set Odie down. 'Accident of some kind, might be.'

Odie scampered up the steps into her caravan.

Errol was sitting at the top of the steps in fraying jeans and a flappy white silk shirt, pineapple-printed scarf wound below his dreadlocks. He smiled at Agnes, propping his chin in his hand. The sun crazed the front of his shirt, making it hard to keep looking.

'I should check on my dad,' she said.

Bette nodded. 'I haven't seen him,' as if she usually did.

As if Adrian came out of the caravan when Agnes and Christie left and stood chatting with Bette, sharing a cup of tea and a plate of biscuits, being a good neighbour.

Her stomach shrivelled, her feet sweating in her shoes, hands sweating too. 'I'd better check.'

Christie was ahead of her, going up the steps into their caravan. Bette called after him, 'Thanks for taking the mutt for a walk. Hope he was good for you?'

'Yeah.' Christie nodded across his shoulder. He'd slipped the backpack to the front, holding it tight to his chest. He couldn't take his new treasure to the shed until the ambulance had gone.

'It was fun to walk him, thanks for asking us.' There was more

Agnes should say, something from earlier, about hot tea and Errol being in bed. 'How's your cold?'

'Under control.' Bette clucked her tongue at her grandson. 'He's getting some fresh air at least.'

'Who's he?' Errol called back. 'The cat's grandson?'

Bette batted this away with her hand. 'Let me know if you need anything.' She fixed Agnes with her sentry's stare. 'Any time.'

'Come by later,' Errol told Agnes. 'Please.'

'I'll try.' She wanted to tell him about Iris but it would have to wait. Family first.

Inside the caravan, Dad sat staring at the TV. The volume was muted, the screen full of the suntanned faces of holidaymakers. Christie didn't bother saying hello, just bumped through to the bedroom he shared with Agnes. The caravan smelt of overheated plastic and bodies. Dad hadn't washed in a while, his hair plastered to his head. The summer's tan was long gone. He looked old and tired. An empty plate sat at his side, cling film rolled into a ball. He'd eaten her sandwich at least.

'I'm making a cup of tea, if you'd like one?'

She waited, knowing it took a while for words to reach him. He turned his head from the TV, staring at her with his sad eyes. Pain twisted in her chest. It was easy to pity Dad but she couldn't do it without knowing how rarely she pitied Ruth, even when her mother deserved or needed pity. She'd fallen into the habit of blaming Ruth for all her problems. Growing up, Dad was so often working away from home. All her childhood terrors and adolescent demons, every mistake she made, each slight she suffered, fell on her mother's shoulders. Agnes didn't even call her 'Mum', wielding 'Ruth' like a weapon because she couldn't afford the loss of her defences. That's how it had felt, as if adolescence was a war and she was losing it. An image stormed into her head of Iris here, intent on interrogating her family, wanting her story. But she'd been at Black-thorn Ashes *before*, at the barbecue. Why was Iris at the barbecue?

'Thanks, love.' Dad switched his eyes back to the TV. 'Tea would be nice.'

Agnes pushed the thought of Iris to the back of her mind. She made two cups of tea, carrying them to the sofa, moving the empty plate out of the way so she could sit beside him, close but not facing; eye contact was hard at the best of times and they were a long way from the best of times.

Her father was wearing his old work jeans with a checked shirt, the same casual uniform Trevor favoured. His socked feet looked vulnerable and his hands too, callused from work, a light litter of nicks and scars across his knuckles. He'd built the shelves in her bedroom, put up the basketball hoop for Christie. When he wasn't selling houses, he was fixing stuff, humming a tune with a mouthful of nails or screws. The archetypal dad. A simple man, Ruth called him although she never said it viciously, only ever fondly, 'Your father's a simple man.'

There was nothing simple about his depression, or his silence. Agnes sipped at her tea, tasting salt from the tears she was holding back. It was an odd feeling to grieve for someone still alive, some-one sitting beside you on the sofa. Ruth had tried writing to him (lists of things that needed fixing in the caravan), stopping short of shouting. The caravan took every sound and multiplied it, crowd-ing out the space until you couldn't open the cupboards without finding the noise in there, or drink from a glass without tasting it.

'Dad, can I ask you something?'

He kept his eyes on the TV. She could smell his sweat. That's all it took. Not even a proper question, just the suggestion of one. His jaw clenched. In a moment, she'd hear it pop, if she asked him what she wanted to ask.

'About Trevor,' she said instead. 'Not about you.'

It was cheating. Any question about Trevor was a question about Dad. For years, they'd done everything together. Except for the summer Agnes was sixteen, the summer Christie was born.

'What?' His voice creaked on the question mark.

'How did you two meet? Was it at college?' The further back, the safer he'd feel. She wanted to take him years away from Blackthorn Ashes, lead him to safer ground. 'Or school?'

'Sixth form.' He reached for his tea. 'Tertiary college.' He drank a mouthful, wincing because the tea was hot. 'Studying architecture, the pair of us. Or trying to.'

'And you've been friends ever since.'

He pointed his chin in a nod, his eyes on the TV.

Agnes waited to see if he'd relax. Laura had taught her to read body language. Social cues were hard but she'd learnt to recognize a few. Raised eyebrows, a taut brow or half-open mouth – these were signs of fear. Curved shoulders signalled a sense of threat. Red skin and a clenched jaw were anger.

'I saw him yesterday,' she said. 'Trevor.'

Dad didn't move but he gave off such a strong pulse of sweat that her own armpits dampened in alarm. He pressed his fingers to the sides of the hot cup.

'I suppose I thought he'd leave,' she said. 'Like Barry and Janis. Get as far as possible from what happened.'

She should stop. She was nearing the cliff edge, as close as she could get and still be safe.

'He said something strange, too.'

Her father was staring at the TV as if willing it to explode, as if he'd sooner the caravan burst into flames than hear what she had to say.

'He said he knew stuff about us. Secrets. He was warning me to keep quiet.' She sipped at her tea, forcing her throat to swallow. 'I was wondering if I should tell Mum what he said.'

Dad's knuckles turned white, their scars standing out like silver.

'Best not to worry her.'

'She's worried anyway. We all are.'

'Still,' there was a crack in his voice, 'she's enough on her plate.'

They'd met in Ruth's first year of college, Mum dropping out of her course, pregnant at nineteen. The three of them – Ruth and Adrian and Trevor – inseparable, until Agnes.

She let the silence take shape before she asked, 'What was he like at college? Trevor.'

Dad's mouth stayed tight. Remembering his best friend back when they were fresh-faced, full of learning. She wanted him to remember. It didn't matter if he didn't answer her questions as long as he didn't forget, didn't let it slip away from him, the way he was letting so much slip. His work and family, his life. She knew how it felt to lose yourself that way. And they needed him. Maybe not now but soon. When the investigation turned in their direction, as it surely would, as it must. She was afraid by then he'd have drifted too far, beyond their reach. This was the only way she knew to keep him anchored. He'd closed all the doors in his head. It was what she did when she was afraid. Laura said, 'You go away. Lock up the house and you just . . . go.' Agnes had tried to explain how it felt – as if time was folded into a paper fortune teller and she could open and shut it to find all the other Agneses, the ones from before. A twitch of her fingers taking her to that summer she was sixteen, the taste of beer on her lips. Sometimes she thought if she turned fast enough, she'd catch her sixteen-year-old self, watching.

'I bet you got up to all sorts.' She stayed on the sofa beside Dad. 'You and Trevor.'

She wanted to open a door in his head, help him to remember who he was. If she could do that, she could bring him back. She didn't need him to speak to her, just remember who he'd been when he believed in Blackthorn Ashes, before it all came undone.

'He had a temper,' Dad said finally.

'At college?' Trevor's temper was like sparks coiled in smoke. 'What did he do?'

'Whatever he could get away with.' Dad's face caved at the cheeks as if his skin had lost its grip. 'Same as always. Same as in that place.'

'Blackthorn Ashes?'

'You stay away . . .' His voice sank to the back of his throat. 'Why can't you stay away?'

He *knew*? Where she and Christie went every day after Mum left for work? How long had he known? Cold clenched the back of her neck.

'You can't stay away.' He wet his lips, eyes sliding away from her. 'Can you?'

She should have been happy – she'd brought him back, just for a moment. But the shock of it silenced her. The idea of him knowing, and doing nothing. Her hands curled around her teacup, wanting to throw it, see it smash against the wall behind his head. In that moment, she didn't just understand Christie's anger, she *felt* it, burning through her.

Their father sat with his head bowed, giving no sign he'd spoken, wrapped in silence again.

What else was inside his head, hiding? What words were waiting in his mouth for her to pull them out in her clumsy bids to break his silence? Recriminations, confessions, what?

Be quiet, she thought, *go away again, wherever it is you go when you're not here. Go.*

By the time her mother was home, the ambulance had gone. Christie didn't mention it, Agnes following his lead. She'd prepared their supper, ready for Ruth's return. Mum looked wearier than ever but she'd found work for a couple of weeks. It was good news, she said. The meal passed more comfortably than Agnes had hoped. Dad congratulated Ruth on the job. 'That's great, love.'

Agnes caught Christie looking between them, softness edging its way into his face. This was how little it took to mend her brother's broken heart. He just wanted to be happy again, and he could be. She pinched the memory into her wrist. If they could hold this pattern, keep the frail shape of their family from tearing apart, it would be all right.

She washed the dishes after the meal. Dad and Christie settled on the sofa to watch TV together. By the time she'd made coffee, Ruth was arranging her work notes at the table.

She took the cup of coffee, saying, 'Thanks, love.'

'Thank *you*, for finding work.' Agnes fought the urge to fidget, unused to this peace between them. 'I wish I could do more to help.'

'You're here. That's a lot.' Her mother held her gaze. 'I know it's a lot.'

'There was an ambulance here earlier.' She'd meant to keep it secret but it blurted out. 'Bette said it was the family from the trailers. Jonelle.'

'I don't know them . . .' Her mother's face clouded with a frown. 'Did Christie see?'

'Yes, but he was fine. Do you think—'

'I need to get on.' Ruth cut her short with a smile. 'Lots to do tonight.'

She didn't want to listen to speculation. She believed in the power of silence, of not saying out loud the thoughts that were in your head. *Keeping mum*, they used to call it.

'There's something else.' Agnes needed to warn her about Iris. 'Someone else.'

'Not tonight.' Ruth lost the smile, fanning her fingers over the paperwork. 'Please.'

It was growing dark by the time Agnes left the caravan. Sunset was a distant streak against the trees. Birds chorused high above her. A slice of cold had crept into the breeze but the evening felt like late summer. She shook back the cuffs of her shirt to cool her wrists. Her head was throbbing, her bad tooth nagging. She nursed it with her tongue, discovering a grain of black pepper hiding there, a sudden hot shock on her tongue.

Errol was sitting on the steps to Bette's caravan, smoking a cigarette. Its scent made her stomach flip hungrily. He'd switched the white shirt for a silk dressing gown, turquoise patterned with gold tulips. He slid along the step to make space for her, offering his half-smoked cigarette before remembering, 'Hang on,' digging out the packet so she could take her own.

She couldn't smoke someone else's cigarette. Laura used to say she'd never have a proper romantic moment until she did. Errol held out his lighter, lit her up. 'Thanks.'

'You're welcome.' He slipped the lighter into his pocket.

They smoked in silence. It was the happiest she'd been in a long time, if happiness could be the absence of a thing, of sadness. After a while, she realized how much of an effort Errol was making to keep quiet. He wanted to chatter, the way he always did. The effort showed in the arch of his feet and at the inside of his wrist when he lifted the cigarette to his lips.

'What happened with the ambulance?' she asked.

He shot her a look of relief; she'd been right about the silence.

'Well . . . It took her away,' a swooping gesture with the cigarette, 'but she was sitting up. Walking wounded, you might say.'

'What sort of wound?'

She was seeing the butcher's block in Whitethorn, shiny handles like spines, Trevor's shadow staining the glass of the door.

'Oh, nothing so dramatic.' Errol inscribed a smaller circle with the cigarette, outlining his nose and mouth. 'Oxygen mask, and one of those silver blankets.'

'Shock blankets.' She remembered their insect sound, the tacky feel of foil under her fingers.

'Bette said it could've been an asthma attack. Or these . . .' He tilted the tip of his cigarette, considering it for a long second. 'She was wearing yellow Crocs.' He wrinkled his nose as if this were a symptom the paramedics had failed to diagnose: death by fashion disaster.

'That's what you meant by walking wounded.'

Errol arched his eyebrows at her.

'Yellow Crocs.' She mimed a shudder.

He gave a crow of laughter. 'Funny girl!' poking his elbow at her ribs.

She slid away before his elbow could connect.

'Oops.' He pulled a face. 'Sorry.'

They reverted to silence, finishing their cigarettes. Agnes hated the taste of the filter, never smoked more than half a stick, but this wasn't hers to waste. When Errol rubbed his filter on the step, she followed suit, holding the stub in her hand. He took it from her without touching her palm, the tips of his fingers as precise as tweezers.

'Drink?' he said then.

'Please.' She put her head back as he stood, dazzled by the golden tulips on his robe, a sudden flash of sculpted thigh.

'Oh, hello. Where'd you spring from?'

His voice arched, making space in their closeness for whoever he'd seen standing a few feet away.

Agnes climbed upright, dusting the palm of her hand on the leg of her jeans.

Iris Edison stood where the ambulance had parked earlier. In her snakeskin leggings and tan ankle boots, a khaki jacket full of pockets. Her chestnut hair fell sleekly about her shoulders.

Errol stared from Iris to Agnes and back, exaggerating a look of intrigue.

'Hello.' Iris took a step towards them, smiling. 'I hope I'm not late.'

As if they'd had a date, arranging to meet like this, tonight. Agnes could have corrected her but it would have meant explaining to Errol how she and Iris had met again, and that she'd failed to share this information with him. Her family was in the caravan, six feet from where Iris was standing. Christie and Ruth and Dad whose story Iris would love to get her hands on.

'We were about to get drunk actually.' There was a possessive note in Errol's voice, under the curiosity. He stood shoulder to shoulder with Agnes, his left wrist loose at his side, fingers crooked towards her, close enough for her to reach and take his hand. He was protecting her, as if he sensed Iris might be a threat. He made a strange champion in his exotic clothes, naked underneath.

'Drunk? That sounds fun.' Iris cocked her head at Agnes. 'We could do this later . . .' She let her stare travel around Indigo Park. 'How's Christie?'

A bark from inside Bette's caravan and Odie dashed out, barrelling down the steps to bounce up against Iris's knee. She laughed, 'Hello again!' and made a fuss of him, lavishing attention.

Errol drew a sharp breath and looked at Agnes, his eyes demanding answers.

'They met on our walk.'

She didn't know what else to say. It was slipping away from her – the happiness from a moment earlier, sitting at his side on the step.

'This place is amazing.' Iris moved nearer, Odie dancing attendance at her side. 'How many people live here?'

Errol watched her with Odie for a moment before he said, 'Do you drink vodka, Iris?'

'Only when there's no whisky, Errol.'

Sixteen-year-old Agnes watched the pair of them with her heart foundering in her chest. Other kids – holidaymakers – formed gangs so easily, coming together like metal filings pulled by the summer's heat. She'd watch them and imagine what it must be like to find a way into those loose knots of arms and legs, become part of the group. It had never bothered her, being on the outside, but it was different now. Seeing the ease with which Iris moved into Errol's orbit, mirroring his body language, loosening her hips, arching her eyebrows. She made it look so easy, being alive. Sixteen-year-old Agnes was hollow with envy.

An animal sound brought her back into the moment – the beat of wings or the scrabbling of claws, or nothing at all. They were in the middle of the countryside but Indigo Park was full of homes; the sound was more likely to be someone's television or laptop.

'Sorry,' she said, addressing Iris. 'But we should get going.'

Errol flung her a look of hurt surprise. She hated hurting him but it would be worse if Iris stayed, if they got drunk and she made Errol tell his secrets, teasing them out of him until he had nothing left. Agnes didn't know what secrets Errol was keeping but she knew Iris. Not logically but instinctively. She knew the sort of person she was, what she wanted. Even if she never wrote a story about Errol, she could hurt him. By emptying him out, the way she wanted to empty Dad and Agnes and anyone with a story about Blackthorn Ashes. People needed their secrets. You couldn't go around dragging them out, passing them from hand to hand as if you were at a child's party, playing a game. Secrets weren't separate, they were part of who we were, like blood or skin or teeth. Laura was the first person to understand how important Agnes's secrets were to her. In the end, though, her secrets had been too much, even for Laura.

'We could sit out here,' Errol said. 'I could bring a tray . . .'

Agnes shook her head at him. 'We have to go.'

Iris switched her stare between them, calculating. She knew Errol might have something worth knowing, something he'd seen or heard or thought about what had happened at Blackthorn Ashes. Agnes could use that – if Iris was distracted with Errol, she might forget about Dad, at least for the night. The way Errol liked to talk, it would be midnight before they were done. Time enough to warn Ruth and come up with a plan to protect her family. But if she did that, Agnes would be using Errol, substituting his secrets for hers.

'Come on.' She made herself put her arm through Iris's, turning their backs on Bette's grandson. She could feel his hurt like hands behind her, pushing her away.

Iris waved at him across her shoulder, letting Agnes lead the way towards the big trailers at the end of Indigo Park.

For preference, she'd have taken the cliff path. It was dark which meant Iris wouldn't be able to see her face when she lied. But the cliff path was dangerous, too many places where they might lose their footing. Agnes was used to walking the route alone at night. Iris wasn't. Or else she was, in which case Agnes was in even greater danger than she realized.

'I heard about the ambulance,' Iris said. 'That must've been a bit déjà vu-ish.'

'They have ambulances everywhere.'

'Still . . . When was the last time you saw one? Or the first time, at Blackthorn Ashes? I'd like to hear about that. I'd like your story from the beginning, back before it started to go wrong.'

How far back would they need to go for that? Before Agnes's diagnosis, certainly. Pre-school, when all she had were 'funny habits', games she played that made sense to no one but herself. Or back to when she was newborn and Ruth said she lifted her head to look her mother in the eye but when Ruth told the midwife, she said, 'Baby's neck's not strong enough for that yet,' so then Agnes did it again, only this time she fixed the midwife with her stare, provoking a startled laugh in response. Should they go back further even than that, to when Ruth was pregnant at nineteen? Or a year earlier, when she wasn't. When she hadn't dropped out of college and didn't have morning sickness or puffy ankles or the awful fear she wouldn't be a good mother or any kind of mother, that she couldn't be one. *Back before it started to go wrong.*

Agnes led Iris away from the big trailers – Elvis playing inside, a low crooning – to the rear of Christie's shed where two cane chairs faced the blackness of an unlit field. Enough light leaked from the trailers to show the places where the cane seats had frayed and sagged.

'What is this place?' Iris tried to peer through the shed's grimy windows.

'Nowhere, just a place.' She sat, waiting as Iris turned the second chair to face her.

Iris pushed her hair from her face, smoothing her expression into one of attentive expectation. 'Can I record this?' She reached for her phone, dislodging a ball of blue paper from her pocket.

'I'd rather you didn't.' Agnes leant to pick up the ball of paper, smoothing it in her fingers. 'And first I need you to tell me what story you're writing, or planning to write.'

A cartoon was drawn on the blue paper, next to a name: *Dearman*.

Panic bubbled in the pit of her stomach.

'If you tell me about the story, then I'll know if I can help you or not.'

Iris had written *Dearman* and drawn a dog's face with zigzag ears like bolts of lightning. 'Do you want this back?'

She shook her head at the piece of paper. 'Just a bad habit, doodling. I've done it since I was a kid . . .' She slipped a thumb inside the neck of her orange top, adjusting a bra strap. 'Fair enough about the recording . . . I suppose you'd say I'm writing an exposé.'

Agnes could hear her own heart beating. 'Exposing what?'

'The truth of what happened, why those people died and who those people were. I know they've said it was carbon monoxide, volatile organic compounds, whatever. But we both know it was more than that.'

Agnes put the scrap of paper into her pocket. 'I don't know any more than that.'

'We could've stayed for drinks with Errol.' Iris looked at her through the darkness, her eyes yellow as a cat's. 'It must be hard to make friends after everything that's happened.'

'I was friends with Errol before. And anyway, most people have been kind.'

'To the other families, sure. But to yours?'

Iris put her hand into her pocket before leaning to pick a slim branch from the ground. 'Your dad's the closest they have to a scapegoat . . . He was involved in the development from the concept stage, that's right, isn't it?'

Her hand stayed in her pocket; Agnes was sure she'd switched a button on her phone to record what was being said.

'He's not a developer, just a contractor. A salesman, really.'

'He was just doing his job?' She stripped leaves from the branch with her fingers. 'Of course you want to defend him, I get that. But you knew the people who died. Three adults and three children, one of them a baby. You were there, you witnessed it. That's a heavy thing to carry.'

Her tone implied she was doing Agnes a favour, helping her to lay the burden down. She stripped more leaves, smoothing the branch to a switch.

'It was meant to be paradise but it must've been hell, watching what happened.'

The cliché grated; surely she wouldn't write a line as clumsy as that?

She was trying to spook Agnes but she hadn't the first idea. You couldn't spook someone who'd been haunted her whole life.

Agnes tipped her face to the sky. The dark was shredded by clouds as thin as tissue paper. It was too soon to see stars. The air had lost its chill from earlier. She could smell the earth in the field and the smoky scent Iris was wearing.

'What's so funny?' Iris's voice didn't change.

'You.' She curled her legs up into the chair, laying her arms along its back. 'You think you're intimidating but you don't know anything.'

'I know people died.' Iris ran the switch through her hand. 'They're blaming the builders for that, and the planners. All the *contractors*.' Emphasizing the word Agnes had used to describe Dad's role. 'The land wasn't safe to build on, the construction faulty from the start.' Her voice sharpened in self-defence. 'I've done my homework, seen the plans. Those concealed heating systems weren't safe. Flue pipes weren't connected securely, some ventilation wasn't connected at all. There were actual *loose* pipes inside the walls, unfinished. How does your dad explain that?'

She was talking about the first show house, Hawthorn, rushed through so sales could start. The ventilator hood over Hawthorn's oven hadn't been connected to the extractor pipe that took steam and smells outside the house. Ditto the extractor fans in the bathrooms. In the days immediately after evacuation, investigators opened the walls to find pairs of pipes lying inside, waiting to be connected. The work was meant to be done before the houses were made habitable, Dad said. It was scheduled to be done, he didn't know how it got missed. But Tim and Val didn't die because of unfinished extractor flues. They died of carbon monoxide poisoning. Like Felix and Chloe and baby Sasha. All this was explained to them at the hospital. Children take more breaths than adults, making them more susceptible to airborne toxins.

Iris said, 'Those poor little kids,' as if reading her mind.

Dad weeping into Ruth's lap. Christie standing, staring. The sweeping lights from the ambulance. Tim and Val's bodies waiting to be found, like Emma's in Silverthorn.

'Even those of you who got out might have health issues. Permanent tissue damage, heart problems . . .' Iris stripped the last leaves from the switch in her hand. 'Anxiety. Depression.'

Something moved at the base of the trees, scratching at their roots. Agnes caught the sharp stink of a fox. In London, the foxes sat on cars or bins. One night, she and Laura watched a fox and her cubs on the scrub of grass at the back of their flat. The foxes stared back at them, unfazed. Out here in the countryside, humans were the invaders. Agnes and Iris, Errol and Bette. The field was full of mice and rats, shrews, weasels, foxes. The fields belonged to them.

'You seem depressed to me,' Iris said softly. 'Your brother too. It must be hard to have seen what you saw. And to be stuck waiting to find out whether or not your dad's going to be charged with manslaughter. He *was* only one of the contractors but he was deep in the pocket of the developers, their golden boy, their Midas.'

She was speaking in headlines now, the piece already written in her head. It wouldn't matter what Agnes said, what anyone said. This was Iris's show, everyone else a spectator.

'Why were you there? At the barbecue. Before anyone died. You were there.'

Bloodstained hands, and questions, 'Can I use your bathroom?' and Agnes led her upstairs, left her alone next to Ruth's room and Christie's, too.

'You know what I was doing. Delivering meat.' Iris's answer sounded rehearsed. 'I'm freelance, can't earn a living from my writing, not yet. I take on odd jobs to pay the bills. It's funny how often they turn into stories. Nothing like this, though. Blackthorn Ashes was a first, in every sense.'

Somewhere above them, an owl hissed, warding off a predator. Agnes closed her eyes. The night was soft as ink against her face. Iris shifted in the cane chair.

'I think you're brave. To go back there, to be able to do that.'

Agnes opened her eyes to see her bending the switch into a circle.

'I don't think I could do it . . .'

'But you did. You were there. It wasn't your first time today. You'd been back before.'

'You and your brother aren't the first people I saw on-site.' Iris lifted one shoulder in a shrug. 'Some builder's been hanging around. He was there at the barbecue, with the blonde in the pink bikini. But your dad hasn't been back. Has he?'

Some builder . . . She was talking about Trevor.

Agnes slid her little finger into the rotting weave of the cane seat, out of sight. The weave was razored, biting the tender tip of her finger.

'He's too upset.' Iris offered up the words as if trying them for size. 'Your dad. Or too ashamed.'

She held back the word *guilty* but it was there on her tongue, the word she'd write in big black letters, in her headlines.

'He's not supposed to go on-site,' Agnes said. 'No one is.'

'Hmm . . . Does he know you and your brother go back there?'

'No.' She could lie to this woman because she had to.

'What about your mum? Does she know?'

Adrian Gale, *guilty*. Ruth Gale, *complicit*. Or would Ruth be guilty too? Complicit wasn't a word Iris would write. Too soft, not sufficiently emphatic. Ruth Gale, *guilty*.

'Does my mum know?' Agnes echoed. 'How old do you think I am?'

'I know exactly how old you are. You're twenty-nine. But your mum would want to know, wouldn't she? That you and Christie are going back there. And she'd want to know why.'

Agnes drove her finger deeper into the cane seat.

'You and your brother . . . I remember him, that day in the house. What was Errol's joke: "Exit, pursued by beer"!'

Iris laughed as she loosened her grip on the switch. It sprang free, quivering in the soft dark air. 'Why do you keep going back? What're you looking for?'

'Odie. He runs away sometimes.' She felt eerily calm, as if floating. Only her finger was real, anchoring her to the chair, keeping her here. 'He won't stay on the cliff path. There're holes in the hedges at the backs of the houses, I'm sure you know that.'

'Like the holes in the walls . . .'

'Maybe. Yes.'

'I love dogs,' Iris said. 'I love all animals. Do you?'

The change of topic threw her.

'Do I love animals? Yes, of course.'

'Not *of course*. Plenty of people don't.' Her voice changed, becoming quieter but at the same time more ferocious. 'Some of the cruelty out there, you wouldn't believe.'

Agnes felt a lurch of almost-understanding. They were close for the first time to the real reason Iris was here, that was how it felt.

'What sort of cruelty?'

But Iris shook her head, saying only, 'You wouldn't believe.' She knotted her hair into a ponytail before dropping her hands into her lap. 'My parents died in a house fire. It was my dad's fault, that's what the investigation concluded.' Another change of subject. 'He was drunk, and he was smoking. His fault, they said.'

Just as Blackthorn Ashes was Adrian Gale's fault?

Agnes felt the conversation slipping away from her. She listened with the sense that Iris was telling her a story. Perhaps it was true, perhaps not, but she was telling it in the hope Agnes would share the stories *she* wanted to hear. She was young to have lost both parents, if she had. She couldn't take anything Iris said at face value.

'I suppose I've been a bit obsessed with domestic disasters ever since...'

Iris straightened, holding her hands out in front of her, their fingers fanned.

'What happened to Emma Dearman?'

The field was a churned black sea at their feet, nests of mice knotted in its hedges. A stoat, sinuous, threaded its way along the bank. All of the night was moving, full of secret things.

'She didn't die of carbon monoxide poisoning,' Iris said.

She placed each word like a stone, smooth and white in the darkness.

'Her death is unexplained. Not suspicious, not yet, but un-explained.'

Leaves ticking in the trees, an owl's harsh hiss.

'I was thinking, the other day, how easy it would be to do that.'

Agnes's finger was bleeding, cut by the cane. She pushed the pain away, needing to focus on the threat from Iris. She wanted to stand and run, anywhere but here.

'To hide a death among all the other deaths. All those people falling ill and with panic all around. It would be the perfect place to hide a death, if that's what you wanted to do. If it's what you needed to do.'

Agnes saw Emma outside Silverthorn, narrowing her eyes against the glare.

'Agnes?' Iris's voice reached her slowly. 'How well did you know Emma Dearman? She lived in the house across from yours. Her husband broke his foot. He was on crutches at the barbecue.'

'He tripped in the garden...'

'He broke his foot in the garden. That was his explanation? Is it what really happened?'

'It's what we heard.'

Her heart was in her mouth, beating black and thick as tar.

'And his wife?' Iris said. 'What happened to her?'

A light went off in one of the big trailers, dropping them down into darkness.

In the darkness, Agnes saw Ruth's face on the night of the evacuation and before, when she was five or six, peeping through the gap in the bedroom door, seeing her mother's stony face that might split at any moment. She felt the press of Iris's stare on her skin.

'Did you know Emma Dearman? Agnes?'

The creak of the chair as she leant forward.

'Do you know how she died?'

12

Adrian rolled free of the sofa's grip, resting for a moment with his head in his hands until the noise of the siren faded. A dream or an echo from earlier when an ambulance came shuddering to a stop outside the caravan, bringing with it all of his worst fears, his guilt and his grief.

It was dark outside but not yet midnight; Agnes hadn't returned and she was never late, not since Ruth lectured her on the dangers of causing more worry for everyone. Adrian had delivered a lecture of his own, he remembered with a cringe. He'd only half known what he was saying, something about staying away from Blackthorn Ashes. She'd been pushing him, poking into the murky reaches of his memory in the hope of helping him stay present. He didn't blame her; they were each trying to cope in their own way. Ruth pushed everything down below the surface. Agnes tried to bring it back up. Adrian didn't know what Christie was doing to cope and he wasn't sure he wanted to; his son had been a closed book to him for weeks.

He stood, walking the short distance to the caravan's front door. It opened soundlessly, letting in the smell of butane and burnt

toast. He put his hand across his nose reflexively. He'd been smelling burning for weeks, since before the evacuation. When he shut
his eyes, he saw flames and smoke. No fires had broken out – the
faulty alarms weren't made to detect smoke – but when he shut his
eyes he saw Blackthorn Ashes in flames, Indigo Park eaten by fire,
gas canisters erupting, plastic windows warping and melting. His
family burning. *We're burning.* With shame, with rage . . .

'Adrian?'

Ruth was in her pyjamas, sleep softening one side of her face.

'Go back to bed,' he told her.

'What is it?' She lifted a hand to scrub the softness from her
cheek. 'What's happened?'

'Nothing. I just needed some air.'

Her face changed as he stood watching, becoming the rigid
mask she'd worn since the night of the storm when the ambulance
came for Barry's kids. The sight of it sparked a flare of fury – his
wife, the doer, standing knee-deep in the death of his dreams without ever once, even for a second, losing her composure.

'Is Agnes back?' she asked.

'Not yet. Soon, I expect.' He shut the door, driving his resentment down. God knows, it wasn't her fault he'd failed. 'Christie's
sleeping?'

'Or on his phone.' Ruth stayed where she was.

Did she feel it too, the awful sense of normality creeping back
in? No, not normality, that wasn't possible. This was like looking
through someone else's holiday photos sent to you in error. All the
ingredients were there, the familiar apparatus of family life: caravan hired for the summer, tins in the cupboards, boots by the door

in case of rain. But it wasn't the weather or the caravan that was wrong. It was them.

'Do you remember that night?' he asked Ruth. 'The night of the storm.'

'No.' She shook her head.

'No, you don't remember?'

'No, we're not doing this.' She moved towards him warningly. 'Get some sleep.'

'I remember.' He raised his voice. 'Barry telling me he couldn't believe the kids slept through it—' His voice cracked in half. 'Even the baby . . .'

'Be quiet. You'll wake Christie.'

Panic clawed at his throat. 'We should talk to him.' He couldn't live like this, knowing and not knowing, keeping quiet at all costs, any cost. 'We should talk to him about Emma.'

'Shhh . . .' Ruth's lips were against his mouth. 'Adrian . . .'

She kissed him until he was quiet, her body pressed against his from knee to neck, closer than she'd been in months. He could smell the cheap shampoo she'd used and a trace of her old expensive lipstick. He stiffened in spite of himself but it wasn't arousal, not in any usual sense. It was fear. As aphrodisiac, or simply as fear.

'Please. Let it go. We're a *family*. Your job is to protect this family. *Your* family.'

She kissed him again, making sure he couldn't respond even if he wanted to. He didn't want to. She'd killed the panic in him, driven it back down. She was good at that.

Behind them, the caravan door opened and then shut. Ruth broke the kiss and stepped away, disappearing into the bedroom.

'Dad?' Agnes clicked a switch and the room blazed with light.

'Hi, love.'

'Are you okay?' She was pale, her eyes huge in her face. 'You look—'

'Couldn't sleep.' He worked the ache from his jaw with his fingers. 'You're late.'

'Not much.' She stripped off her jacket, hung it up.

Something had happened out there. He saw it in the way she moved, as if every part of her was tender, aching like his jaw. The thought came too fast for him to stop it: *this family's made of secrets.*

'Be careful,' he warned Agnes.

'Of what?' Those big eyes, watching him.

'Christie.' He swallowed, tasting bile. 'He's sleeping. Your mum doesn't want him waking.'

'Okay.' She pulled her hands inside her sleeves, making herself smaller. 'I'll be careful.'

Just a boy, Ruth had said, your son. *Your family.*

Adrian watched his daughter cross the room in the direction of her brother. When he shut his eyes, the smoke was there and the fire too, roaring and red at its heart.

Twenty days before abandonment

———

13

Christie was shooting hoops when he heard the buzzing. He'd gone outside to empty his head, wanting the *thwap* of the ball on tarmac, the sting of it in his hands, the *clunk* against the hoop, the *rattle* down the pole. In the silence as he gathered the ball to start over—

Buzz-buzz. Buzz-buzz-buzz.

At first he ignored it; hearing noises was his sister's thing, not his. He wasn't going to encourage her by joining in. Mum was over the road with Mrs Dearman, asking if she could help with their shopping after Mr Dearman came home on crutches. He'd slipped in the garden which Dad said was daft of him since it hadn't been raining and the decking was brand new and super solid. Only Mr Dearman said he hadn't slipped, he'd put his foot in a hole in the lawn which made even less sense. Whatever, Mum was talking with Mrs Dearman so it wasn't her making the buzzing. And it wasn't Dad, who was with Trevor talking about the builders who needed a good bollocking for leaving the site unfinished.

'Lazy fucking arseholes,' Trevor had called them.

Christie liked listening to Trevor, hearing the rough edge in his voice, the smell of beer and cigarettes reminding him there was a whole world of adult stuff waiting for him at the end of this summer and the next. He'd sneaked a Brew Dog from the fridge, sucking it straight from the can. Next day he didn't brush his teeth, liking the sweet-starchy taste in his mouth. He'd started watching Felix's mum who sunbathed in a bikini and sometimes drove to the shops in short shorts and tight tops, although usually the baby was strapped to her, hiding the view. Trevor liked watching Janis, too. Casually, like he didn't care. Women always eyed him, even mums like Janis. Trevor liked blondes best, like Sandra who was his girlfriend even though they fought most of the time. Christie studied the way Trevor walked and the way he stood. He got into the habit of being outdoors as long as he could, working on his tan. He was saving up for a pair of cowboy boots. Shooting hoops was giving him muscles.

Buzz-buzz. Buzz-buzz-buzz.

The sound was coming from the family bathroom upstairs at the front of the house. He bounced the basketball a couple of times then held it to his chest, listening.

Agnes was upstairs. He was surprised she wasn't down here, asking if he could hear that and wasn't it spooky, didn't it freak him out? She'd been worse since the rabbit died. Walking round like a ghost, pulling at her hair and scratching her face. Yesterday he'd yelled at her to shut up and she'd lunged at him, spinning at the last second to start wrecking her bed instead, clawing at the duvet and pillow, slapping her hands like a lunatic. 'Shit,' Dad'd said, staring down at her bed. Christie went to look, imagining blood or puke or worse but it was just two wasps crawling in the sheets near her pillow. Big fat wasps, their feet leaving sooty marks on the cotton. Agnes had backed herself into the corner. She kept dragging at her hair, slapping her head like there were more wasps in there, like her hair was a nest and wasps and beetles and worms would burst out of it, emptying down her shoulders, all over the floor. Christie thought he might actually puke. He went to his room, slamming the door to let them know what he thought of this latest bullshit. He heard Mum and Dad moving around, pulling furniture away from the walls. Of course, she'd be saying the wasps came out of the rotten leaking walls of this house she hated so much.

Buzz-buzz. Buzz-buzz-buzz.

Christie held the basketball to his chest, trying to work out if the noise could be wasps again. Dad said they must've come down the chimney, that's why they were covered in soot. He said he'd seen some crawling on the kitchen window but Christie hadn't seen any wasps. Dad probably made it up to get Agnes to calm down. He and Mum buried the wasps in the garden, Agnes refusing to watch. Christie was surprised she wasn't screaming right now, given how loud the buzzing was.

Unless *she* was making it.

His mind skipped to chainsaws, masks made of human flesh, family massacres. When his heart slowed, he dropped the basketball and went inside the house, climbing the stairs two at a time to get it over with. The sound grew louder the nearer he got to the bathroom. He shouted her name, to show he wasn't scared and to warn her he was coming so she could stop whatever mad thing it was she was doing.

Buzz-buzz. Buzz-buzz-buzz.

The bathroom door wasn't locked, wasn't even shut properly. He pushed it wide, seeing his sister bent over the sink. Grey vest and shorts, bruises behind her knees. The whole room rang with the buzzing. She *was* the one making it: Dad's hair clippers, glossy-black in her fist. She was shaving her hair off.

All of it, the hair falling into the sink and landing in black scribbles on the tiles by her bony feet. She was doing it like it was someone else's hair on someone else's head – one hand pushing her head down, the other running the clippers from the back of her neck to the front, over and over until he could see the shape of her skull which was small like a bird's and weirdly beautiful with just a silvery fuzz left by the clippers. She stroked her hand over her scalp, dusting the last of the hair away. Then she straightened and saw him in the mirror, watching her.

'I'm sorry,' she said.

It made him wonder if he looked sick or scared. Because that's how he felt seeing the black curls on the bathroom tiles and clotting the sink – like a little kid who'd never understand what was wrong here, with his sister, or his house, or his family.

'I want to show you something,' she said.

He didn't want to see anything she had to show him. He'd already seen too much. All the bones in her skull on show, the naked state of her head. She needed to clean up the mess she'd made. He pointed at the sink. 'That'll clog the drains.'

'It doesn't matter. Look—'

'Clean it up!' he yelled. 'Mum'll have a fit when she sees it!' He didn't know if he meant the mess or her shaved head. He'd shaved himself a couple of days ago, cutting his face with the razor, Mum shouting at him when she saw the blood.

'I'll clear it up.' Agnes put her hands together in a prayer shape. 'Please let me show you. I want you to believe me about what's going on here. Binka died and the wasps . . . The wasps have a nest in the walls.' She ran a hand over her head, making it sizzle. 'That's why I did this. It creeped me out having them crawling in my hair but it's okay. That's not what I want to show you.'

'I don't care,' Christie said. His chest heaved. 'Whatever it is, I don't care.'

But he went with her down the stairs and out of the kitchen into the garden.

Agnes knelt where she'd been sitting with Binka in her lap. 'See?'

She put her hand flat to the grass and it disappeared. Like the ground had swallowed her hand right up to the wrist.

Christie squatted to see what she'd done, so he could tell Mum and Dad about her latest load of shit, whatever story she was making up now.

'It's right across the lawn.' She swung her arm at the elbow, her hand staying out of sight, buried in a trench that ran all the way to the rabbit's hutch.

Christie's stomach dropped the way it did on a roller coaster. 'What've you done?'

'It wasn't me.' She pulled her hand from the trench, brushing soil from her fingers. 'It's the garden. It's splitting. All over the place. It's like . . . it's sliding, somehow.'

Christie bent over the trench which was about fifteen centimetres wide and thirty deep. The grass was long enough so you couldn't see anything was wrong until you were standing right over it. Inside, the earth was wet and stank of rust. The trench didn't look like it'd been dug with a spade. It looked like the lawn had split open, just as she said, the kind of crack you saw in roads and houses after an earthquake.

Agnes was watching him, waiting to see what he'd do. He

wanted to ask what she'd used to make the lawn look like this. But at the same time he knew she hadn't done it.

'I bet this is how Luke broke his foot,' she said.

'He slipped on the decking, that's what Dad told me.'

'Luke said it was a hole in the lawn.' She traced the edge of the trench with her fingers. 'I bet this is happening in all the gardens. In all the houses.'

Christie thought of the kids next door. Felix who was his friend, and Chloe and the baby. They were out with Janis now but he'd heard Chloe earlier, crying about a lost toy. He pictured it lying in a trench like this one, hidden from sight. A trench full of foam bullets from Felix's blaster gun, red enough to look like the lawn was bleeding.

'This's mental.' He stood up. 'I'm getting Dad.'

Agnes climbed to her feet. 'Do you know where he is?'

'With Trevor, down the end.'

He felt wobbly, the way he did after stepping off a waltzer.

'Where's Mum?' she asked.

'With Mrs Dearman . . .'

He took a step towards the house then stopped to see if he could still see the trench. He couldn't. Just the grass growing a bit long, in need of mowing. He stepped forward: *there*. Stepped back: *nothing*. Like a magic trick.

He looked at his sister, standing with her shaved head. This mess suited her, was exactly what she'd wanted. Because now she was the one in the right and they were the crazies. After Binka died, she'd kept saying, 'I told you,' and he hadn't believed her but it was true, it was happening. The whole place was cracking up, like her.

Christie made a promise to himself then. He didn't care how he did it but he was going to stop her. He was going to stop his sister from wrecking this place.

He was being made to choose a side, that's how it felt. He could choose Blackthorn Ashes, where Dad had worked so hard for so long, Dad and Trevor and Christie too, signing all those bricks with his name. Or he could choose Agnes, who'd left for London when he was a baby and only come back home because she was desperate.

Easy. He chose Blackthorn Ashes.

14

Agnes began the day by lying to her family. She told her mother she needed time off from watching Christie, she wasn't feeling good, not enough to be in charge of her baby brother. Mum said she'd take him into town with her for the day. Christie glared at Agnes but she could live with his resentment, and with Ruth's disappointment, as long as they were safe. She had to keep everyone safe. Last night, she had struck a bargain to keep Iris out of Indigo Park, away from Errol and Bette, and from her family. In return, she would do her best to help Iris find the proof she needed to write her story about Emma Dearman's unnatural death.

She began by lying and then she stole: Mum's keys from her bag, separating their old front door key from the ring, hoping Ruth wouldn't notice it was gone. Lying, and stealing. The trespass hardly counted, in the scheme of things. After all, she and Christie had been trespassing for days.

It was lonely, walking to Blackthorn Ashes without him.

The weather had dipped to cloud, the threat of rain banked blackly at the horizon. She didn't go directly to the houses, walking instead to the trampoline trapped in the hedge, standing there a long time before turning back, taking the route she and Christie always took, which ended with the hole in the hedge into May-thorn's garden.

Iris was waiting outside Blackthorn in her snakeskin leggings and an acid lemon top, busy on her phone.

'Do you fancy her?' Christie had asked. She'd avoided a straight answer because it was muddy in her head. She was afraid of Iris, more than ever after last night. Yet at the same time she wanted to touch her tanned shoulder, feel the smoothness of her skin. Iris was so strong and sure of herself. Laura said some people were attracted to weakness, 'You're not like that, you prefer strength,' but Laura grew weary of always being the strong one. In the end, in a way, that's what had finished them.

Iris didn't look like she'd ever tire of being strong. And she was hard, which Laura never was. The only way to tackle Iris was head on. No soft spots, no places Agnes could breach as she'd breached the hedge into Maythorn's garden where the paddling pool stirred with dead leaves.

Iris pocketed her phone, spying her at last. 'I was starting to think you'd changed your mind.'

'I had to wait until my parents were out.'

Last night, by the empty field, Agnes had lied about Dad, saying he went with Ruth every day down into town to look for work. She didn't want Iris knowing he was confined to a caravan, easy prey for someone able to charm or pressure her way into your home. The way she'd charmed Agnes and Errol on the day of the barbecue. Agnes hadn't seen Errol since last night, had no way of knowing how hurt or angry he was. But she knew he was safe. As long as she was the focus of Iris's attention, everyone else was safe.

'I hadn't changed my mind.'

She held up the key she'd stolen from Ruth's bag.

Iris smiled. Last night, she'd said, 'I can't believe they let you keep your keys. Surely the whole place should be under lockdown?' Then she'd shrugged. 'Why bother locking down a deserted housing estate, I guess, especially one as toxic as that.'

That was when Agnes knew for certain what she was up against. When Iris shrugged about six lost lives. She was playing out a game in her head about broken families and failure or maybe about a full-time job, a way to earn a living doing what she loved. As long as the game lasted, she wouldn't stop. The only way to make her stop was to let her get so close she could see and hear and *smell* the horror of what happened. Close enough for the ghosts to get their hands on her.

'Don't touch anything in the house,' Agnes warned her. 'Christie will know. He will tell our parents and they will report it.'

'Really?' Iris looked sceptical but she nodded. 'I won't touch anything.'

Inside, Blackthorn smelt of the summer's dust. Dead flies, sealed windows, stale air and, underneath, the same bloodied badger's sett smell as all the other houses.

Agnes walked Iris to the kitchen, hating the narrowness of the hallway with the other woman close behind her. Their kitchen looked the same, its marble island messy with mugs and bowls. One of the big glasses Christie liked to drink from lay on its side under the hot water tap. Apples had rotted in the fruit bowl, leaving a cidery scratch in the air. The fridge was massed with magnets from family holidays: glazed pottery cat's face, miniature surfboard, tiny jar filled with Spanish sand and sea shells. Odd, intimate reminders of her family's happiness. She wanted to protect them from Iris's scrutiny. It struck her this was how Christie felt when she came home from London, a stranger invading his home. Sadness stung her eyes at the thought of her brother seeing her that way.

'This is where you first noticed something was wrong?'

Iris was at the back door, looking into the garden.

'Cracks in the lawns? Sinkholes in the flower beds? Killer wasps?'

A dead rabbit. Binka never made the news. Who cared about a rabbit when children had died?

'I can't believe it took them so long to figure out what was happening.' Iris fingered her phone. Agnes had said no photos but, of course, she was recording this.

'What was it really like, living here? Before it all went wrong, I mean. And afterwards.'

'You were in this house, the day of the barbecue. What did it feel like to you?'

'Honestly? It felt like you were all trying too hard and it was exhausting you. You looked ill, like your dad. And your brother, from what I saw of him.'

'We were poisoned.'

'Before, though.' Iris studied the garden. 'Back at the beginning. What was it like then?'

'It was exciting.' Agnes borrowed from her brother's vocabulary. 'A fresh start. Everyone who moved here said that. It was so different to anywhere else, so much more exciting.'

'Forever homes.' Iris turned to face her.

The light was dim, nothing like the dazzling backdrop it was during the summer, making woodcuts of everyone who stood where Iris was standing now. Part of Agnes prayed for a shadow to loom behind her. Broad-shouldered, cowboy-booted. Casting Trevor in the role of rescuer – she must be losing her mind.

'It's what we're supposed to want,' she said. 'Isn't it?'

'Look no further for your forever home.' Iris quoted the brochure. 'And then this happens.'

'You called it a war zone, remember?'

'Yes, that was uncanny of me.'

'I thought it meant you knew. About the things that were going wrong. Did you? Is that what you were really doing – investigating the holes in the gardens, Luke's broken foot?'

'Maybe.' But Iris sounded distracted, as if she wasn't really hearing Agnes. 'Why did the Dearmans come here, do you know? And the Masons. All of you. Why did you come?'

'I told you, for a fresh start. That's what it was for us, anyway. I don't know about the others.'

What else was life but the repeated attempt at a fresh start? Ruth dropping out of college to have a baby then trying again with Christie, searching for a firmer foothold in motherhood. Adrian learning to be a dad at nineteen, bringing his family here to begin again. Barry and Janis wanting to raise their children in a place of open spaces, big skies.

Blackthorn Ashes was right at the edge, where land met sea. It should have been green and blue and white but it was black and rotten. Worn through with an ancient, arcane evil that preyed on their weaknesses. Reopening old wounds between Agnes and Ruth, exaggerating Christie's need to be a man, making Dad make promises he knew he couldn't keep, promises no one could keep, tempting Trevor to cut corners and cheat. Every one of them trapped here, a slave to the fantasy of a forever home. Even Luke, with his petty bureaucratic rage against the world.

Everyone who came here was running away.

The thought pierced her, coming from nowhere, from the dead air in the house. Everyone was running from something that bored or trapped or threatened them. She knew how it felt to run away. She'd been doing it all her life. Seven weeks ago, she'd told herself she had to stop. Here in Blackthorn Ashes. No matter how uncomfortable or unhappy life became, at some point you had to stay and be still. She had tried to do that in this house. Had she? Christie would say no, that she'd fought from the first day.

'How many of them did you know? Your neighbours?' Iris smoothed a finger at the fridge door, tracing the shape of the magnets. 'Did you make many friends here?'

'Of course.'

Ruth taking the shopping to Emma – did that count?

'Only six houses were occupied during this first phase. That's right, isn't it?'

'You were here.' Every word Iris spoke drove the fear deeper into her bones. 'That day, you asked these questions. It's not why we're here now. So ask me what you really want to know.'

'I want to know how much *you* know, about the other families.'

Iris took the tiny jar magnet from the fridge and shook it. The sand and shells made a gritty sound against the glass.

'We can start with the Dearmans, if you like, or with you. Your mum was sceptical, did you know that? She'd requested land contamination reports. Your dad might have been sold on this place but she was smart enough to have her doubts, just like you.'

'I thought this was about Emma?' Agnes kept her voice light. 'That's what you said.'

'All right . . .' Iris replaced the magnet, wiping her hands on her hips. 'But you may as well show me the rest of the house, since we're here. Give me a flavour of what it was like to live this fantasy. I didn't exactly get a guided tour the day of the barbecue.'

Agnes showed her to the sitting room where Iris examined Ruth's paperweights and tweaked at Ruth's cushions. Her curiosity was intrusive, voyeuristic. She picked over the books on the shelves, searching for colourful titbits perhaps, to bring her story to life. She'd promised not to write about Dad. Her source would be anonymous, a whistleblower, that was the promise Agnes had extracted. In the end, though, Iris would write whatever she wanted. Dad's name was headline-ready – 'Gale in Storm over New Houses' ran on a news site the day after the evacuation – and Agnes had let her back into Blackthorn, the house Dad chose for them. She had lied about the other houses, said she didn't have a key to Silverthorn where Emma's body was found at the foot of the stairs, or to Maythorn where the children died. In Blackthorn, Iris could touch cushions and books – put her hands anywhere she wanted – but she hadn't lived through it, just that glimpse at the street party. She wasn't here when the headaches started and the nausea, red eyes, sore skin. Christie had blamed Agnes for Ruth's dermatitis and Dad's chest pains but it was the house, their proximity to the old power station, the toxic land stolen from the sea to build Blackthorn Ashes. Iris wasn't here when the lawns split open. She hadn't hidden as Agnes had, behind boxes in the garage while Ruth and Adrian fought in whispers about what was happening and what they should do.

'Upstairs?' Iris suggested and Agnes led her to the bedrooms, one after another.

She couldn't see what, if anything, Christie had taken from Ruth's room. After that, she took Iris to the garage, to show her the place where wasps had made their nest.

Iris scooped up Christie's basketball, bouncing it from hand to hand. Her eyes searched the garage, snagging on boxes but with little interest. Agnes was showing her how they had lived when what Iris wanted was how they had died, or survived. In all likelihood, it would bore her to hear about the afternoon Agnes hid behind the boxes.

'We have to tell someone!' Dad hissing, his face at full stretch.

'Can you calm down for a second?' Ruth putting up her hands, trying to make him stand still. 'Look at me. *Adrian*. Listen.'

'You saw the state of the lawn! Luke broke his foot, for Christ's sake! Everyone we speak to has a headache or a cough! I can't just pretend it's not happening. What if Christie breaks a bone or Agnes gets sick? What if we're next?'

'No one's going to be next. It's summer and we're in the countryside. It'll be hay fever or—'

'Agnes's been feeling unwell since we moved in.' Dad was pacing up and down. Ruth tried to get hold of him, to make him stop, but he swerved from her angrily. 'What if Christie doesn't wake up one morning because I said nothing about how unsafe these houses are?'

Crouching out of sight, Agnes put a hand across her mouth to stop a sound of distress escaping. They *knew*. Her parents knew – and they'd said nothing.

'Stop panicking and *think*.' Ruth put her hands on his elbows, shaking him. 'Are you aware of any evidence that tells you *for certain* these houses aren't safe? *Evidence*, Adrian. Are you? Because I've looked – believe me, I've looked – and I haven't found anything.'

'I know we cut corners!' Dad shook her off. 'The finances are fucked, Trev says. He more or less told me we'd have to find savings and it wouldn't be in the soft furnishings which're already paid for because we had to have those bloody show houses open on time.'

'He more or less told you,' Ruth repeated.

'You're not listening.' Dad pulled away. His voice rose until Agnes didn't recognize it. 'You don't want to hear it but it's true. This place . . . We started out wanting to make somewhere special. *Unique*. But we needed it open for the summer because that was the sell – sea and beaches. We were full of ourselves, full of *shit*.'

A furious sob broke from him.

'This was supposed to be a paradise project but people don't need paradise, not for living in. For holidays maybe, but here? They just need to be safe, to know their families are *safe*. We've failed them. Don't you get it? We *failed*.'

The basketball rattled through the hoop, bringing Agnes back into the present.

Iris dusted her palms. 'Show me Silverthorn.'

'I told you, I don't have the keys to any other house. Why would I?'

'We can go into the famous garden, though. Where he broke his foot. Allegedly.'

Just for a second – the time it took the basketball pole to stop juddering – Agnes wanted her mother. Not the woman who'd argued with Adrian in the garage or the one who'd warned her to put her family first. Her mother in the red sundress, the one person in the world who could put things right, shield her from what was coming.

'You were a bonfire,' Laura said, in London. 'You and Ruth, a bonfire.'

There was enough truth in that to hurt. She was the viper in her mother's bosom, sharper than a serpent's tooth, and Ruth her Medea, high priestess of her distress. Their story was old, nothing special. But now they were in a place without signposts. Agnes didn't know how to get back; she'd never wanted to go back before. Her life had been about moving on, getting away. Blackthorn Ashes changed that. She was desperate to help her family survive this crisis but she didn't know how to do it. Everything was changed and she was lost without Ruth. Without her mother, who was there to pick her from an old school photo or recognize her handwriting from when she was ten? And who was there to blame, for everything that'd gone wrong in her life?

Outside Silverthorn, dust was circling, blown from the building site. Plastic sheeting shifted on the unfinished houses. The word *demolition* came into her head and wouldn't leave.

'Luke and Emma Dearman.' Iris was staring up at the house. 'They lived here.'

Died here. Agnes's skull clogged with pain. *Demolition.*

Iris took out her phone, waiting. 'You agreed to tell me, you know.' She switched her stare to Agnes. 'About what happened. *How* it happened.'

'I said I'd tell you what I know.'

Iris's eyes narrowed, intent on her face. Such sharp eyes but blind. Missing all the details that mattered so much. She was a predator focused single-mindedly on the hunt, seeing only bone and muscle, assessing the threat, calculating how long it would take to bring down the kill. Not seeing a living thing at all. Only a dead one in waiting. She tapped her phone against her thigh.

'What were they like? I saw Luke at the barbecue. But what was she like? Emma.'

Hunting was what she did. It was who she was, and she wouldn't stop.

Agnes needed her to stop.

'She was struggling, after Luke went into hospital. Mum helped with the shopping, kept an eye out for her. It's what we tried to do for one another. But you don't believe that, do you? You think we looked the other way while . . . what? You said he broke his foot *allegedly* but you saw him at the street party, he was on crutches.'

'Oh, he broke it.' Iris gave a tight smile. 'Just not in the garden.'

Coldness clenched her skin. 'What is it you think happened? Exactly?'

'Exactly? Luke had a history of violence, did you know that?'

'No . . .'

She tried to conjure a picture of the man, short and balding, always angry. No, that was after the accident. What was he like before? Ruth had described the Dearmans as good neighbours but something about the phrase made her heart skitter. *Demolition.*

'Of course he had an alibi,' Iris said. 'That broken foot came in handy, trips to the hospital, more than once. But there's doubt over exactly when she died, because of the heat in the house, faulty electrics and so on. Time of death's difficult to pin down . . . You know she hit her head?' She began walking away. 'She collapsed on the stairs, they think. Fell and hit her head. They found brick dust in her hair . . . Show me their garden.'

Agnes followed, pushing her hands in her pockets, trying to keep the pictures of Emma out of her head. Iris's story kept shifting, changing shape. Agnes couldn't get an angle on precisely what she intended to write. *She fell and hit her head.*

She followed Iris up the side path into Silverthorn's garden where the decking was greased with rain and moss, no longer Dad's weatherproof, hardwood promise of Siberian larch. The decking, like everything else, had been a lie.

'Well, it's slippery enough now.' Iris poked the toe of her boot at the moss. 'To fall and break your foot . . .'

Her eyes wandered to the grass, grown too long to see the damage hidden there. She picked her way across it, stopping when she discovered the trench.

'Oh, okay, you could definitely break your foot in here . . .' She dropped into a squat, taking out her phone. 'I know we said no pictures but I need to be able to describe this.'

Agnes turned away, looking up at the bedroom windows. Was that where Luke beat his wife or whatever it was Iris suspected? In one of Dad's master bedrooms with interior-fitted wardrobes, polished chrome handles. A history of violence. *Demolition.*

'I remember Luke at the street party,' Iris said. 'Blaming your dad for everything, throwing himself on the barbecue so he'd be back in hospital when it happened. When his wife died . . .'

As if the accident had been a stunt, an alibi.

'What about after he found out about the carbon monoxide? He was threatening your dad before the worst of it even happened. Has he been in touch since?'

'I don't think so.' Her skin was damp with panic. 'I don't know.'

'He wanted your dad strung up, just for this trench.' Iris straightened, the sun sitting on her shoulders. 'I'd have expected him to be leading the charge for a conviction, wouldn't you? Corporate manslaughter, at the very least.'

'His wife died. He's grieving.'

'He wasn't in hospital the whole time. I checked their records. He could've come here, killed her and gone again. As I said, handy alibi.'

Agnes saw their faces reflected in Silverthorn's windows, two young women with an unhealthy obsession with death. Needing to know what happened here, as if knowing could make it better.

Iris had seen something at the foot of Silverthorn's garden, was striding in that direction. Agnes followed, watching as Iris planted her feet in the lawn, reaching to pull whatever it was from the shrubbery. A metal cage, big enough for a cat or a small dog, fitted with a sturdy-looking latch.

The cage was empty, rusting in places, its door falling open when Iris shook it.

She dropped it in the same movement, stepping back as if a wild animal had escaped from the cage.

'What is it?' Agnes asked.

'Nothing.' Iris dusted her hands, sounding shaken. She turned to look back at Silverthorn. 'When was the last time you saw Emma alive?'

'The morning of the street party.'

Standing on her doorstep in her red fleece dressing gown.

'But she wasn't *at* the party,' Iris said. 'I didn't see her there.'

'She stayed away. With Luke the way he was, we just assumed he'd told her to stay away.'

Iris thought about this for a moment. 'I didn't see the Prentisses either. Valerie and Tim. Did they take Luke's side against your dad?'

'I don't think so. They left early because they weren't feeling well.'

Agnes pictured Val and Tim, the last time she saw them alive. They'd looked ancient but they weren't much older than Ruth and Adrian. She had hardly known them. It weighed on her mind how little she had known them, how small of an effort she'd made to make friends. When she conjured the ghosts at the cliff each night, roll-calling her father's pain, Tim and Val came reluctantly, as if to underline the fact she'd missed her chance to get to know them.

'Did they get on with Luke and Emma?' Iris was watching her intently. 'They were the closest to them in age.'

'Val and Tim were nice.' From things her mother had said. 'They wanted everyone to get along.' Like Dad. 'We *did* get along, except for Luke.'

'Let me guess. He kept himself to himself.' Iris gave a short laugh, devoid of humour. 'They both did. Seemed a nice couple, pleasant.'

'You knew them,' Agnes realized.

This was personal. Iris knew the Dearmans. Luke with his history of violence, Emma who had fallen down the stairs and died.

'You knew them. Didn't you?'

'Are you sure you don't have a key?' Iris pushed at Silverthorn's door. 'I'd love to get in there.'

And do what, search for blood spatter or broken teeth? What evidence did domestic abuse leave behind? Smashed glass, shattered furniture, pages torn from photo albums. Or was all the evidence on Emma's body, in the morgue now? She had died of carbon monoxide poisoning – that was the story they'd told themselves, no one thinking to question it on the day of the evacuation.

Carbon monoxide was the serial killer inside the houses, claiming victim after victim. Emma breathed poison until she passed out and fell, hitting her head. She died like Tim and Val, like Felix and Chloe and Sasha. On the night of the storm, when the wind brought down power lines and picked up the trampoline, tossing it towards the sea.

'Why do you care?' she asked Iris. 'About Emma? Why about her, especially?'

'Don't you?' Iris curled her hand against the glass of the door, peering inside. 'The truth either matters or it doesn't. The truth about a person's life, and their death. I happen to think it matters.'

'*Did* you know them?'

Iris turned to stare at her. 'Did you?'

'Not really. It was only six weeks, we were only here six weeks.'

'That's another myth they spun about this place then. That you were all one big happy family, a community who cared, looking out for one another.'

'Is anyone like that, anywhere?'

'In remote locations, sure.' Iris gestured around them. 'I'd like to think people give a shit in a place like this, given how cut off you all were from the rest of us.'

'The rest of us? You're local then.'

'Not any more. But I grew up not far from here. I guess you'd say that's what drew me back.' She rubbed a finger at the outer edge of her eye. 'I expect you think I'm a ghoul but some stories you don't choose. They choose you. I knew I could write about this place. I used to come up here with my friends when it was all just fields and what was left of the power station.'

'The power station was here when you were growing up?'

'Bits of it. Like . . . bones. It was spooky, a sort of dare, to come up here.' She pushed the toe of her boot at the decking. 'Spookier now, though.'

All around them, the houses were silent, windows dark where the day's shadows sat.

'Can't you feel it?' Iris said. 'All that . . . death.'

Agnes bit the inside of her cheek to stop herself from speaking.

'I want to know what happened here in this house with these people. What if we're telling the wrong version because it fits the bigger picture? That's what they did with my dad. *He-was-a-smoker-and-a-drinker-and-the-house-burnt-down.*' She machine-gunned the words. 'Can you imagine what it's like to have something that huge – the death of your parents – reduced to something so *small*?'

She made a box shape with her hands, squeezing her fingers until the shape was gone.

Agnes understood then what she had only glimpsed last night. How intent this woman was on finding the truth. How she hungered for it and would fight for it, with her bare hands if necessary, with her teeth and her nails.

Iris wasn't only a reporter after a story. She was a distillation of grief and need and nostalgia, of everything she'd seen and survived. Like anyone, everyone. Like the earth disturbed by the building of Blackthorn Ashes which for decades had held the ingredients for catastrophe: rot and erosion, pollution, blight. From the unfinished houses, she heard the plastic sheeting sigh against the bricks.

'I want to know the whole truth of what happened because what if Emma didn't die of carbon monoxide poisoning?'

Iris dusted her hands. Her face changed, becoming hard again.

'If she was murdered, that *matters*.'

She fixed Agnes with her yellow stare.

'It should matter to you, too.'

24 AUGUST

One day before abandonment

———

15

Agnes was better after shaving her head. Apart from looking like she'd escaped from an asylum, obviously. They used to drill holes in people's skulls to get rid of their mad ideas so maybe it was like that. Or maybe she got calmer because she saw what was coming, the only one of them who did, until the night of the storm.

Everyone had a headache that day. The air was heavy, wet-feeling, the sky yellow-black. Christie had been feeling out of it for days, like he was watching sample game play instead of the real thing. Mum and Dad had powered down, that's how it felt, everything taking twice as long. Meals, showers, shopping. When they first moved in, Christie helped Dad and Trevor fix things – sticking doors, loose floorboards – but he hadn't had the energy for that in ages. Every house had an issue that needed looking at. They were getting grief because of Mr Dearman's broken foot. Mum tried talking to his wife who was wound up, Dad tried talking to Dearman who was pissed off. Everyone was pissed off but no one had the energy to do anything about it, that's how it felt.

'Supper's ready.' Mum was turning forks in a bowl of salad.

Lettuce and peppers, green and red. Zombie colours. Christie's head felt thick on the inside like it'd been packed with the stuff they'd used to insulate the walls.

Mum shook oil from the forks before dropping them in the sink. Then she put her hands on the marble island, leaning there. 'Tell Dad, and Agnes.' She sounded drunk.

Christie went to the foot of the stairs and shouted his sister's name. It hurt to raise his voice, his throat raw and scratchy. He looked for Dad and Agnes in the sitting room but they weren't there. Just looking at the stairs knackered him but Mum was in a shit mood or close to being in one so he climbed the stairs to his sister's room, dragging his feet.

When he kicked at her door, it swung open on an empty room. *Great.* She'd fucked off and now it'd be his job to find her, and Dad too. He looked in the rest of the rooms but they weren't in the house.

In the kitchen, Mum was putting plates on the table. Her wrists were scaly. She needed to dye her hair, it was full of grey roots. She pushed it behind her ears, squinting at him. Her eyes were red like her wrists. She looked really old.

'I can't find them.' He dragged out his stool.

'Well, where are they?' She frowned. 'The food's ready.'

'I don't know.' He kicked at the island. 'I looked and they're not here. It's not my fucking fault.'

'Christie!' She rapped her knuckles at the marble. 'Don't use that language.'

'Why not? You do.' When she looked shocked, he said, 'I *heard* you. You and Dad talking about the Dearmans and their stupid fucking garden.'

'We were frustrated.' She wet her lips, looking away. 'It doesn't mean you can start swearing.'

'He's threatening to sue.' Christie had overheard the whole conversation, could tell it wasn't the first time they'd argued. 'Dad should tell him to piss off. There's nothing wrong with the garden and even if there was, he should look where he's bloody well going like the rest of us.'

'Mr Dearman has a broken foot. He's probably not feeling great right now.'

That made him angrier, being talked at like a baby who didn't understand the adult world where people got sued. 'You didn't take his side when you were shouting at Dad.'

'I wasn't shouting at Dad.' She gripped the lip of the island. 'No one was shouting. We were discussing what's best to do.'

'Dad should tell him to piss off, that'd be best.' Christie stabbed his fork at the salad, spearing some of it onto his plate. He didn't even like salad but it felt good to stab something. 'He should tell him to stick his crutch up his bloody arse.'

'Christie!'

'That's what Trevor said.' He started sawing up his chicken. 'I heard him and Dad. Everyone's shouting at everyone else and it's *shit*. I'm sick of it.'

'You heard your dad and Trevor fighting?' Mum leant into the island. 'About what?'

'Same thing as you and Dad: the Dearmans and their dumb garden.'

He cut more chicken, trying to ignore how she was standing there with her face a funny colour, white with red patches like he'd slapped her.

'Our garden's messed up too but we're not breaking our feet in it, not even Agnes and she's been bitching about this place since we moved in.'

This place. It was the first time he'd called Blackthorn Ashes that, like it wasn't *home* any more. He wanted to bawl his eyes out. It was Agnes's fault but it was Mum's too. She should've told Mrs Dearman to fuck off when she first started stirring things.

'This's screwed up.' He shoved a piece of chicken in his mouth to stop himself from crying. It tasted salty, rank. 'I'm sick of it.'

Mum sat down, reaching for the salad bowl. 'It'll be all right,' she said tiredly.

She was making an effort to keep him calm. She did the same thing with Agnes. It shouldn't have worked on Christie because he knew she was faking but the chicken dislodged itself from his throat and went down, letting him swallow. Mum started to eat too and even though it was just the two of them and the sky was the colour of desert camouflage, it was okay. He wished Dad was here but Christie was used to him being away when he was working. He was glad Agnes wasn't here, now the rest of them had caught up with her. Panicking, whispering, fighting.

She'd wanted to start a war here and she'd done it.

Blackthorn Ashes was a war zone.

'Luke's a fucking lunatic, don't know why you give him headspace.' Trevor was fussing with a spirit level so he didn't have to look at Dad. 'Last week you told him yourself that garden was solid. He hadn't a leg to stand on – that was *your* joke. Now you're losing it because his bitch of a wife's added her voice to the chorus?'

Agnes had come to the end of the estate to find her father. She'd been trying to catch Dad on his own since she'd heard him arguing with Ruth. But, of course, Trevor was down here; he'd been here nearly every day since they'd moved in, another reason she felt so ill, poisoned by the past.

Trevor said he was working on the next phase but he was alone, all the other contractors had left when the money started drying up. No work had been done down here in weeks. The cement mixer was shoved aside, its empty mouth marked by a scrim of dry cement. On a makeshift work table in the half-formed sitting room, Trevor had spread plans held in place by the spirit level.

Her back prickled at the sight of the spirit level, remembering the day he'd shown her how it worked. 'Keep still.' Stretching her arms out at her sides. 'Very, very still . . .'

'Emma's not a bitch.' Dad rested his knuckles on the work table. 'And Luke's not a lunatic. They're ordinary people who thought they were buying a luxury new-build because they believed what *we* told them. They've a right to be pissed off. I'm pissed off, aren't you? And not just about the gardens. The *houses*. Wasps in the walls, dodgy water pressure, crap ventilation . . . Our bathroom's growing mould, for God's sake. We've not even been here three months.'

'Exactly.' Trevor lifted the spirit level, using it to point at his best friend. 'The houses're still settling. Give them a chance to settle. That's what we always do, isn't it?'

'That's not what's happening here.' Dad lowered his voice to a hiss. 'They're falling out of plumb.' He pointed back at Trevor. 'Have you used that spirit level inside any of the houses in the last month? Because I have.'

Falling out of plumb.

Agnes didn't know what it meant. Nothing good, that was for sure. From where she was hiding she couldn't see Trevor's face but his shoulders stiffened defensively.

'What'd you know about the construction, Ade? That's my area of expertise. You're the sales guy, I'm bricks and mortar.'

'You should've *told* me.' Her father's voice was full of splinters. 'For pity's sake! Why didn't you tell me?'

'You're unhappy with the decisions *we* made? Because we're a team, isn't that what you told everyone? No one's going to believe we weren't a team.'

Agnes crouched lower, suppressing a shiver. Trevor was threatening Dad, that's what she heard. Threatening to lay the blame at his door.

'You cut corners,' Dad said, 'that's what you're saying. You cut corners without telling me and now this whole site's a lawsuit waiting to happen. Or worse . . . We need to come clean before someone does more than break his foot in a bloody big trench in the lawn.'

Something was happening to the air, turning it heavy, the sky bronze and blackening. Agnes doubled under its weight.

The sheeting was tight to the windows as if the house had taken a breath and was holding it. A seared metal smell seeped through the bricks. A storm was forecast for the weekend but it was coming sooner than that. Now, tonight. She should get back to their house. It was after six, supper would be spoiling. She didn't dare move from her hiding spot.

'We all need to move out,' Dad was saying. 'Before one of the kids gets sick.'

'No one's getting sick,' Trevor scoffed. 'You need to stop panicking and sit tight.'

'Sit tight?' Dad echoed. 'I'll tell you what's *tight* – the fucking house. You think my voice is meant to sound like this?' Hoarse, too high. 'That I'm choked up with emotion? I'm getting chest pains. Ruth's skin's a mess, Christie looks like a zombie . . .'

'He's thirteen. It's the summer holidays, he's entitled to a lie-in.'

Trevor set the spirit level on the table, tucking his hands into his pockets with a shrug. Agnes knew he was using his best smile, the one that made everyone weak at the knees.

'Look, man. Supposing you're right and there's more than settling to be done here, yeah? Say the houses are too tight, whatever . . . No way you'd be getting symptoms so soon after moving in. It takes months for that shit to affect anyone. You're letting yourself get stressed because Dearman broke his foot and wants compensation, and because his wife's being a bitch to Ruth. He's trying to make you feel guilty enough to give him what he wants. You've just got to nut up till he shuts up.'

'Nut up,' Dad repeated. 'That's your advice? With all this shit going down? *Nut up* ?'

'Or ask me to have a word with him.' Trevor gave a short laugh. 'I'd be happy to.'

Agnes knew that laugh, it made her skin flush between her shoulder blades. She wished she'd never come looking for her father, that she'd gone with Errol and Bette to the caravan or stayed home with Christie and Ruth. It was the first time she'd called this place *home*, as if Blackthorn Ashes for all its broken promises had won her heart. Because her family was here. They had been healing until it started to fall apart, but even now they were here. Together.

Trevor wanted to keep the lies going, and the deceit. That's where the danger lay, Laura said. Lies could be forgiven but only after they'd been exposed. Trevor's lies were like the spidery cracks that ran down the walls, looking like nothing until you got up close.

'You're a fucking *prick*!'

Dad grabbed the spirit level from the table and swung it so violently Agnes ducked, afraid of shrapnel, splintered glass, blood. The spirit level hit the wall, sending echoes chasing one another around the half-built house.

'Steady on, mate!'

Trevor had his hands up, play-acting surrender, but his voice wavered, as if Dad's sudden rage had taken him by surprise, scared him as it had scared her.

'Prick,' Dad repeated.

He threw the spirit level to the floor and walked away, taking the last of the air with him so that Agnes, needing to breathe and stay hidden, felt her lungs stagger in her chest.

It was after dark before the thunder came, rolling in off the sea like all the weather here. The storm mustered at the horizon, steel-coloured clouds giving way to a sunset like distant forest fires. The heat was unbearable, pushing at everything and everyone.

Christie would not stop moving, pacing from room to room, his phone case sweating in his hand. Agnes offered to bring him a cold can from the fridge but he said the ice maker had packed up. He kicked the wall as he said it, as if he hated the house now. Their mother was in the sitting room listening to a podcast on her phone. Dad was in the garden, folding away the loungers in case of storm damage. The storm was needed, that's how it felt, to break the bad mood that had descended on the street since the party. The last of the balloon arch sagged and dragged in the dead air. Agnes lay on her bed, sweat crawling from her temples, watching the sky through her window.

The first split of thunder sounded like an axe through wood.

All her attention was on the sky, the treetops where the storm was pressing. Another axe blow opened a seam of white in the darkness. *Lightning*.

She went to the window, put her palm to the glass. The house was trembling as if heavy traffic was passing at a distance. Two fat splats of rain hit the window then nothing. Silence.

A stirring in the trees. The sharp shape of a bird flying from its branches, away.

Thunder rolling, on and on into silence again. The glass shuddered against her skin. The house was thrumming with blood fit to burst. A sound from behind made her turn.

Christie with his phone in his hand, his eyes shadowed. She put out a hand to him and he crossed the floor to stand at her side.

Wind buckled the tops of the trees, rain hitting the window like a handful of gravel. The sky was lit from beneath by a long jagged line of lightning, a hot high wind pressing at the house.

Silence followed but it didn't last, thunder cracking to a fork of lightning as the storm settled directly overhead. The rain when it came was heavy, thick against the pane.

Wind roared through the gardens, clattering furniture.

Deep in Blackthorn Ashes, glass shattered, high and shrill. Voices shouted in alarm, lights coming on in the houses, banging in the blackness like searchlights. A gull crazed across the sky, crying.

Agnes could smell her brother's skin and sweat. The sky was sulphurous, wind whipping the scent of the sea into the house.

'Shit!' Christie pointed towards the garden two houses from theirs.

Blurred by the rain, it looked like a spaceship trying to take off. Black body, silver fins – a trampoline, tugged by the wind, turning somersaults as it hit the hedge and went over, away.

More people began shouting as the lights went dead. Power cut. The darkness only lasted a moment before lightning cracked, dazzling all the windows into brightness. At her side, Christie flinched. She offered her hand and he took it, gripping tight.

Crashing from the gardens as furniture and potted plants blew over and broke. Car alarms shrieking, and people too. Over it all, the endless percussion of the rain, beating down.

Agnes was the first to hear the ambulance, its siren a reedy note under the drumming of the storm, coming from the other end of Blackthorn Ashes where the new tarmac drive met the old road, Ashes Road, that ran into town.

3 SEPTEMBER

Nine days after abandonment

———

16

Indigo Park was quiet when Agnes returned from her trespass with Iris. In the caravan, Dad was asleep on the sofa, shoulders curled towards the wall. Ruth and Christie wouldn't be back until suppertime. It was her job to prepare the meal they'd eat seated around the table like a happy family. She searched the cupboards and fridge, finding tins of tuna and a bag of dried pasta, a tube of tomato puree, a cube of hard cheese. The meal wouldn't take more than half an hour to prepare.

Dad's sandwich sat untouched on the counter. She carried it to the table by the sofa. The back of his neck bore a tidemark of dirt. His hair looked dusty, his skin giving off a heavy, sour scent.

'Dad,' she said softly. 'What happened?'

He didn't stir but the rasp of his eyelashes against the pillow said he was awake.

'What happened to Emma Dearman?'

Nothing, not even the sound of his breath.

All the fight had gone out of him as the first of the ambulances arrived on the night of the storm. Almost overnight, he changed.

One day tall, tanned and smiling. The next shrunken with his face slumped to one side as if he'd suffered a stroke.

Shock consumed them all in the days immediately after evacuation. Agnes couldn't stop thinking about the children dead in their beds. When the coroner came, Christie stood watching with her, his face shuttered and empty. His friend Felix was in the biggest of the black body bags but even that bag was small. She'd tried to get her brother out of the house, afraid he'd be next. His skin was grey and his breath rank. Their parents talked in whispers or not at all. Dad was already gone, replaced by a ghost who flinched when anyone went near him. It made her sorry for the years she'd lost by leaving home. Eleven years of his smiles, of the highs and lows of normal family life. Now they were as far from normal family life as it was possible to get.

'Dad,' she asked again in the caravan's hush. 'What happened to Emma?'

He wouldn't answer, she knew. But she had to keep trying. Ruth said the important thing was to move forward, away from what had happened. She didn't see how it was tangled around Dad, holding him hard. Agnes saw because it held her too. Not just Blackthorn Ashes but Laura in London and Trevor when she was sixteen, Ruth all her life. You could run or you could stop and look, try to learn.

Iris was looking. Agnes was grateful for her fixation on Luke, who was a stranger for whom she'd felt no special affinity. She'd never fought with Luke or run away only to return, never made his life more difficult or unfairly blamed him for her problems. And he'd never stood with his face turned to stone, insisting she guard her family with her life.

She took Christie's broken Game Boy from their bedroom,

putting it on the kitchen table while she searched for what she needed. Cotton buds, an old toothbrush, sandpaper and surgical spirit from her father's toolbox. Years ago, she had fixed her brother's broken toys, discovering she had a skill for taking things apart and putting them back together. She took Christie's console apart now, separating each of the components. Soaking the cotton bud in surgical spirit, she cleaned the rubber pads and button contacts. The battery contacts she treated with sandpaper, carefully removing the build-up of corrosion. Her fingers moved instinctively – pinching, lifting, pressing – a dance her hands had done dozens of times, just not for years.

She waited for the parts to dry before reassembling the console and switching it on. It was working again, she'd fixed it. She took the Game Boy to the bedroom, leaving it on Christie's pillow. On a shelf above his bunk, he'd stood one of his toy soldiers. What did he call them, Ultramarines? She touched the tip of her finger to the model's chest, thinking of Trevor and her brother's hero-worship. She would fight to keep him safe from Trevor's influence. Her own ferocity shocked her; there was nothing she wouldn't do to stop Trevor wrecking her brother's life the way he'd wrecked hers.

Outside there was no sign of Iris, just Errol sitting on the steps to Bette's caravan, one knee drawn up, a cigarette burning between his fingers. Black jeans slashed at the knee, Doc Martens, an oversized red jumper cobwebby with age. His dreadlocks were freshly bleached; she could smell the peroxide.

'Hello.'

He dipped his head in response, smoke coiling from his lips. Not speaking.

'I'm sorry about last night.'

She put a foot on the bottom step, waiting to see whether he'd tell her to go away. He didn't but nor did he ask her to stay. His clothes were different today, very *fuck-off-and-leave-me-alone.*

'Did you have fun with Iris last night?' He tapped ash from the cigarette, not looking at her until he reached the question mark when he put the stick back in his mouth.

'Not really.' She wanted to tell him the truth. 'Iris isn't interested in fun.'

'She was keen enough on a drink, until you dragged her away.'

'I had to.' Agnes saw Bette's shadow moving inside the caravan. 'She's not . . . a good person.'

Errol considered this before he said, 'So you weren't even having fun?'

'The opposite.'

He leant to scrub the cigarette into a china saucer at his feet. 'Where'd you go?'

'I'll show you if you like.' She nodded in the direction of Christie's shed. 'It's not far.'

Errol climbed to his feet like an old man, as if his whole body hurt. Was he unwell? There was a guardedness to him, which was new. She'd thought he was angry with her but it wasn't just that. He was too thin, like her. When he turned his head to call to his grandmother, she saw the bones in his jaw and face. He looked held together with wire.

'I'm going for a walk with Agnes!'

He waited until Bette called back: 'Take Odie!'

'We're going the wrong way. See you in a bit!'

To Agnes, 'Quick, before she gets the lead.'

They walked in the direction of the trailers. Errol kept step with her, his hands loose at his sides. She liked walking with him, better than with Iris or Christie; their steps matched. The sleeve of his jumper kept brushing the back of her hand but it was so soft it hardly mattered.

When they reached the big trailer, Errol said, 'Lidl does Las Vegas . . .' He sounded delighted. 'Will you look at that?'

The Graceland sign was sagging, stained by rain. A dog yapped from inside the trailer but no one came out, all the lights switched off.

'It wasn't an asthma attack, by the way. Jonelle, the ambulance? Bette says they don't know what it was but it wasn't asthma.' Errol toed an empty can out of his path. 'Where's Christie? It's odd not seeing you together.'

'He went with Mum, into town.'

She was taking a risk bringing Errol to the shed. Christie would be furious if he found out. Secrets were the only things keeping him and Agnes close.

'This's where we came last night, me and Iris.'

Errol eyed the groundsman's shed. '*Okaaay . . .*'

He walked to the nearest window, peering inside. 'I'm starting to think you meant it when you said she wasn't interested in having fun.'

'It's better inside but I didn't let her in. I didn't want her finding out what's in there.'

Errol looked at her for a long moment. 'Okay,' he said, more seriously this time. He wasn't going to push her. He knew how hard she was trying to make up for last night.

'I'll show you, if you'd like.'

He glanced down at his clothes. 'Not sure I'm dressed for it . . .'

'You're perfect.' She took out the key, fitting it into the lock. 'Come on.'

Inside, the shed smelt of creosote and rubber. Light lay along the floor in stripes, softened by the grime on the windows. Errol scuffed a boot at the dust, stirring up shadows. Agnes went to the filing cabinet, fitting the key she'd taken from Christie's keyring. She'd never opened the cabinet before, had no real idea what it might be hiding.

Errol was poking at piles of old flowerpots and the broken bits of furniture stacked against the walls. He stopped when she slid open the top drawer of the filing cabinet, coming close to see.

'Ohhh . . .' he said on a long note of surprise. 'Now you're making more sense.'

The drawer was full of colour. Green and gold and red: a red leather coin purse lying on top of an emerald silk scarf patterned with gold crowns. She lifted the purse from the drawer, shaking free the scarf before offering it to Errol. He took it from her delicately, holding it by two corners so it fell in a big silk square across the chest of his jumper.

'You do know this is Hermès?' His voice was breathy with reverence.

'Is it?' She was looking inside the purse, at a few coins and a house key.

'I only mention it as you might not like to let it *rot with damp* in this shed?' His voice arched on a note of disapproval. 'Hermès, darling!'

'The shed's not damp. It's drier than our caravan.' She watched Errol sling the scarf around his neck, tying it in an elaborate knot, stroking the silk with his thin fingers. 'You should keep it.'

He stared at her. 'Don't toy with me.'

'I'm not. It doesn't belong to anyone else and it suits you.' She paused, shutting the purse. 'Just don't wear it when my brother's around, okay?'

Errol looked at the purse in her hand then back at the filing cabinet. He'd guessed the whole of it: Christie's scavenging during their trips to Blackthorn Ashes, the stashing of his treasure here, with Agnes's passive assistance. Everything. Perhaps it was obvious. Probably it was.

'What's in the purse?' he asked.

'Nothing much.' She put it into her pocket, sliding the top drawer shut.

The second drawer held fridge magnets, CDs and a painted wooden box the size of a paperback book. The box was empty. She moved on to the next drawer. Errol peered over her shoulder but he didn't touch anything, or speak. She was grateful for his silence. In the bottom drawer, the scatter diamond rattled loose, alone. She was certain there'd been more treasure in this drawer. She squatted on her heels, Errol doing the same at her side. Nothing, just the diamond. No sign of whatever Christie had taken from their parents' bedroom on the day Iris intercepted them. But the ambulance had come for Jonelle, preventing him from getting to the shed. He must have stashed that particular treasure in their caravan, along with whatever it was he'd removed from the bottom drawer of the filing cabinet. Agnes shut the cabinet, locking it up.

'Are you sure about this?' Errol fingered the scarf. 'I think maybe I should put it back.'

'And let it rot?' The red purse was in her pocket, hot against her hip. 'Keep it.'

'Won't Christie notice it's gone?'

'Yes, but he won't say anything.'

Not to Errol. Agnes was the one he'd confront with the theft of the scarf and purse. Well, it was time she and Christie talked about what was going on, before Iris made it her business to find out. She and Ruth needed to talk too. About Iris but mostly about Emma. Silence wouldn't keep them safe from what was coming.

Agnes locked the shed, taking Errol to the chairs where she'd talked with Iris the night before. He dusted a cane seat and sat, crossing his legs, swinging one booted foot.

'Are you going to tell me?' He said it lightly, as if it hardly mattered.

'Iris is a reporter.' Agnes sat beside him. 'She's writing a story about Blackthorn Ashes. She thinks I must have some good gossip because Dad was on-site from the start.'

'Isn't it being investigated officially? Can't she just wait for that?'

'She could, yes.'

'I mean, what happened was horrible.' Errol reached to dust the knee of his jeans. 'Especially the children. But carbon monoxide poisoning isn't exactly the crime of the century.'

'She thinks one of the deaths was murder.'

Errol's foot stopped swinging. 'That's different, of course.'

He looked so serious she struggled to recognize him. The silk scarf should have been incongruous with the punk clothes but it wasn't. He was all punchy colours and textures, keen edges. He saw such a lot, didn't miss the details the way Iris did. He knew Agnes needed a friend to confide in, that she had questions which needed answers. She didn't expect him to have answers but to be able to ask them out loud to someone she trusted meant more than she could have imagined.

'Why do you live with your grandmother?' she asked instead.

Errol took his time to answer. He picked at the cuff of his jumper, rolling a thread of red wool into a ball before flicking it away.

'Because my mum and dad can't stand the sight of me.'

When Agnes blinked, he shrugged. 'You asked.' His voice was light, unconcerned.

'I'm sorry . . .'

'I'm not. I love living with Bette.'

'She seems very nice.'

Errol let the platitude pass. He turned his head, resting his eyes away from her. She thought he was doing it for the sake of his privacy but perhaps also because he knew she found it easier to talk without making eye contact. 'You said a murder . . . ?'

'It's what Iris thinks. That Emma Dearman was murdered. Luke was abusing her, maybe. He has an alibi but Iris seems to think that's suspicious.'

'Don't Luke Now,' Errol murmured, remembering his joke from the street party. 'He was always very angry. Not making much of an effort to cover his tracks if he was an abuser, or a killer.'

'It's Iris's theory, not mine.' She scratched at her ankle, wondering what'd bitten her. An ant perhaps, or a flea. 'But she says Emma's death is being treated as suspicious.'

'How would she know? There's been nothing on the news.'

Agnes thought of Iris picking through the fridge magnets, grabbing at the books on their shelves in the hope of finding her story hiding there.

'Maybe she has sources, being a reporter.'

'Maybe she was there,' Errol said. 'She came to the street party in disguise. Hiding in plain sight. The bloodstained hands might have been a huge clue . . .'

He was joking but Agnes shivered.

'She knew Emma and Luke, I'm sure of it. She's obsessed with what happened to them.' She remembered the animal cage hidden in the shrubbery at Silverthorn. 'And she's angry.'

'Why was she hanging about at the barbecue, did she say? I mean, this was *before* anyone died.'

'She's been interested in Blackthorn Ashes since the planning stage. She's local, used to come up here as a teenager. A dare, she called it.'

Errol pulled at another loose thread, working it free from his cuff.

'I saw Christie up there once. With your dad and Trevor. Back at the planning stage. Before you came home from London.'

'What were they doing?'

'Working, I guess? Going in and out of the houses. Your dad had a tool belt.' Errol wound the loose thread around his index finger. 'All of them in hard hats, Trevor with his cowboy boots . . . It was very Village People.'

'Dad and Trevor were inseparable once.' Her ankle itched. Perhaps it was a tick that'd bitten her. From the beach or the woods. 'Before it all went bad.'

'The friendship, you mean?'

'The houses. Everything.'

Errol gave a slow nod. 'I was nosey. Like that day you and I met, and I talked and talked . . . I wanted to know what it was like to live there.' He unwound the thread from his finger, smoothing it on the thigh of his jeans. 'Something about those families got in my head. I mean, *everyone* was talking about Blackthorn Ashes. Whenever we took the bus to the shops or into town. Bitching about the property prices, or swooning over them. *Paradise*, that's the word I kept hearing. Bette remembers the power station, though. She was making dark mutterings long before anyone else.'

He looked sideways at Agnes. 'I went to look because I was jealous of the families who could afford to move there. Of the families full stop. All those mums and dads and picture-perfect kids. Only it wasn't like that, was it? The houses looked fancy, and the cars. But the families? No black or brown faces, for starters. Everyone in a nice straight couple, no surprises there.' He ghosted a smile. 'It was like someone went catalogue shopping in the suburbs and bought up all the Normal.'

I'm not normal, she thought. But she didn't say it because Errol was right.

'How could you stand it there?' he asked, as if he'd read her mind. 'I mean this in the nicest way but you didn't fit in, did you?'

'I'd no choice. I lost my job in London, Laura'd broken up with me. I've debts you wouldn't believe. I was lucky they took me back.'

'Your mum and dad?'

'Especially my mum.'

'She looks pretty tough but Bette likes her.' Errol was knotting the red thread into a loop. 'That's usually a good sign.'

'Yes. It's only when it's the two of us together, you know?'

A bonfire, still burning after all these years. Teenage rebellion for kindling and hormones for fuel, a ritual feeding of twigs and coals; Trevor, and her meds, the late diagnosis, her autism passing undetected until adolescence. Her mother's mistakes, and hers.

And now this latest pain – the poison from Blackthorn Ashes balanced on top of all the burning, yet to catch light.

'So this murder . . .' Errol said. 'Emma. What's that about?'

'Honestly? I've no idea.' She stretched in the chair, feeling stiff and old. 'Might just be Iris, an idea in her head. I think she's dangerous. It's why I didn't want her near my dad last night. Or you.'

He arched an eyebrow. 'Do I look like someone who can't take care of himself?'

'I didn't mean—'

'I'm joking.' He gave a gurgle of laughter. '*Of course* I look like that.'

He fanned the fingers of his right hand. 'I can slap a bitch, if I have to. But I'd rather watch old movies with my gran and drink my own body weight in daiquiris.'

'I don't trust her,' Agnes said. 'Iris. I'm scared of what she's going to uncover.'

He stopped laughing, his eyes serious. 'What's to uncover?'

'I don't know. Maybe nothing. Emma and Luke looked like all the others, like you said, a straight suburban couple living the dream.'

Errol rolled the loop of thread onto his ring finger. 'You never saw him hit her?'

'Never.'

'No bruises or anything like that?'

'He was the one on crutches, not her.'

'So maybe *she* was abusing *him*. It happens that way, more than people like to think.'

'I know. But Iris says he's the one with a history of violence.'

'Sounds like Iris says a lot of things.'

'That's true.'

It helped to talk with him. Iris was shrinking back to human size, no longer crowding out the space in Agnes's head.

'She's determined to find a story, though. A scandal.'

'Six dead people not enough for her?' Errol frowned. 'I wouldn't go near that place for a bit. Bette says she's hearing rumours of looting. She hears all kinds of stuff when she's down in town.'

'*That* was looted.' Agnes nodded at the scarf. 'I suppose you'd say. I can put it back if you'd rather not take the risk.'

'What risk? Of looking *fabulous*?' He tossed his head but his eyes remained grave. 'What happened to you in London?'

She thought for a moment before she answered. 'I wrecked everything. It's what I do. I fight to get something then when I've got it, I ruin it.'

'That sounds . . . exhausting.'

'It is.' She reached for the branch Iris had stripped of leaves last night. 'It was.'

'I thought I'd love London.' Errol stretched a leg, studying his booted foot. 'But big cities are only ever fun when you have money, or friends with money.' He relaxed deeper into the cane chair. 'I prefer it here.' Closing his eyes. 'With Bette.'

Agnes watched the lush curve of his mouth, the long curl of his lashes. He was too beautiful to be in a caravan park in the middle of nowhere. But perhaps he'd been too beautiful for London, she could see how that might be true. London loved beautiful people the way fire loves paper. She shut her eyes, seeing the bonfire Laura had described, and the bonfire Agnes gave her – a parting gift after the tears and pleas and brittle silences. She'd brought it all down, everything they'd made, all they had. After Laura had picked up the pieces of her and made her whole again. For what? So Agnes could burn the life raft for fuel as soon as she was safely on dry land? She tightened her face against the threat of tears.

Remembering would ruin what was left of her resolve. She had to stay strong for her family's sake. For Adrian and Ruth and Christie. She hadn't wanted to come home to them but here she was. And they were in danger. She wasn't sure how, not yet. But she could taste it on her tongue as sharp as a drop of wine, or poison. Her family was in terrible danger.

Sixty days before abandonment

———

17

Laura came home smelling of the oils she used at work, of lavender, rosemary and lemongrass. Her hair was tied away from her face. Agnes could see the place above her left eyebrow where she'd wiped the back of her hand.

'How was he?' She'd poured wine for the pair of them, their ritual on a Friday night although Laura had started cutting down the measures, warning Agnes about mixing alcohol with her meds. She was starting to sound like Ruth. 'How was his foot?'

Laura hung her jacket on the back of the door, not answering right away. She glanced around the kitchen, seeing the mess Agnes had made while making supper. Ratatouille. The kitchen smelt of the vegetables she'd sliced – fiery peppers and watery cucumber. She took a gulp of wine to calm her giddiness. This was always the worst part. When Laura was first home and the flat was a different place to the one it had been during the hours when she was alone. Then it was small and shambolic but safe. Now it was four rooms full of things she had failed to do. A bed she hadn't made, a bathroom she hadn't cleaned, this kitchen spattered with peelings and pips.

Laura said, 'You know I can't talk about my work. Or my clients, anyway.'

'You used to talk about them.' Another gulp. Had she taken her meds? Of course, why else was her heart racing in her chest? 'I liked hearing about him. The soldier, his missing foot.'

Laura shook her head, dismissing the intrusion. She was wearing her denim tunic dress with black leggings and green sandals, her toenails painted pink, two gold toe rings.

Agnes saw the soldier lying face down, watching those gold rings flashing as Laura moved around the table, stroking his skin. He'd lost his right foot to a landmine but still felt it, asking her to massage the phantom foot when she was working on his right leg. Not to stop where his leg stopped but to take the weight of his missing foot in her hands, hold his heel and the arch of his instep, all the way to his toes. Laura did as he asked because that's who she was – someone who took other people's hurt and tried to ease it. Each week, she massaged the soldier's missing foot. Her slim fingers stroked his toes in turn, bringing them back to life for the hour when he was lying on her table. Agnes had started dreaming about it, alone in the bed while Laura slept on the sofa because they were falling apart. Agnes wasn't here any longer, that's what Laura said. She'd gone away, out of Laura's reach. She knew it was true; she kept seeing herself from a distance growing smaller and further away but she didn't understand why Laura couldn't love her, why she couldn't touch her and hold her and bring her back. The way she did with the soldier's missing foot.

'I made supper,' she said.

'I can see.' Laura rolled up her sleeves and began clearing Agnes's mess, rinsing the knife under the tap, sweeping seeds from the counter into her cupped hand and carrying them to the bin, pressing the pedal – a blast of rotting fruit and teabags – before swiping her hand clean. The bin needed emptying. Another job not done.

Agnes's temples throbbed. The flat, so small during the day, expanded now. Bloating about her, bobbing with unwashed plates and abandoned books, clothes dumped on the floor instead of put away the way she was supposed to, the way she'd meant to. Time on her hands. She looked at her hands, their empty palms facing upwards. What had she done with her day? Laura used to ask her that, back when Agnes was first out of work. She had stopped asking when the answer became obvious, scribbled across the dirty sinks and floors, written all over Agnes's unwashed face and clothes. *Nothing.* She had done nothing with her day. To begin with, Laura was sympathetic. She took time away from her own work to put a schedule in place, guarding against the threat not of boredom but a lack of structure. Agnes needed structure, an order to her days, and it needed to be written down so she could see it.

The schedule helped, at the beginning. Until the flat started to change size, rooms telescoping, getting lost inside each other. Time played the same trick, folding in on itself. One minute she'd be making the bed she and Laura used to share, the next she'd be screaming at Ruth not to touch her things, 'I'm sixteen! I'm not a little kid any longer!'

She wasn't losing her mind, she didn't scream out loud. She didn't see Ruth, other than in her mind's eye, and she knew she was twenty-nine not sixteen. It was just . . .

All the padding was gone, the boxes she'd built in her brain to keep the past in its place so she could live in the present, in London with Laura. She'd packaged it all up – her and Ruth, and Trevor – put it away like the purple suitcase shoved under the bed.

Laura was picking pips from the kitchen counter. At her sandalled feet, a tiny starburst of silver: the last little piece of glitter from their Christmas, trapped in the jute matting. The sight of it brought tears to the back of Agnes's throat.

One morning, a week after losing her job, she'd lain in bed trying to summon the energy to get up and look at Laura's schedule. Every day until that one she'd got up as soon as Laura was gone. Made the bed, showered, dressed. That morning she did none of those things. She turned on her side and pulled Laura's pillow towards her, pressing it to her face until all she could breathe was Laura, until she couldn't breathe. Then she lay on her back, staring at the ceiling, thinking of the distance between the bed and the bathroom where her meds were waiting in a giant pill bottle on a miniature glass shelf like a prop from *Alice in Wonderland: Take Me.*

She stared at the ceiling until the bed began to fight her, prodding the small of her back as if something was rearing up, a big dog or a wolf. It had been there since she'd moved in, asleep under the bed. Now it was awake and trying to stand, arching its back. The only thing under the bed was the purple suitcase. She had pushed it there herself, the one thing she took from home that wasn't hers. Ruth's suitcase: a wolf with its lips stretched back from its teeth.

That was the start of the strangeness, the telescoping of the rooms, present sliding into past. It had been going on so long now, it no longer felt like strangeness. *Strangeness* would have been a return to the way things were before. She had tried to explain to Laura how it felt being in the flat on her own. Laura suggested she get out more, just short trips, nowhere too loud or busy. She had managed the commute to work after all, week after week without a hitch. Laura didn't understand why it was suddenly impossible for her to step outside their front door, why she couldn't put on her noise-cancelling headphones and go for a walk, 'It's not good for you being cooped up in here all day.' It wasn't good but it was worse outside. Noise slamming at her head, people crushing up close, smells and colours making her sweat, making her shake.

'Have you taken your meds?'

'You sound like Ruth.'

Laura stopped tidying the kitchen. She rolled down her sleeves, looking tired and sad. 'Because I care about you?'

'Because you think I'm sick even though you know I'm not. *She* thought I was sick, for years and years. Bipolar, that's what she decided I was.'

'It was hard,' Laura said after a pause. 'The late diagnosis. Hard on both of you.'

'Poor *Ruth*?' Her face stung as if Laura had slapped her. 'After everything I told you? About what she said, how she treated me?'

'I'm not excusing that. But it can't have been easy.'

Laura turned her hands up in surrender. All day she treated other people's pain, chasing it away with her hands. All day. Holding the soldier's dead foot, stroking a ghost.

'Not knowing how to help you. I understand a little of how hard that must've been.'

Tears blinded her, hot and self-pitying. 'She ruined my life.'

'But she's *not* your life. She hasn't been for years. You've had nothing to do with her for eleven years.' Laura was trying to be patient, her face making painful shapes. 'You know what would help, you but also *us*? To admit you have a talent for self-sabotage, for picking at things until they fall apart. I know it's because of what happened to you, I know how hard that was and I'm sorry, really I am. But you keep *letting it happen*. Get help. Please. Therapy or whatever you need. You know I'll support you but *you* have to make a start. That has to come from you.'

'You said you weren't trying to fix me.' Agnes let the tears fall, wanting them out of the way, needing to be angry because it was all the protection she had. 'That's what you said. You can't fix me because I'm not broken. I'm not *sick*. You said you understood that.'

'I did. I do. But you make things harder for yourself than they need to be. And much harder for us. All this digging at the past, dragging it into the present . . . It's a pattern, a form of self-harm. You know that's true. We've talked about it many times.'

'When things go wrong it's my fault. Is that what you mean?'

'No.' Laura sighed. 'That's not what I mean.'

'Like when I could smell mould in the bathroom before you could and then the tiles started falling off the walls. Like that? So I *caused* the mould. Is that what you think?' She rattled through the words, leaving no room for Laura or anyone else. 'I suppose if I heard gas escaping and then there was an explosion, I'd have caused that too. Or if I tasted poison in the meal I made – if I was the only one who could taste it – then I must have put it there, to poison us.'

Laura was staring at her, silent now.

'I didn't,' Agnes said. 'Poison us. Not in the food, anyway. Just . . .' She gestured at the space between their bodies. 'Like this. By being here, being me.'

Her throat was closing up, panic pinwheeling at the edge of her vision.

In another minute, she'd reach for a glass or a plate and throw it.

Not because she was angry. Just to try and stop the sensation that she wasn't here, wasn't real. She was spinning out of Laura's reach. The smashing would bring her back but it would also make everything so much worse.

Laura was staring at her. Agnes could see tears pouring down her face. The tears weren't there but they had been, and would be again. The past folding into the present and back again, into the future. She left, the next day.

After Laura went to work, she dragged the purple suitcase from under the bed and filled it with her things, zipped it shut and went.

Out through the noise and smells and the crush of colour, of people.

Onto a train and home, to Ruth.

Ten days after abandonment

———

18

Christie went straight to his bunk when Ruth brought him home, shoving the mended Game Boy from his pillow. He had a new modelling magazine and made a point of reading it, shutting Agnes out when she tried to ask about his day.

Ruth told her to leave him alone. 'Is supper ready?'

'I'll start it now. It won't take long.'

Her mother looked around the caravan, her eyes passing over Dad on the sofa in his pyjamas. 'You might've tidied up.'

'I'll do it after supper.' Agnes didn't want to fight but she recognized the need in Ruth to do exactly that, her mother searching for a place to put her day's frustration. She took an ovenproof dish from the cupboard. 'How was town?'

'Busy.' Ruth pressed the back of her hand to her forehead. 'Too hot for September.'

'Was there any work?'

A strange question to ask a forty-eight-year-old former executive, as if Ruth were a farm labourer from another century. Her suit was creased at the shoulder from the car's seat belt. She smelt of supermarkets and petrol stations.

'Nothing new.' She shrugged off the jacket, hanging it from her hands. She worked so hard at being the strong one. It had to be exhausting.

'Were you and Christie able to spend some time together?'

'Only in the car . . . You're feeling better, I take it?'

'Yes, thanks.'

Agnes filled a saucepan with water, clicking on the stove. Her mother was making her nervous. She should have prepared the meal earlier, when she was free to focus.

'Well enough to spend time with Errol, smoking.'

'What?' Agnes turned to face her.

'I can smell it on you,' Ruth said flatly. 'He's the only one who smokes around here. Or he was.'

'He was smoking, I wasn't. We spent a bit of time together, that's all.'

'You can smoke, if you can afford to.' Her mother shrugged. 'You're a grown woman. But I'd thought you weren't well enough to look after your brother today. That was my understanding.'

'I slept.' She was sweating, in danger of stammering. 'I felt better when I woke up.'

'Just not well enough to tidy up or prepare the supper.'

Agnes needed to stop this, and sensed Ruth did too. There was a wildness in her mother's eyes, flickering almost too rapidly to see but Agnes saw it. Ruth was afraid of fighting tonight.

'I'll do better,' she said. 'Tomorrow.'

Ruth started to say something then bit her tongue; Agnes saw her wince, could almost taste the pain in her mother's mouth.

'What?' she asked, as softly as she could. 'Tell me.'

But Ruth just moved her hand, shaking her head. She didn't

believe in Agnes, or in tomorrow. She needed things to be better here and now, in the caravan where the kitchen was too small to fit the awkward elbows of their battling, this war that went on and on.

'I could go,' Agnes offered again. 'Back to London.' To Laura, whose hands would smell of lemongrass from stroking the soldier's missing foot. Her throat closed. 'I could.'

'Stop saying that. You know it isn't possible.'

'The investigation might take months.'

'It *will* take months.' Her mother reached past her for a bottle of water from the fridge. 'That's obvious. There's no sense of urgency from their side.'

Their side. As if the investigators were the enemy. Ruth was good at battlelines. She'd been drawing them all her life. She thought she knew where all the risks lay – out there with the health and safety investigators. Agnes should tell her about Iris. And she should ask about Emma and Luke, his history of violence. She watched her mother unscrew the cap from the bottle of water, shutting her eyes as she drank. When she opened them, the wildness was still there, a pulse beating in her throat so strongly Agnes could see her blood under the pale of her skin.

Dad joined them for the pasta supper, sitting with the light in the lines of his face. He didn't speak more than a handful of words. Christie pushed the food around his plate in silence.

After the meal, while her parents were drinking coffee, Agnes tidied the living space, brushing the sofa free from crumbs and the dull strands of her father's unwashed hair.

The cushions were gritty, reminding her of holidays long ago, sand in the sheets. She stooped to collect the ball of cling film from the carpet and for a second she was back there, folded into the past: the fizz of lemonade on her tongue, laughter in her throat, her mother's arms catching her as she leapt. In the caravan, she brushed orange sand from the sofa into the cupped palm of her hand.

Ruth glanced across at her. 'What is it?'

'Just rubbish.' She straightened, showing Ruth the ball of cling film before crossing to drop it into the bin.

At the sink, she washed her hands, watching as the water took the sand away, rinsing the last grains of it down the plughole until it was gone.

The next morning, the sun had gone behind a bank of putty-coloured cloud. Agnes could smell rain. She felt it in the joints of her fingers, a dry fractious sensation.

Their mother left for work almost as soon as Agnes and Christie were up. Breakfast was bowls of cereal. Ruth didn't look at Dad on her way out. Usually she flicked him a glance, even on days when it was clear she hadn't the patience to talk to him. Now she'd stopped looking altogether. It was what Dad wanted, Christie said. For the rest of them to stop seeing him, judging him, 'He *wishes* he was invisible', but Agnes knew her father was making himself smaller because he was ashamed of how much space he took up in the world. She was afraid for him. He was like the rain – a warning pain in her bones. Something was coming. It had been coming for days, pushing at the caravan while they slept and woke and ate together, pretending to be a family.

As soon as Ruth was gone, Christie was at the door in his

hoodie and rucksack. He didn't speak to Agnes or wait to see if she'd follow, just left, shutting the door behind him. She pulled on her jacket and boots as quickly as she could. No time to make Dad a sandwich. She had to stay close to Christie, the mood he was in and with Iris out there.

Outside the caravan, there was no sign of her brother.

Errol was drinking a cup of coffee on Bette's steps. 'He went that way.' Pointing to the duckboards. 'Not looking much like a morning person . . . I said hi but he ignored me.'

'He's pissed off with me.' Agnes zipped her jacket against a squall of wind.

'Coffee?' Errol offered up his cup, nodding at the thermos flask at his bare feet. He was wearing his peacock-patterned robe.

'I'd love to.' The coffee smelt good. 'But I'd better get after him.'

'Where's he going?'

'The only place he ever goes.'

'Then you know where to find him. And you look like you need a coffee.' He took the steel lid from the thermos, filling it with a measure from the flask. 'Before you set off.'

Christie was smart; if he saw Iris, he'd duck out of sight. Agnes sat with Errol, sharing his flask of coffee, their silence comfortable. Wind tugged at the caravan park, running into crawl spaces, fluttering at flags: a cheerful sound like beach windmills from her childhood. Bette had hung a basket of blush-pink begonias above the door, their spicy scent mixing with the roasted beans.

'This is really good coffee.'

'You will miss it when you leave Casablanca.' Errol did that elegant thing with his wrist. He was quoting a line from a film. 'Not that Indigo Park is much like Morocco . . .'

'But you love it here.' She watched him. 'Don't you?'

He put his hand over his heart. 'There's no place like home.' He repeated it a couple of times, tapping the heels of his feet together.

'Would you come with me?' she suggested. 'When I go looking for Christie?'

'Now, you mean?' Errol eyed the duckboards, flicking his thumbnail against the lip of his cup.

When had he last left Indigo Park? Not since the evacuation, she suspected.

'It's a nice walk, along the cliff path. There's a shortcut through a hedge – you'll want to dress down.' She paused, aware of how tense he'd become. 'I could use the company.'

He swirled the dregs in his cup and drank them, climbing to his feet. 'Give me five minutes.'

She waited with her face tipped to the sky until he re-emerged in his ripped black jeans and a long-sleeved T-shirt – purple with the word 'Lucky' printed in blue below his left shoulder – a black cotton bandana tied under his dreadlocks, Doc Martens in one hand. He sat next to her while he put them on, lacing the boots up his ankles and calves. The clothes were close-fitting, showcasing his thinness. But when he climbed upright, he was tall and looked adventurous as a pirate. He held out his hand and, for a second, she nearly took it. Then she realized he was asking for the lid to the thermos. She handed it up before getting to her feet. 'Does Bette want us to take Odie?'

Errol shook his head. 'She's walking him herself.'

'You're both feeling better. That's good.'

'How's your dad?' Errol pushed his hands into his jean pockets, shrugging up his shoulders as they negotiated the greasy gangplank of duckboards out of Indigo Park.

'He's sad. He sleeps most of the time. I wish he'd get out but he's not ready to do that.'

Errol nodded as if he understood. He did, of course. They walked until the sky was free of trees and pylons, a big bowl of sky over their heads. It felt good to be out in the open. Errol was quiet, keeping step at her side. If she listened hard, she could hear the stress in his breathing, a tight sound from the top of his chest. He wasn't used to leaving the caravan park any more than Dad was. But he surprised her: 'Bette said she saw your dad yesterday. Going out. While you and I were at the shed.'

Agnes stopped, turning to look at him.

Errol folded his arms around his torso. 'She wasn't keeping watch or anything.' He sounded awkward. 'She doesn't do that. I only mentioned it because you said he never went out.'

'Did she speak to him?' She tried to picture her father and Bette, Odie running back and forth between them. 'Where did he go?'

'She was baking, elbow-deep in flour, she said. She saw him through the window but didn't get the chance to say hello.' Errol shivered. 'I didn't mean to freak you out. She didn't think it was odd, just nice to see him getting some fresh air. She worries about him – about all of you. But she's not nosey. She wouldn't say anything—'

'Where was he going?' Agnes cut him off, needing information, not apologies. 'Did she say?'

'This way.' He nodded ahead of them. 'Out of the park.'

'This was when we were at the shed?'

She and Errol had talked for a long time, sitting in the rotting cane chairs. It was mid-afternoon by the time she returned to Dad sleeping on the sofa. Just as she'd left him, she'd thought.

Errol rubbed at his wrists. 'Look—'

'What was he wearing?'

His work shirt and jersey pyjama bottoms, that's what he'd worn at supper last night. Was he wearing the same clothes when he left the caravan?

'She didn't say.' Errol sounded sick. 'I'm sorry. I shouldn't have said anything.'

Agnes made herself stop and look at him. He was so changed, out here. She'd thought him invincibly flamboyant, loud and colourful. On the cliff path, he looked boyish and lost, his face thinned by cold. She felt a rush of protectiveness towards him, different from her feelings for her brother but no less intense. 'Do you want to go back?'

He shook his head. 'We're getting Christie, aren't we?'

They walked on in silence. Agnes tried to keep her mind from jumping through the hoops of what he'd told her. Dad outside the caravan, walking in this direction. Her chest tightened against the pictures in her head.

When they reached the hedge, she shouldered her way through, Errol following, pausing on the other side to pick leaves from his T-shirt. They stood for a beat in the back garden of Maythorn before Agnes led the way up the side of the house to the street.

Errol was alert, his eyes everywhere, fresh tension in his face and body. It was how she and Christie should've been, every time they came here. Not just revisiting their old home or trespassing in condemned buildings – walking through a graveyard, ransacking rooms where people had died. Remorse flooded her, a wave of heat that moved so fast it left her breathless.

'Where'll we find him, do you know?' Errol worked his hands into his pockets.

'In one of the houses . . .'

She scanned the estate, roll-calling the homes Christie had already been inside, like one of the looters Bette warned her grandson about. What would Errol say if he knew Agnes was no better? But he did know; she'd given him the silk scarf from the filing cabinet. The red coin purse was in her pocket. She was afraid she'd seen it before, in Emma's hand as Luke's wife counted out coins to pay for the shopping Ruth had done.

The wind wrapped around their shoulders, sending a scurry of cloud and sun across all the empty windows. Errol ducked his head, a flash of fear in his face.

'It's just shadows.'

'It looks like people.' His voice was hollow, drum-tight. 'In the houses.'

'I know. But there's no one. There hasn't been in weeks.'

'I don't know how you can stand coming back.' He grimaced at the sound of his boots on the tarmac. 'It's like a funfair without the fun. Just ghost trains and mad mirrors.'

'And no candyfloss.'

'You like candyfloss?' He shot her a look of gratitude for the small talk. 'I *love* candyfloss.'

'I like toffee apples better but my teeth hate them. Have you ever had a toffee strawberry? They're better than apples, much easier to eat.'

Before Errol could answer, Christie came into view, running

from the far end of the estate, his rucksack bumping on his back. Agnes raised a hand but didn't call his name, afraid of hearing it echoed back at her. She fizzed with fright; the way he was running . . .

Something wasn't right.

'Is he—' Errol stopped.

He'd seen Christie's face. A pale disc, unmistakably afraid.

Agnes said, 'Come on,' breaking into a run of her own.

Christie nearly swerved when he saw them, alarm fracturing his face into wide eyes and a flatlined mouth. He hadn't recognized Errol. When Agnes put her arms out, he skidded to a halt ten feet from them. Agnes stopped, Errol close behind.

'What is it, what's happened?'

Freckles stood out on his white face. His hands were trembling at his sides.

'Christie? What's happened?'

'Bricks . . .' His voice was high, scrambled with terror. He jerked his head in the direction he'd been running from – the building site at the bottom of Blackthorn Ashes.

Agnes closed the gap between them, holding out a hand for his. 'Tell me.'

He shied from her hand, his eyes wild on Errol. 'What's he doing here?'

'Hello to you, too.' Errol sounded shaken rather than offended.

'We came looking for you.' She was two feet from her brother, close enough to see his blown pupils. 'Has something happened on the building site? Is someone there?'

Iris. Trevor.

'Christie?'

Her brother's chest was hitching. He kept switching his stare between Agnes and Errol as if he couldn't talk to her while a stranger was here. She half turned towards Errol.

'Give us a minute?'

He nodded and walked away from them.

'Tell me,' she said again.

'Why'd you have to bring him?' Christie put his hands on the backpack's straps, pulling it tight to his body. 'This's our place.'

'And he's our friend. Who're you running from?'

'He's not *my* friend.'

His voice was returning to normal and his face, just a bit tattered at the corners of his mouth where he was trying to summon a scowl that wouldn't come.

Agnes knew that trapped look. It was the same wildness she'd seen in Ruth's eyes last night. She stared across his shoulder to the building site, remembering the day she'd hidden behind a half-built wall while Dad argued with Trevor about the Dearmans. 'Tell me. Or I'll go and see for myself. But Errol's coming with me.'

'Go on then.'

He'd flattened the fear into anger, looking at her with the same hate she'd seen in his face all those weeks while she was trying to convince her family this place wasn't paradise but something else entirely.

'Stay here,' she instructed Christie.

She walked to where Errol was scuffing a foot at the tarmac.

'Come with me? I don't want to do this alone.'

He glanced across at Christie. 'Did he say what freaked him out?'

216

Agnes shook her head. Errol's eyes went to the unfinished end of the estate.

'So we don't know what's down there?'

'He won't say. He's pretending it didn't frighten him. Maybe it's nothing.' She owed it to Errol to forewarn him. 'It could be Trevor.'

'The cowboy?'

'He might've given Christie a scare, to get him to stay away. He doesn't like us being here.'

'He has a point.' Errol bit the inside of his cheek.

'Are you coming? It's probably nothing but I'd like to be sure.'

'Or we could call the police.'

'We're trespassing. Look, if it was looters, we'd have heard them by now. Or seen them. If it's Trevor, I can deal with him. But I wouldn't mind some back-up. He can be a bit of a creep.'

Errol's stare grew sharp then softened abruptly, as if he'd guessed all her secrets in a single swoop. That idea unnerved her more than anything lurking in the houses.

'All right,' he said. 'But he'd better come with us. Unless you want to lose him again.'

Agnes walked back to where her brother was scowling at his phone screen.

'Last chance to tell us what you saw down there before we go and investigate.'

She kept her voice light, giving him a toehold out of his anger.

'I don't know what it is, all right?' His thumbs punched at the phone, his head angled away from her and Errol. 'Thought I heard someone but it was probably just a seagull. It freaked me out so I legged it. You're the one making a big deal of it.'

'Come with us, then.' She waited until he looked up at her. 'If it's no big deal.'

His eyes flickered but he shrugged. 'Fine.' He jammed his phone away, sliding his stare past Errol. '*Jesus . . .*'

He sounded like Trevor and he looked like him, the way he swivelled on his feet, fixing his eyes dead ahead, cocking his hips as if he wore a builder's belt full of tools, or guns.

They walked together to the building site, the rain joining them halfway. By the time they reached the first of the unfinished houses, it was running down the plastic sheeting with a sizzling sound that died abruptly as it landed in the sand.

More rain hit the roof, hissing against the tiles as they approached. Agnes glanced at Christie. His jaw was jutting. He'd made fists of his hands but he dropped them when he saw her looking. The rain made everything smell of iron.

Errol murmured, 'Tell me when we turn and run . . .' He could've been speaking to Christie or Agnes, or to himself. She saw the site through his eyes and it was worse. Haunted.

'Which house?' she asked her brother. 'Where you heard the seagull – can you tell?'

He shrugged. 'Maybe that one.' Pointing away from the first of the unfinished houses to another standing some distance from the others. But his eyes crept back to the first house.

Agnes walked towards the first house, feeling the tug of her brother's resistance at her back. Errol kept step with her, his face fiercely focused, different again from the flamboyant young man at the caravan park and the thin-faced boy on the cliff path.

This place changes everyone, she thought. She was still thinking it when Trevor stepped out of the half-built house, dressed the same as always but unrecognizable, his face pulled sideways.

Errol came to a standstill, the back of his hand touching her wrist.

Christie was two steps behind. When she checked across her shoulder, she saw his mouth open in surprise; he hadn't expected Trevor. Christie saw her looking and shut his mouth with a snap, his teeth grinding together.

Trevor said, 'What the fuck are you doing here – and who the fuck are you?' to Errol. His voice was thick, as if he'd swallowed wet sand.

He stood in the doorway to the house, directly under the lintel. The front of his shirt was dark with rain. Behind him, the aborted living space was solid with shadow, unseeable. Rain seethed softly. It had found a way through the roof into the house.

'What's happened?' Agnes asked him.

Trevor stared at them in turn, his expression switching as it tried for the right expressions: avuncular concern for Christie, narrow suspicion for Errol. He couldn't quite manage it, though, his face unable to hold on to anything.

'Christie thought he heard something. We came to check no one was hurt.'

'You came too late.' Trevor wiped a hand across his mouth. 'You're not the only trespassers.' His voice skidded, braking hard: 'I warned you this place was a death trap.'

Agnes moved closer. 'Let me see.'

He shook his head but stepped aside as if afraid of being touched by her.

Errol was close behind. He seemed to scare Trevor too.

Rain was puddling on the concrete floor of the house. That iron smell again, a brackish taste in her mouth. A heap of bricks had collapsed against the wall with a smaller heap lying huddled at its base: snakeskin tangled with a long chestnut coil of rope.

No, *hair*.

Chestnut hair. Legs twisted under her, arms outstretched, face turned away. Rain fell on her jacket, soaking its pockets. It ran over her smooth, tanned calves, whispering against her wrists.

Iris Edison. *Dead.*

Agnes had never seen a dead body before but it was obvious from the way the wind lifted the flaps on her pockets, and the way the rain ran over her. She was dead. Not dying but dead.

Errol said, 'Have you called an ambulance or the police?' His voice was altered, angry. He was addressing Trevor. 'Have you?'

'Literally just found her, mate.' Trevor snapped the answer. 'So, no.'

Errol pulled out a phone and walked away, out into the rain.

Christie was standing out there. He hadn't tried to enter the house with the others. His face was pale, hair plastered to his head.

Agnes stayed where she was, looking down at Iris.

There was no blood that she could see and no bruises, just a few frail curls, golden-brown against her cheek. A sweet, ripe smell came from her body.

'What happened?' she asked Trevor again.

'D'you not hear what I just told your little friend? *I just got here.*' His voice shook until he closed his teeth around it. 'I've no fucking clue how it happened.'

His boots made a grinding sound as he paced, tracking rain and sand across the floor. Agnes watched him for a moment before she asked, 'How do you think it happened?'

'How do I *think*—?' As if she were quizzing him on astrophysics. 'How the *fuck* would I know?' He gestured savagely at the half-built walls. 'Maybe she went climbing up those bricks and fell. Or she tripped and bashed her head. This place's a fucking death trap. It was all over the news. Why the hell anyone would come poking around here is a fucking mystery to me.'

'But you come. And Christie comes. Looters, too. Did you know her, who she was?'

She watched closely for his reaction.

Trevor shook his head but his rage had a different flavour, off-key. His eyes twitched away from Agnes, up to the roof where the rain was getting through.

'This *fucking* place . . .'

'An ambulance is coming.' Errol ducked back inside. 'Police, too.'

'Well done, Shaft.' Trevor curled his lip.

Errol arched an eyebrow, unmoved. 'They said we're to stay here.' He nodded at Trevor's clenched face and fists. 'You might want to dial down the rampage.'

'Little prick . . .' Trevor pushed past him, out of the house.

Errol came to stand at Agnes's side. 'Are you okay?'

Was she? She should have been more upset, she knew that. Shaking or weeping. What did a normal person do when they found the corpse of someone they'd spoken with just the day before? *A delayed response to sensory stimuli* – could that explain the numbness she was feeling? Her fingers and toes were icy from the rain but there was a dark fizzing in the centre of her chest like the sensation before a storm breaks, a build-up of electricity.

Sand sounded under Errol's feet as he stepped closer, taking her hand in his. He couldn't see the pictures Agnes was seeing, each a bright burst against the blackness in her skull . . .

Laura's kitchen floor littered with smashed plates, sharp shards everywhere like the sand and broken bricks in here, and Agnes with her fingers throbbing, the shape of the shove still hot in her palms. Plates, bowls, cups – all of it knocked from the table to the floor in the frantic second when the scream in her throat wouldn't come out and she'd thought her skull might burst from it. The next second she was on her knees, poleaxed with shame and remorse, picking the shards from the floor, saying, 'I'm sorry, sorry,' over and over again.

Errol let go of her hand and she shivered.

'Where's Christie?' she asked.

'With Trevor. He's okay, I think. I mean . . . He must've seen her, that's why he ran.'

'He didn't do this,' Agnes said automatically.

'What? *No.* Of course not. God . . .'

Errol's feet scraped at the floor.

'Why would she come here?' Agnes stared down at grey puddles, sand silted over cement. 'It was the other houses she was interested in, the ones where people lived. Silverthorn . . .'

'Silverthorn?' Errol echoed.

'Where they lived. Emma and Luke.'

Agnes turned away from Iris. She was tired suddenly, so tired she could hardly see.

'Not here. There wasn't anything here . . .'

'It's a death trap,' Errol said tautly. 'Trevor got that much right. Look at the state of the roof. And there're loose bricks everywhere . . .'

'She was strong.' Agnes shut her eyes for a second. 'She had a mountain bike. She wasn't—'

Going to stop. Iris wasn't going to stop. The hunter's fire in her yellow eyes, that stark single-mindedness. 'If she was murdered, that matters. It should matter to you, too.' She was going to track down the truth of what happened in Blackthorn Ashes, no matter the cost to anyone.

Rain plinked from the cuff of her jacket.

Light fell through the half-finished roof to make the floor shift and dazzle – and to send a shadow leaping from Iris's fingers to touch Agnes's own cold feet.

Nine days before abandonment

———

19

Most days, Dad and Trevor were busy. Christie liked to tag along to lend a hand, even when he hadn't the energy to get out of bed. He'd been helping since before the families moved in, going from house to house with his dad or with Trevor, carrying tools, handing out pliers or spanners or hammers. Trevor let him wear the tool belt sometimes, weighted down with wrenches and batteries. Sometimes, like today, a power cut fritzed a few electrics and that's when Trevor asked if he could borrow Christie while Dad was tied up talking to pen-pushers about insurance.

'He's handy to have around,' Trevor said.

He never treated Christie like a little kid, more like one of his mates down the pub, 'Hold this will you, mate?' handing him a box cutter with a blade so sharp you could slice yourself just looking at it. He expected Christie to use his common sense, 'Fuse switch's tripped. Reset it, yeah?' No crap about taking care up ladders or not touching stuff. Trevor trusted him to get it right.

Once, he gave Christie a claw hammer with a solid steel shaft and told him to hit the shit out of a wall they were having to rebuild because the cement was dodgy. He didn't even make Christie wear safety goggles. Trevor had his own hammer and they went at the wall like a couple of crazies, smashing it until Christie's arm was shouting with pain, his nose stuffed with dust. When he finally stopped, his arm floated up from his side like it weighed nothing without the hammer to hold it down. That was a good day, a great day.

'Nice one, mate.' Trevor had grinned. 'Your dad'd have a fit if he'd seen that. And don't tell your mum. She'll have my balls for a bracelet.'

Christie swore not to tell. He liked keeping secrets with Trevor, who was the smartest person he knew. Not tied down, living as he liked, going on holiday or out drinking, living off takeaways or those microwave burgers Christie was always begging Mum to buy. Lucky in love, too. That's what he told Christie, tonguing his cheek as he said it so Christie knew he was talking about sex. He even won the lottery once, not millions but at least ten thousand. Okay, so he didn't live in Blackthorn Ashes but that was good luck too with all the crap about the lawns and wasps and water pressure.

'Wouldn't live here if you paid me,' Trevor said. He grinned at the look on Christie's face. 'Not having a go, mate, just stating a fact.'

When he was around Trevor, Christie felt the luck rubbing off. That's when he found all the best stuff, for starters. People didn't care what they left lying around. It was the only odd thing about Blackthorn Ashes, back before all the other stuff started – the lack of security. The houses had big windows so you couldn't help seeing all the expensive shit. After dark, you didn't need to be standing right outside to see what was on offer. You could be across the street in your room with a pair of binoculars or that toy telescope you got when you were ten.

Any night after dark you'd lose count of the screens and consoles and iPads, each one lit up like a bat signal. He didn't understand why people didn't put it all away at the end of the day. He locked his stuff in the cupboard Dad built for him, not just his iPad and laptop but the things left lying around in the other houses. Nothing too big or obvious; he didn't steal consoles or phones. Little things like boxes of matches and packets of razor blades, to start with. Later, he took better stuff. Pieces of jewellery, or clothes. To see if he could as much as anything. To see when people would start to notice someone was pinching their stuff, and to see what they'd do about it. No one noticed, not for weeks.

A couple of times, Christie thought Trevor noticed. Like that time he was stuffing a green scarf into his pocket and when he turned round, Trevor was right there in the room with him. Not looking at Christie, busy sizing up the job to be done. If he'd noticed, he didn't say anything.

When they went into the houses, they always ended up in the bedroom. 'Upstairs lights're tripping,' and they'd head up, Trevor leading the way, Christie following.

Trevor'd flick the light switch a couple of times before testing the lamps. He'd sit on the bed and bounce, 'This's seen some action,' or, 'Reckon he does her up against this headboard?' grinning at Christie who always grinned back. Sometimes he beat Trevor to the punchline: 'Reckon she's got carpet burn on her knees from this rug?' and Trevor'd put his head back and laugh until he cried.

After that, Christie went looking for Trevor when he needed a laugh. Everyone else was so serious it gave him toothache. He was used to it from Agnes but now Mum and Dad had gone over to her side. When they weren't whispering in the garage, they were on their phones or laptops looking like the world was about to end. It was doing his head in. Mr and Mrs Dearman throwing a fit about the state of their garden, Felix's dad wanting to know how rain was getting through their walls and windows, not much rain but some and it was a first-class fucking catastrophe, apparently. It started as low-level bitching but levelled up into full-blown outrage.

'These houses are a disgrace!' Mr Dearman stomping round on his crutches to give Dad an earful before breakfast. 'Did they even meet building regulations?'

Dad said he'd call in the builders to come and fix any defects.

'Our warranty covers you for that, but weather damage is different. We've not seen a lot of rain but this heat's taking a toll.'

'You lot'll worm out of anything, if you can.' Dearman was red in the face with rage. 'There's condensation all over my floors from your bloody shonky windows!'

'We'll come round and see what's what. I can promise you that.'

'You wouldn't know a promise if it punched you.' Lifting one of his crutches to jab at Dad.

Christie hoped he'd fall over and break his other leg.

'Fall asleep to the sound of the sea?' He laughed, more like a growl. 'I'm lucky if I sleep for five flaming minutes! We've mould growing up all the curtains.'

Christie wanted Dad to stand up for himself. He'd have liked to see Dad punch Dearman: 'How's that for a promise?' or at least tell him to piss off and let him finish his breakfast in peace. But Dad kept nodding and turning his hands up, saying sorry over and over like Dearman wasn't some nutter spoiling for a fight. It made Christie want to puke.

He went looking for Trevor on the building site.

'Well, Dad's pussy-whipped.'

'I'm not arguing but how's that?' Trevor was rolling a cigarette, packing it tight.

'Luke Dearman.' Christie kicked his foot at a pile of bricks. 'He came round on his crutches to give him shit about his curtains. He reckons the windows are shonky. I bet his wife's the one doing most of the moaning. Who complains about *curtains*?'

'Your dad didn't tell him to do one?' Trevor licked the Rizla, sealing the cigarette. 'I guess you can't fight a man in a plaster cast.'

'He could've stuck up for himself.' He kicked the bricks harder. 'For this place!'

Trevor watched him. Christie thought he'd warn him to stop but he didn't. He put the cigarette in his mouth and lit it with the battered silver lighter he kept in his jeans pocket. Christie liked the noise the lighter made, the thick *clunk* of the flint.

'So Dearman's blaming the building, not the weather. That's what he said?'

'He's blaming Dad for making promises he couldn't keep, said Dad wouldn't know a promise if it punched him in the face. I'd like to punch *him* in the fucking face.'

A year ago, Trevor would've told him not to curse. Now he just watched Christie taking it out on the bricks while he smoked his cigarette.

'Can I have one of those?' Christie asked.

He wanted to be on Trevor's side. Not just for Trevor to be on his. He wanted to be standing here not giving a shit about Luke Dearman or anyone else, smoking and not giving a single shit.

'If you can roll it, sure.' Trevor shrugged. In other words, *no*.

Christie's foot was starting to hurt.

'So how's everyone else? Your mum. Agnes. They survive this heatwave okay?'

'Agnes loves extreme weather, only thing that's more of a diva than she is.'

'Your sister's a diva?'

Trevor streamed smoke from his nose like this was news to him.

'Have you *met* her? 'Course she's a fucking diva.' He gave up on the bricks and started pacing round the concrete floor. 'She's having the last laugh now, with the shonky windows and power cuts. She's been bitching about this place since she saw it.'

His sister was a witch, that's what he wanted to say. Like the ones in *Macbeth* they'd made him study at school. She put cracks in the garden and wasps in the walls. Probably killed Binka, too. And brought on the heatwave that was wrecking the windows. Sitting on the floor in her room making some stupid spell, putting her dead hair and Binka's bones in a bowl, setting fire to the lot. She was such a freak.

'She was gone a long time.' Trevor spat a shred of tobacco from his teeth. 'Eleven years. I guess she's different now.'

'No, she's not, she's exactly the same. You know she's mental, right? On pills for it.'

'For what?'

'She sees stuff. Has these attacks.'

'You mean fits?'

'Panic attacks. Probably had them in London, that's why her girlfriend kicked her out.'

Trevor smoked, watching him pace. 'She has a girlfriend?'

'Had. In London. Not any more.'

'Right.' Trevor looked pissed off, or bored.

Christie wished he'd never mentioned his mad sister. She was such a buzzkill. Trevor would've preferred to swap insults about Luke Dearman, or to be left to smoke in peace. Only a scrap of his cigarette left. He pinched it between the tip of his thumb and finger, sucking the last of the smoke before snapping his fingers to get rid of the ash.

'Any sign of Dearman's wife? Last I heard, she was bitching just as much as him.'

Christie shook his head. 'Just him this morning. D'you think we should check on the other houses? Some of the electrics could be fritzed.'

Trevor gave a short laugh, as if he knew exactly why Christie wanted to get in the houses. Like he'd seen inside the locked cupboard in Christie's bedroom, all the dumb things he'd stolen like women's clothes (not even sexy stuff) and magnets and cheap ashtrays. His neck burnt.

'Your Mum know what you get up to while she's off at work?' Trevor asked.

'She works from home.' He had a sour taste in his mouth, to go with his sore foot.

Trevor was laughing at him but he wouldn't laugh if he knew the whole story, about what'd happened before they moved here, *why* they moved, what his mum called 'the trouble at your school'. Christie should tell Trevor about that, just to see the smile slide off his face, or grow into a grin. Trevor might reach a hand, not to ruffle his hair like he would've a year ago but to grip his shoulder, 'Nice one, mate. No one messes with you.' The temptation to test this theory nearly made him puke. He had to clench his teeth to stop the words coming out. He concentrated on the look on his mum's face if she found out he'd spilt his secrets, never mind to *someone outside the family* because Dad didn't know, at least Christie didn't think he did, and Agnes definitely didn't.

'Tell your mum I was asking after her,' Trevor said. 'I'll call round later, see if I can help your dad retrieve his balls from whichever pouffe they've rolled under.'

It was a joke they'd made in Silverthorn, the day Dearman went into hospital for his broken foot. His wife had this crushed velvet stool the colour of mouldy raspberries. Trevor said it was called a pouffe, 'Better not sit there, you might never shit straight again.' The thought of his dad's balls being under a raspberry pouffe made Christie cringe but at least Trevor thought *he* had balls, at least *he* wasn't pussy-whipped or a diva like Agnes. Probably he could tell Trevor the secret he'd promised Mum he'd never tell and Trevor would say, 'Cool,' and teach him how to roll cigarettes which they'd smoke in here, sitting on the pile of bricks Christie had been kicking, away from all the bitching and panicking because Blackthorn Ashes had turned out not to be paradise after all, like paradise existed anyway let alone in the middle of nowhere in Cornwall.

'Shall we check out the other houses?'

Trevor wiped his hands on his jeans. 'You got your dad's keys?'

Christie dug them from his pocket, seeing Trevor's face split into a grin. 'I've got them.'

4 SEPTEMBER

Ten days after abandonment

———

20

Iris's corpse felt like the only thing in the half-built house.

Agnes couldn't see the collapsed bricks or makeshift work-bench, or the abandoned plans curling in tatters across the floor. She knew these things were there but she could only see Iris. She'd never been close to a dead body before but she guessed they always did this – emptied out the place where they were found until they were the only thing left, all you saw.

'Who found her?' the police wanted to know.

A man and a woman, their hi-vis jackets slick with rain, big black drops of it on their radios and the equipment stashed inside their pockets. Agnes was shutting down by the time they arrived. She'd taken in too much. Iris's brown legs, the long rope of her hair. Trevor's hostility, and Christie's. The relentless falling of rain on Iris's jacket and Iris's skin. She had texted Ruth to let her know what was happening. Christie had shouted at her but she'd done it anyway. Ruth needed to know where they were. No one wanted to wait in the rain but waiting in the house was worse.

'Who found her?'

'That would be me,' Trevor said and the police turned to him, their bodies blocking the view of whatever was happening to Iris now.

More people. Paramedics and two men in suits, one much older than the other. Detectives? The thought of their hands on Iris made Agnes breathless with distress. She shivered next to Errol, Christie a few feet away. She'd tried to stay close to her brother but he'd kept moving off, away. In the end, she'd stopped so he could do the same, at a safe distance from her.

'No idea . . . I was checking the site was secure.' Trevor stood with the police, answering their questions. 'I'd heard talk about looting, sounded worth a check . . .'

A flurry of wind brought the smell of him – sweat and sweet tobacco and a staleness that matched the twist at the edge of his mouth. He was hiding it from the police but he was furious. Agnes didn't understand why unless it was because they were all here, caught up in this. Agnes and Christie and Errol. Trevor had taken against Errol on sight. She could guess the reason for that, Trevor being every kind of bigot rolled into one. 'I've known men like that,' Laura had said, 'blaming everyone else for their problems.' Except Trevor never had problems, his girlfriend always took him back. 'Sandy Bitch,' he called her but she took him back. The sun shone out of him, that's what Christie thought. It was one of the reasons Agnes wished they'd never come here, giving her brother the chance to study his hero at close quarters. Trevor encouraged the hero worship, even when it set Christie against Adrian and Ruth. Sometimes she thought Trevor wanted nothing better than to drive a wedge between his best friend and his son, as if wrecking their family was a goal he'd set himself, starting that summer she was sixteen.

From inside the house, she heard the harsh sound of a zip and knew it was on the heavy black bag they'd brought for Iris's body.

Christie was watching Trevor for clues as to how to behave around the police. For weeks, she'd watched him aping Trevor's mannerisms, cocking his hips, jutting his chin. Even now, with rain blurring his face, Christie had the same sour twist to his mouth.

She shut her eyes and leant into Errol without asking if that was okay. He found her hand, curling his fingers together with hers. She felt a small stab of guilt for taking comfort from him, and for dragging him into this morning's mess.

The policeman was telling Trevor, 'We'll need statements from everyone here.'

The thought of putting into words everything that had happened since she and Errol pushed through the hedge into Maythorn's garden was exhausting. She wanted to lie down in the dark, pull a blanket over her head and rock herself to sleep.

Errol murmured, 'This'll be why I don't leave my room unless I can't help it.'

He meant to lighten the mood but she shrank inwardly. He thought the extent of the damage was trespass and petty theft. He had no idea about the real danger because she'd given him no clue. At least Trevor was giving Christie clues.

Iris had come here to prove one of the deaths was murder, and now she was dead. The police were eyeing Errol with suspicion; he'd been right to remark on the lack of black faces in Blackthorn Ashes. Given the chance, Trevor would deflect in Errol's direction, she knew. Rain ran down the side of her neck, creeping into the collar of her shirt.

She thought of the last time detectives came, for Felix and Chloe and baby Sasha, the sound of Janis screaming, the only sound a parent can make on finding her babies dead. Detectives went in and out of Maythorn all morning. Finally, they brought out the children in small black nylon shrouds. Janis screamed again when they were driven away. The detectives had stood looking at the other houses. Hawthorn where Val and Tim's bodies were waiting, and Silverthorn where Emma lay at the foot of the stairs. Luke was back in hospital after the barbecue, didn't know his wife was lying dead in their new home. Unless he did, unless Iris was right. She'd tried to uncover the truth; it was why she was in the half-built house where the paramedics were huddled away from the worst of the rain. Where was Luke now? Why *had* he stopped demanding recompense from Dad?

'We need to keep this rain out . . .'

The older detective was crouched by Iris's side, the shoulders of his suit black with wet. He had a West Country burr, *rain* rolling from his tongue.

Agnes could hear Errol's heartbeat, light and fast in his chest. He was in shock, scared like her.

She saw it again, the half-formed picture in her head – a red coin purse in Emma's hands as she paid Ruth for the shopping. Agnes had never seen Emma in a green and gold scarf but perhaps that was hers too. Christie was in and out of the houses, almost from the first day.

A cold spot cleared in her chest, making space for this new, intrusive thought: her brother rummaging through Emma's wardrobe, caught red-handed. What would that have done to Ruth?

*

235

In Indigo Park, the rain had brought the mud back to life. Everything was flat, a cardboard cutout of itself. Agnes kept her eyes on the ground to avoid looking; it was her only survival tactic when she felt like this – as if someone was pushing solid blocks of colour and sound and smell into her skull, through her eye sockets and down her ears, up her nose. She was weaving, struggling to stay upright, the duckboards a mudslide of footprints. Errol held her arm to help her. She couldn't feel his hand. She didn't feel real. Paper skin, glass bones, a bursting skull.

Ruth was waiting outside their caravan. 'Christie,' she said, opening her arms for her son. She reached a hand for Agnes too, their fingers brushing in passing.

Errol got Agnes into the caravan, past Dad – bare feet, big toes gritty with sand – and into her bunk. Errol didn't try and have a conversation, didn't ask if she was okay. He unlaced her boots and pulled them off, waiting until she was curled on her side before covering her with a blanket. She couldn't thank him or ask him to stay, the words wouldn't come. Her eyes were squeezed shut, acid pinwheels on the inside of their lids. After a moment the air thinned, and she knew he'd gone.

It was dark when she woke. Not night, just rain falling from a black sky, almost silently, like static after a TV's switched off. The caravan was silent too.

Agnes felt numb and clean, washed right through. She blinked at the wall, tensing for the sound of her family. The bunk above hers was empty. She could smell Christie's socks but there was no flickering across the ceiling from his phone or console. It was strange to lie in bed without his shadow over her.

She rolled upright, waiting a beat before she tried standing.

By moving slowly and keeping her focus narrow – not looking at too much too soon – she was able to navigate the space between the bedroom and bathroom, leaving the light off while she used the lavatory. She washed her hands for a long time, avoiding the mirror and reflective surfaces.

In the kitchen, she clicked on the kettle.

Rain sent shadows over everything, long squirming rivulets down the windows and across the floor. She set two mugs on the counter. Ruth and Christie must have gone out, a trip into town or to the shops. The clock said it was only just 4 p.m., early still.

'Dad, I'm making tea . . .'

She didn't expect an answer but the quiet from the sitting room felt uncanny. She put her head round the door and stopped, her chest crowding with panic.

The sofa was empty, Dad's pyjamas on the pillow.

When she looked, she saw his shoes and coat were missing, too. He'd gone with Christie and Ruth, had he? Leaving her to rest and recover.

She pulled on her jacket and boots, checking for a text from Ruth. Nothing. Her phone needed charging soon but it could wait.

The caravan had been locked from the outside.

She used her key to let herself out into rain that was thick and soupy, not cold as she'd expected. Pulling up her hood, she went across the duckboards to Bette's caravan, knocking on the door. Errol's bedroom was in darkness. After half a minute, Bette answered the door in her pink fleece and red trousers.

'Come out of the rain,' she invited.

'Thanks.' Agnes stayed on the step. 'Is Errol . . . ?'

'Out with Odie.' Bette dusted flour from her hands. The sweet smell of pastry drifted from the kitchen. 'For his sins.'

'His sins?' Agnes echoed stupidly. She wasn't quite awake.

Everything shook at the edges, as if an articulated lorry had passed on the main road above them, the tremors from its tyres only now reaching Indigo Park.

'Come in and wait. He won't be long and you'll cheer him up. He hates walking the dog nearly as much as he hates the rain.'

'I can't right now.' She had to find Dad, and Ruth. 'But can you let him know I called round to say thanks, for earlier?'

Bette nodded. 'If you're sure.'

Agnes wanted to ask her what she knew, whether she'd seen her parents and Christie leave in the car and, if so, which direction they'd taken, whether the police had been round and what Errol had said about Iris's death. But she didn't know how to frame the questions. She returned Bette's smile, retreating down the steps.

Mum's car was missing. It would be suppertime soon. Perhaps they'd gone to get fish and chips. The idea tasted vinegary in her mouth, and idiotic. Ruth knew Christie had seen a dead body. She knew he'd spoken to the police.

Agnes turned in the direction of the groundsman's shed, seeing the big trailers lit up, solid under the rain.

The duckboards sucked at the mud as she walked. The back of her neck was leery, damp inside her hood. She kept hoping to catch sight of Errol and Odie but of course they'd walked the other way, out onto the cliff path.

A shadow moved inside the groundsman's shed, light wobbling

from a torch or phone. She nearly turned back when she saw it but kept walking until her outstretched hand touched the door.

Christie barrelled out of the shed, pushing past, too fast for her to stop him.

She turned to follow but a hand grabbed her arm, 'No you don't,' hauling her inside, slamming the door shut, dragging her hood from her head.

Broken furniture piled behind him, a mountain range made of peaks and valleys.

The windows were dim but she saw his eyes, pale as pencil beams. The front of his shirt was soaked with rain. He smelt like a thunderstorm.

'Came looking for your swag, did you?'

Trevor bared his teeth at her. 'Too late.'

To her right, the filing cabinet stood open and empty. Christie hadn't been wearing his rucksack when he pushed past her. There were no bags by Trevor's feet. The cabinet had been emptied by someone else. All of Christie's treasure taken, by someone else.

'What've you done?' She was glad her voice was steady despite the skittering of her pulse, all the blood jumping to her feet and fingers. 'What's wrong with Christie?'

'Your little brother's pissed off.' Trevor dug a hand into his pocket, taking out his tobacco tin. 'I guess he got a fright earlier.'

That's how he chose to describe Iris's corpse. *A fright.*

'Why are you here?' she demanded.

'My assistance was required.' A glint from the tin as he flicked it open with his thumb. 'To get rid of certain . . . evidence.'

'Required by who?'

'You've no idea what's really going on, have you?'

He ran his stare over her as he rolled a cigarette, the task so familiar he didn't need to look down as he pinched tobacco into the paper.

'You come back after eleven years in London with your *girl-friend*,' speaking the word like an obscenity, 'expecting to pick up where you left off. Telling lies, fighting with your mum, tearing it all down. But you haven't the first idea what's going on.'

Agnes had caught a flash of Christie's face as he'd pushed past her – strained and white, anger and fear slogging it out for pole position. Dad was gone from the caravan. Ruth, too. Where were they? And why leave Christie alone with Trevor, when he was the one found standing over Iris's body in the derelict house? How many warnings did her mother need about the sort of man he was?

'So tell me,' she said. 'What's going on, if you know so much about it?'

Trevor propped his shoulders against an empty strip of wall. He was enjoying himself, relaxing into his old role as her tormentor.

'Ask your mum.'

'Or I could ask the police.' Her palms were crawling but she kept her expression blank. 'I bet they know a thing or two by now. About Iris Edison, if nothing else.'

'I'm not talking about her.' A flare of anger as if she'd dropped a stone in the road, forcing him to steer around it rather than follow-ing the path of his choosing.

'Why not?'

Because you killed her?

Trevor put the cigarette between his lips, snapping his lighter. The flame threw mad shadows around them for a second before the darkness crowded back in.

'She was here,' Agnes said. 'Two nights ago.'

She let her gaze travel around the shed. 'I hope you wore gloves while you were clearing it out.' She rested her eyes back on his.

His face contracted into an expression she'd never seen before, a sort of savage hunger. Not for her – for something she couldn't see. She'd thought she knew what he'd wanted when he dragged her in here but it wasn't that simple. He wasn't the same man he'd been when she was sixteen. He wasn't even the same man he'd been yesterday.

'We sat out there.'

She gestured through the window to where the field was black under the rain.

'Me and Iris. And we talked. About Blackthorn Ashes, what really happened there.'

His mouth sneered around the cigarette. 'Like you know anything about that.'

'I know you're hoping my dad will take the blame.'

He blinked, refocused on her. 'What?'

'My dad, your best friend. You're hoping he'll be the one who goes to prison, not you.'

Smoke streamed from Trevor's nose. He'd gone very still, waiting to hear what else she'd say.

She was close to the truth, closer than she'd imagined. It gave her an edge but she could undo it by saying too much. Better to let him talk, give her the evidence she needed.

When he didn't speak, she said, 'He told me about the pair of you, what you were like in college. Best friends, taking on the world. The two of you against the world.'

Until Ruth. Until me.

'Yeah?' He laughed without humour. 'Look at us now.'

The college detour was a welcome relief, which meant this was nothing from the past. It was something here and now, breathing with them in the shed's strange dryness as the world thundered with rain outside.

'It can't be easy to turn on your best friend after all these years. And there's Christie – you care about him, I know you do.'

That was better, closer. His left hip tightened, his foot stirring at the leaves on the shed's floor.

'He looks up to you.'

Trevor took the cigarette from his mouth and looked at it before putting it back between his lips.

'So? What's your brother got to do with any of this?' He relaxed his hip, rocking his shoulders back into the wall. 'How cold you are, how cold . . .' A sing-song sneer.

It was a game they'd played when she was sixteen. *How warm you are . . .*

She learnt a lot that summer. Didn't he know how much you learn when someone puts his hands on you? He'd taught her all about him.

'Christie's a part of this or you wouldn't be here. You'd let my dad take the blame. Or Ruth, although you were close to her too, once upon a time. But Christie? Christie's different.'

He eyed her through the dying smoke. His cigarette was done, just an ashy twist of paper sticking to his bottom lip.

'Christie,' he said, 'is a fucking nightmare.'

It took her by surprise, a choppiness in her throat. What did he know?

'Yeah.' Trevor nodded. He picked the scrap of ash from his lip.

'You're out of date there, too. Still thinking your kid brother's into trains or models, all that shit. He grew up. Did it so quickly it left scorch marks.' He pointed a thumb at the filing cabinet. 'You knew about that, the stealing.'

'Stealing isn't *growing up*.'

'Stealing's the least of it.'

He shoved away from the wall, his shoulders uncurling like a cat's. 'We could talk about Christie, or about your mum and dad.' Closing the distance between them but slowly, at a prowl. 'I could catch you up on the last eleven years, and the last eight weeks.'

'In exchange for what?' She held him off with a look. 'Sex?'

Such a small word but it filled the shed, the sibilant like the rain which was licking at the windows, trying to find its way inside.

'If that's what you want.' Trevor shrugged. 'It was always about what you wanted, remember?'

'No. It was about what you took.'

He was right up against her now, breathing smoke.

'You wanted me to take it, An-*yes*.'

'I didn't know what I wanted.' She stood her ground, cold-fishing him because fighting never worked, only ever made him hungrier, more grabby. 'I was a child.'

'At sixteen? You were never a child, that's what Ruth says.'

Her mother was right here between them, the way she'd always been and always would be, until Agnes put a stop to it. This wasn't about Trevor. He was a distraction, a detour. She had better things to be doing.

'Ruth is wrong about a lot of things.' She reached for the door. 'You should pay attention to that. If she asked you to help clear up this mess,' nodding at the filing cabinet, 'it's because she has a use for you. It's nothing to do with loyalty, or blackmail.'

'I'm blackmailing her?' Trevor stayed where he was, laughing. 'That's your excuse for how she behaved back when you were sixteen?'

He raised his voice as she walked away. 'Ask her again!'

Agnes stepped out into the rain. It was changed, colder now, fresh against her face. She left her hood down, let the wet run over her head as she walked away, taking care on the duckboards, not wanting to slip in case he caught up with her. She couldn't hear him following, just the hum of electricity from the big trailers. The lights were on in Errol's bedroom. She moved in that direction, stopping when she heard Ruth's car parking up.

Dad climbed from the passenger seat with his head down, shoulders caved. Ruth paused at the driver's side, slamming the door, her eyes on Agnes.

Footfall from behind their caravan.

Christie, stopping short when he saw his sister. A warning zipped between him and Ruth, quick and clear as death.

No one moved, all three of them standing there, under the thinning rain. After a second, Dad lifted his head to join the other two, staring at her.

Three sets of eyes on her face, so familiar and so alien.

Her family.

Strangers.

21 AUGUST

Four days before abandonment

***

21

After the street party, Blackthorn Ashes changed again. Not just the people – circling one another at a distance, staying indoors – the houses changed too. When Agnes walked home from the woods, Redthorn and Silverthorn seemed to turn away, hunching against the skyline. An undercurrent of violence ran from house to house, its high-frequency vibration charging the air. Blackthorn Ashes was on the brink of something.

Chloe Mason cried a lot since the incident in the sandpit, all her happy ferocity gone. Agnes was used to her piling out of the car after a day on the beach, sand in her hair, ice cream on her chin, bickering with her brother. Felix holding her toy just out of reach as she jumped and shouted, 'Give it *back*!' Baby Sasha lifted from her car seat, little head and legs lolling, fast asleep. Maythorn used to ring with the sound of them shouting and playing but now it echoed with the thin noise of Chloe's weeping.

Most days, Agnes crept away as soon as it was light. To the beach or deep into the woods. The summer she was sixteen, she lived on the beach. Ruth, expecting a new baby, had no time for her when all they did was fight. Agnes knew she should be glad of the break in hostilities, that she was no longer the sole focus of her mother's attention. But Ruth's judgement – so quick and piercing – turned out to be the thing keeping her grounded. Without it, she began to spiral. It started as fretfulness, a small fraying at the edges of everything. Her hands shook, she got dizzy for no reason. She paced, picking things up then putting them down. Colours hit her in sharp little slaps, stinging the skin around her eyes. Smells and sounds did the same. Ruth's sudden silence ripped a hole in her routine. Words she was used to saying or shouting died behind her teeth, leaving a foul taste. The beach was the best place to spiral. If she lay flat on the sand and shut her eyes, she could feel the world tilting under her, taking her with it. Grass was too soft and full of thrumming life. The beach was hard, impacted sand with no give in it. The beach was like Ruth.

Agnes didn't sunbathe. She wore long-sleeved T-shirts and jeans, covering her head and face with a wide-brimmed hat. Like that, she could spend all day with the sun drilling down. It wasn't good for her but she wasn't looking for *good* – she was looking for *the same*.

'Nice tan,' Trevor joked when he saw her returning one afternoon.

The heat was draining out of the day, her limbs weak and trembling. He was on the path in front of her, smoking a cigarette. All of a sudden, she was freezing cold.

He reached a hand to touch the base of her throat. 'Goosebumps.' He lifted his thumb as if she should be able to see her goosebumps imprinted on his skin.

He wore bleached jeans and a white T-shirt that gleamed so

hard it was fluorescent. He was long and lean and roped with muscle. She was afraid of him, for the first time.

The cigarette hung from his lips; she could taste it, bitter on her tongue. She could smell the sea's salt in his hair. He slouched his hips, tucking his thumb into the belt loop on his jeans, holding smoke in his mouth before letting it stream from his nose. In the smoke, she saw dragons, and lizards on arid rocks. Dizzy from the sun, the tips of her fingers were cold and clenched.

Every evening, he was there waiting for her to come up from the beach. The first few times he pretended it was coincidence, talking about her mum and dad, the new baby that was coming. After a day or two, he stopped talking and started touching. Hardly at all to begin with, a finger and thumb plucking a thread of seaweed from her shoulder, a palm dusting sand from her sleeve. It was hard to find places he could touch bare skin, she was always so overdressed.

'Don't you get hungry?' he asked after touching her throat. 'You're down there all day.'

She shook her head but her gut griped as if it had needed this reminder. Ruth was the one who prompted her to eat, and to take her meds. She was busy nesting, that's what Dad called it, folding tiny vests and muslin squares, packing and repacking her suitcase for the hospital. 'I was stupid to try and have you at home,' she'd said. 'A first baby and I was only nineteen. I know better now.'

Trevor leant nearer, tapping ash from his cigarette onto the stony path under their feet. 'You must be hungry.' He stayed close, half turning his head to look out at the sea, his profile taut. He smelt of leather. She saw hawks and gauntlets.

'I should get back.'

Her skin was twitching, restless. Her throat burnt where he'd put his thumb. A strange pain sat in the pit of her stomach, the place she'd seen Ruth massaging with the palm of her hand. 'The baby's head,' she'd murmured, as she massaged herself.

Everything was badly blended, colours and flavours running into one another, sweet and sour and salty all at once.

'I need to get back,' she repeated.

To Ruth and their holiday home, crowded out with the *any-day-now* new baby, the air parched and thorny. Ruth was so changed, monstrously calm. Sitting on the sofa as if the baby were already in her lap, her bump so big it was always in the way. Lying on the bed with her sweat running into the pillows, smelling of milk and blood. Everything about her was alien, frightening.

Agnes tried to move past Trevor but he was too solid, his shadow a long furrow of shade, looking like a place she could rest. He'd soaked up the day's sun, his skin spicy with it.

'Come back to my place,' he said indifferently. 'There's beer in the fridge. I can cook steaks, give your mum a night off.'

The beers were frosty. She drank from the bottle, holding the glass to the side of her neck, under the fall of her hair. His caravan was bigger than theirs, all sleek silver surfaces. The steaks were bloody, rich with butter. Her chin, greasy, had to be wiped.

'Come here,' he said.

His fingers were hot and dry, moving over her. Pink paint had dried on the heel of his left hand. She put out her tongue to taste it. It tasted of the shelves Dad had built for her, back at home.

Christie was born the next day. Quickly, in the hospital. One minute Ruth was huffing out breaths while Dad held her hand, the next she was taken to the labour ward, leaving her last huff hanging with a feather from her pillow, turning slowly as it fell towards the floor. The next time Agnes saw the pillow it was propping her new brother to her mother's breast. Christie was red and skinny, his face squashed into a terrible shape they said was normal, the shape he made coming out of their mother. Everything was worse after that. Mess and stains and strange noises in the night; Agnes was less afraid of Trevor than she was of Ruth and Christie.

In Blackthorn Ashes, baby Sasha was pink and sleepy, her head lolling in the car seat, a sunhat strapped under her chin. Agnes watched the Masons the way she always watched other families, searching for clues in the shapes they made.

Chloe and Felix trailed into the house, their mother following with Sasha. Barry locked the car, lingering over the task as if to delay the moment he'd join them in the house. Agnes watched him bend to brush sand from the car seats, opening the boot to check inside before closing it again, resting his hand there for a long moment. He looked as if he wanted to get back into the car and drive away, keep driving. He was poisoned, she found out later. They all were.

It explained the tiredness that came like a cloud to blot out the sales-brochure sunshine. Ruth's sore eyes, Dad's chest pains, Christie's headaches. Maybe it explained the way Barry leant against the car that afternoon, looking as if he'd give anything to escape. If he'd known how near he was to losing his children, he'd have raced inside, holding out his arms to gather them one last time. It was terrible to think like that, of lost chances, moments you could never have back. Eleven years of seeing her father's smile, of watching Christie grow, trying to mend what she and Ruth had broken. Eleven years of wishing she'd taken the turn on the stony path, away from Trevor and back to them.

Eleven days after abandonment

22

That night, Agnes didn't sleep. Lying in the bunk below Christie, alert to every sound her brother made – playing on his phone, falling asleep, waking and playing again.

The shadows on the ceiling shifted as the rain cleared overnight, weather moving inland from the sea. Indigo Park fell quiet just before dawn. Until then there was the hum from the trailers and a smatter of voices, sometimes raised, sometimes whispering, under the soundtrack of rain on plastic roofs. Christie wasn't speaking to her. Dad wasn't speaking to anyone.

'What's happened?' she'd asked her mother yesterday, after Ruth had locked the car and they were all inside the caravan. 'What is it?'

Ruth shook her head, 'Not now,' as if she were a child who couldn't be trusted with the information which was destroying her parents' faces, making them unrecognizable.

She waited for Errol to return from walking Odie, intending to escape to Bette's for a nightcap. She was desperate to talk with him about Iris. But Ruth was watching her too closely.

'No one's leaving here tonight,' she said.

She'd wanted to tell her mother to go to hell, she was an adult and would do as she pleased, but the look on Ruth's face shut her up. Something terrible was happening. Worse than Iris, worse than Trevor threatening to bring it all down around them. *No one's leaving here tonight.*

Dad stood blinking at the sofa until Ruth slipped her arm through his and walked him away to the big bedroom at the back of the caravan. Agnes followed her brother, to their bunks.

Now Christie muttered in his sleep, rolling onto his side in the bunk above her.

Dawn drew lines across the ceiling, slight and wavering. She waited another half an hour before she slid from the bunk, still dressed in her clothes from yesterday. She crouched to find her shoes, staying down until she was sure Christie was asleep. Easing the door open, she looked for light coming from the other rooms. The caravan was in darkness. She slipped from the room, soundless on her bare feet.

In the sitting room, she saw the empty sofa pricked with half-light from the windows. Dad was sleeping in the double bed with Ruth for the first time since they moved to Indigo Park. Where did Ruth take him in her car yesterday, and with what purpose? He was in her bed now, as if she were afraid to let him out of her sight.

Ruth wasn't afraid of anything, that's what Agnes had come to believe. But, of course, it wasn't true. Everyone was scared, sooner or later, of something or someone. No one lived their whole life without feeling fear.

'What're you doing?' Ruth had wrapped a cardigan over her pyjamas. Her voice was low, her eyes cutting to the rooms where Dad and Christie were sleeping.

Agnes turned. 'I couldn't sleep.'

They stared at one another across the unlit space.

'Go back to bed,' her mother instructed finally.

'I'd rather go for a walk.'

'It's pitch black out there.'

Agnes wanted to say, 'It's worse in here,' but she knew better than to argue with Ruth in this mood. Pushing past her mother would be impossible, like pushing at a cliff face. Agnes was nearer to the door, she might make it out of the caravan if she was quick. But she was too tired to try, soaked through with an exhaustion that felt like fever.

'Why did you take Dad away? Yesterday, in the car. Where did you go?'

'Go to bed.' Ruth looked exhausted too, her face burning white. 'We'll talk in the morning.'

'Why don't you trust me?' It came out like a whine, her sixteen-year-old voice.

'You took your brother back to that place.' Ruth's voice clamped down. 'Day after day.'

'He wanted to go. I couldn't stop him.'

'Did you try?' Ruth didn't blink, not an inch of give in her anywhere.

'He's scared. You don't know what he's like when you're not here.'

'I don't know what he's like?'

The echo in her mother's voice meant something. She was saying *Agnes* was the one who didn't know. Agnes was the one in the dark. Trevor had said the same thing in the shed yesterday: 'You haven't the first idea what's going on,' he'd said.

'It was you.' Like a light coming on in her head: that bristle of attention every time she and Christie walked the cliff path. 'Watching us. Whenever we went to Blackthorn Ashes. It was you.'

Not in town, looking for work. Or not all day. How long could it take to read the noticeboards in the shops in a town that size? An hour, maybe. But not *hours*. Not all day.

Ruth let her shoulders drop. 'What?'

'We were being watched, I could tell. But I never saw anyone . . . It was you. You didn't go into town. Not always, anyway. You followed us because you didn't trust me to take care of him.'

'I was right, wasn't I? You couldn't take care of him. You didn't.'

'If you knew, why didn't you stop it? Why let us keep going back?'

But her mother wouldn't answer, her face closed again, its expression wiped clean. Both of them were listening for sounds from the other rooms, of Christie, of Dad.

Dawn was right around the caravan now, the day crouching just out of reach. The sun would be up soon. Agnes would pack a bag and leave. She'd say goodbye to Errol then she'd walk to the bus stop and on, to the train station. Board a train to London. Not to Laura unless she had no other choice but far away from here, as far as she could get. Because no good could come of this. She knew her mother. No good was coming.

'Go back to bed,' Ruth said.

In their bedroom, Christie was awake, playing on his Game Boy.

'Did you fix this?'

Agnes nodded and he said, 'Thought so, thanks.'

His smile was sleepy, contented. She couldn't leave him, how could she?

She said, 'You're welcome,' and her brother tucked the console under his pillow, folding himself back down to sleep.

Adrian lay very still as Ruth climbed back into the double bed. He kept his breathing deep, his face slack against the pillow, feigning sleep for the time it took her to settle.

She'd been arguing with Agnes. He'd heard the rise and fall of their whispers in the other room. It'd taken him back to the summer Agnes was sixteen, the summer Christie was born. Ruth had insisted they go away, despite the nearness of her due date. Cancelling their annual holiday and staying home would be an admission of defeat and Ruth hated to admit defeat. So they went away, despite the heat and the hugeness of her belly, the looming prospect of an early birth. And Trevor went with them because that's what they'd done for years, the three of them a family long before Agnes and Christie were born. Adrian and Ruth usually took a room in a B&B, Trevor sleeping in his tent because he didn't want to pay for a bed. Later he got the campervan and kitted it out, 'Saving myself a small fortune in the long run, and no house rules about who I can have back in my bunk,' winking at Adrian, eyeing whichever blonde was behind the bar. The blondes always winked back. Everybody loved Trevor.

In the caravan, Adrian breathed through his mouth, as silently as he could.

Next to him, Ruth lay with her eyes open. He could hear her blinking, could almost hear the cogwheels in her head as she tried to find a way out of this. He'd told her, 'It's over,' but she wouldn't accept it, wouldn't even admit it. Trevor had helped empty the shed where Christie was keeping the things he'd stolen from Blackthorn Ashes.

'Not a problem, mate,' Trevor said.

It was what he always said. He'd said it about everything that went wrong with the houses, from a loose screw to a wall that needed rebuilding. He said it when Adrian had to apologize for Agnes, who'd refused to sit down to a meal with them because Trevor was at the table. She'd been happy to be back with them, as happy as they were to have her home. But she'd wrapped her arms around herself and turned away, that happiness wrenched from her face because Trevor was there.

'Not a problem, mate.'

Adrian's chest convulsed, snatching at air because he'd forgotten to keep breathing. He turned the noise into a snore, rolling away from Ruth to face the wall. Now he could open his eyes like her, blinking into the blackness.

'We're saying nothing,' she'd told him yesterday. 'To Agnes, or Trevor. This stays between us.'

But it was too much for them, he'd told her that. They'd needed Trevor to help them carry it, the way Adrian had needed Trevor to help sell the houses in Blackthorn Ashes, and to try and fix the things which went wrong. Trevor made it all seem much less than it was, like someone folding a huge ordnance map into a neat square small enough to be slipped into a pocket.

'It's an illusion,' Ruth had snapped. 'Trevor isn't our friend. He certainly isn't yours,' but when Adrian pressed her to explain, she shut up, telling him to do the same.

Not a problem, mate.

He pressed his thumbnail into his palm until it sent a flare of pain spreading through his hand. In the other bedroom, Agnes was in the bunk below Christie, waiting for the morning to come. Adrian could feel the hum of her through the wall. Since Black- thorn Ashes, he felt his family more keenly than ever. Where they were, if they were close by or faraway. He'd known before Ruth that they went back to the houses, Christie looting the deserted rooms while Agnes kept watch.

Ruth thought he didn't notice things any longer, that he lived under a cloud of remorse, sedating himself with daytime television and endless cups of tea. But he saw more than she did, more than she allowed herself to see.

'This stays between us,' but it was already too big. Sprawling across the double bed and out into the sitting room, filling the bedroom where Agnes was waiting and Christie was sleeping – the only one of them who could. It sprawled and spread and stretched its arms through the caravan's windows and out into the dark, into the fields and across the cliffs to the sea.

23 AUGUST

Two days before abandonment

———

23

After the street party, Christie got given a curfew.

It was dumb, just because Chloe cut herself in the sandpit and Dearman was back in hospital after cooking his arm on the barbecue which'd actually been pretty fucking funny at the time. The curfew was a way of keeping him home where they could watch him. Mum had guessed what he was up to. She'd figured it out. Well, it was about time.

He'd been with Trevor down on the building site, helping make it secure after the party. 'It's all coming a bit unstuck,' Trevor said but he didn't look that bothered, asking Christie to help him fix batteries in the alarms for smoke and carbon monoxide.

'Some of the alarms look dodgy,' he said.

Christie carried the batteries while Trevor climbed the ladder to fit them. He'd expected Trevor to hand down the dodgy batteries but most of the alarms didn't have batteries fitted in the first place. Christie kept his mouth shut about that. More people should keep their mouths shut, Trevor said.

When he got home, Mum was waiting in his bedroom, sitting in his gaming chair next to the cupboard Dad built.

'Where's the key to this?'

She was in her green dress. He'd liked the dress when she bought it but she didn't look good in it any more with her scaly wrists and neck. There were gross bags under her eyes. She looked old and angry, like Dearman's wife.

'The key to this cupboard. Where is it?'

'I lost it.'

It was an excuse he'd dreamt up for when she asked about the key. He'd known she'd ask, sooner or later. He was surprised it'd taken her this long.

'Don't lie to me.'

'I'm not fucking lying!' He kicked the foot of the cabinet where his Ultramarines were watching. He was sick of being treated like a kid. Sick to death.

'Don't use language like that.' She narrowed her eyes. 'I'm warning you . . .'

'Warning me *what*? Not to lose stupid keys to stupid cupboards that don't have anything in them anyway? This's *dumb*.'

'Sit down. And be quiet.'

'You're the one asking questions! In *my* chair. Where're I'm even supposed to sit?'

'Christie.' She pointed at his bed. 'Sit down.'

He flung himself on the bed, lying full length because it was *his* room, she was trespassing. So much for having privacy here. He put an elbow across his eyes so he didn't have to look at her. She was staring at him, he could feel it, like she didn't know where to start, even though she did. They'd done all this before, in the old house, while Blackthorn Ashes was being built. Before his sister came home from London. Back when there were no houses, let alone alarms with no batteries in them to warn people about carbon monoxide and smoke and everything else.

'I spoke with Emma Dearman,' Mum said.

His stomach flipped. 'Who?'

'Mrs Dearman, from Silverthorn.'

'The one with the mad husband.' He kept his elbow across his eyes, bouncing the heel of his trainer on the bed. It made him tired, though. Trying to be mad at her. It made him really tired. 'The old bastard who's always round here talking shit at Dad.'

'What did I *just say* to you, about language?' She was hissing now, like one of those imaginary sounds Agnes kept hearing. Gas escaping, or a snake in the walls.

'What about Emma Dearman?'

He wanted to get it over with so he could go back to the building site and hang out with Trevor. He'd had enough of his family.

'She's found things missing from her house.'

Mum was taking care suddenly, tiptoeing around the real reason he was in trouble. She was going to drag this out to make a point.

'So? What's that got to do with me?'

'It was after you'd been in her house, helping Trevor fit a handrail to make it easier for Luke to get up and down the stairs while he's on crutches.'

'We shouldn't have bothered. He can fall down and break his bloody neck for all I care.'

Silence. His heart was making fists in his chest. It really, really hurt. He was probably having a heart attack because of this, because Emma Dearman was as much of a bitch as her husband.

Mum said slowly, 'She's missing a scarf.'

He wanted to shout at her, rage at the unfairness – how

everything was always his fault – except the rage was draining from him like she'd stuck a knife somewhere and he was bleeding out. Every second she was in his room, he felt weaker and more tired. Why didn't she go away?

'Someone stole the scarf. It was expensive. A purse was taken too.'

'So?'

'So I'd like the key to this cupboard. I'd like to look inside.'

'I told you, it's empty.'

'Christie.'

Her voice was a warning: *last chance.*

The purse had been stupid, he knew that. People always freaked out over money. But Emma Dearman was a cow for going to Mum, making accusations when she couldn't possibly know it was him. He wished he'd taken more stuff, that he'd done what burglars did – pissed in her wardrobe or shat on her pillows. He wished he was back there right now, telling her what he thought of her, *showing* her what he thought . . .

'Christie, look at me.'

He kept his elbow over his eyes. If he concentrated, he could see himself in Silverthorn with Trevor, that day he helped out. He'd had a handful of screws arranged in his palm, magnetic heads facing outwards. It felt impossible now, that he'd ever had the energy to do that. Arrange the screws or pass them to Trevor, or plug the electric drill into the socket at the top of the stairs.

'Careful,' Trevor had warned, 'that flex's dangerous. Someone trips, they're going to make a mess on the floor down there.'

'Look at me, Christie. I'm asking you about Mrs Dearman . . .'

Fuck Mrs Dearman.

That's what he was seeing as Mum kept up her interrogation – the handrail half finished like the houses down the bottom of the estate. The drill's flex strung like a tripwire across the top of Silverthorn's stairs, floorboards at the bottom sticky and spreading red.

5 SEPTEMBER

Eleven days after abandonment

———

24

'Go back to bed,' Ruth had said and Agnes did as she was told, falling asleep in the small hours. When she woke, the sun was up and the bunk above hers was empty, Christie gone. She'd dreamt of him ransacking the houses in Blackthorn Ashes. In her dream, he was a giant, not a boy, lifting roofs and rummaging his hands inside, bringing up furniture and fireplaces, a whole staircase, fistfuls of wire hanging like entrails from his fingers.

She sat on the side of the bunk, rubbing sleep from her shoulders. Stupid to think the scavenging was the extent of it, that he had no other secrets. Stupid to have imagined herself his trusted accomplice, kept close from nostalgia or in the hope of mending their broken relationship. He was clenched with secrets, she saw that now. Further away from her than ever. Whispering in the shed with Trevor who was his first and preferred accomplice, whose poison was in his blood and had been for months. The boy she was remembering hadn't existed for a long time.

In the caravan's bathroom, she washed her face and hands and armpits, brushing her teeth to get rid of the night's taste. The bathroom was foggy from someone else's shower. She had to wipe the mirror before she could see herself in it. From the cabinet, she took her meds, measuring each dose carefully, chasing the pills with a handful of water. She changed her underwear and top, choosing a long-sleeved T-shirt. She could smell bacon frying; someone was making breakfast.

Ruth, she guessed, but she was wrong.

Dad was in the kitchen, in his work clothes, using a spatula to turn bacon in the frying pan.

'Morning, love.' His voice was rusty with disuse, his smile rusty too. 'Sleep okay?'

'Can I help with that?' she offered.

He shook his head. 'You sit down. There's coffee in the pot.'

Agnes caught a flash of summers long ago, before Christie, before things with Ruth began to unravel. Sitting in a caravan like this one, swinging her sandalled feet under the table, digging her spoon into a big bowl of Rice Krispies, snapping and crackling on her tongue. Mum and Dad laughing, leaning into one another. She'd taken it all for granted. The breakfast and the sunshine waiting outside, her happy family. It hadn't occurred to her that she was lucky or that she should fix any of it in her mind because one day it would all be gone, out of her reach.

Dad turned the bacon in the pan. 'This's nearly done . . .'

Her mouth flooded with the memory of marmalade sandwiches and milky coffee from a flask carried to the beach with towels and windbreakers, inflatable armbands. 'Kick your feet! That's it . . . That's it, kiddo. You're swimming!' Salt water stinging a cut on her foot where she'd stepped on a razor shell. Dad carrying her across the pebbles, Ruth bundling a towel around her, dusting sand from between her toes with talcum powder shaken from a pink and white bottle.

Agnes gripped the edge of the table, fighting a blaze of tears. Her family . . .

She'd do anything for them. Not from nostalgia or as penance but because they were broken and hurting and she loved them, she'd never stopped loving them.

She sat, filling a cup from the coffee pot with her hands shaking, watching her father at the stove. He'd showered, his hair damp at the collar of his shirt which was full of square creases as if he'd taken it fresh from a suitcase. His jeans hung at his hips from the weight he'd lost. He added two eggs to the frying pan, flinching as fat spat at his hand. Bacon and eggs. She couldn't remember the last time she'd eaten either but she'd have to eat these, Dad was trying so hard to get it right. Ruth must have talked with him last night when they were driving back to Indigo Park after dumping Christie's treasure from the shed. She could hear her mother's steady voice listing the rules, rearranging everything to make space for this fresh danger. Had she told Dad to take care of Agnes, keep her from asking too many questions?

'Drink up.' Dad's smile was forced. 'We caffeine fiends must stick together.'

She swallowed a mouthful of coffee. The police would be coming to Indigo Park, one of the last places Iris was seen alive. What had Ruth done with Christie's treasure, dumped it in litter bins a long way from here? She couldn't picture a safe enough place but she could picture her mother's panic: a cold thing, in the process of being frozen. Ruth wouldn't let it ride her, not for long.

She'd taken Dad from here yesterday to be sure he understood the danger they were in.

'Breakfast is served.' He put the plate down with a clumsy flourish that tugged at her heart.

'Thanks.' She took up her fork, breaking the eggs, yellow yoke running to the edge of the plate. 'Where's Mum, and Christie?'

'They went into town.' Dad pulled out a chair and sat with his own plate, looking at the food as if he had no idea where to start with it. 'He needs a few things for school.'

She ate a mouthful. 'What happened yesterday?' The eggs tasted slippery, salty.

'Yesterday?' He began loading his fork, a tremor in his fingers.

'You went out in the car, you and Mum.'

'Oh, yes. Just for a spin . . .' He filled his mouth as if he wanted an excuse to stop talking.

Swinging her sandalled feet under a table like this one, cereal snapping in her bowl. Dad and Ruth leaning into one another by the window, sunshine trapped in her mother's hair, Dad's lips against Mum's neck, kissing. Milk, on her own chin. Something tugging at her mouth, she reached for the memory – a smile. She was smiling, swinging her feet as the caravan filled with sunshine and her parents leant into one another and whispered, their faces hidden from her.

Bette answered the door in olive jeans and a jade-green jumper. 'He's in his room but he's decent, you can go on in. I'll make a pot of tea.'

'And biscuits,' Errol called.

The caravan smelt of porridge and oranges. Odie looked up from the kitchen floor before putting his head back down. 'You go on,' Bette said. 'I'll bring a tray.'

'There's no need. I just ate a big breakfast.'

'He didn't.' Bette nodded in the direction of Errol's room. 'And it's making him teazy,' using a Cornish word to describe her grandson's scratchy mood.

Errol was sitting on the bed in his slashed jeans and red jumper, scrolling through his phone. He moved his bare feet out of the way so Agnes could settle herself there.

'I wanted to say thanks, for yesterday.'

He fired a look from under his eyelashes then lowered his phone. 'What's happened?'

'Nothing.' She felt a prickle of surprise that softened swiftly to relief. He could read her and she was glad. 'Dad made breakfast. First time he's done that in weeks.'

'Where's your mum?' Errol held the phone against his thigh, tension in his neck and shoulders. 'And your brother?'

'They went into town.'

He reached a finger to flick at his ankle, dislodging a dog hair. 'And you're all right?'

'Yes. Are you?'

'Well, the dead body was a surprise but more for me than you; I wasn't there for the others—' He broke off when Bette knocked at the door. 'Hello?'

His grandmother swept the beaded curtain to one side, bringing the promised tray with two brown glazed mugs of tea and a plate of ginger biscuits. She set the tray on the bedside table. 'Eat,' she told Errol firmly.

'You bet.' He reached for the biscuits.

It sounded like an old joke between them: *You, Bette. Me, Errol.* His grandmother rolled her eyes, bending to pick a pair of socks from the floor before leaving them alone. The curtain swayed in her wake, beads tapping. Agnes reached for the tea. The mug was a lovely shape, perfect for cradling. The tea was scented, Earl Grey, just a splash of milk.

Errol broke a biscuit and put half into his mouth. 'So it hasn't made the news yet,' he said through the mouthful. He joggled his leg against his phone. 'I've been checking.'

'I guess they have to inform next of kin.'

Agnes hadn't checked for news of Iris's death. She'd been too busy worrying about her own family. Iris had said her parents were dead. She hadn't mentioned other relatives but someone, somewhere, had opened a door to police officers with grave faces.

'Your dad's friend's a charmer. Trevor. Can't say I'm sad I never had the pleasure of meeting him when we were staying in Quickthorn. He was at the barbecue, of course, but I seem to remember he had his lap full at the time . . .'

'He's dangerous.' She hadn't meant to say it.

She wasn't even sure it was true, not now. Trevor had preyed on a lonely teenage girl but that was low-grade work for a predator, easy pickings.

'He took a shine to me.' Errol brushed crumbs from his jumper jerkily, all his elegant edges blunted by what he'd seen yesterday.

'He's a bastard.'

Agnes wished she'd never taken Errol back to Blackthorn Ashes. She thought of their first meeting there, Errol in his orange kimono, dazzling her. His loneliness calling to hers, despite the show he put on.

'Do your friends really call you Jackie?'

He smiled, for the first time since yesterday. 'They might.'

'Can I call you Jackie?'

'Any time you feel like it.'

She smiled back at him. 'I'm sorry, for dragging you into this.'

'Are you kidding?' He sat up, happier now, reaching for his tea. 'It's the most action we've seen round here since – oh, wait. A week ago?'

He wasn't joking about the deaths, just following her lead, trying to lighten the mood. She didn't know how to tell him she was thinking of going back to London.

Last night, she'd thought she might ask him to go with her, imagining the pair of them sharing a flat – Errol's beaded curtain and posters, her books, pot plants they'd buy together in Camden Market. She could live like that. She could be happy. But Errol had lived in London once before, 'I thought I'd love London but big cities are only ever fun when you have money, or friends with money.'

Odie was snoring in the kitchen, a comfy sound like a small engine. Agnes wondered what her father was doing now, what Ruth's instructions had been. *Take care of Agnes, keep her from asking too many questions.* While Ruth took care of Christie?

'What happened after you brought me back here yesterday? What did I miss?'

'Your mum was waiting.' Errol sipped at his tea. 'She's scary . . . I nearly brought you here instead.'

'Did she say anything?'

'Didn't need to, she was giving me the dragon eyes . . . Christie copped most of it, though.'

'What did she do?'

'Took him off down the end.' He waved a long arm in the direction of the groundsman's shed. 'I didn't see where, too busy putting you to bed. They were still at it when I'd finished, though.'

'Did my dad go with them?'

'He must've. He was in the caravan when I was putting you to bed but gone by the time I was leaving. I was worried about the door, leaving you alone in there.'

'You didn't lock the door?'

'Are you saying it was locked when you woke up?' His stare sharpened. 'From the *outside*?'

'I guess they wanted me to be safe. I have my own key so it's not like I couldn't leave. I let myself out once I woke up.'

'Shit,' Errol said. 'You were *out* of it. You could've—'

'Nothing happened.'

'That's not the point. You're not their . . . You're not a *dog*.' His eyes flared. 'Who locks another person in a caravan?'

'My mum,' Agnes said peaceably. She didn't want him to be angry. The room was too small. 'You said she gave you the dragon eyes?'

'Well, not me specifically, more the whole situation. Like she was Godzilla and we were Tokyo.' He mimed Godzilla with laser eyes, rampaging.

'Sounds familiar.'

They were back on safe ground. After a bit, she said, 'So the police didn't come yesterday? While I was out of it, I mean.'

'Nope.' He handed her the plate of biscuits, saying, 'Before I eat them all.'

'I had breakfast with my dad.' She rubbed her stomach. 'Stuffed.'

'I'm glad he's feeling better.'

She could see Errol wanted to ask questions but he didn't. Iris did that and look where it got her. She bit the inside of her cheek, surprised by her own callousness. She'd felt threatened by Iris but she hadn't wanted her to get hurt, let alone—

'I was walking Odie,' Errol said. 'Yesterday. Bette said you called round.'

Not questions – something he needed to tell her.

He'd been waiting to see what mood she was in or because he wasn't sure how far he could trust her, maybe. After seeing Iris's body and the way Trevor and Christie reacted, her brother running, Trevor's rage at their arrival. Errol had stayed close to Agnes but really, who was she to him? She was a stranger.

'I wanted to thank you.' She kept the smile in place. 'It was raining pretty hard for a walk.'

'It was pissing down.' He picked at the cuff of his jumper, working a thread loose. 'Look . . . I saw Christie. Yesterday when I was coming back from the walk. At least, *I* didn't see him. Odie went nuts, that's what gave him away.'

'Gave him away?'

'He was hiding, that's how it looked.' Errol kept his eyes down, worrying at the thread. 'Round the back of your caravan by the storage box.'

Where the gas bottles were kept. Agnes could picture it. A waterproof, fireproof box the size of a school locker. Her mouth was dry. She drank tea, picturing Christie crouched there, rain soaking down. Why hadn't he gone inside the caravan to wait for

Ruth and Adrian? Why hide in the rain? He'd run from the shed, leaving Trevor. Leaving Agnes.

'Odie found him and made a fuss, jumping up, mud everywhere. Your mum'll probably send us a bill for washing his clothes . . .'

Errol was trying to find a way back to the place where they'd laughed but the path was too slippery, like the duckboards after rain.

'Did he say anything to you? Christie.'

Errol shook his head. 'Just looked pissed off. But that's normal, given the state of Odie.'

'Mum and Dad had gone in the car. I guess he was waiting for them to get back.'

'Where were you?' Errol looked up, at last. 'You said you let yourself out, after you woke up. Where'd you go?'

'Down to the shed, the one I took you to.'

'The one you took Iris to.' He'd looped the loose thread into a ring which he was rolling on and off his finger. 'With the filing cabinet.'

She watched his thin fingers fidgeting, all his fear focused on the frail loop of wool. He deserved the truth, what little she knew of it.

'Christie was in the shed with Trevor. He ran away when he saw me. I guess he'd had a fright, earlier. Maybe that's why he was hiding by the locker.'

Or he was looking for a new safe place for his treasure. Waterproof, lockable. She still didn't know what he'd taken from Ruth's room in Blackthorn Ashes.

'Wait,' Errol said. 'You were alone in that shed – with Trevor?'

'Just for a bit.'

'What did he want?' The flare was back in Errol's eyes. He

snapped the thread, dropping it onto the bed. 'Did he threaten you?'

'With what?' she asked, stalling for time.

'I don't know. Keeping quiet about earlier, about Iris. He was pissed off, he made that clear.'

'He knows we talked to the police. Well, he talked to them too.'

She felt outside of herself, as if she were watching the scene unfold on a big screen: a young couple seated on a narrow bed, Harry Belafonte smiling down at them from the wall. That was the name of the handsome actor she'd failed to recall the first time she was here. Harry Belafonte.

'You said he was dangerous.' Errol hooked an elbow around his drawn-up knees. 'Trevor.'

'He can be.' She watched understanding take form in his face. It made him look older but also more vulnerable. 'Don't,' she said suddenly, seeing him on the ground, bruised by Trevor's fists.

'Don't what?'

'Look like that. Think – like that. It was a long time ago. He can't do anything, not now.'

'Then why're you so scared?' Errol demanded. 'You're terrified. You have been for days.'

'No . . .'

'*Yes*. You have.'

She wanted to say, 'You don't know me. You hardly know me,' but she couldn't. Any more than she could explain how he'd known to bring her home to bed yesterday, removing her boots without speaking, covering her with a blanket. She picked up the loop of red thread. 'My dad could go to prison.'

Errol went still. Finally, he said, 'You mean . . .'

'For what happened with the houses. Failed safety standards, incomplete land surveys.' She slipped the thread around her thumb. 'He and Trevor said the local authority failed to declare the extent of the contamination. There was nothing on the land registry. They dug up three hundred tons of hazardous soil and took it away but it wasn't enough. The remediation work was never completed because the local authority ran out of money and failed to register the amount of contamination left in the soil before they started building. But none of that caused the poisonings.'

'Carbon monoxide, the papers said.'

'Faulty boiler systems, bad ventilation, subsidence putting cracks in the flue pipes.' She recited the list, knowing it by heart, by the pain in her heart and in Dad's eyes. 'Concealed pipes running through the ceilings and internal walls so you couldn't easily access the flue to check for damage.'

'What I've never understood is why the houses didn't have carbon monoxide alarms. That's a legal requirement round here, the store up the road sells batteries in bulk for the alarms.'

'They had alarms, yes.'

She took the ring from her thumb and placed it on the bed.

'But they didn't go off?'

'No alarms went off.'

'Why not?' Errol was watching her, wanting answers.

'I don't know.'

Christie and Trevor were in and out of the houses, she knew that much, Trevor needing Christie to help him check the batteries in the alarms, that's what he'd said.

'The alarms weren't working.'

Or batteries were never fitted in the first place. Was that

possible? An oversight of that magnitude and Trevor *knew*, using her brother to cover his tracks?

Odie started barking just before someone thumped on the caravan door.

Agnes turned to see the shadows of two men outside Errol's window.

Bette called out, 'I'll get it!'

Errol leant forward. 'What is it?'

'I don't know.' But she did.

Police. Detectives. Who else would it be?

The bead curtain began tapping as Bette opened the caravan door. Agnes could feel the weight of the men on its steps. Odie kept barking, too loudly for them to hear what was being said. Then Bette knocked at Errol's door, saying his name, a world of warning in her voice.

'What?' he called back.

He looked confused, hadn't guessed what was happening.

'Police.' Bette opened the door, standing between her grandson and the strangers. 'They've a warrant . . .' She was fighting a shake in her voice as she pointed to his boots on the floor. 'You'll want to put those on. We're to wait outside, apparently.'

Errol got up from the bed, reaching to pull on his Doc Martens.

Agnes stood, feeling dizzy and sick. The red thread was lying on the bed. She wanted to take it, tuck it into her pocket and keep it safe. She didn't even know why.

The detectives nodded as they went down the steps to stand outside the caravan, letting them know they hadn't been forgotten, that this had always been their plan: to get a warrant and come here, find what they were hiding. More police stood at the door to

Agnes's caravan. She couldn't see Dad. He should've been outside, waiting while the detectives searched the caravans for whatever evidence they were after.

'Where's Dad?' she asked.

Bette put an arm around her shoulders. 'Now, then.' She had Odie's lead wrapped around her other hand. The little dog was fretting at her feet, whining.

'Excuse me?' Errol walked to where the police were standing guard. 'Where's Mr Gale?'

'Move away, please, sir.'

'I am moved away. I've been moved away from my caravan. This's my friend's caravan. She's wondering where her dad is. Adrian Gale?'

The police officer flicked his eyes at Errol then away. 'You'll need to wait there.'

'Errol, come here. Odie's getting his growl on.' Bette's arm was steady around Agnes's shoulders but she was unhappy, afraid of what was happening.

Errol came back to her side, taking out his phone. 'I'm calling Leye.'

'We'd rather you didn't make any calls at this time.' One of the detectives was behind them, standing in the doorway to Bette's caravan. 'Put the phone away, sir.'

Errol arched his eyebrows but did as he was told. Something caught his attention, behind them. 'Oh, great. Rent-a-tweet.' He said it under his breath, between his teeth.

Agnes saw a small crowd was gathering outside the big trailers. She turned away, concentrating on her own caravan. Was Dad inside, answering questions? Or had they taken him to one of the two cars parked on the gravel – a marked patrol car and an unmarked silver Audi. She couldn't see anyone in either car but the Audi's windows were tinted and the police car was parked in the shadow of the trees. She needed to reach Ruth and Christie, warn them what was happening.

'Errol Argall?' The detectives were coming down the steps from Bette's caravan. One had a clear plastic bag in his hand, an evidence bag, filled with something green.

'That's me,' Errol said.

Agnes couldn't look at him, or at Bette.

All she could see was the evidence bag coming closer, swimming with light and shadow. Green . . .

A green and gold silk scarf.

At her feet, Odie started to bark again. He didn't stop, even after the car had taken Errol away and the crowd had dispersed and Bette's arm was gone from around her shoulders, leaving her cold and shaking.

25 AUGUST

Abandonment

25

The road which brought the police cars and ambulances was called Ashes Road. Its name made Agnes think of fires – coal which was once trees and its embers, sometimes called *clinker*. The word *clinker* was in her head as she came home from the woods on the morning they were told to leave Blackthorn Ashes. It had been a long time coming but in the end everything happened swiftly, after the storm and the coroner coming to Maythorn to take the children's bodies away.

The morning after the storm, she rose early, while the rest of the house was sleeping. Alone in the kitchen, she made a sandwich of peanut butter, wrapping it in foil. She took an apple from the fruit bowl and a bottle of water from the fridge, packing these provisions in a small rucksack. She wore a long-sleeved shirt and jeans, hiking boots for those parts of the wood flooded by the storm. She left her family sleeping, curtains drawn at all the windows.

The sun was rising pale behind the trees, a quiver of cold in the air. The houses watched her as she walked, each locked in its own silence. She could taste a cliff edge, raw and white. The deaths in Maythorn were unspeakable but there was no sense of a full stop.

Only of a hurtling, unchecked, to whatever was waiting ahead of them.

In the woods, she felt insulated; the hurtling would have to take down all the trees before it reached her. She wished she had a tent so she could live out here until it was over. It couldn't be long now, surely. No one would want to stay, with the children gone. It was an effort just to move from room to room, or up and down the stairs. They were poisoned but they still didn't know it. Only Trevor had any energy, fizzing as he came to the house to call Christie away, 'Tour of duty,' as if Blackthorn Ashes was a war zone, just as Iris had said at the street party. It looked even more like a war zone in the wake of the storm, with cables trailing and gardens tumbled, white faces at the windows, hands raised to draw down blinds.

The woods were cool, smelling of pine needles and tunnelled earth. Rain had put potholes into the paths, the trails spongy under her feet as she walked into the heart of the woods where the trees were too closely crowded for rain to reach. She found a stone ledge and sat, eating the apple and listening to birds – disturbed by her arrival – returning to their nests. She was thinking of Dad, the questions he'd be made to answer in the light of the deaths. She had no idea how the children had died but she knew it was the houses, that death had been waiting for them here from the very start, from the first brick laid with her brother's name written on it. She knew there would have to be a scapegoat, a scalp. Trevor wouldn't take the blame, not even a part of it. No dirt ever stuck to him.

She finished the apple, dropping the core into the pine needles at her feet. An ant found it, crawling into the grooves left by her teeth. Above her, a crop of abandoned nests built too low for safety clung to the branches. Instinct drove every living thing to make a home for itself. She thought of tiny vests and muslin squares, and of fresh starts in wild places poised between land and sea. Something moved through the undergrowth, dragging teeth and claws. She shivered and stood, dusting the legs of her jeans. She should get back. This day was not like the others. Today was going to be different.

By the time she returned, Blackthorn Ashes was shiny with cars. Everyone was up, and busy. She counted four police vehicles. She didn't stop to ask what was happening, making her way home to find the front door open, the garage door too. Dad was packing boxes into the boot of Ruth's car.

'Go inside.' He didn't look at her. 'Find your mother.'

Ruth was upstairs, emptying the bathroom shelves into a carrier bag. She thrust the bag at Agnes, 'Finish this,' heading in the direction of the bedrooms.

'What is it?' Agnes called after her but Ruth didn't answer.

She did as she was told, filling the carrier bag with aspirin, indigestion remedies, her meds. For good measure, she added plasters and antiseptic cream, toiletries from the shelves above the bath. When the bag was full, she went looking for her mother, finding her in Christie's bedroom, crouched beside the cupboard Dad built. When she saw Agnes, Ruth straightened, shutting the cupboard door and locking it, tucking the key into her pocket. She had a second carrier bag filled with whatever she'd taken from the cupboard, its neck wrung tight in her fist.

'Get what you need from your room. Essentials only. You have three minutes.'

'What's happened?'

'If you'd been here, you'd know.'

Ruth swung past her, out of the room. She was wearing yesterday's clothes, her hair wet from a shower, dripping in a dark vee down her back.

Agnes went after her. 'Tell me.'

'We're being evacuated.' Ruth stopped at the top of the stairs, her hand gripping the banister. 'They say the houses are unsafe. We need to leave.'

'Unsafe how?'

'Carbon monoxide. It's what killed the children, and the Prentisses.'

'The Prentisses are dead?' Agnes felt a scrabbling in her chest.

Her mother blinked once, then pointed a finger. 'Hurry up.'

'Where's Christie?'

'With your dad, packing the car.'

'He's not. I was just there.'

'Then find him. I have to pack my work papers.'

Ruth was gone, back into her bedroom.

In her own room, Agnes shoved clothes into the purple suitcase, along with her phone charger and passport, the box file with her birth certificate and other paperwork. She worked fast, trying to separate out her feelings of relief and dismay. Three minutes, Mum had said.

She carried the case to the car, asking Dad if he'd seen Christie.

'He's with Trevor.' Dad looked as if all his energy was going into staying upright. 'They went across the road.'

'To Silverthorn?' She slid the purple case into a gap in the boot. 'Luke's in hospital, isn't he?'

'Not the Dearmans . . .' Dad was looking around the garage, distracted. 'I'm not sure where they went to be honest. Where's your mum?'

'Upstairs getting her work papers. She told me to find Christie.'

'You'd better do that, then.' He pressed the ends of his fingers to his eyes. 'Quickly.'

Christie's basketball was in the corner of the garage, at Dad's feet. Loss hit her out of nowhere, so hard she couldn't breathe, the magnitude of what this had meant to her brother and her parents. Their fresh start. Dad's pride in being their saviour, the prize this house had been. Glittering, yes, but needful too. Because it was bound up in what it meant to be a family, to be back together again.

'It'll be okay,' she said. 'Dad?'

'It won't.' He raised a haggard face to hers. 'It can't be.'

It was the last meaningful thing he said in a long time.

Outside, police were gathered between Hawthorn and Silverthorn, their faces grim and steady. She heard one of them say, 'It's a blood bath,' and she turned away, feeling sick.

Christie and Trevor were coming up the road from the building site, Christie running to keep up with Trevor's long stride. Trevor's face was a woodcut, dark and unforgiving. The police moved down the road from the other direction, overseeing the evacuation, knocking on doors to check everyone was out or getting out.

Christie was saying, '. . . batteries?'

Trevor cut him short. 'Your sister's turned up, anyway.'

Christie's head swung towards her, his chin retracting. His face was bunched around his eyes. Blaming her, even now.

'Mum's looking for you,' she said.

Christie peeled away from Trevor at the last second so that

when he was gone she was standing near enough to hear Trevor's heart knocking in his chest.

He said, 'You got what you wanted, then.'

'Did I?'

'This place's finished. Dead. You'll never have to come here again.'

'And that's what I wanted?'

'Isn't it?' He looked down at her. The sun was in his eyes, wiping them out. 'To get away and never come back. That's your MO.'

'Because I wanted to get away from you, you mean.'

He laughed, cutting it short. 'I was thinking about before that. What you were running away from when you found me.' He glanced to where Ruth was coming out of Blackthorn, carrying an overnight bag. 'What you're still running from.'

They drove to the hospital first. For check-ups, blood tests, charts. Agnes caught sight of Barry and Janis Mason in the hospital, ashen-faced, Barry clutching a baby blanket, Janis hugging her empty arms to her chest. *It's a blood bath . . .*

She saw a young man in running gear talking urgently to a nurse, and wondered if he was related to Val and Tim Prentiss. She'd hardly known them, she realized, as if they'd been dead long before it happened. Guilt buzzed in her skull.

After the blood tests and checks, they were free to go. Not back to Blackthorn Ashes, which the police were treating like a fire or flood, as if the houses had been burnt to the ground or half washed out to sea. Safety investigators warned they'd have questions for Adrian Gale and Trevor Kyte, and everyone else responsible for the planning and construction, and the sales since these'd been rushed. Adrian, in particular, had to stay close to the investigation. Agnes wasn't sure why so much of the spotlight shone on her father but she suspected Trevor steered them in that direction. Her phone was buzzing.

'You can come here,' Errol said. 'Bette's found you a caravan.'

By the time they found their way to Indigo Park, it was growing dark. After Blackthorn Ashes, the caravan park looked crude and carnival-like, neon firing from the big trailers.

Inside, the caravan smelt of some other family gone away for the summer.

Dad headed for the sofa and sat down, looking stunned. Christie called top bunk in the room he'd be sharing with Agnes.

Ruth was the only one operating on anything like full power. She unpacked the suitcases and carrier bags, putting pyjamas on everyone's beds, arranging meds along the shallow shelf in the bathroom, cracking open windows to let the stale air escape.

'We'll get fish and chips,' she decided, forcing a bright note from her voice, as fake as the diamonds left behind in the show house.

Dad said nothing, leaning into the sofa and shutting his eyes. Christie kicked his heel at the bunk, busy on his phone. At least there was a signal here.

'Agnes, you'll come and help me carry everything?' Her mother framed it like a question but it was a command.

Agnes wanted to run. Out of the caravan into the gathering darkness, away from her fractured family. Heat raced through her, leaving her cold at the core. She wanted to find Trevor wherever he was holed up. A place far better than this, she was certain. She wanted to find him and hit him and keep hitting him, not just for the past but for everything that was out of her control, all this mess pressing in on every side, stealing her father and drumming her brother's heel on the bed, turning her mother's eyes to chips of dark glass.

Ruth drove them to the coastal town, not speaking until she reached a fork in the road where she took a narrow lane to a car park at the head of the cliffs. The car park was deserted. Agnes didn't ask why they were taking this detour. She'd known her mother wanted more than fish and chips, that she'd brought her here for a reason.

Ruth faced the car seaward, where the last of the sunset clung to the horizon. She switched off the engine, easing her hands from the wheel. She was vibrating with tension.

Agnes sat waiting for her to say whatever it was she needed Agnes to hear. A pep talk possibly, seasoned with recrimination for the part Agnes played in unpicking their paradise. 'You need to do better,' how many times had she heard that? She slipped her hands under the seat belt, waiting for Ruth to begin.

Below them, the sea ran smoothly into the rocks, with hardly a sound. There was a complicated edge to their silence, staticky.

'The police are going to come, tomorrow or the next day.'

Ruth kept her eyes on the oil tankers on the horizon, lit by pin-pricks of light.

'They're going to ask questions about what happened back there. Everything that happened.' She paused. 'Do you understand?'

'They'll want to know what's wrong with the houses—'

'No,' Ruth cut her off. 'Not that.'

Their breath was starting to cloud the windows. She could smell her mother's stress. The sea swept at the rocks, a shushing sound. Agnes focused on that. *Hush.*

'Something happened in Silverthorn.'

Ruth's voice was steady, the one she used when Agnes was spiralling out of control; a voice to hold her down, keep her quiet.

'With Emma and Luke.'

'Luke's in hospital, isn't he?'

'Yes.'

'And Emma went with him?'

'No.' Her mother reached a hand to clear a circle in the mist on the windscreen. 'She didn't.'

'Then . . . the police will have evacuated her. This morning, with all the others.'

Ruth wiped the wetness from her fingers onto the skirt of her dress.

Again she said, 'No.'

Agnes wished she were far away, up in the sky where clouds shredded the darkness, miles from her mother's awful stillness.

'Tell me.'

'She's dead. I asked one of the police officers, the one who found Val and Tim. He said we were the only ones who made it out of there. Barry and Janis, and us.'

Only us. All that's left.

'Does Luke know?'

'I imagine so. By now, if not before.'

'What happened? You said something happened in Silverthorn?'

'You don't know?'

Ruth shot her a look, so sudden it landed like a slap on her skin.

'No . . .' She recoiled, her fingers flinching under the stiffness of the seat belt.

'Are you sure?' Her mother's face was razored with suspicion.

'I don't know what you're talking about.'

But a flood of shame ripened in her belly, flushing her cheeks, the sensation so familiar she almost leant into it. 'Tell me,' she said again, hearing a whine in her voice. It made her want to bite her own tongue, spit the taste from her mouth.

'I thought you knew . . .' Her mother let out her breath, very slowly. 'You used to be so close when you were living at home. You and Christie.'

Agnes should have gone then. Ripped the seat belt from her body, shoved open the door and run. Down to the rocks and the sea, or back to the road to flag down a passing car, beg a lift to the police station. Or else she should have made her way deep into the woods to hide. Anywhere but in the car with Ruth and her half-secret.

Lights winked on the oil tankers, blurred by their breath on the glass. Wind pressed into them, the seat belt chafing Agnes's hands. The only sound was the insect-ticking of the engine as it grew cold. She tried to concentrate on these things, to stay grounded.

'What does this have to do with Christie?'

'He was in the house,' her mother said. 'In Silverthorn, with Trevor.'

Her voice splintered on Trevor's name, as if she'd taken a hammer to it.

'Fixing the batteries, in the alarms.' She rubbed her index finger at the steering wheel. 'That was his excuse.'

'Christie's? Excuse for what?'

'Stealing. I assumed you knew.' Ruth drew a breath. 'It's why he had to leave his last school, why this fresh start was so important. He was stealing and . . . lying about it.'

Wind rocked the car, whistling against the windows. Agnes saw her brother jogging to keep up with Trevor, his pale face bunched, blaming her. He was just a boy, she wanted to say. She wanted to shout it: *He's just a boy!*

Emma Dearman was dead. The word hurt, the touch of her tongue against the back of her teeth: *dead*.

Somewhere a lorry brayed, rocking around the bend in the road as it headed into the town. Ruth turned in her seat to face Agnes.

'Look at me.' She waited until Agnes did as she was told. When she spoke again, her voice was threaded with steel. 'It was carbon monoxide. It is in all the houses. That is why we were evacuated. Because Blackthorn Ashes is toxic. No one was safe there.'

'But you're saying that's not—'

'Blackthorn Ashes was *toxic*. You know that. You were the first to know it.'

Every part of Agnes was cringing, at bay. Her mother seemed not to notice, or noticed and didn't care. Because Agnes was always like this, because *Have you taken your meds?*

'You came back,' Ruth said. 'To us. You came back home.'

From London, she meant, and Laura. A crash of colour across her mind – plates, smashing. Shards of china like daggers, the sting of it in her hands. *Demolition*. She'd confessed what she'd done, the night she came home, wailing into Ruth's lap, 'I didn't mean it,' while her mother stroked her hair, 'Of course you didn't, of course not.' She knew everything, how Agnes fell apart after losing her job, how she'd fought with Laura and lost her. In the car, she clenched her hands around the stiffness of the seat belt.

'What matters now is that we stay together,' Ruth was saying. 'You and me, Dad and Christie. It's going to be hard and I'm going to need you here. *Properly here*. Do you understand? Not going off to the beach or into the woods or lying in bed all day because you feel like it or it's *too much*. It can't work like that, not now. I'm going to have to try and find work. The money's worse than we thought. My job was tied to Blackthorn Ashes just like your father's. There won't be any cash coming in and there are debts. I don't know how bad it is yet, we're still finding out, but it's bad. Your father isn't going to be—'

She bit off the rest of the sentence but Agnes knew: Dad wasn't going to be much use for a while.

'This is going to fall on us. You and me. I need to find work and you need to look after your brother. *We need you*. Do you understand?'

Did she? Understand? Six people were dead and her mother wanted to talk about money, about debts and work and babysitting her brother. They were about to buy fish and chips as if they were on holiday, taking the food back to the caravan where they would sleep within a few short feet of one another, a plastic wall separating her head from Ruth's, and Ruth's from Christie's.

'I can't—'

'Yes, you *can*. Agnes, look at me. You can.'

The car was thick with their breath now, like drowning. Air staggered in her chest, her skull filling blackly with London, with Laura picking pieces of broken plate from the floor, filling the palm of her hand with the daggers Agnes had thrown.

'It will be all right,' Ruth said. 'We're going to be all right. This is temporary, while they're conducting the investigation into the gas boilers and flues. They'll find all the answers you wanted us to look for weeks ago. You were right, something was wrong.' Her voice slipped sideways into the old sing-song that had swayed Agnes to sleep when she was small and settled her when she was older. 'You were right. The first of us to see the houses weren't safe. No one was safe there. We were lucky we got out when we did.'

Cotton wool was taped to the inside of Agnes's elbow where the needle had gone in for the blood tests at the hospital. Ruth's elbow had the same small puncture wound. After breathing carbon monoxide, the nurse told them, it enters your bloodstream and mixes with haemoglobin to form carboxyhaemoglobin. If this happens, your blood can no longer carry oxygen and your body's cells and tissue will fail and die. Neither Dad nor Ruth, nor Agnes nor Christie had breathed enough carbon monoxide to need emergency oxygen therapy. The nurse had told them to go home and rest. Their bloods were in transit to a laboratory.

Agnes thought of those phials now, each sealed with a rubber cork, travelling together through the darkness. In another world at some other time, the technicians who ran the tests might have been able to work out what went wrong between her and Ruth. By spotting their blood onto glass slides, putting the slides side by side under a microscope to reveal the truth in tiny red cells, round fragmented platelets.

'We were lucky,' Ruth said. 'We got out. Now we need to stay together.'

———

26

Ruth and Christie didn't return to Indigo Park until after dark. Agnes waited with Bette for news of Errol, and of her father. He'd been in the police car with the tinted windows, taken away like Errol to answer questions. She'd tried calling him and Ruth, even Christie. No one was picking up. Bette phoned the friend of a friend, a lawyer, for advice. After an hour, the friend called back to say Errol had a duty solicitor with him at the police station. She didn't know any more than that.

'It's my fault,' Agnes told Bette. 'I gave him that scarf.'

'But where's it even *from*? It can't be anything to do with that poor lassie who died.' It wasn't a question, Bette knew her grandson. Agnes was the one she didn't know. 'I saw the scarf, very nice but nothing a young lass would wear.' She was talking about Iris.

'It was stolen. From one of the houses at Blackthorn Ashes.'

Bette's stare sharpened. 'By you?'

Agnes dug her thumbnail into her wrist. She could tell the truth, name her brother as the thief and try to claim back a little of this woman's warmth and sympathy. But it wouldn't be the whole truth. She'd gone with Christie, not on the day he took the scarf but every other day. 'It's my fault,' she repeated. 'I'll tell the police that as soon as I can get to the station.'

Bette was shrewd enough to read between the lines. Her face softened a fraction. 'How's your dad mixed up in all this? They took him in for questioning too.'

'I don't know. It doesn't make any sense.'

That was a lie. The sense it made was so ugly she was afraid to look directly at it. She kept seeing a knife her father had owned when she was small, a complicated multi-tool like a Swiss Army penknife but with more blades, some as thin and wicked as razors. She'd picked it up once, cutting her fingers despite the fact all the blades seemed to be tucked safe inside its handle. The cuts were so delicate she didn't notice them at first, only a frozen sensation at the ends of her fingers before stinging red beads of blood came up.

Odie lay at their feet with his head turned towards Errol's room. Every now and then, Bette reached to pet his ears.

It'll be over soon, Agnes wanted to tell them.

The police will bring Errol back, or Ruth will come home. Whatever happens next, it will be over.

Luke must have given the police a list of everything missing from Silverthorn, including his wife's scarf and coin purse. Agnes could prove she gave the scarf to Errol because she had the purse that was taken at the same time. She would have to tell the police it was Christie who took the scarf and purse; she didn't know enough about where in Silverthorn he'd found them, or when exactly he'd taken them. She'd have to tell the police about the keys from Dad's toolbox, the filing cabinet in the shed and the storage locker behind their caravan where Errol had seen Christie hiding. If she told them Ruth cleared out the cabinet on the day Iris was found dead, the police would search Ruth's car and find evidence she'd transported the stolen goods from Indigo Park to dispose of them elsewhere. What would her mother do then? This was a murder investigation. Why else were so many police involved? Agnes pinched the skin at her wrist, hard.

Had Errol already told the police Adrian Gale left his caravan on the last day Iris was seen alive? Even if he hadn't, Bette would. It was only fair, with her grandson caught up in this for no good reason and Dad like Agnes – a stranger.

Had they found some of Christie's treasure in their caravan, was that why Dad had been taken for questioning? Or had Trevor decided to drop Dad in it, needing to shield himself from scrutiny since he was the one found at the site where Iris died? Knowing his best friend was so eaten up with guilt he'd accept the blame even if it belonged elsewhere.

Agnes thought of the silent plea she kept seeing in her father's eyes. He'd welcome the blame – a place to put his shame about Blackthorn Ashes, the broken promises and lost lives.

Bette was checking her phone again. Odie whimpered at their feet. Agnes reached a hand to pet him. Her head ached, filling with the puzzles of the last few weeks. Dad's misery, and Christie's fury. Ruth keeping watch from a distance, making sure she knew where Christie went. Trevor watching too, looking for an exit strategy, refusing to let this mess swallow him the way it was swallowing Adrian and his family. Then Iris coming with her questions and her hunter's eyes, like a fox slinking into their hen house. Agnes gave the stolen scarf to Errol because she wanted a friend. But in doing that, she'd offloaded evidence, sending the police in Errol's direction instead of Christie's. Could she have done that on purpose, even subconsciously? Family came first, Ruth said. But Agnes wasn't Ruth. And Errol was her friend, her *family*. Odie put his ears back at a sound from outside.

Bette said, 'Just someone changing a gas bottle.'

'I should get back, make a start on supper. Unless I can help with anything here?'

'No, you go.' Bette climbed to her feet. She looked old for the first time, worry lines deep around her eyes. 'I'll be getting on with our own supper. He'll be hungry when he gets home.'

'How will he get back?' Bette didn't have a car and Errol didn't drive. The two of them always took the bus when they went down to the shops. 'Does he have money for a taxi?'

'Enough for a bus, anyway. He'll manage.'

'I could go down there,' Agnes offered. She'd offered this twice already. 'Then we could come back together.' She looked towards the window. 'It's getting dark.'

'He's a grown man. He'll phone if he needs anything.' Bette straightened, holding the empty mugs to her chest. 'It's not the first time they've had him answering questions. Whenever there's trouble round here, they come looking for the first black face they can find.' She moved her mouth painfully. 'We're used to it.'

The storage locker at the side of their caravan was padlocked. Agnes searched for the key in all the places she could think of. She couldn't find it. Perhaps it was in her brother's pocket. Judging by the pristine state of the padlock, the police hadn't tried to open the locker when they searched the caravan. But they might think of it later, come back with bolt cutters. They'd been through the caravan's cupboards and wardrobes, searching for whatever they thought was hidden here. Where was Ruth?

Agnes tidied the sitting room and kitchen, washing up the breakfast plates Dad had left undone. The caravan smelt of bacon and eggs; it felt so long ago, that breakfast together. Had she missed her last chance to talk to her father, to tell him she loved him? Had she missed that same chance with Christie and with Ruth? She'd tried to talk to her mother in the night but Ruth had shut her out, thinking silence was the solution. Perhaps it was. If Agnes had been quieter, gentler, easier, perhaps she'd be with Ruth and Christie right now, trusted to help her family weather this storm.

In Ruth's room, the duvet was folded back from the bed, both pillows indented. Agnes put her hand in the hollow left by her father's head, looking at the matching ditch in her mother's pillow. What happened if they never came home, her parents or her brother? What would she do? The questions were too big, crowding her mouth.

She went to the kitchen, searching for something to cook for supper. Before she'd taken the first tin from the cupboard, car tyres sounded in the gravel. Her heart thudded with relief. She put the tin back, wiping her hands clean.

Outside, Christie was climbing from the passenger seat of Ruth's car. His face was white, chin wobbling. He didn't look at Agnes, pushing past her into the caravan.

Ruth stood at the side of the car with her head bent over her phone, its screen bleeding blue light through her fingers. Agnes waited for her to look up, for a word about Dad or Errol. Whatever she felt towards Ruth – and her feelings had never been more complicated – her mother held the answers. When they'd fought it was never because she believed Ruth was wrong; they'd fought because she knew Ruth was right. She no longer thought it. But some grain must have stuck because she was waiting for her mother to tell her what to do, how they were going to get through this.

'Get in the car,' Ruth said.

It wasn't what she'd expected. 'Why?'

'Just get in the car. I'll be back in a minute.'

She walked past Agnes into the caravan where Christie had gone. To tell him what? That she and Agnes were going for a drive and he needed to get supper for himself, keep his phone close so he could call her if Dad came home? It seemed incredible she would leave Christie on his own when he looked half his age and scared to death.

Not knowing what else to do, Agnes got into the car, fastening her seat belt. Bette was at the window of Errol's room, watching. She must have hoped the tyres were a car bringing her grandson home. Seeing her, Agnes suffered a pang of homesickness. She didn't know which home she was sick for, unless it was here in Indigo Park – where she could be certain of Bette's kindness and Errol's friendship. She wanted to go back two days, to when Iris was alive and the worst she'd had to fear was Christie's retribution for sharing their secret with a stranger.

Bette dropped the curtain across the window, switching off the light in Errol's room. She said the police made a habit of coming for him whenever there was trouble, 'We're used to it,' but Agnes doubted it was a thing you could get used to, being suspected of something you hadn't done and would never do. Errol was arch and funny and flamboyant but he was also the gentlest, kindest man she'd ever met. He would no more loot an abandoned house than wear yellow Crocs. The thought of him in a police cell was a blade between her ribs. If she managed nothing else in the next few hours, she had to clear his name, bring him home to Bette.

Ruth got into the car, firing the ignition and letting the engine idle while she fastened her seat belt. She put her phone into the moulded shelf inside the driver's door, out of Agnes's reach.

'Will he be all right?' Agnes asked. 'Christie, on his own?'

Ruth didn't answer. She backed the car from the gravel onto the lane that led in the direction of the cliffs, driving a short distance until she found a parking spot by a hedge of blackthorn. She tucked the car into the space and switched off the engine, opening the driver's door and getting out, taking her phone with her.

Agnes struggled with her seat belt for a second before she followed. Her mother was making no sense. She had to break into a run to catch up with Ruth who was striding towards the cliff path with her hands in her pockets and her head down.

'Where're we going?'

The sunset was spectacular, splashed across the horizon, setting the oil tankers ablaze. The hawthorn sheltered them a little from the rocking of the wind but it was cold. Each step drove a fresh chill into Agnes's bones.

'Why did we take the car? We could've walked.'

'And have your brother follow us?' Ruth threw her a look, as knife-like as the thorns. 'He knows this path rather too well, doesn't he? You both do.'

So that was it. They were here so Ruth could punish her for her part in Christie's transgressions. Agnes matched her step to her mother's, not shrinking. If this was a battle about who'd done what over the last seven weeks – who'd kept whose secrets – she had questions of her own. Ruth's green dress glowed in the sunset, her hair too. She was brimming with an energy Agnes hadn't seen in a long while but which she remembered from eleven years ago; her mother was drawing a sort of fury to herself, getting ready to fight. When they passed the trampoline, Agnes almost suggested they take turns punching it, the way she and Christie did, to work out their rage. At the cliff head, Ruth stopped.

The sea was striking the rocks below them. Agnes drew its salt into her lungs. She was ready, readier than she'd been eleven years ago, readier than she had any right to be after the last few weeks of stress and confusion. She thought of Iris sitting in the cane chair pretending an interest in an empty field when all of her attention – every cell in her body – was focused on getting the answers she wanted to her questions. Ruth had hold of the same energy now.

'Do you know why we came here?' Her mother wrapped her arms around her chest, holding her elbows in her hands. 'To Blackthorn Ashes, I mean.'

'For a fresh start.' Agnes pushed her own hands into her pockets. 'You told me, Christie told me. It was meant to be a fresh start, only I ruined it. I should've stayed away.'

'This isn't about you,' her mother snapped. 'It just *isn't*. Are you going to listen?'

She was scared, Agnes realized with a shock. Ruth was scared. The skin under her eyes was strained, every taut line in her face battling against outright terror.

'Christie was getting into trouble back home. He was suspended from school. We had the police round. I told you about the stealing and the lying but it was worse than that. He'd been getting into fights. He broke a girl's nose.'

Agnes's mind turned emptily, seeing her brother putting his fists into the trampoline, not stopping until he was out of breath, until his hands were black.

'The stealing didn't stop. Well, you know all about that.'

'It was only' – wind knocked against her shoulders, shaking her – 'in the empty houses.'

'No. It started before we moved out.'

Ruth caught at her hair, dragging it behind her ears. For a second, her eyes rested on Agnes's cropped head as if she wished she'd done the same, shaved it all off.

'Trevor knew. All those times he took Christie to fix fuse boxes, fit batteries . . . Christie was stealing things. Trevor knew but he said nothing, until it suited him.'

'That sounds like Trevor.'

She took care not to put any emotion into the words but Ruth fired another sharp look at her.

'You know,' Agnes said simply. 'What he's like.'

Her mother studied her in silence. Agnes waited, watching the sky change colour as more of the sunset flattened itself at the horizon. It was time they talked about this. Not shouted, or fought. Just talked. It was time.

At last, Ruth said, 'This isn't about you.'

'If that were true, we wouldn't be standing here. You'd have left me in the caravan and taken Christie away, somewhere safe.'

'*Where?* Where is it you imagine we can go? There's no money. There's the investigation. And now there's the police.'

'Has Dad been arrested?'

'Not yet. Not that I know of. But the way things are looking?' She showed her hands, their empty palms turned up. 'Who knows?'

'And Christie,' Agnes said. 'Will he be arrested?'

Her mother shut her hands into fists, shaking her head. A shudder went through her, cold or fear. She closed her eyes then opened them, fixing her stare back in place.

'Trevor helped you get rid of the evidence,' Agnes pressed. 'From the shed at Indigo Park. The things Christie stole. He was keeping them in a filing cabinet.'

'Trevor *helped*.' Ruth's teeth snapped shut. 'Oh, he was right there when we needed him. And he made certain we did.' The air was soaked with her fury. 'He's an expert at being indispensable.'

Agnes felt a barb in her chest uncurling.

'He's threatening to tell the police about the stealing?'

'Of course he is.' Her mother looked exhausted suddenly, wrung out. The red in the sky stained the side of her face. 'Of course.'

'And you're telling me because you think I can do something? Talk to him or—'

'I'm telling you because it's *over*. You need to understand that.' Her voice dulled. 'You need to know what to do now. We'll all have jobs to do.'

'This isn't about the stealing.'

The wind hit like a hand. Agnes had to brace her feet against the grit of the path. The trampoline screeched in the hedge, blackthorns scraping at its frame.

'Is it? Or not just that.' She thought of the last time Ruth brought her up here. 'It's about Emma Dearman. It's about what happened in Silverthorn.'

Her mother half turned from her, to face the sea. The wind lifted her hair at the nape of her neck, showing the narrow bones there.

'I found her . . .' The words left Ruth like a sigh. She blinked at the horizon, keeping her eyes shut a second too long, as if she didn't want to open them again. 'That was me.'

'You found . . . ? What do you mean?'

'At the bottom of the stairs. Her neck was broken.'

Another slow blink. 'She'd been dead a while.' And another. 'She was starting to smell.'

Agnes wrapped her arms around herself to try and stop the shaking. 'When?'

'The morning of the storm.' Ruth's voice was flat, flavourless.

'But the police didn't come until the next day . . . You didn't call them when you found her?'

Her mother's jaw moved drily. 'Evidently not.'

'Why?' Agnes stopped, tried again: 'It was carbon monoxide.'

'Of course I'd have called them if that's all it was.' Pain twisted Ruth's face. 'You think I haven't thought about that, every day? How I might've saved the children if I'd called the police that morning . . . But I couldn't be sure how she died. I didn't *know*.'

A falling sound made them turn, staring into the dark of the path.

Footfall on the loose stones, heavy and quick.

Someone was coming their way, moving with purpose, not caring if he was heard. Agnes saw his head first then his shoulders, fiery from the sunset.

Fear fell through her, the sea tilting across her shoulder. At her side, Ruth had gone still. Her eyes were focused, bright. She'd been waiting for this. For him. That shimmering energy was back, carving something fierce from her face.

Trevor said, 'This'd better be fucking good.'

'You came,' Ruth said. 'That's good.'

'You said this was about Christie.' He jerked his head at Agnes. 'What's she doing here?'

'Bearing witness. In case you get any more funny ideas.'

He laughed but it didn't sound right. His shoulders were stiff and wary like his neck. 'Your kids are the ones with the funny ideas.' He tossed a look at Agnes. 'No offence.'

'Some taken.'

Agnes did her best to match her mother's tone, rewarded by a flare of disquiet in his eyes. He'd been summoned by Ruth, hadn't expected to find Agnes on her side.

'I mean, Christie's a thief. But this one?'

'Worse things to be.' Ruth closed in on him, a narrow movement of her head prompting Agnes to follow suit. 'Like a murderer, for example.'

Trevor came up short. His smile slipped, losing its footing on his face.

The wind hit him squarely in the chest and he shifted, trying to recover lost ground. Now he was the one with his back to the sea, standing at the cliff's edge squinting into the darkness at Ruth and Agnes. 'What the fuck's this about?'

'Iris Edison.' Ruth spoke the name coolly. 'You killed her.'

Agnes held her breath in her chest, blunt pressure under her ribs. She saw the coil of Iris's hair in the unfinished house, Trevor standing guard, Christie running in fear.

'Are you mad?' The tips of his ears were red from the sunset, demonic, making a carnival mask of his face. 'I thought *she* was the one on strong meds?'

'She's autistic. She's not insane.'

It was the first time Agnes had heard her mother acknowledge

301

her diagnosis, the first time the word 'autistic' had left Ruth's mouth.

'That's not what you said all those years ago.' Trevor curled his own mouth, shadow eating his upper lip. 'Then, you told me she was bipolar.'

'I was wrong.'

The first time Ruth had admitted to making a mistake.

'Yeah? Maybe you're the crazy one. Dragging me out here to fling accusations.'

'I know you killed her. I can prove it. So you'll shut up and listen to what we've got to say.'

She'd wanted Agnes with her, safety in numbers; she was her mother's back-up. The idea made her want to laugh, and weep. How long had she waited for this? Ruth taking her side and making her peace. Except it wasn't peace. It was war. Ruth was waging war on Trevor. Sixteen-year-old Agnes had longed for that but now it was here and she was afraid. Afraid of Ruth, afraid of Trevor.

'I don't imagine you meant it to happen,' Ruth was telling him. 'Apart from anything else, it ruined your plans for getting Adrian to take the blame for Blackthorn Ashes.'

Trevor squinted, trying for a better fix on Ruth's face. His hands were bunched in his pockets, every inch of him ready to fight. Agnes could smell the rash of sweat under his shirt.

'You didn't mean to kill her, I'm sure. You should make certain the police understand that when you tell them. Did you think she was after a bit of rough? In any case, she underestimated you, thought you were just a builder, someone she could use to get inside the houses.'

Her mother had known all this, without saying a word to Agnes.

She'd known Iris wanted a way into the houses, that she'd seen Trevor and mistaken him for a builder. Had she been eavesdropping the night Agnes made her bargain with Iris to leave them alone? She'd thought she was alone in that bargain, but Ruth knew all about it.

'I imagine it was a stupid, clumsy accident,' her mother said evenly. 'Like most murders. You didn't plan it or want it but it happened, and you didn't know how to get out of it. Then you thought of Adrian. You were already halfway to getting him to take the blame for the development. Why not this, too?'

Trevor's boots rasped on the gravel but he wasn't moving, staying where Ruth had put him at the cliff's edge. *There are two of us,* Agnes thought, *and only one of you.*

'You lost your head a little, I expect. One thing to get your best friend to take the blame for failing building regulations, another to pin a murder on him. It's why you were so angry when you were found with her body, because you were panicking. Your plan was coming apart at the seams.'

'Prove it.' His pupils were pinheads. 'You crazy insane bitch.'

'Oh, I can. Trust me. The police are already looking for you, in fact.' Ruth's voice iced over. 'Did you really think I was going to let you fuck with my family a second time?'

Trevor flinched then, staring as if Ruth was someone he'd never seen before. He was afraid of the words she was speaking – of the truth.

Everything Ruth was saying, Agnes had known. Standing in the unfinished house with rain coming through the roof, seeing Iris on the bricks. Frail gold-brown curls on her cheek, a sweet ripe smell from her body. Not decay. *Tobacco.* Shreds of Trevor's tobacco, sticking to Iris's dead cheek. She raised a hand to her own cheek, remembering. Those shreds found their way everywhere, in her hair, behind her knees. Her sixteen-year-old body had been a crime scene. Never investigated, no charges brought. But Iris was an active investigation; her hands sealed in bags to preserve evidence from defensive wounds, broken fingernails, torn cuticles – Agnes held the answers in the flavours on her tongue. Trevor's temper, always so close to the surface, too easily flared. She *knew*.

'Where's your evidence?' he demanded.

'Right here.' Ruth brought her hand out of her pocket, holding a sandwich bag sealed across the top. Inside, a small metal tin, battered blue and gold. 'Yours, I believe.'

'You thieving bitch . . .' Trevor's hand went to his own pocket, slapping its empty shape. 'You're no better than your boy.'

'How do you think I got hold of it?' Ruth returned the bag to her pocket. 'There's more evidence back at the caravan park. In case, as I said before, you're getting any funny ideas.'

'*I'm* getting funny ideas?' He stared, blood crazing the whites of his eyes. Unable to believe he was being played at his own game. Outwitted by two women. 'You bitch. I helped you get shot of the evidence from that shed.'

'And planted some of your own,' Agnes said.

Trevor's stare swung towards her.

'The sand on Dad's clothes.'

She'd felt its grit on her fingers when she swept the sofa cushions, reminding her of holidays when she was a child. Except the sofa's sand was rough and orange. Builder's sand, not beach.

'You lured him to that building site after you killed Iris, asking for his help, knowing he couldn't refuse because he's feeling guilty. You were going to frame him for the building work, in any case. That's why you stayed close, pretending to be on our side, *helping* us.'

It was so clear in her head, every frame of it mercury-bright.

'Dad was your get-out-of-jail-free card. Of course you thought of him after Iris died. After you killed her. Dad was going to be your fall guy again. You made sure he got sand in his clothes, knowing he'd walk it right back to the caravan. I'm willing to bet you were the one who tipped off the police this morning.'

'You don't need to bet,' Ruth said. 'It was him. Your father's phone has texts this bastard sent to get him out to the site that night.'

'I asked for Ade's help making the site secure because we had *trespassers*.' Trevor flung a fierce stare at Agnes. 'He stayed on site after I went. *He* stayed on site.' He bared his teeth at them. 'What he got up to after that? That's for the police to find out.'

'Your tobacco was on her face,' Agnes said. 'I saw it.'

'So? I *found* her. You were there.' His jaw knotted as he tried to stare her down. 'You pair of sick bitches . . . What makes you think anyone's going to listen to a word you say? You're on anti-psychotics, for fuck's sake. As for *you*, you can't keep track of your own kids let alone your husband. Your son's a *thief*. If I talked to Ade about the insanity up at the site, it's because I knew he was losing it. He's been losing it for weeks, in case you give a shit. You think he's copped out but it's more than that. If you cared, you'd have noticed. He needs all the friends he can get right now.'

'And that's what you are, is it? His friend.'

'The only friend he's got.'

Trevor searched Ruth's face, finding only hardness there.

'So I texted him, so what? There's nothing to prove I touched her, let alone killed her.'

'You have a criminal record.' Ruth's voice was full of flints. 'For assault. Did you really think I wouldn't check up on you, after what you did? And what you're trying to do?'

'Yeah? Funny how you never lifted a finger to stop this,' pointing with the flat of his hand between his body and Agnes, 'all those years ago. Pretty sure *she's* not forgotten that.'

He was right. Agnes kept her expression blank but her whole body burnt with the need to hear her mother explain why she'd taken Trevor's side over hers.

'You think if I'd known I'd have let you get away with it?' Ruth's voice was low, lethal. 'I would have taken a knife to you. As for Adrian, he'd have skinned you alive.'

'Instead, I get a lecture about flirting—'

Trevor broke off when Ruth made a savage movement with her hands.

'So you didn't know. Fair enough. I'd like to know what sort of parent that makes you, missing a thing like that.'

'I was wrong. About a lot of things. That doesn't mean I haven't been keeping count.' She faced him down. 'I have a record of everything my daughter told me about you, eleven years ago. And everything my son's been telling me ever since.'

The papers Christie took from her room at Blackthorn Ashes and hid in the storage locker at the caravan – was that what she meant? Ruth's insurance policy.

Agnes shuddered, the coldness of it freezing her right through. It was freezing Trevor, too. But he'd learnt to expect no consequences to his actions. Ruth was going to lose this bluff because she'd trained Trevor not to be afraid of her.

The cliff path was shrinking into night, clouds across the sky like camouflage. Below them, the sea held its breath, no longer beating at the rocks.

'So you thought you'd lure me up here to listen to your sick little stories and then what?' He folded his arms. 'I'd break down and confess to killing someone I'd never even met? That's how this's supposed to go?'

'You'd met her,' Agnes said. 'Iris told me. She called you a cowboy builder.'

'According to you.' He nodded as if humouring a slow child. 'Makes sense you'd say anything to protect your dad, since he's the one in custody.'

'He's not in custody,' Ruth said flatly. 'He's helping the police with their enquiries.'

'Oh, wake *up*! What d'you think that means? I bet Christie knows.'

His face grew dark. 'He was doing okay, you know that? Until you got to work on him, putting whatever poison you've put in his head to get him spying and stealing from me. He's a kid, for fuck's sake. No way you're making him give evidence in a police station, let alone a court. In any case he's off the rails, it's why you brought him all the way out here, isn't it? To see if he could behave himself, give him a second chance. That turned out well.'

'You care about Christie,' Ruth said in her coldest voice. 'I'm aware of that.'

'Oh, you'd better not've dragged me all the way up here because you think I give a shit about *anyone* in this fucked-up family!'

Trevor snarled a laugh. 'Because right now I'm thinking I need to get as far as possible from the lot of you.'

He turned the snarl on Agnes. 'Your dad's going down for this. Your brother, too.'

'Adrian isn't as pussy-whipped as you'd like to think.' Ruth's voice was frigid. 'That's the expression you taught Christie, isn't it? How you encouraged him to think of his father. Well, if it's how *you* see Adrian, you're in for a shock. Because right now he's telling the police what he saw at Blackthorn Ashes the night Iris Edison died. How you and he fought about what you were asking him to do, how he refused to help. How angry that made you.'

'And he's not fucking whipped?' Trevor's laugh was incredulous. 'You controlling cunt.'

Agnes held her breath, seeing that night – Trevor killing Iris, his temper finally released from the cage he'd kept it in during the building of Blackthorn Ashes. Here on the cliff, she saw him frown, summoning the memory of everything he'd said to Adrian as they'd stood over Iris's body, wondering in what ways he'd incriminated himself. Not many or he'd be more shaken at the prospect of Dad's phone in the hands of the police.

Fear ran its rash across the back of her neck; Ruth was going to lose. Despite his temper, Trevor had himself well under control.

'This doesn't look much like a police station to me.' He spread his hands. 'More like a picnic spot. If you had any evidence, you'd have taken it to them. You're pissing in the wind.'

He was right, there was no purpose to this standoff or none that Agnes could see. Ruth didn't take risks but this was monstrously risky, for both of them. Who confronted a killer at the edge of a cliff? At best it was melodramatic. At worst . . .

The sea slapped the rocks, salt adding its tang to the fiery air.

Ruth was less than a foot away, holding her ground at Agnes's side, shoulder to shoulder. Was that why she'd brought them here, to clear her debts in some way? It didn't sound like Ruth but perhaps she'd wanted Agnes to witness her confronting Trevor with what he'd done, not just to Iris but to her. She hadn't asked for Agnes's forgiveness but this felt like atonement. Was that enough to explain the risks she was taking?

'That's it?' Trevor dropped his hands to his sides then shrugged them into his pockets. 'That's all you got?'

Agnes thought of those hands on her, and on Iris.

Had he meant to kill her? Or had Iris opened the cage of his temper, pushing with her questions at the edges of his arrogance? Was there a moment when she realized what she'd done, the price she was about to pay?

'You can keep your little souvenir, that tin you swiped. Should give the police a laugh, if nothing else.'

His face relaxed into its old lines, cocksure and confident. He wasn't going to make the same mistake twice, by losing his temper when Ruth had nothing.

'Waste their time just like you've wasted mine. See what good it does you . . . Are we done?'

Ruth's silence was charged but it didn't register with Trevor.

'I'll be going then.' He shouldered past them, heading back down the path.

Agnes waited until she heard his car start, the spit of gravel against tyres.

'What was that?' she asked Ruth. 'What were you trying to do?'

Anger found its way through her confusion. Her friend and

her father were with the police, she should be at the station telling them about the scarf, clearing Errol's name. Instead, she'd been dragged up here to witness a standoff that'd ended in deadlock.

'Are you even going to tell the police about the tobacco tin?'

'Perhaps.' Ruth's voice was distant and distracted. She was looking at her watch.

'Well, I'm going to tell them about the scarf. The one Christie stole.'

Ruth looked at her. 'No, you're not.'

'Errol is my friend.'

'Christie is your brother.' Those dragon's eyes on her face. 'Your blood.'

Agnes shivered, in spite of herself.

'You were telling me about Emma Dearman—'

Her mother cut her off a second time. 'We should get back to the caravan.' She swept her hair from her eyes, glancing at the horizon as if she'd timed this whole thing to the slow slinking of the sun until all that was left was a thin red line on the water.

Four days after abandonment

———

27

Indigo Park was a dump. Anyone would've thought that even if they came from a crappy council estate. Coming from Blackthorn Ashes, it was a kick in the teeth. When Christie told Trevor how bad it was, Trevor laughed, 'I'll have to check it out.'

His camp was ten minutes away, along the edge of a field. He thought the big trailers were cool, 'Like Elvis died and went to Devon,' and he fancied the woman from the flashiest trailer who had big tits and tight clothes which Trevor said was the best of both worlds. Jonelle liked Trevor, too.

Next time Christie went to Trevor's camp, he heard thumping inside the motorhome. He sat by the fire pit, poking a stick at the ashes, wanting Trevor to come out and talk to him. Jonelle was first out, snapping at her bra and skirt. She grinned at Christie, 'This your lad?' reaching to ruffle his hair. Christie jerked his head away. Trevor laughed, 'Not a chance!'

He was always laughing. Some days it pissed Christie off but hanging out at Trevor's camp was better than being stuck in Indigo Park. For one thing there were loads of great hiding places.

Back in the caravan, Christie couldn't hide anything. He used the filing cabinet in the shed but Agnes knew about that and even if she never said anything, it wasn't the same. He missed having a proper place.

Most of what he took wasn't worth anything to anyone else. But it was stuff only he knew about, that's what made it special. Like the last of the bricks with his name signed on it in black marker pen. It should've been in one of the houses at the end of the estate, where they'd stopped building when the money ran out. Every house in Blackthorn Ashes had a brick in it signed by Christie. It was one of the reasons he'd been so proud to live there and so fucked off when they had to leave.

In Indigo Park, he'd hunted for a new hiding place for that last brick, not wanting it anywhere Agnes and Mum might see it and ask questions, or worse – feel sorry for him. It was no one's business how it made him feel, having that brick. Being able to take it out and hold it in his hands whenever he felt like it. He'd hidden the brick in the filing cabinet in the shed, wrapped in the scarf he'd stolen from Silverthorn. If Mum found out, she'd have a fit.

Trevor said, 'Your mum's kind of scary, mate. You know that, right?'

He didn't make use of any of the hiding places at his camp. If you walked in by accident, you'd think it was some SAS-grade shit with the fire pit and tripod to heat water and beans. Mostly, though, Trevor lived in the motorhome with its microwave and chemical toilet, a bunk bed with a duvet instead of a sleeping bag. He liked to be comfy, 'And slags don't like sleeping bags.'

He'd shagged Jonelle in the bunk bed while Christie sat by the fire pit waiting for them to finish so he could find a good place to stash the house brick. The motorhome had tons of empty cupboards, ones that slid out from under the bunk or opened over the toilet. It stank of sweat and smoke and whoever he'd been shagging but it was still better than the caravan at Indigo Park which wasn't even on wheels. Trevor could kick leaves into the fire pit and collapse the tripod, pack it all up and go, any time he wanted.

Christie's vision shook when he thought about how easily Trevor could escape. Not like Dad and the rest of them stuck in that dump, day after day after day. Indigo Park was making Mum worse. Sometimes Christie caught her looking at him and he *knew* she knew. All of it. Not just about the stuff in the shed that wasn't worth anything to anyone else but about the brick and why he needed a special hiding place for it, why his secrets mattered so much even though he was supposed to be better now, different. Changed.

Inside the motorhome, Jonelle was yelping like a dog.

Christie reached for a twig and snapped it savagely, adding it to the fire. Trevor had all the luck. It wasn't fair, his chest burnt with the unfairness of it; why should he get away with everything when the rest of them never could?

Just once he'd like to see Trevor lose something – his home or even something small like his tobacco tin or his lighter – just so he could feel how Christie felt, so there'd be one person who got it, who understood how his chest felt full of fire and knives and stones and he had to do something – anything – to make it stop.

6 SEPTEMBER

Twelve days after abandonment

———

28

When Agnes woke the next morning, the first things she saw were her brother's gloves on the floor at the foot of their bunk. Last night, when she and Ruth returned to the caravan, Christie was on the sofa, the TV remote in his fist, flicking between channels. They'd seen the light from the television, a fast flickering of colour from inside the caravan. Just for a second, Agnes had thought their home was on fire.

'Go to bed,' Ruth had told the pair of them.

'What about Dad?' Agnes asked.

Christie kept his eyes on the TV but blindly, not taking anything in. Agnes recognized the look. She'd been seeing it on her father's face for weeks – feeling trapped, looking for a way out.

'He'll be back soon,' Ruth said. 'Go to bed.'

Christie's face was too pale, every freckle standing out, but he'd lost the wobbly look from earlier, seemed wired, one foot popping at the sofa. 'I'm not tired.'

'Aren't you?' Ruth stood watching him, her face wiped clean of the emotions she'd revealed to Agnes on the cliff path, eerie in her calmness. 'You should be.'

Christie jabbed the remote's buttons with his thumb. 'I don't want to go to bed.'

'It's been a long day. We all need some rest.'

'I *know*.' His voice rose an octave. 'Okay? I just said I wasn't tired. *Jesus* . . .'

'Christie, that's enough. Go to bed. You, too.'

Ruth didn't look at Agnes, keeping her eyes on her son. Christie swore under his breath, tossing the remote onto the table.

'I said *enough*. Bed.'

'*Fine*. I'll fuck off, then.'

'You do that.'

The way they spoke to one another made Agnes's scalp tighten. As if they had a special code, one she didn't know and could never crack.

She and Christie did as they were told and went to bed, Christie climbing into the top bunk without a word to her. She lay listening to his breathing for a long time, wondering how to keep him safe or if *safe* was what he needed.

Dad's absence was like the pain in her tooth, nagging. Her dreams when they came were muddled, twisting away from her.

When she woke, Christie was gone. She picked his gloves from the floor, returning them to his pillow. Rain was falling with the dry sound of sand striking the windows.

As she dressed, tyres turned in the gravel.

She was outside in time to see Bette's door closing and the taxi driving off. *Errol was home*. She wanted to run to him but he needed time with his grandmother, to rest and recover from what must've been a night answering police questions. He might not want to see her, anyway. So much of this was her fault. Either way, she had to wait.

The kitchen was deserted. No dirty plates or cups in the sink. When she held a hand to the kettle, it was cold. The caravan was empty, she didn't need to search its rooms to know that. Ruth and Christie were gone, again. She filled a glass with water and carried it to the sofa, sitting where Christie sat last night, where Dad had slept every night until the one before the police took him away. The glass was heavy in her hand. She held its coolness to her cheek, staring at the wall in front of her. On the other side of the wall was the storage locker where Christie had stashed whatever treasure he'd salvaged from Mum's clear-out of the shed. Had Ruth discovered his new hiding place? It would explain this fresh tension between them. And there was the trouble he'd been getting into at his old school. Fights, Mum said, a girl with a broken nose. Did Dad know?

Someone knocked at the caravan door. She set the glass down to answer it, finding Errol on the doorstep in his red jumper and ratted jeans, head cocked to one side.

'Aren't you *at all* interested in my story of police brutality?'

He had a flask of coffee, a packet of biscuits tucked under his arm.

'Only I saw the car was out, thought this might be a good time.'

'You're okay.' She reached for him in her relief, stopping short of touching. 'Come in.'

They sat on the sofa, Errol curling his bare feet under him. Looking at him more closely, Agnes saw he was exhausted. His face was thinner than ever, his eyes spacey from lack of sleep. 'They didn't question you all night?'

'On and off. Mostly off.' He unscrewed the flask, pouring them each a measure of coffee. 'I had time to memorize *all* the graffiti so if you ever need a list of who's shagging who around here and with how large an appendage, I'm your man.' He drained the cup in a few mouthfuls, refilling it straightaway. 'The tea in that place was revolting . . .' He was strung out on adrenaline, talking too fast, one foot fidgeting, like Christie last night.

'Did you see my dad at the police station?'

Errol shook his head. 'They didn't mention him, either. Wanted to know about Iris, how come my name was on this note she'd scribbled on the back of a parking ticket . . . And about the scarf of course, what I was doing with that, how I got hold of it and what else had I nicked. Keys, money, credit cards, et cetera. Her phone . . .' He struggled with the seal on the biscuits, trying to break into the packet.

Agnes took it from him, opening the end of the wrapper before handing it back.

'Her phone?'

'Is missing,' Errol spoke through a mouthful of biscuit, 'allegedly.'

'It wasn't on her body?'

'Or in her car. So that's crazy, right? The police said they searched the whole site. Then they found this old parking ticket in her car where, *allegedly*, she drew a cat next to my name which of course the police thought *highly* significant . . .'

Another doodle, like the one Iris dropped from her pocket by the shed: Dearman and a cartoon dog. Errol and a cartoon cat. Or had she written his surname, *Argall*?

'She was murdered by the way.' Errol finished the biscuit, pausing to pick crumbs off his jumper. 'Did I mention that already?'

'I guessed, from how long they kept you there. And Dad, too.'

She should tell him about Trevor and Ruth on the cliffs last night. Should she?

'He isn't back?' Errol blinked about him. 'Where's everyone else?'

'Mum and Christie went out before I got up. I'm hoping they went to get Dad.'

'The police weren't questioning him. At least according to my duty solicitor who looked about twelve but still.'

'But they let you go without charge?'

'In the end.'

'Ruth said my dad went with the police to make a statement.'

'About what?' He reached for another biscuit. 'Not Iris.'

'Iris and Trevor.'

Errol halted the biscuit midway to his mouth. '*Trevor?*'

'He killed Iris. It was an accident probably but Mum thinks Dad knows, one way or the other.'

Errol took a bite of biscuit, frowning. She should tell him about the standoff that'd ended in Trevor walking away, certain he'd won because Ruth had no real evidence, only the tobacco tin Christie had lifted.

'When the police searched your caravan, they were looking for Iris's phone?'

'They wouldn't say. But they have a list of everything missing from the houses.' Errol dunked the rest of the biscuit in a fresh cup of coffee. 'It's how they identified the scarf.'

'I'm sorry.'

He shrugged. 'You told me it was stolen.'

'Was it Luke who told them about the scarf?'

'They didn't say but I guess so. Didn't Iris suspect him of topping his wife?'

'Yes.'

Had Iris shared that suspicion with the police, scribbled it down the way she'd scribbled Errol's name? If so, the police would have wanted to speak with Luke. It made sense he'd tell them about the items missing from the house after Emma died.

'Did you and Christie wear gloves?' Errol asked. 'Only I'm pretty sure they're going to be lifting prints from inside all the houses as part of the murder investigation.'

Agnes didn't own a pair of gloves but Christie did. She'd picked them from the floor and put them on his pillow. He hadn't worn gloves on any of their return trips to Blackthorn Ashes but he'd been wearing them yesterday while Agnes and Ruth were on the cliff path. Ruth who was happy to leave Christie alone while she went to confront Trevor. Ruth who had kept looking at her watch.

'It's odd they couldn't find her phone,' Errol was saying, 'unless it was a mugging. But who kills someone for a phone? Around here, I mean. I'm sure even Trevor has a phone of his own.'

'She might've been using it to record conversations.'

Iris had done that in Blackthorn, and in the cane chair by the empty field, slipping her hand into her pocket after promising Agnes she wouldn't record her. Taking photos in Silverthorn's garden.

'I'm glad you kept her out of our caravan in that case . . .'

'I was stupid. I spoke with her, let her talk me into taking her to Blackthorn Ashes. If she was recording me and the police find her phone . . .' Agnes trailed off, not wanting to think about the consequences of that.

'Maybe she recorded whoever killed her,' Errol said, 'and that's why Trevor took the phone. If he did.'

'It would explain why he was so angry when we walked in on him. If he'd killed her and couldn't find her phone and if he went back to search for it . . . Once it sank in, I mean. What he'd done.' She glanced at Errol. 'How did she die?'

'The police didn't say but from what we saw? I'm guessing he hit her and she fell on those bricks, bashed her head.' He pulled a face. 'I didn't see much blood, did you?'

'No . . .'

'Or he could've strangled her, I suppose.'

Those lean tanned fingers, had he ever put them around Agnes's neck? He'd liked to stroke her throat, she remembered. And plenty of times he'd hit her.

'I think Ruth's right,' she said. 'It was an accident. A punch makes more sense.'

Iris falling, her phone skidding, lost under a pile of bricks. Trevor panicking in the heat of the moment, unable to find the phone but knowing there was evidence on it which would damn him. Phoning Adrian and asking for his help, getting nowhere with that. Returning the next morning to search more thoroughly because his first plan hadn't worked, to frame his best friend for murder.

'He called my dad out there, the night it happened, said he needed his help making the site secure. Ruth thinks he was trying to set Dad up.'

Errol chewed the inside of his cheek. 'Shit . . .'

'Dad wouldn't have helped, not with something like that. He feels guilty about everything but a dead body?' She shook her head. 'He'd have refused and they'd have fought over it. Dad must have known he had to go to the police.'

After Ruth took him back into her bed and talked him into it. He'd kept quiet until then. 'I mean, I don't know. But that seems most likely.'

'So Trevor goes back the next day to search for the lost phone.' Errol poured the dregs of the coffee into his cup. 'Only to find it's gone. That's why he's pissed off when we discover him there with her . . . But if he didn't find her phone, who did? Who took it?'

Agnes didn't answer but she saw her brother, clear as day. Running from the unfinished house, his face white with shock. Christie with his magpie's eyes, spying treasure everywhere. His gloves on their floor this morning. The long confrontation on the cliffs last night. Ruth stalling for time, finally admitting she had no real proof, nothing to take to the police, after keeping Trevor there while they argued back and forth . . .

Tyres hissed to a halt in the gravel outside.

Errol swung his feet from the sofa to the floor, dusting crumbs from his jeans. From the window, Agnes saw her mother's car parked under the trees. Light shifted over the car windows, settling to shadow as her father pushed open the passenger door.

'Dad.' She was out of the caravan before he was out of the car.

He opened his arms, catching her in a hug.

'It's okay . . .' His voice was bruised. 'It is . . .'

Agnes lifted her head from his shoulder, met her mother's eyes across the roof of the car. Ruth's face was sewn shut with her secrets. Christie climbed out, blinking, to stand at Ruth's side. His stare was glazed, focusing on nothing.

By the time they were inside the caravan, Errol was gone, taking his flask and biscuits.

Dad headed for the bathroom, 'I need a shower and a shave,'

while Christie peeled off in the direction of his bunk, leaving Agnes alone with her mother in the sitting room.

'Has Trevor been arrested?'

Ruth set down her car keys. 'Is that what you've heard?'

'I've heard nothing. It's what I'm guessing.'

Agnes listened for sounds from Christie or Dad. 'And it's what you planned.'

Her wrists were pricking, and her thumbs. 'Last night on the cliffs, keeping him busy while Christie—' She stopped at the look on Ruth's face.

'Outside.' Her mother fastened steely fingers around her wrist. 'Now.'

Agnes broke her grip but she followed Ruth from the caravan, her mother striding in the direction of the groundsman's shed. The day was damp, the sun hidden from sight. All the trailers were in darkness. When they reached the shed, Agnes faced Ruth.

'You planted Iris's phone in Trevor's place. His camp, or his van. Last night. You got Christie to take it there while you and I were keeping Trevor busy on the cliffs.'

She waited for Ruth to deny it but her mother didn't speak.

'Christie told you about finding the phone or else you found it on him. Why didn't you just take it to the police?'

'Why do you think?' Ruth was pale, her eyes blazing. 'Your brother's prints were all over it. He's in the system because of that nonsense at school.'

'He broke a girl's nose. That's not nonsense.'

'It's not *murder*. What, you think he killed that woman? It was *Trevor*. You know it was.'

'But you couldn't prove it. Not until you found the phone.'

322

Agnes was shaking in the pit of her stomach.

'You made Christie take it to his camp. No wonder he looked so terrorized last night. Why do you keep putting your kids in the firing line?'

'My whole family's in the firing line,' Ruth shot back. Fury tugged at her face. 'Or hadn't you noticed? Your father's been under suspicion for *weeks*. Now Trevor's trying to frame him for this murder. You must have seen that last night. It was glaringly obvious.'

'Did your plan even work? Has he been arrested?'

'He will be.' Her mother smoothed her face into something more solid. 'And not just because of the phone. The woman from the trailer,' she nodded in that direction, 'Jonelle Teague. She reported Trevor for assault. It's why the ambulance came to take her away that day. They'd been having sex and he turned violent—' She stopped suddenly. Pain clouded her eyes. 'I'm sorry. For everything.' The words spilt out of her.

She didn't mean Jonelle Teague. She meant Agnes, and Trevor.

'I didn't know, not back then. I *swear*. But when you came home to us and I saw how you were around Trevor – it was suddenly so clear to me. I thought it might even be clear to your dad but he was distracted by the houses, everything going wrong all at once.'

She pressed her hands together in front of her heart.

'I was pregnant, it was complicated. The pregnancy, Christie . . . It was difficult. Dangerous, that's what they told me. I nearly died.'

Agnes blinked. Blood beat in her temples. 'What?'

'It doesn't matter now.' Her mother put the past aside with a movement of her fingers. 'But at the time it was the only thing that mattered. It was hard to concentrate on more than one danger – more than one *catastrophe* – and of course he was making threats. About you, about me.'

'What threats?'

'That you seemed ... unstable.' Ruth's voice hitched, on the edge of tears. 'I should've known then, what he was doing. But I couldn't believe it. I thought maybe it was ... flirting, that he was flirting with you. I thought if I warned him off ... And there was your dad, the business they had together. But if I'd *known*, I swear ...'

'You'd have taken a knife to him.'

Agnes made herself smile, needing her mother to stay strong, focused on what mattered right this minute, now.

Ruth said, 'Then he threatened to tell your father Christie wasn't his.'

Something cried out in the empty field, a desolate sound. A gull, or a fox.

'He's Christie's dad?' Her tongue was furred, thick against her teeth. 'Trevor?'

'*No.*'

The word was a stone thrown from her mother's mouth.

'But your father would have believed it. He lives in Trevor's shadow, has done for years. In college, Trevor was the one all the girls wanted. Your dad was half-crazed with jealousy, couldn't believe it when I picked him.'

Her stare was far away, lost in the past until she pulled it back.

'Of course Trevor couldn't be happy for him, or us. He started stirring at it right from that first week, making your dad doubt his luck, making him suspicious of everything I said and did ... If he'd said Christie was his, he'd have believed Trevor's lies because he couldn't believe in us.' Bitterness marred her face. 'It was always easier for him to believe Trevor. So, *yes*. He'd have swallowed the lie that Christie isn't his son.'

Agnes thought of her father in the caravan, saying he knew she and Christie had been back to Blackthorn Ashes but doing nothing, sitting with his silence like a force field, keeping them all out.

'He'd have believed him,' Ruth said, 'because that's what he does. And because I kissed Trevor, once.' Her lips twisted in distaste. 'Years and years ago but your father never forgot.'

'You—' Agnes felt sick, unable to repeat her mother's words.

'Adrian thought the sun shone out of Trevor, in spite of all the evidence to the contrary. He never stopped listening to him or following his lead.'

Ruth turned her blazing eyes on Agnes. 'I've seen the way he looks at Christie sometimes, even now. And Christie feels it, at some level. I know he does, the way Adrian holds him at arm's length . . . It's why your brother spends so much time with Trevor, aping him. Which of course makes Adrian jealous all over again. It's a vicious circle. I sometimes think Trevor set out to destroy this family. It's as if he believes it should've been his. *His family*. And if *he* can't have us, then—'

She pinched her thumb and forefinger together, showing Agnes the mean shape it made. 'You have no idea on how *little* all this is built. Or how hard I work every day to keep it together.'

She dropped the shape, her hand falling open. 'It's why it meant so much when we moved to Blackthorn Ashes. Away from the trouble Christie was in, more space for us to be a family. To try to be a family. When you came home, I had so much hope. We all did.'

Agnes struggled to swallow the blockage in her throat.

She'd talked to Dad about Trevor, imagining she was evoking happy memories, hoping to use those memories to bring him back into the present, to what mattered. All the time she'd been reminding him of the reasons he had to be jealous of Trevor and to doubt his own son. She'd opened that door without knowing what danger and pain was stored behind it. She'd done that and now . . .

'You've seen how he is,' Ruth said. 'Your dad. How easily he slipped into this depression.'

She was watching the warring expressions on Agnes's face, and she was watching Indigo Park too, her eyes returning to the trailers as if she feared being overheard.

'Being depressed doesn't make you weak.' Agnes drew her fingers into fists, tamping down her misery into something more useful. 'If Trevor's threatening our family, Dad has a right to know. He'd fight for us, I know he would.'

'Take a knife and skin Trevor alive?' Ruth shook her head. 'I want to believe that but if he found out what was done to you? I think it would break him once and for all. It nearly broke me, and I'm stronger than your dad right now. Perhaps I always was . . .'

She steeled her shoulders. 'This mess? You and I have to sort it, between us. If you can do that, if you can forgive me for everything I failed to do, thirteen years ago.'

Wind whipped at their faces, dragging Ruth's hair across her face.

'You were pregnant,' Agnes said.

'I was scared.' Her mother cleared the hair from her eyes. 'I thought I was losing the baby, they said that might happen. I think I spent every waking hour in a state of panic.'

Her mother never panicked, that's what she'd thought. She

remembered Ruth's pregnancy as a time of waiting, of monstrous calm, but her mother had been afraid. Terrorized, even. She'd seen something between her teenaged daughter and her husband's best friend, dismissing it as flirting, warning Trevor away without asking Agnes for the truth. It was years ago, in the past.

'Tell me about last night,' Agnes said. 'And Iris Edison.'

'You've guessed it anyway.' Ruth leant into the side of the shed, tiredly. 'Christie found the phone before he realized what it was, before he saw her body. He was scavenging, of course. It was dark and he was scared, so he ran. When he went to put the phone back where he'd found it, Trevor was there. Then you and Errol arrived. Everything happened so fast, he didn't know what to do.'

'Tell me about Dad and Trevor, the night before.'

The night she died.

'Trevor messaged your dad, asking for his help securing the site. Looters, supposedly, you heard his excuses. Your dad says Trevor tried to make him search her body for the phone.'

'Why would he do that?'

'I don't know, Agnes.' Her mother's voice frayed with frustration. 'Because he didn't want his DNA on her corpse? Because he was squeamish? Or because he wanted to see your dad jump through yet another hoop . . . You'd have to ask him what his motives were.'

'What did Dad do?'

'He refused. Drew a line, finally. It took a stranger's murder but he woke up to the kind of man Trevor is.' Ruth rubbed at her eyes. 'I told him he had to go to the police. I thought of trying to clean your brother's fingerprints from the phone but I don't know enough about the tests they might run. I wanted your father to take the phone to Trevor's place but he couldn't. He'd worked himself up into a state over it . . . That left you, or Christie. Your brother's been in and out of that camp enough times to know what he's doing, his fingerprints are already there.'

'You could have asked me to go with him.'

'I needed you with me. I was afraid to be alone with Trevor.'

'You're not afraid of anything.'

'I'm afraid all the time.' Her mother shuddered. 'I've been afraid for years.'

Agnes couldn't look at her any longer. She dropped her stare to where Iris's switch lay on the ground, a slim branch stripped of its leaves.

'So . . . Christie found her phone and he gave it to you. Did you listen to the recordings? I think Iris recorded everything.'

'I know she recorded Trevor making a pass at her then making threats when she turned him down, accusing her of trespass, breaking and entering . . . That should be enough to convict him.'

Agnes waited before saying, 'She recorded me too. Did you listen to that?'

Her mother shook her head. 'I tried not to handle the phone more than I had to.'

'But you did handle it. And then you wiped it clean, which means Christie's prints weren't on it. You could have taken it to the police, told them you found it.'

'*Where?*' Ruth demanded. 'I was never at the crime scene. My husband's a suspect. My son's in their system. When they start looking, they'll find *your* connection to Trevor. I'm the last person they'll believe.'

Her face was pulling out of shape again. 'Trevor tried to frame your father and he'll do the same to Christie if he can. I needed his attention on *us*.'

'You distracted him with the tobacco tin.' Like a magician's trick. 'Christie stole that for you.'

'Forget the tin. It's the phone that will prove everything.'

Ruth spread her hands. 'I had to get the phone into his camp. Christie knew his way around and, yes, it was risky. But less risky than doing nothing and letting him get away with it, with framing my family.'

Agnes wanted to shout, 'You sent a child into a killer's camp!'

She shut her teeth against the accusation, hearing her mother's name in her head and the word that ran out from it: *Ruthless*.

'I'd die for him. For Christie. And for you.'

'Not for me, don't lie.' Agnes recoiled. 'You don't need to do that.'

'For you, too. You've never understood. We've never understood one another and now it's too late but it's what you feel when you're a mother, you have no choice. You'd die for your children.'

Agnes's whole body was trembling with adrenaline, and exhaustion. She wanted to lie with the hard ground under her head. She wanted her mother to stop talking.

'When you were a baby, you cried all the time. I couldn't make you stop, it didn't matter what I did. No one helped me, not really. We were all alone, together. And it was as if . . . we were at war. I was afraid to sleep, even when you slept, afraid to wake you because it would start over . . . The awful noise of you not trusting me, the *mess* of us.'

She pushed her hair from her eyes. 'I was so tired it was like . . . hot tar was running through my veins instead of blood. Most days I could hardly move. But the nights were the worst.'

Her face closed, a prisoner of the past. 'We slept in the same room and it smelt . . . scorched. I was afraid to open a window in case you caught a chill, afraid to leave you alone in case of cot death, afraid of *you*.'

Her right hand crept to the neck of her dress. 'You were sick every night, sometimes all night. You fought me. I had these bruises . . .' Her fingers brushed her throat. 'When you were quiet, if you ever were, I felt like shouting. It was as if I'd won, at last.'

Her voice dropped with shock. 'I was horrible, a terrible mother. But it felt . . . as though you'd hollowed all the love out of me.'

Agnes didn't move, didn't speak. She could feel the earth under her feet and the ocean under the earth, fathoms deep. A word from her now would be like a pebble dropped into all that darkness, falling and falling, on and on for ever.

'I suppose it was post-partum depression but no one diagnosed it, they just gave me . . . strategies. I put up a blackout because they told me to. But the dark was always ruined by this *glare* from all the bottles and the boxes of baby wipes, and from the whites of your eyes when you woke . . .' A shiver went through her. 'You'd get me in your sights and cock your head and your whole face would turn red before you started shouting. More than anything else, I was scared of you shouting.'

She made a sound like a sob. 'I'd hold you close and rock you and sing to you . . . do everything I could to soothe you, desperate to help, for you to see how I loved you. But you'd shout and shout into my face. My eyes would be streaming, every bit of me would be jumping.' Her hands went to the front of her dress. '*Feed me! Feed me!* You had every bit of me under siege. You'd yell yourself hoarse, until you were in pain too. I couldn't bear it. I didn't know

how to make it better, for either of us. Nothing I did made a difference, you didn't do any of the things they said a baby should do.'

She stopped, swallowed. 'The Spanish have a saying: in every
good harvest you must expect a few thistles. It felt . . . we had nothing but thistles.'

Agnes waited for Ruth to run out of words, making herself as
small as she could.

'It was so quiet when you stopped shouting. We could've heard
a pin drop, you and I.' Ruth pressed her hand to her sternum. 'Your
heartbeat was so close it got into my chest. And when you smiled!'

Her face altered, opening wide. 'Colic, they all said. But that
smile was what saved us. Like green grass pushing through concrete . . . All I wanted was to hold you and kiss you and see it again.
Your smile saved us. I could see that you knew we loved you.'

She brought her eyes back to Agnes's face. 'Then when you
were older and you were so unhappy, you started hurting yourself . . . Before anyone knew what was wrong or how to help you,
before we *understood* you . . . I felt as if I wasn't able to do it any
longer. *Be your mother.* I know that sounds terrible. I don't understand it, even now. But without that smile . . . I didn't know how to
do it. I felt so lost.'

Agnes couldn't speak, could barely breathe.

She could only think how everything at Blackthorn Ashes was
an echo of what had happened, was still happening, between her
and Ruth. Things falling apart, cracks running wide, no extension
joints to dictate where the damage would be. She saw Ruth at
nineteen, young and green with her life in front of her, gleaming
with possibility. Then this tiny person corroding her confidence,
curtailing her freedom. Lights going on in the dead of night, stairs

shrieking, sticky green doors cut from trees before they were ready – all of it was echoes. Her mother's stolen life was so close she could stretch out her hand and touch it. But she knew she must never do that. Because it belonged to Ruth, alone. Agnes could look at what her life had been, see its clothes and colours, the slim gold necklaces (no good for a baby's grabby hands) and trembling earrings (no good, no good) but she must keep her hands to herself, never touch. Never know.

'What will happen to us?' she asked.

The thought of going back to their caravan was too much, pushing like a tide at a shrinking margin of sand. She saw her mother shake herself back into the present.

'Trevor will be arrested.'

'Not that,' Agnes said. 'Everything else. Blackthorn Ashes. What will happen to us?'

'I think they'll leave us here,' Ruth said after a beat. 'Out of harm's way. Who are we, after all? We got sick but we survived. No funerals for us, no people to mourn. We're anomalies. We should have died, all the houses had the same faults. Carbon monoxide could've killed any one of us – *should* have killed . . . They didn't even learn from us, our bloods didn't teach them anything they didn't already know, that's what the hospital said. We can't help them find answers, only give them more questions.' She moved her hands as if they hurt her. 'There's no peace in us.'

'What should we do?' Agnes asked.

This time, her mother didn't hesitate: 'It's your job to protect your brother.'

'From what? If Trevor's in prison—'

'From himself. Christie needs protecting from himself.'

Agnes saw her brother's face transfigured by fear and anger. He'd swallowed Trevor's poison, all of his machismo, aping his strut, thinking Trevor the pinnacle of manhood. But he was just a thirteen-year-old boy, scared and lonely.

'It's Christie's fight,' she told Ruth. 'With Trevor gone, he might win it. But it's his fight. He has to find the path himself. And he has to face the consequences of whatever it is you're afraid he's done. Without consequences there's no redemption, or recovery.'

That was the truth she kept seeing in her father's eyes. He desperately needed to be made to face the consequences of the failure of Blackthorn Ashes so he could move forward, get better. Her mother's strategy of retreat was no good, not in the long term.

Ruth stared at her as if she were a stranger. She didn't deny being afraid Christie had done something for which the consequences would be severe, even insurmountable.

'Tell me,' Agnes said, 'what really happened to Emma Dearman.'

Her mother glanced towards the trailers but there was no sign of life inside. There was only the wind pushing at the pair of them, pulling echoes from the empty shed.

'Christie was out with Trevor every day. In and out of the houses, the two of them. What Trevor's done to him . . . It's not the same as what he did to you, I know that. But Christie's so changed, unpredictable. I think . . . he's dangerous.' It hurt her to speak the word. 'Or he was, at Blackthorn Ashes.'

'You think he killed Emma.' Agnes fought to keep her voice level. She was light-headed for a moment. 'Christie.'

'I didn't know what to think. And there was no *time*. Everything happened so fast after the children died. Before that it was different, as if time were standing still. Everyone circling each other, no one knowing what to think or do other than come knocking on our door, asking questions of your dad, demanding answers he didn't have. Answers no one had.'

'Like Luke.' Agnes saw the man puffed up with indignation, lifting a fist to hammer on their door. Christie watching, eavesdropping on Luke's accusations, furious when Dad didn't stand up for himself. 'He gave the police a list of what was missing from their house.'

'The scarf, and Emma's purse.' Ruth nodded. 'Christie took them.'

She'd known and said nothing. Done nothing.

'I gave the scarf to Errol. It's why the police took him away.'

Her mother dismissed that. 'Errol isn't part of this. He's not family.'

'He's my friend.' Agnes stooped to pick up Iris's switch. 'Trevor helped you clear the shed, all of Christie's treasure. What will you say when he tells the police about that?'

'I'll say it was his idea. He poisoned my son, who's a child, made him do things he wouldn't normally do. Trevor is violent. Jonelle Teague will bear witness to that. He deals with his problems with threats and violence. The police will see a pattern because it's there. It's the truth.'

It's the truth about you, too.

Ruth made Christie plant the phone, using Agnes to keep Trevor busy, distracted. Ruth solved her problems with violence, just like Trevor. Except she hadn't killed anyone. Trevor killed Iris. Was it possible Christie killed Emma?

'He stole the scarf and purse, I know that. But *murder?*' She shook her head. 'Iris said Emma didn't die of carbon monoxide. She suspected Luke. That's more likely, isn't it?'

Than a thirteen-year-old boy, her brother, a killer.

Iris had implied the accident with the barbecue was deliberate, a way for Luke to shore up his alibi. She'd been full of theories, freely shared. Agnes frowned.

'Or even Iris herself. She was there the day of the street party. She knew the Dearmans and she was angry at them, I don't know why but it's possible she—'

'No,' Ruth said. The full stop was solid, impassable.

'What else do you know?' Agnes felt sick. 'You must know something, to suspect him of . . . that.'

'It's better you don't know.'

'You're asking me to lie for him because he's my brother. I need to *know*.'

'Bricks,' Ruth snapped. 'All right? I found bricks he was hiding, with his name written on them. It was your dad's idea, a brick for every house. I'm sure Christie told you about the bricks.'

Agnes wasn't thinking about her brother. She was seeing Iris striding to Emma's house, throwing words across her shoulder: 'She collapsed on the stairs, they think. Fell and hit her head. They found brick dust in her hair.' She was seeing the filing cabinet's empty drawers. Her brother's name on every brick. Of course he had to get rid of them.

Her mother hadn't finished.

'One brick . . .' Her voice twisted. 'There was blood, and hair.'

Agnes turned to face her.

'It was hardly anything, really.' Ruth's fingers twitched at her sides. She wiped them on her skirt to make them stop. 'It's possible he hadn't noticed.'

'Emma's blood,' Agnes said numbly. 'Her hair.'

'I had to assume that, yes.'

Her mother's face was haggard. Agnes saw the brick, sticky with strands of greying hair, her brother's signature washed in red.

'What did you do with it?'

'I put it back.' Ruth sounded bewildered by her own actions. 'I didn't want him knowing I knew. It might've been nothing . . . One brick, a couple of strands of hair. It might not even have been blood, I might have got that wrong. He wouldn't have kept it, would he, if that's what it was?'

All this time, she'd been afraid. Terrified for Christie, and *of* him. Not knowing what he'd done but fearing the worst. Believing her child to be a killer.

'When did you find the brick?' Agnes asked.

'The day we were moved out. The day we came here.'

'You didn't say anything, to anyone.'

'I didn't *know* . . . only that I had to protect him.'

Ruth moved her eyes away, as if the sight of Agnes was too much.

'I thought I could count on you to do the same. But the pair of you have been so odd together. Fighting then inseparable . . . I couldn't make sense of it.'

At Blackthorn Ashes, Christie's hostility had been unequivocal but here in Indigo Park it was more complicated, bound up in the ritual of their return trips.

'You found Emma's body but you left it where you found it. You didn't tell anyone.'

'I knew they'd think it was another death like the others. There were no batteries in the carbon monoxide alarms, they'd forgotten to fit them. It's one of the things Christie and Trevor were busy doing, trying to cover up the mistakes that were made. *One* of the mistakes . . . Either they fitted new batteries in Silverthorn, or Emma did.'

Ruth swallowed. 'I took the batteries back out. I knew the police and investigators would see it wasn't working and assume she died like the others.'

She made a swift, urgent movement with one hand. 'She *might* have died like that, like the others. Breathed in fumes and fallen, lost consciousness. If they tested her blood and found she was poisoned . . . It's the simplest explanation.'

'Except for the brick. With her blood and hair on it.' Agnes ran Iris's switch through her hands, concentrating on its smooth-rough feel against her skin. 'Where is it now?'

'Where?' Ruth looked confused.

'The brick. You cleared everything out of the filing cabinet.' She nodded towards the shed. 'Did you take the brick too?'

'It wasn't *in* the filing cabinet. I don't know where it is. I was stupid . . . I should've taken it when I first found it but I couldn't bring myself to touch it.'

'Christie got rid of it, then. Or he found a new hiding place.'

The storage locker at the side of the caravan. Had Ruth looked there?

'Didn't you ask him about it when you were clearing the shed? Oh . . .'

She was surprised to find she could read her mother's face.

337

'You still haven't told him, have you? That you saw the brick. And that you suspect he used it to kill Emma.'

Agnes shaped Iris's switch into a circle, hiding the shiver in her bones. It made a perfect circle, bending easily in her grip. A dog barked in one of the trailers.

The sound of it shook Ruth back.

'Christie needs me. Just as you needed me once. I can't fail again.' She hardened her face. 'I won't.'

She'd taken the batteries from the alarm, left Emma for the police to find. She'd done this to protect Christie, and to save her family. A terrible sacrifice, is that how she saw it? It was how she wanted Agnes to see it. No price too high to keep her brother safe.

'If he killed her, it was an accident. He's a child. He needs help.'

'He'll go to prison. The age of criminal responsibility is ten. *Ten*. He will be in prison for years. It would change him, for ever.'

The blaze in her eyes was like blackness, swallowing everything.

'We would lose him, *for ever.*'

'What are you going to do?'

'What I failed to do for you.' Ruth turned away, in the direction of the caravan where Christie and Dad were waiting. 'I'm going to keep him safe.'

29

'You've got this.' Ruth was filling an overnight bag, rolling a change of clothes around a washbag, packing it all tight. 'You have.'

It wasn't the first time she'd said it, just the first since she'd settled on this insane solution to the nightmare they were in.

'The kids need you. This is the best way.'

'You, confessing to a crime you didn't commit?'

Adrian kept his voice low, afraid it would carry to the room where Agnes and Christie were sleeping. 'You think you can fix this but you can't.'

Talking was like dragging rusted nails from the back of his throat. His skull was full of wasps, buzzing blackly. 'No one can.'

'Adrian.' She shot him a look, not pausing in the packing. 'I need you to keep it together.' Her voice was full of warning but it was too late for that, too late for anything.

'Keep *what*? It's all gone. Over.'

He wanted her to stop. *Needed* her to stop, to stand still. She was always racing ahead, away from him. He felt more alone than he'd ever felt in his life.

'Aren't you scared? I'm scared.' He heard the shake in his voice, despising himself for it but he needed her to stand still with him. He needed his wife.

Ruth halted what she was doing. For a split second, she kept her eyes down, on the bag. When she looked up, her stare was so cold it burnt. 'Would you die for them?'

'What?'

'The kids. Our kids. Would you die for them?'

'Of course! How can you even—?'

'Then *live* for them.' Her voice shook but not from fear, from fury. 'Whatever it takes, that's what I need you to do.'

'Letting you go to prison.' His blood was like water, making him light-headed. 'Letting Trevor go to prison . . .'

'It's what he deserves.'

Ruth moved in front of the light. He couldn't see her face, just the intense whiteness of it, demanding he look and listen. 'He's deserved it for years.'

'It was me.' His voice was like water, weak. 'Who killed that reporter. You *know* it was me.'

The words shook the air between them. The secret – unspoken until now – scalded his lips as it spilt out. He expected Ruth to recoil, or to strike him, or to weep. He wanted to weep but the tears wouldn't come, a solid plug of bitter salt in his throat.

Ruth did none of the things he'd expected. She stood her ground, immovable and unmoved.

'*I don't care.* Do you understand?'

'How can you say that? I told you it was an accident, I told you everything . . .'

The lack of light in the half-built house, ghosts whispering, the children's voices raised in play and Iris Edison with her phone out, demanding a statement, 'What do you say to the families of those who died, to your own family? What sort of father are you?' His reflection trapped in her phone screen and all he'd wanted was to free himself, to get out of that half-built house where he could hear the children playing.

'How can you say you don't care?'

'Because I *don't*. And because Trevor needs locking up. He's needed it for years.'

'What are you talking about?'

Her face frightened him.

'What do you mean, *years*?'

'Thirteen years, Adrian. What does that mean to you? Summer, thirteen years?'

'Christie was born. You were pregnant with Christie.'

He wanted to ask what that had to do with Trevor but he was afraid of the answer. She'd always denied it. *Always*. Dismissed his fears as nonsense, as jealousy; of course Christie was his, how could he doubt it? How could he?

'I was pregnant with Christie,' Ruth agreed. 'Do you remember how hard that was?'

'Of course I remember.'

Sleepless nights, swollen ankles, sudden bursts of blood. Ambulances.

'Of course you remember,' she echoed. 'You were there.' A beat. 'Where was Agnes?'

'What?' He felt lost, further away from her than ever.

'When you were rushing me to hospital or finding me a change of clothes or telephoning the midwife.' Ruth set the flat of her hand on the lid of the bag. 'Where was our daughter?'

'She was . . . on the beach, in the woods.' He saw Agnes between the trees, a pale flitting figure. 'She went to the woods.'

'She was with Trevor.'

Ruth zipped the bag shut, slapping it to the floor. 'Your best mate. Good old Trevor, charming the pants off everyone, ducking and diving and letting you carry the can. All that summer he was grooming our teenage daughter.'

Her words landed like blows, staggering him. 'She was—'

'Sixteen. A child. A vulnerable child. But never mind what *she* was. I'm talking about Trevor, what *he* was. What he still is.'

Ruth drew a breath, as if summoning fresh rage from the pit of her stomach.

'A predator, a rapist.' Her eyes scanned his face. 'If I'd known, I'd have killed him. What would *you* have done?'

He made a fist of his fingers, seeing hammers and chisels, a smashed spirit level, broken bloody bones, Trevor's smile hanging sideways from his face. He saw Agnes refusing to sit down at the table in Blackthorn, Trevor shrugging off his apology, *Not a problem, mate.*

'Why didn't you *tell* me?' His voice was high, inhuman.

'I didn't *know*! I was trying to keep Christie alive, fighting to take him to full-term. Most days I was out of my mind with pain or worry. Where were *you*?'

She made a blade of her hand, stabbed it at the air.

'*You*. Her father. Where were you?'

'You've just . . . you *said*. I was telephoning doctors, taking you to the hospital . . .'

'Or drinking with Trevor, or working away. Not just that summer, every summer, every holiday. It was on *me*. All of it, all the time. You weren't *there*. For us, for our kids.'

She squared her shoulders, straightening to her full height. 'Well, you're going to be there now.'

'You can't just dump this on me and go! If Trevor did that . . .'

She was watching his face too closely, there was nowhere to hide his disgust and guilt and shame. But still she didn't see it, why couldn't she see it? All she saw was Christie, all she cared about was sparing her son – *their* son? – from prison, by confessing to killing Emma Dearman. She knew Adrian was responsible for what happened to Iris because he'd told her – broken down and told her – but because of Christie, because her son was a killer, she was tasking *him* with Christie's rehabilitation and Agnes's too, if what she was saying about Trevor was the truth.

'*Listen,*' he tried again to tell her, 'it's not what you think—'

She lifted her hand to silence him. He'd been silent for so long, was that it? She couldn't hear him, and he couldn't reach her. She'd made her mind up about him years ago, years and years. And because of that she'd chosen this version of the truth now – plucked it from the rubble of their lives and dusted it down to present to the police. It hardly mattered what he did, what he'd *done*. And part of him, a dark rotten place under his ribs, didn't want her to listen. Let her fix this the way she'd planned. She was the doer, he was the dreamer. Except all his dreams were nightmares now, boiling like wasps in his skull.

'They *need* you.' Ruth softened, looking like his wife again instead of a stony-faced stranger. 'Their dad.'

She was going to prison because she believed her son was a killer. Adrian's guts twisted, everything knotting, his throat closing reflexively.

Ruth stepped close, put a hand on his hand. 'They need their dad.'

———

30

Christie kicked at the wall of the house savagely. He wished he could kick it down, this house and all the others. He wanted Blackthorn Ashes to burn to the ground. His foot hurt but he kept kicking, harder and harder.

Somewhere in the wall was a brick with his name on it – a fucking joke. He'd told Dad it was a joke. He may as well've autographed a pile of shit. Dad said no, the bricks were special, 'We built something special, together,' sobbing as he said it.

Christie was ashamed of him, crying like a girl. He told Dad they should bury the rest of the bricks, the ones he'd signed, or else smash them to bits. It wasn't like they were ever going to finish the other houses now.

'Your name,' Dad said. 'Your name's on all these.' He was cradling one of the bricks like a baby. Christie felt like he might actually puke. 'It *means* something.'

'It doesn't mean *shit*.' He pulled the brick from Dad's hands, throwing it as far from him as he could manage. It hit the ground, turning until it came to rest in the grass. 'It's nothing!'

Dad went down on his hands and knees after the brick like Christie threw something valuable, precious. He wanted Dad to find it and chuck it – through a window or at Luke Dearman except he was back in hospital after barbecuing his arm.

He watched Dad kneeling in the grass and he wanted to scream at him to *do something*. Stop being a pussy and a walkover, get up and fight back!

He didn't understand why Dad put up with all the shit from the Dearmans, making himself a punching bag for every whiny bitch who couldn't fit their own batteries or fix their own lights. No matter how bad it got, Dad soaked it up. All the anger and blame, every insult they flung at him, down on his knees trying to please everyone all at once. If Christie did that, he'd explode. But Dad just kept smiling and saying sorry and doing *nothing*. He made Christie sick to be his son.

'You should've told her to shut up! Just because her old man's not here to give us shit, doesn't mean *she* has to start!'

Dad hunched forward, hiding the brick in his chest.

'What do you mean?' His voice was like the rest of him, weak.

Christie would've shut up if Mum had been there, or if Trevor had. But it was just him and Dad and he was sick of shutting up, rolling over, playing dead. Dad did enough of that for both of them.

'I saw you go over there.' He pointed at Silverthorn. 'I bet you went to apologize *again*. You should've told her we've had enough of her and her stupid husband.'

'You saw me?'

Dad kept his face hidden, like the brick in his lap. 'Did Mum see me?'

God, now he was scared of *Mum*.

'No. She's out with Agnes, picking up her meds.'

He looked down at his dad in disgust. 'I'm the only one here. No one else saw you creeping to that pair of freaks *again*.'

'Christie.' Dad sucked a big breath like he was about to make a speech about how important it was to keep everyone happy, how it was his *job* to creep to freaks like the Dearmans.

'I *know*! Okay? They're our *neighbours* and this whole place was *your* idea and of course they come to you with their problems and everyone's worried sick right now *blah-blah-blah*.'

How many more times did he have to listen to the same tired crap? He wanted to run away, live with Trevor or on the streets, anywhere but here.

'Did she make you grovel? I bet she did.'

Dad climbed to his feet like he was climbing a mountain slowly.

'Did who make me grovel?'

He looked at Christie and he was so . . . *old*. Grey and knackered like all the life'd been sucked out of him, shrivelled up. He made Christie think of vampires and zombies, the undead.

'You know who!' He jerked his head at the house across the road. 'Mrs Dearman!'

Dad shook his head. He was gripping the brick with both hands like it was really heavy. He didn't look like Christie's dad any more. He looked like a bad drawing of his dad done by someone who didn't like him and didn't care how accurate the drawing was.

Christie wished Mum was here. She'd know what to do. He

wanted his real dad back, his dad from before. Not this one with his wet, scared eyes.

He tried to think of something he could say or do to shock Dad back to him. Maybe he could tell him about the stuff in the cupboard in his room, the stuff he'd stolen. But this dad wouldn't care, this dad'd just cry and wrap up his stupid brick in Mrs Dearman's stupid scarf and rock it to sleep.

'I need to take a shower.' Not-Dad's voice was wrong, too. 'Can I ask you a favour?'

'What? Go across and apologize to her? We've all got to grovel now?'

'*No.*' Dad nearly shouted, which was just great, perfect in fact. He couldn't have shouted at that old bitch, had to save it for his son? He'd been weird with Christie for weeks, never mind how hard Christie worked to help out round here, all the times he lent a hand with Trevor.

'I need you to *stay away* from there,' Not-Dad said. 'From *all* the houses. I know you and . . . Trevor like to help out.' He choked on Trevor's name like it was a bone. 'But it needs to stop. Please, Christie. You need to stop.'

It was the *please* that did it. The idea his dad was begging him the way he begged everyone now. Down on his knees, taking a beating. *Please.* That's when Christie knew he might as well give up on Dad once and for all. He'd never stick up for himself or the rest of them. He was whipped, just like Trevor said. That was the day Christie stopped speaking to him, the day his dad stopped being Dad and became nothing, no one, invisible.

Later, in Indigo Park, he'd remember and feel horrible, sick with guilt. It would feel like he'd lost more than his dad, as if he'd left part of himself in the empty houses at Blackthorn Ashes and he could get it back if he searched hard enough – he could go back and put it right. But at that moment, seeing Dad clutching the brick, he felt only rage. Coming up through the ground where he stood, squirming through his shins and into his stomach, burning all the way to his eyes.

31

Ruth took a taxi to the police station alone, leaving the car, leaving everything. Adrian sat in the caravan waiting for the kids to wake, working over the words he and Ruth had chosen to explain to them what had happened. Mostly, though, he was thinking of Barry Mason on the night of the storm.

He and Janis must've thought it was a miracle, the kids sleeping through all that noise – through the wind and rain whipping at the windows. The baby, especially. Then the power cut and one of them decided they'd better check on Sasha who wasn't a light sleeper at the best of times or perhaps it was time for her feed, Barry's turn, but Sasha wouldn't wake and when Janis checked on Felix and Chloe – that's when the screaming started. Ruth had reached for her coat when she heard the screams. 'I'd better go and see if they're okay,' she'd said. She hadn't needed to wake Adrian. He was already up. He hadn't slept in days, not since the street party, Luke's arm sizzling on the barbecue. He'd gone to Silverthorn the following morning, to see if Emma needed anything and to plead with her about his paradise lost. That was his mistake, thinking it was his private hell when it was everyone's, they were all lost.

She hadn't answered his knock on the door or his call from the hallway when he ventured inside, fearful for no good reason. He could still smell Luke's arm burning.

'Emma?' Climbing the stairs, scared by the silence in the house, carrying his peace offering tenderly in both hands. 'Mrs Dearman?'

She'd come out of the master bedroom to stand at the top of the stairs, wrapped in an old red fleece dressing gown and a new rage.

'You're a pathetic puppy, aren't you?' Her eyes raking his face before dropping to his hands. 'Bringing that ridiculous brick in here like a dead rat.'

Another mistake. He'd thought the brick would move her, proof of how deeply his whole family was invested in Blackthorn Ashes.

Christie's name was on the brick, for pity's sake.

Instead, 'You've failed.' Nothing but contempt in her voice, just like her husband. 'This place is ruined. You're a failure. Everyone can see it, even your own family.'

'Please don't bring my family into this.'

'That daughter of yours with her shaved head, I've seen her, smoking drugs with that black boy who wears women's clothes . . .'

'Mrs Dearman, please. I came here to see if there was anything I could do—'

'*You*? You can't even sort out your own family. What kind of father are you, exactly? Your boy's a thief, I told your wife but she wouldn't have it. You're lucky Luke doesn't know about that.' Her mouth twisted, mocking him. '*My* husband's a man. He doesn't hide behind his wife.'

'I've tried.' He turned his back. 'I'm going now, before I say something I'll regret.'

But, 'Don't turn your back on me, you pathetic puppy!'

Grabbing for his arm and missing, her fingers snagging in his sleeve, shoving him so the pair of them lost their balance and fell, no time to scream or shriek, thudding down the stairs, thumping, a clumsy slow-motion mess until that single, sickening crack as her head hit the bottom.

He was underneath, thought for a second he'd broken her fall. But when he moved his arms he found Christie's brick in his fist, as if he'd glued it there, refusing to let go. He could smell talcum powder and toothpaste and her blood, hot.

His heart punched in his chest. He couldn't catch his breath – soaked right through with horror and shock and *relief*. Appalling, wonderful, eclipsing relief. Because everything had stopped. The madness and anger that'd been battering inside his skull for weeks – stopped. Silence, deep and black, drifted him like a sea.

It didn't last, of course. How could it?

In the caravan, he blinked, steadying his hands on the lip of the table, listening for sounds from the room where his children were sleeping. He was certain they must have heard the violence in his head, that awful crack as she landed. It was so loud, even now.

'That happened.'

He made himself say it out loud because he'd kept it inside too long. Buried under the wreckage of the days that followed. The storm, the children. Hiding it, even from himself. Until Iris Edison came with her questions.

At the hospital, they were told carbon monoxide poisoning causes confusion and paranoia, even hallucinations. That's how it'd felt, in Silverthorn. He'd convinced himself he couldn't be sure how it happened so what hope was there of explaining it, or describing it to the police? He would never be free, though. He knew that now. Until he faced it and was made to pay. He wanted to be made to pay.

He twisted his fingers together, raising the fist they made and hitting his forehead dully, again and again.

Ruth was gone. She'd taken it with her, his chance to be made to pay. If he confessed now, she'd go to prison for perjury. The kids would be left alone and Ruth was wrong about Christie being a killer but she wasn't wrong about everything. It would all fall on Agnes. Ruth didn't believe Agnes could carry that, or else she'd have come up with a different plan.

He forced his hands down, listening.

By some miracle, the kids were sleeping through this. But that's what Barry Mason had believed, the night of the storm, and he was wrong.

Perhaps Adrian was wrong too, and Ruth. Agnes was here. She'd come home to them and she'd stayed, even when everything was smashed to pieces right in front of her. He felt a fresh surge of rage at Emma, her contempt for them all, even Agnes.

That daughter of yours with her shaved head . . .

Her face a mask of disgust. *What kind of father are you?*

22 SEPTEMBER

Twenty-eight days after abandonment

32

It was fifteen days since Agnes had last seen her mother. She was alone in the caravan with her father and her brother. The three of them had fallen into a new routine, Dad taking Christie to school and bringing him home, Agnes taking care of the cooking and washing, watching her brother from the edge of her eye, wondering.

Her mother's trial was scheduled for the spring. Trevor would stand trial for manslaughter. He would plead not guilty despite the evidence against him. Ruth, against whom there was no compelling evidence, was going to plead guilty. Unless Agnes could find a way to stop her.

'Your mum told the police she lost her temper, just for a second.' Dad had sat with them on the morning of Ruth's arrest, looking sick to his stomach. 'They were upstairs, Mum said. Emma was upset about Luke's foot and all the problems with the houses. Mum was trying to explain how hard we were working to put it right.'

Christie made an impatient sound in his throat.

Dad glanced at him, then away. Agnes could feel the heat coming off Christie, his anger at being made to sit and listen to this.

'Emma didn't believe we cared. It was all about money, she said, and we'd failed.' Dad's stare shifted around the caravan. 'Your mum couldn't make her understand. She reached out to try and take her hand – just to take her hand – but Emma didn't want Mum touching her. She pulled away and that's when she fell. Lost her balance and . . . went down the stairs.'

He blinked twice, as if to clear the images in his head. 'It was an accident.'

He paused on the word, weighing it against their silence. 'We know your mum would never hurt anyone. She's told the police everything. It was an accident.'

'Can we go now?' Christie had been kicking at the table leg the whole time Dad was talking. 'Are you done?'

That night, he'd crept out of his bunk and into hers.

Agnes was curled on her side when he slipped under the duvet to lie next to her, staying there until his breathing deepened into sleep. She lay awake for a long time with the heat of him at her back. Thinking of the storage locker whose key she'd yet to find. Christie wasn't hiding treasure, not now, not in days. All his secrets were inside. She'd wanted to roll away, find a cool spot where she could sleep. But she'd made a promise to keep him safe. Ruth trusted her to mend what was left of their family.

Fifteen days since she'd made that promise.

She wanted to visit the prison but for that to happen Ruth needed to add Agnes to her visitor list. So far, the only name on that list was Dad's. This morning, he'd been to see Ruth for a second time, between taking Christie to school and bringing him home. Her brother had been in his bunk, playing on the old Game Boy Agnes had fixed.

'How was Mum?' She set the mug of tea on the table.

'Thanks, love.' Dad touched the rim of the mug. 'She was . . . the same. The same as always.'

'It must be hard, going there. Seeing her there.'

'It's easier the second time.' He put a hand across his mouth, fingers spanned. 'Harder for her.'

'It isn't right. What she's doing, taking the blame. It isn't right.'

'I've tried. We thought . . . there was no evidence. Nothing to prove she did it.'

'Of course there isn't. But then why haven't they let her go? Or charged her with something else? Obstructing the course of justice . . .'

'Agnes . . .' His palm was a muzzle but his eyes shouted with horror and pain. 'She told me today, it's all changed. They have evidence, a motive.'

'What?' She felt blank. 'But they *can't* have.'

'Her solicitor says they've arrested Luke.'

'*Arrested* him?' Her heart leapt. 'For Emma?'

It would solve everything.

Her mother could come home, Christie would be cleared.

'*Luke* killed her?'

But Dad shook his head. 'They searched Silverthorn.' He rubbed at his face with stiff fingers. 'They found . . . cages and poison. A lot of poison. Pellets, traps . . . They're saying Dearman isn't even their real name.' He sounded bewildered.

'Poison?' Agnes touched her fingers to the table to ground herself. 'Traps?'

'To kill rats. But they weren't trapping rats. Some of the cages were big enough for dogs.'

Odie limping towards her, his paw raised. Iris finding the cage in Silverthorn's garden then dropping it, as if the cage had burnt her. Because she knew the purpose it was put to? That night by the field, she'd said, 'Some of the cruelty out there, you wouldn't believe.' She'd known the truth about Emma and Luke, tracked them from wherever they'd been before Blackthorn Ashes.

'They were convicted of animal cruelty,' Dad said. 'When they lived in Exeter. Dozens of dogs and cats were found dead or in cages, in terrible conditions. They were running away from . . . that. When they came to Blackthorn Ashes. They were hiding.'

Running away. Not all the poison came from the land, or the houses. Some of it was brought by the people, abandoning their old lives but not their old selves. Emma and Luke putting down pellets and traps, injuring Odie.

Agnes shuddered. 'But if they've arrested Luke . . .'

'For animal cruelty and fraud, using a false name. Not for Emma.'

Dad blinked ahead of him, as if trying to bring an impossible picture into focus.

'When your mum confessed, there was no motive. That's what we were holding on to. But now they think . . . Emma killed Binka.'

Agnes stared at him. He stretched a hand for hers then stopped himself, gripping his own wrist as if afraid of what his hand might do. 'They exhumed her, love.'

Something in her silence seemed to ground him.

He spoke more calmly than he had in a long time. 'They exhumed Binka and they found poison that matches the pellets in Silverthorn. Emma's prints were on the packet. Not Luke's, just hers.'

Binka, limp in her lap. Mum trying to comfort her, Christie

sitting on the grass at a distance. She'd blamed Blackthorn Ashes but it was Emma. *Emma* killed Binka.

'But they can't think Mum . . . Not because of that, not for Binka. We all loved her but she was just a rabbit. It's not a motive for murder.'

'Manslaughter.' Dad winced reflexively. 'They've never called it murder. We were poisoned, they know that. Carbon monoxide causes mood changes and paranoia, even hallucinations. None of us were in our right minds. We weren't ourselves.' That plea was in his eyes again. 'That place did so much damage, love. We might never know how much.'

'Then they think Mum was . . . mad? Or Emma was?'

'Mum didn't have packets of poison in her house or cages, or boxes full of broken glass.' Dad's eyes darkened. 'They think Emma may've put the broken tin in Chloe's sandpit.'

Agnes felt ill. 'But *we* know. It wasn't Mum. She's taking the blame because she's scared Christie—'

Dad cut her short. 'She knows best.'

He put his hand back across his mouth, fingertips white where they gripped at his cheekbones, eyes pleading with her.

'She always . . . knows best.'

'She could get fifteen years in prison.'

And you, she thought, *you could get fifteen years for corporate manslaughter.*

Christie would be her age by the time they got out. Agnes would be middle-aged. It had only been fifteen days but already the loss of her mother was like a stone in her throat. How could she live like this, for fifteen years?

———

33

'We're celebrating.' Errol held up two frosty bottles of beer. 'It's three weeks since I was released from police custody.'

'You weren't in custody,' Agnes corrected. 'You were helping with their enquiries.'

'Well, it's three weeks since they arrested Trevor for murder. We can celebrate that.'

Errol scanned her face, a flicker of worry in his eyes. He was wearing his peacock robe over blue jeans, a dazzle of colour on her doorstep. Here to check up on her. Not to celebrate but to make certain she was holding it together.

'Let me in?' He peered past her shoulder into the caravan. 'You're alone, right?'

'Not any more.' She smiled at him. 'I have you.'

Errol chinked the bottles together, breaking into a big grin. 'You do.'

'Let's go out.' Agnes reached for her jacket.

It was a beautiful morning, the sky pearly with autumn sunshine. Errol needed fresh air. They both did.

'I'm not dressed for it,' but he fell into step at her side, tipping his face to the sun.

They walked the cliff path, in the direction of Blackthorn Ashes. The hedges held on to the night's rain, shimmering on either side. When they reached the trampoline, Errol opened the bottles and they stood facing the sea, drinking cold, crisp beer.

He wouldn't ask about her dad or her brother, or about Ruth. He'd stay close and give her the space she needed, waiting until she was ready to talk. He'd waited three weeks already.

Each day, he brought a flask of coffee and a slice of Bette's cake, or a serving of casserole. Each day, she thanked him and Bette and held her tongue, biting it against the threat of tears. She'd cleaned the caravan inside and out, washed down walls and bleached drains, turned mattresses, aired beds. Each day after Dad left on the school run, she sat on Christie's bunk until Errol came, grateful for the rhythm he gave to her days.

He leant into the trampoline, drinking beer from the bottle. A breeze brushed the sleeves of his robe from his wrists. His eyes were half-closed, the sun on his face.

'There was a moment,' Agnes told him, 'when I thought she'd frame me for Emma's murder. She was so desperate. Probably she believed I'd survive prison, the routine and so on. Better than Christie anyway.'

Errol waited. When she didn't continue, he said, 'She was ruthless. I was thinking how odd that was, her name being Ruth . . .'

Now I am Ruth-less. We all are.

'She made me promise to take care of Christie.'

Errol flicked a fly from his face. 'That was a hard thing to ask.'

'Not really. I mean, yes. But at least it made sense. Not much of this makes sense . . .'

Agnes turned from the sea towards Blackthorn Ashes, its high sloping roofs like an alien moonscape. *Akiya*. Ghost houses.

'Christie invested everything in our new start. Wrote his name on the bricks, ended all his old friendships . . .' She drank a mouthful of beer. 'I think that's why he took the scarf and the other things. Because it was *his place*, that's how he felt about it. Not in an arrogant way, or not to begin with. He loved it, every brick of it.'

Each time she said *brick* she was aware of a tiny flinch at the base of her throat.

'Ruth couldn't let him go to prison. She said he might as well be dead.'

Errol raised his eyebrows. 'What sort of prisons has she been visiting?'

He wouldn't forgive Ruth for what she'd done. Not now, maybe never. It was different for Agnes. The journey she'd been on with Ruth hadn't prepared her for what happened at Blackthorn Ashes but it kept her from tipping too easily into recrimination.

'She told me what it meant for her, becoming a mother. My mother. She felt she'd failed. Not by getting pregnant but as my mother. She'd failed and she kept failing, every day. She wanted it to be different with Christie. I guess . . . it was different.'

Errol lifted the beer bottle to his lips. His own mother had turned her back on him, Agnes remembered, and his father too. In many ways, she was blessed.

'I went back through the hedge,' she told him. 'Into Blackthorn Ashes.'

He lowered the bottle in surprise. 'When?'

360

'Two days ago. Don't look like that . . . I didn't go into any of the houses. I just wanted to see if it looked any different.'

'Did it?'

She shook her head. 'Not really.'

The only difference had been a white campion growing in the road outside Silverthorn, a frail flower but fierce enough to find its way through tarmac into the autumn sunshine, pricking the air with the faint scent of cloves.

Errol said, 'The papers have stopped running stories about Iris at least.'

'For now. Did you know she had no family? Her parents died in a house fire.'

Iris had told the truth, that night. Agnes hadn't trusted her but she'd told the truth about how her parents died. Her father, fairly or unfairly, had been blamed for the fire.

Errol held his bottle to the light, studying the sea through its brown glass. 'D'you think that's why she latched on to the story in the first place? Because it was about families.'

'Maybe.'

Agnes thought of Tim Prentiss lining a spirit level along a blank wall, measuring the space for a painting they'd choose together, Val polishing the hall mirror, uncomplicated in her happiness. She thought of Felix and Chloe racing around their square of lawn while baby Sasha sat on the grass, Janis and Barry leaning into one another in the doorway, watching and smiling. All those lives lived so ordinarily in the shiny new houses with their wild promises. Someone should keep faith with Blackthorn Ashes, that's how it felt. Someone should stand where she had two days ago, where the road curved towards the sea, and know how lucky they were to escape the dream of luxury living, how fortunate to be stuck in poky houses with families who loved them and who understood they could never afford to be in a place like this, that the price was too high.

'I should get back,' she told Errol. 'They'll be home soon.'

She said goodbye to him by Bette's caravan, hearing Odie bark with excitement to have him home. Bette waved from the window, her friendship like her grandson's, inexhaustible.

Inside her own caravan, Agnes took tins from the cupboards and made a start on supper. At the table, she laid three places. Three glasses and three plates, three sets of cutlery. When the food was cooking, she went to the bedrooms, opening windows to freshen the air, making sure the beds were neat. Yesterday on her walk, she'd picked a handful of wild pansies, setting the flowers in a small vase on the table beside the double bed in her parents' room. Christie's bunk had fresh bedding, his pyjamas washed and folded on his pillow. She smoothed her hand at the pillowcase and tidied its corners. Everything was ready for their return.

That morning, she'd tried to reach her father through his sadness: 'I could collect Christie from school for a change. We'd catch the bus. Why don't you take the day off?'

'Thanks, love.' His face was ghost-grey. 'But it's best to stick to our routine.'

His pain was eating him up. She was afraid of the damage it would do if he didn't let it go. Christie's silence felt different, as if he might be healing. The heat had gone out of him, that fretful rage which infected him in Blackthorn Ashes. It gave her hope, like the white campion growing outside Silverthorn. Three weeks ago, he'd been burning up.

She smoothed a hand at his clean pyjamas. She wanted every-thing perfect for when they got back, fresh flowers on the table, fresh milk in the fridge. She needed to keep busy but there weren't many jobs left to do. She'd vacuumed every inch of the caravan, liking the neat stripes it left in the carpets and the rhythm of it, back and forth, a satisfying ache in her arm. She couldn't clean the carpets again but she could vacuum the upholstered furniture.

In the sitting room, she pulled the cushions from the chairs and the sofa, running the nozzle into the recesses to collect any last resi-due of dust. She left the sofa till last, knowing it would be holding on to crumbs from Dad's toast and Christie's crisps.

The vacuum made a gritty sound, snatching at something trapped down the sofa's side seam. She switched off the power and crouched to push her hand into the gap, finding nothing there. When she peered into the neck of the nozzle, it was empty.

Her hand hovered over the On button before she reached to pull the plug from the socket in the wall. It took both her hands to unfasten the vacuum's dust compartment but only one to sift through the debris and dust for what it had swallowed.

A scrap of blue paper, lined.

She sat back on her heels, smoothing it flat against her thigh.

Scribbled in black ink: a cartoon snake. Like the dog drawn for *Dearman*, and the cat for *Errol*. A snake with fangs curling from its upper jaw.

She looked for the name Iris had written under the doodle. Black ink on blue paper made it hard to read unless it was the heat behind her eyes where the threat of tears was pressing because Iris hadn't written Trevor's name or Ruth's.

A car door slammed outside, shocking her to her feet.

She pushed the scrap of paper into her pocket, shredding it with her fingers so no one would ever be able to read what Iris had written, what Agnes had read.

Her family was home. It wasn't the police at the door, not this time. Iris was dead, Trevor standing trial for her manslaughter. Emma was dead, too. Ruth thought she knew Emma's killer but she was wrong. Ruth was wrong.

Agnes tore at the bits of paper in her pocket, making them smaller and smaller until there was nothing left of the five letters written there. *Their* name – hers and her family's – but only two of them shared the same first initial.

Iris had written 'A. GALE'.

Agnes, or Adrian.

Only one of them slept on this sofa and went missing the day before Iris's body was found. Only one failed to put up a fight when his best friend was arrested, and then his wife.

She forced herself to breathe through the panic, her mind skidding to Trevor's bluster at the cliff head. Guilt, she'd thought; he was hoping to frame Dad for a crime *he* committed in the heat of the moment, lashing out because his temper was too near the surface of his skin. Not like his best friend who'd buried his shame so deep his daughter was afraid of the damage it was doing, the damage it had already done—

It's easier the second time.

His hand like a muzzle across his mouth, eyes full of horror.

Agnes fought a sob. She saw her mother on the cliff path, calmly facing down the man she was accusing of murder. Then her icy determination to plant evidence, where otherwise there would be none.

Ruth had known who killed Iris, snatching at the chance to punish Trevor and protect Adrian.

Agnes bent double, her chest clenched because *she'd* known too. For weeks.

The truth lived in her heart like a thorn. All those days and days of him sitting on the sofa, too depressed to speak or wash or talk. Long before Iris died. He'd been a ghost since the street party.

'It's easier the *second* time.'

Iris wasn't the first.

In the caravan, she'd thought his depression was because of the children, his guilt at everything that went wrong. Six people died but the charges against him would be negligence, at worst corporate manslaughter. He wouldn't stand trial for the murder of Emma Dearman or Iris Edison. Those truths would stay hidden, locked away like the brick he'd used to kill Emma. Like this scrap of paper pushed down the side of the sofa. She should search the locker, find the murder weapon . . .

This time, the sob tore from her before she could stop it. She clapped both hands across her mouth, teeth slicing into her lip.

Adrian Gale. Her father. Christie's dad.

Stop it.

Ruth's voice cut through the clamour in her head. *Pull yourself together. We all have a job to do and this is yours.* She could hear her mother saying it.

But Ruth was gone. It was up to Agnes. What was it she'd said to her mother, out by the empty field that last night before Ruth took her false confession to the police?

And he has to face the consequences of whatever it is you're afraid he's done. Without consequences there's no redemption, or recovery.

She'd been talking about her brother but thinking of her father, the lost look in his eyes, his silent plea for her understanding. He needed her to do the right thing.

Outside, Bette was speaking to Adrian, Odie barking at Christie.

Her brother's voice carried, 'You're okay, aren't you, boy?'

He sounded happy, glad to be back.

Agnes picked cushions from the floor and put them back in place. She returned the vacuum to its cupboard.

At the mirror by the door, she paused to study her face: her father's nose, her mother's mouth. Her hair had grown back from the buzz cut, dark curls springing from her scalp.

She touched a finger to her reflection, drawing her mouth into the shape of a smile.

The mirror was coming away from the wall, a screw loose at the back, but she could fix it. She was good at fixing things.

1 JULY

Fifty-five days before abandonment

———

34

'Ade!' Trevor wore his hard hat, striding to sling a long arm about Adrian's shoulders. 'You're just in time to take me to lunch. Pub, yeah? My throat's full of brick dust . . .'

'I've only just got here, can't skive off straightaway.'

'Skive off? Mate, you work harder than the rest of us put together.' He squeezed Adrian's shoulders before letting him go. 'Come and take a look at your new place.'

'In a bit,' he repeated. 'I need to check the show house, see it's shipshape.'

'Everything's shipshape . . .' Trevor lifted his face to the sun. 'Damn, it's beautiful here. Did you arrange the weather, too?'

'Specially for you. Your tan's looking tropical.'

'The ladies love it.' He flashed white teeth.

Adrian laughed. 'Show house, come on.'

Hawthorn shone, despite the dust breezing from the building site. Adrian had two sets of keys in his pocket. To Hawthorn and to Blackthorn, his family's new home. He'd earmarked the house as soon as the plans were drawn up, a big corner plot with space in the garden for a basketball hoop for Christie, a spare bedroom

367

where he'd planned to build shelves for Ruth so she could use it as an office. It was a cliché but Adrian's chest swelled with pride at the part he'd played in all this. A passion project, and a personal one. Hell, Christie had even signed a brick for each house.

'Shoes off,' he prompted Trevor at the door.

The door was a bit sticky – he made a note of it – but the paint job in the hallway was flawless. In the kitchen, the fridge was packed with cans to quench the thirst of potential homeowners. The instant hot water tap worked like a dream. Adrian polished his prints from it with the cuff of his shirt.

Trevor reached into the fridge for a can of Coke, opening it over the sink before sucking a mouthful. He was being careful not to make a mess, which was harder for Trevor than it was for Adrian, walking dust everywhere in his cowboy boots, smelling of wood and glue and sometimes of cordite like fireworks. Appropriate as he had a short fuse although it hadn't been in evidence these past few weeks – too much to keep him busy, plus the sunshine helped. It was pressed against the back door, so much sunshine it made the glass bulge as if it might give way any second, a tidal wave of sunshine slopping and splashing and knocking up against the fridge, washing Adrian off his feet. He shook his head to get rid of the illusion, bending to check the cupboard under the sink; people looked in the weirdest places when they visited a show house. The cupboard was clean, just a bucket under the new plumbing. He made a note to put cleaning products in the bucket in case anyone thought it was there to catch leaks. When he tested the switch, the sunken lights dimmed before they died. In semi-darkness, the quartz stopped sparkling and the floor no longer shivered. What'd looked like hand grenades in a brass bowl were lemons again. He could hear the bubbles bursting in Trevor's can of Coke.

'It's cool, right?'

Trevor's voice was steady enough to stand on, his confidence amplified in order to get Adrian over this final hurdle: the sales that would see them into profit.

'It's cool . . .'

Adrian fixed his gaze on the planter whose shadow spilt along the counter. The hot water tap ticked as it cooled. He had a sudden intrusive image of Trevor tripping and hitting his head on the tap, his neck snapping on the hard marble lip of the island. He took a step back, felt something hot and sharp move against his foot.

Trevor laughed when he jumped.

'Underfloor heating, remember?' He cuffed Adrian's shoulder lightly. 'You'll be glad of it on cold mornings.' A second cuff, with a wink. 'Or cold nights.'

Adrian stepped out of range. He could see himself over by the window, standing behind Ruth with his arms around her waist, chin resting in her hair. Christie was there too, next to the shallow table where acrylic diamonds were scattered as casually as walnuts. Whenever Adrian pictured them here, Christie was off to one side, at a distance. Well, he was growing up, a teenager now.

In the doorway, Trevor's can caught the light, red shadows spilling down the wall.

The pub was half-empty, a proper Cornish pub – wonky floors, ancient whitewash, smelling of hops and vinegar. Trevor headed for the bar, propping one foot to the brass rail at its base. Adrian knew he was grinning wolfishly for the blonde behind the bar who was pouting in appreciation. A worm of unease twisted in his gut. At Ruth's insistence, he'd laid his suspicions to rest. One kiss, she'd said, that was all, years ago. One drunken kiss. But whenever Christie and Trevor were together, he found himself squinting as if another picture was hidden underneath, one he was choosing not to look at. He did a lot of that, he knew. Refusing to see, not allowing anything to get in the way of the project and its success. Too much riding on it. Everything.

'Weather's been a nice surprise lately!' The barmaid was admiring Trevor's tan and he was admiring hers which was probably from a bottle but still.

Adrian checked his phone messages, finding one from Ruth to say Agnes was coming with them at the weekend to see the show house: 'My office may need to be a bedroom after all!' She sounded excited. *He* was excited. Blackthorn Ashes was made for families and it'd been too long since his sat around the same table. His grin was wider than Trevor's in that moment.

'Fish and chips okay? It was that or soused mackerel and I've sorted the sousing . . .' Trevor put two pints on the table.

'I'm driving,' Adrian reminded him.

'Tegan's bringing you tap water.' He grinned back at the barmaid. 'These're for me.'

'The portaloo's going to see some action.'

'Nah, I'll use the bog in your new house.' Trevor caught his eye. 'Joking. But that reminds me, we've got a couple of faulty flapper valves, cisterns overfilling.'

'I'll add it to the list.' Adrian took out his phone, reading the list back to himself. 'This is getting long.' He looked up, saw Trevor shrug. 'Are we falling behind schedule?'

'Not if I can help it.' He nodded at Adrian's phone. 'What's up?'

'Apart from the faulty flapper valves and leaking radiators and wonky underfloor heating—'

'Hey, the underfloor heating works a treat in the show house. You did a little dance to celebrate it and everything.' His grin was infectious. 'I meant apart from the doomsday list . . . You were smiling like a loony just now.'

'Agnes is coming home.'

'And that's a good thing?'

The barmaid brought two plates stacked with battered fish, fat chips, peas and lemon wedges. She set the plates down, returning shortly with a glass of water and two sets of cutlery rolled in paper napkins. 'Any sauces?'

'We're all set, thanks.' Trevor wiped his mouth with his thumb.

Adrian said, 'How's it not a good thing? Agnes coming home?'

'Grown kids coming back to roost?' Trevor picked a couple of chips from his plate and put them in his mouth. 'Long as she's not sponging, I suppose . . .'

'It's not like that with Agnes.' He squeezed lemon over his plate. 'Anyway, there's masses of space in the new house. Her timing's pretty perfect.'

'That what Ruth thinks?' Trevor sliced his fish in half so he could eat it with his fingers.

'She'll want to make it work, you know Ruth.'

'Yeah, I do.'

A couple came into the pub with a terrier on a lead. The dog went to the water bowl by the bar, started slurping.

371

Trevor said, 'Reminds me, the pair who've reserved Silverthorn?'

'Luke and Emma Dearman.'

Adrian had the names in his head. His new neighbours.

'She was back in the sales office this morning, asking about pets. Said you'd give her a call but you'll want to brace yourself. She's got it in for dogs and cats, wouldn't be surprised if she hates bunny rabbits and goldfish too. Doesn't want the lawns digging up or her roses getting pissed on. Husband's not much better, from what I've seen of him.'

'He's fine. They just want everything to be perfect.'

They'd have to get used to pets living in Blackthorn Ashes, all the same; Adrian had promised Christie a dog.

'Makes sense for them to talk to you in that case.' Trevor licked his fingers. 'Mister Perfection.'

They ate in silence, Trevor enjoying Tegan's interruption to see how they liked their meal, 'Very tasty,' turning down the offer of a third pint to Adrian's relief; there was too much work to get done.

Most lunches they worked through, Adrian grabbing butties on the way out from the Travelodge where he was staying. Trevor was in his campervan, had made his usual offer of a bunk but Adrian suspected Tegan might be sharing that tonight. He drank half a glass of water to settle the bubble of resentment in his stomach. Trevor was his best mate but sometimes Adrian thought he'd like to break it off, that their friendship was phony, well past its sell-by date. They'd had nothing in common since he got married, even less since he became a dad.

Sometimes, to his shame, he felt like punching Trevor in the gut, a feeling that came from nowhere and nothing, out of a sunny day on a building site where his family would be living soon, all four of them together. Other days – quite a lot lately with the list of problems mounting at Blackthorn Ashes – Trevor was the one person who could raise a laugh from him. Ruth said Trevor was like a bad habit to be fallen back on in times of stress. Adrian found it hard to argue against that. They finished their meals, Adrian settling up, before heading back to the car.

A silver Lexus was parked up alongside his Audi, a family climbing out.

Boy and girl, maybe ten and six, squabbling over a games console, their mum slow to exit the passenger seat. A blue sundress just about contained her bump. Due any day now, by the look of it.

'It's near here . . .' Her husband had his phone in his hand, frowning at its screen. 'Must be.'

'Give it *back*!' The girl jumped, trying to reach the console which her brother was holding over her head. 'Mum said it's my turn!'

'You can't even play this game,' he scoffed.

'Felix,' their mum sounded at the end of her rope, 'it's Chloe's turn.'

'She can't even play it! She just dies all the time.'

'Let her have her turn . . .' Chloe wrapped herself around her mum with a wail. 'Oh, C'lo . . . Mummy really needs the loo.' She looked close to tears. 'D'you want to come with me?' The little girl hung from her arm, shaking her head. 'Baz, I need you to take them.'

Their dad was frowning at his phone.

'*Baz!*'

'Course . . . C'mon you two, Daddy's in charge.'

Chloe wailed louder. Her brother propped himself to the side of the Lexus, busy on the console. Over the roof of the car, Adrian caught Baz's eye, exchanging a rueful grin.

Trevor was rolling a cigarette by the back door. He stepped aside when Chloe's mum approached, propping the door with his foot as she went inside. Chloe's wail went up an octave, making Trevor wince as he lit his cigarette. Adrian watched him turn away, smoke curling across his shoulder.

Baz picked Chloe up and she clung to him like a monkey.

Adrian remembered Agnes doing the same at that age, whenever he came home after working away. He remembered Ruth's white, drawn face the summer Christie was due – blazing heat and blue skies – Agnes spending every day on the beach. Maybe she'd go back to the beach when they were living in the new house.

'I don't suppose you know how to get to Blackthorn Ashes?'

Adrian switched his focus to Baz. 'Sure, it's seven minutes away. Just follow the sound of the sea . . .' The sales brochure used the same line.

'Yeah, I tried that.' Baz rubbed his temple on the crown of Chloe's head. 'Then I tried the satnav. No luck.'

'You're thinking of moving out here? It's a great spot.'

'Well, it's certainly remote . . .' Baz shifted Chloe's weight on his chest. 'But, yes. We fancy a move. The houses look great on the website. We hear they've just opened a show house so . . .' He nodded in the direction his wife went. 'Not a lot of time to get organized before the new arrival.'

His daughter went floppy in his arms, as if the mention of her new brother or sister had triggered an allergic reaction. Baz gathered her up more tightly. 'You got kids?'

'Two. Boy and girl but she's a bit older than this little lady.'

Chloe wriggled round to stare at him. Adrian smiled: 'Hi,' and she buried her face back in her dad's chest. Families, what else was there that mattered as much?

Baz said, 'You know the way out there?'

'I know a bit more than that.'

He scratched his ear, feeling self-conscious but pleased. 'I'm Adrian Gale, one of the sales team. Well, a bit more than that. I was in on the ground floor, I guess you'd say.'

'In that case . . .' Chloe's dad worked a hand free and held it out. 'Barry Mason.'

Adrian took the hand and gripped it. 'Let's talk houses.'

Acknowledgements

Writing is a solitary pastime, but a book needs a team behind it. *Black Thorn* owes much to my champion editor Vicki Mellor and the wider Pan Mac family, including Neil Lang who designed the perfect cover, and Josie Turner and Laura Sherlock who plotted its launch into the world. I was blessed by a brace of ideal agents in Jane Gregory and Veronique Baxter. As a sensitivity reader, Hayley Webster is without peer. For their friendship, warmth and wisdom, I thank Alison Graham, Erin Kelly, Jane Casey, Paddy Magrane, Andrew Taylor, Mick Herron and Jo Howard, Julie Akhurst and Stephen Brown, Alyson Shipley, Michelle Buckeridge, Fiona Cummins, Anna Britten and Lydia Downey. Still more thanks to my mother, and to my siblings and their partners. My son, Victor, who was the first to support my idea for this book, remains an inspiration. Lindsay Jackson, co-founder of Ledburied, deserves a special mention. As do all the booksellers, librarians, reviewers, bloggers, festival organizers, interviewers and podcasters who work behind the scenes to get books like *Black Thorn* into the hands of readers. Without readers, writing would be a very lonely business indeed.

About the Author

Sarah Hilary's debut, *Someone Else's Skin*, won the Theakston's Crime Novel of the Year and was a World Book Night selection, a Richard & Judy Book Club pick, and a Silver Falchion and Macavity Award finalist in the US. *No Other Darkness*, the second in her DI Marnie Rome series, was shortlisted for a Barry Award. The series continued with *Tastes Like Fear*, *Quieter Than Killing*, *Come and Find Me*, and *Never Be Broken*. *Black Thorn* is her second stand-alone novel, following *Fragile*.